Unthinkable Consequences

BOB RECTOR

Cover art by Richard M. Harrison

ISBN: 1493563483
ISBN-13: 978-1493563487

DEDICATION

To the woman who is my wife, my life, my business partner, my fellow adventurer, the matriarch of our family, a best selling author herself, and my constant inspiration, Marsha Roberts.

1

October 10, 1959. A balmy Saturday night on the northern tip of Key Largo Island, Florida. The eve before America was to change drastically and forever. Thirty-nine year old Paula Taylor didn't care about that. She was focused on the present. Tonight. It belonged to her. Nothing was going to change that.

She approached the bridge over the inlet and slowed to a crawl, hoping to keep its aging timbers from groaning too loudly under the weight of her two-ton Country Squire woodie. She was determined to keep her presence a secret from Kurt. That was important.

Once over the bridge she cut her lights. It was a clear night. The moon was waxing half-full. Paula made her way easily enough, but she'd done this so many times before, she could have driven it blindfolded. The pungent smells of salt water and decaying foliage filled her lungs. The sensory overload made her head swim. She rolled to a stop among a hammock of gumbo-limbo trees, not where she normally parked, but tonight was different. She cut her engine.

A subtropical forest surrounded her, a raw, primitive place unchanged for eons. It flaunted its sensuality brazenly, like those ancient little fertility statues with torpedo-shaped bazooms and bursting hips. The flora here was wanton, shamelessly beckoning to be pollinated.

Like me, Paula thought. I need pollinating bad.

The thought shot a burst of adrenalin through her veins, a tingly sensation that quickened her heartbeat and made her face flush hotly. Pollination, yes -- the act, not the end result nature intended. Tonight, yes. Here in this wild, secret place, yes, yes. She caught her breath.

She listened to the waters of the strait ripple past thick growths of mangroves. Above her, leaves rattled in a prankish breeze. Familiar sounds. Comforting sounds. Sounds from childhood days spent exploring here. Secretly. Sounds that aided and abetted her stealthy arrival.

Perfect.

She savored the moment, not moving, not firing up the Chesterfield she so badly wanted, knowing its glow was visible for miles. Especially by Kurt's hawk eyes.

It was the animal part of him that first hooked her. The brooding danger just below the surface. The reckless eyes. The musky smell. The broad shoulders. The big, wide devilish grin as he reeled her in. She shivered again in anticipation then felt silly for doing so, like she was fifteen again, then thought, well, so what?

It occurred to Paula that not another living soul knew where she was, would never in their wildest imagination think she was here, about to do the unthinkable. Not her nosey neighbor Millie. Not her Pi Kappa son or her dragon-mouthed mother-in-law. Certainly not her husband, lord-and-master of all he beheld.

Well, he wasn't beholding her now.

She was in a secret place doing a secret thing, not behaving at all like the Paula everybody thought she was. This was Secret Paula. Exciting. Daring. Uninhibited in a way that frankly boggled her mind. In the vernacular of her son's crowd she was most assuredly cool. She blushed at the thought of her son ever knowing what she was about to do.

Bad time to think about that, Secret Paula scolded her. So she didn't. Tonight's a night to revel in just being a woman. Not a mother. Not a wife. Not a household administrator. Certainly not a cornerstone of society. She didn't think she'd ever been one of those anyway.

A woman. Ready to dispense enormous pleasure, or tantalizing pain, then demand it back in even greater measure. It was a heady awareness of the true power simmering away inside her, bestowed upon her by God.

Yep. God. He put it in me. Must have had a good reason.

But what if it wasn't God who put it in me? What if it was the devil?

Paula scoffed at the idea. Devil, smevil. If it was the devil then why had all her previous encounters with Kurt been so heavenly? Why did she always feel like singing a few bars of the 'Hallelujah Chorus' after their gymnastics? She giggled at the thought then covered her mouth, afraid Kurt might hear.

Too late for second thoughts. I'm here. It's going to happen. To hell with what anybody else thinks.

Especially if they don't know. Other than herself, Secret Paula was known by only one person. Kurt. He had set up tonight's rendezvous in his usual clandestine way, making it clear he expected her to be here.

But Secret Paula didn't always do what was expected of her.

She envisioned him waiting for her not more than a hundred yards away, restless as a caged tiger, aching for the taste of her.

Time to end his suffering.

Paula switched off the dome light and quietly eased the door open. She stepped out of the safe, man-made environment built for her comfort, into a world where she was surrounded by denizens of the wild, lurking in the darkness. Beady little eyes looked down on her, hidden in the growth. She was a trespasser in this world. Their shrieks of outrage at her intrusion told her she didn't belong here, shouldn't be here. She was a threat to the normal order of things. A troublemaker. Dangerous.

Not so very different from the denizens of Palm Beach, she reflected.

Beady little eyes looked down on her there, too. The difference was she felt safer here. This was a place she had loved and understood since she was a girl. As for Palm Beach, she would never understand it much less love it. She pondered this only for a moment, then the vision of Kurt waiting hungrily for her returned. It pushed every other thought from her mind.

She untied her wrap-around skirt and tossed it onto the back seat. Her tropical print blouse followed, then her sandals. Normally her swimsuit was a standard-issue Jantzen, complete with flowery cap, but tonight she wore a simple cream-colored leotard that fit her statuesque frame like another layer of skin. She was ready.

Was Kurt ready? She smiled knowingly. Of course he was. Kurt was always ready. She caught her reflection in the window and had to admit she looked, well, earth shattering. Watch out big boy, here I come.

After stashing her keys and wallet under an exposed root, Paula followed a narrow footpath through the mangroves down to the water. Typical of late October evenings in Key Largo, the air and water temperatures were almost identical. Having grown up here, Paula was accustomed to the phenomenon. She found the seamless transition of moving through air one moment, liquid the next, invigorating, sensuous in a primeval way.

She closed her eyes, listened to the cacophony of night sounds. Thousands, maybe millions of tree frogs were locked in a grating, rusty harmony, accompanied by the frenzied buzzing of insects, the whispery darting of nightjars feeding on them. She heard the guttural belch of a distant crock too, but knew that contrary to popular perception, crocodiles did not attack humans unless provoked.

No problem. She would save all her provocation for Kurt.

Paula glided silently, effortlessly on the surface. She knew where Kurt would be. They had met at this same spot countless times before. She could have driven to within a few yards of him, usually did, but tonight she had something special in mind.

She arrived at a cluster of mangroves that jutted out into the Sound, blocking her from Kurt's view. She separated a few leaves and peeked through. There he was, all right, unaware of her nearness, naked except for a pair of trunks. A cigarette dangled from his lips. He was lying on his back, his hands tucked behind his head. It accented his bulging shoulders, his broad, hairy chest. It flattened his washboard stomach. One leg was crooked up casually. Paula noticed the lump in his crotch and knew he was thinking of her. It made her smile.

He was the most magnificent thing she had ever seen. Six-foot-four, hairy as an ape, with rock-like muscles that came not from lifting weights, but from being a man. Forty-five years of hard, fast living had chiseled his face into its craggy features. His sandy hair was thick and always seemed to be wind tossed. But it was his eyes, dark and reckless, always challenging her, that held Paula spellbound.

Oh God.

She wanted to strip to the waist, beat her breast, and scream out like a warrior woman.

Instead, she filled her lungs and dropped below the surface. The only sound now was water gurgling past her ears. It was in marked contrast to the jungle drums beating in her blood.

Her plan was to swim underwater until she knew she was right in front of him and then stand up -- a mermaid rising from the sea. She imagined what his expression would be when he saw her and it made her tingle. It made her quicken her pace. A natural athlete and a strong swimmer, Paula plowed effortlessly through the water -- a torpedo locked on course.

Target: Kurt.

Chances of success: 100%.

2

Kurt had been waiting about twenty minutes. When he pulled up at their secret meeting place in his war surplus Jeep, he expected to see Paula's big Country Squire wagon already parked there. She usually arrived first. Correction, she *always* arrived first. Tonight she hadn't arrived at all. It made him uneasy.

Was she in trouble? Did her car break down? Palm Beach was three hours away, an easy, comfortable drive in that big tank of hers, but anything could happen -- flat tire, engine trouble. Once past Homestead it was no-man's land. Was the Overseas Bridge clogged again? No way to know. No way to contact her. Panic gnawed at his gut -- a rare occurrence for him. What if tonight of all nights she didn't show? Weeks of planning up in smoke. His life in jeopardy. Paula's too?

Possibly.

Probably.

He shuddered at the thought, then shook it off, disgusted with himself. All right soldier, get a grip. She'll show. She always has. It will all work out as planned.

To get his mind off it, Kurt spent his time fashioning a passion pit from a thick layer of mangrove leaves covered by a standard issue canvas tarp topped by an oversized beach blanket. He laid down on it to make sure it would accommodate his six-four frame. It did. He fired up a Camel, then locked his fingers behind his head and waited. Now where the hell was . . .

At that exact moment, Paula stood up from the water not ten feet in front of him. She was bathed in the moon's spectral glow, wearing a leotard, wet now and virtually transparent, stretched tight over those inviting hips, those breasts the size of honeydew melons. What an entrance.

It damned near stopped his heart.

No doubt the effect she had intended.

Ah, Paula, Paula . . .

Five foot ten and a half inches of grade triple-A prime woman. A yard or so of velvety legs reaching up to that mysterious dark patch of glory land. A thick copper mane glistening wet, splashing down over soft, creamy shoulders. Full, sensuous lips. Large, green eyes that glowed like polished emeralds. Eyes that were childishly innocent one moment, wantonly carnal the next.

Kurt knew he would always be a prisoner of those eyes.

Paula was proof positive that God was a man. Maybe even a dirty old man. If Eve looked anything like Paula, man never had a chance.

The look in Kurt's eyes was everything Paula had hoped for -- a bull about to charge. Then he *was* charging, over the mangroves, into the water. She only had time to catch her breath before he scooped her up in his arms, those incredibly powerful arms, making her feel weightless, searing her with his need for her.

He slammed her down on the blanket so hard it made her grunt in surprise, then laugh. Kurt towered over her, man in his most primitive form, the hunter-killer, now ready to rip apart his victim. Paula smiled tauntingly at him. Go ahead, Kurt, rip me apart.

He was on her, crushing her, his tongue plunging deep into her mouth, his hardness pressing against her, causing fireballs to explode in her head, fanning the flames of her passion that were already blazing. She screamed out, surprised at how primal it was. His skin was hot to the touch, feverish, yet all she wanted was to hold him closer, closer.

Instead, Kurt pushed away.

The loss of his heat was unbearable. Instinctively she reached for him again. "No, no, Kurt. Tighter."

Kurt brushed the wet strings of hair from her face. His desire for her was strong in his eyes, but something else was there too, something she couldn't decipher. "Easy, Paula."

Paula laughed. "Yeah, Kurt, real easy."

She reached for him greedily, but he grabbed her wrists, pinned them down above her head.

"Hey, cut it out." Paula knew her need for him was written all over her face. What more did he want? "Let me get out of this swimsuit. Come on . . ."

He was silent for a moment, his expression hard to read. "Not yet."

Paula squirmed, giggled. "Come on, Kurt. Do your manly duty."

"No."

"No?" Paula didn't like games. She didn't like to be teased either, especially not when every pore in every square inch of her body was about to explode. She worked her knee up between his legs; applied pressure where she knew it would get his attention.

"Yeah, Kurt. Right now."

Kurt's response was lightning quick. Paula found herself flipping through space then slamming back down again, wrists still pinned, legs splayed wide with Kurt wedged between them. She groaned with such savage wantonness that it surprised even her. "Damn it Kurt, cut it out. Let's just do it, okay? Come on . . ."

He eased the pressure on her wrists but still kept her pinned. His gaze was intense, as usual. In it was all the desire she had hoped for and expected. But gone was the playful twinkle that always made her heart beat double-time, replaced by an earnestness so out of character that it was jolting.

"Hey, what's going on?"

"I wanna hear you say it. I wanna know you mean it."

Paula was at a loss for words. More games? But he looked so damn serious.

"Say what?"

Kurt's nostrils flared. He sucked in a lungful of air like an Olympic swimmer waiting for the gun. "That you love me."

It was jarring. The rhythm was all wrong, the mood destroyed -- a record jumping to the wrong groove. Paula's brain wobbled inside her head. "Huh?"

"Say it, Paula."

"You want me to say I love you?" The laugh came from deep within her stomach, sounding like a bark when it burst from her mouth. "My God Kurt, since when did that matter?"

But Kurt wasn't laughing. "It matters."

A wave jumped the mangroves, splashed against her. Droplets curled across her face. She shook them off. Kurt's eyes were boring into hers. This was too much. She struggled to break his hold but couldn't. "Get off me, Kurt. Let me get out of this thing."

Kurt released her wrists, sat back, a predatory look in his eyes. "I will. When you say it."

Paula was surprised at the anger welling up within her. What was the matter with him? They were here for one purpose only: sex -- raw, wild and abandoned. She was determined to rekindle the fire. She opened her mouth for him, grabbed his hair with both hands, pulled him down to her, but he jerked away.

"Kurt!" Like all men, he could be infuriating. He was proving it now. Paula knew if she was going to win the war, she was going to have to lose the battle. She drew a deep breath. "All right, damn it."

She laid the back of her hand against her forehead in an exaggerated swoon. "Oh my darling Kurt, sweetheart, light of my life, I love you, I do, I really, really do." She fluttered her eyelashes. "There, how's that?"

His eyes continued to bore into hers with such intensity that she thought he was going to explode, but then his familiar, mocking glint was back.

His face broke into a roguish grin, the one that always made her tummy quiver.

"All right then." The velvety growl was back in his voice.

"All right then," she echoed and hoped they'd now move on to the main event. But Kurt wasn't finished.

"You really don't grasp how much I love you, do you, Paula?"

Oh God, please, Paula thought, then smiled brightly, held her hands about eight inches apart. "This much?" She then moved them ten inches apart, her eyes growing bigger. "*This* much?" She flashed him a big, toothy smile, nodded her head enthusiastically. "More?"

To her great relief, Kurt grinned. Hoping to lighten things up even more, she added, "So tell me Mongo, where did you learn about this love thing anyway? Not really your style."

Paula was shocked to see the wounded look in his eyes. "From you."

"Oh." Wasn't expecting that one. "Okay."

"That's why tonight's the night. "

"Well, it's certainly a night, all right." Then, realizing from his expression that she obviously wasn't getting his point, asked, "What about tonight?"

"Tonight's the night you make it official. Tonight's the night you commit."

"Commit?" She was surprised he even knew what that word meant. "Commit to what?"

"Starting a new life. With me."

3

Having heard men describe what it was like to be sucker punched, Paula was sure it had just happened to her. She reeled, blinked away stars, then in a burst of anger jumped to her feet. "Are you crazy?"

She grabbed Kurt's pack of Camels, shook one loose. Her body ached from the lack of him. The night air on her wet skin brought goose bumps. She trembled, longing for Kurt's warmth. A buoy clanged forlornly in a distant channel, echoing the feeling of emptiness lodged in the pit of her stomach. This was hardly the way she had seen the night unfolding.

"You're already getting the best part, Kurt. Don't screw it up. Besides, by all accounts, I'm not very good at the love thing."

Paula was torn between a desire to get the hell out of there and her burning need for Kurt. She balanced the damp cigarette between her lips, lit up, and watched Kurt push to his feet. There was something formidable about his stance. There always was.

"You're wrong, Paula. You were made for love."

She barked out a laugh again. "Oh, really? Tell it to my husband. Or my son. Or maybe my mother-in-law. If I knew anything about love I'd be home with them right now, not here with you. No, I think I flunked the love test. You'll have to settle for lust."

Kurt stepped up behind her, encircling her with his arms, his breath hot on her cheek. "That's not love, Paula. That's marriage. You've never been in love . . ." He jerked her around to face him. "Until now."

He crushed her to him, smothering her with his mouth, lifting her off the ground. When he released her, his eyes were full of challenge. He took the cigarette from her, clamped it between his lips, and walked away.

Paula stood helpless in her desire, watching him stride confidently over to that camouflaged Army Jeep of his. So that's it? Meeting over? Now he's going to just drive away, leave me standing here in this stupid see-through swimsuit feeling like a fool? But instead, Kurt reached into the back, pulled out a T-shirt and slipped it on.

Was she in love with him? She didn't think so. She only knew she had to have him in her life. She was addicted to him. If uttering the three most overused words in the English language was what it took to turn him on, then what the hell? Time for drastic measures.

She raised her arms, ran her fingers through her hair, pushed out the water, aware of how it stretched the leotard tight over the parts of her that Kurt liked best. "Of course I love you. How could you doubt it?"

It didn't have the effect she thought it would. He didn't sweep her up in his arms, rip off her suit, and throw her to the ground. He just stood there, took a long draw on the cigarette, then said, "And?"

"And?"

Bastard. Why is he doing this? "Damn it, Kurt, what are you trying to do? Look, I know all about 'ands'. 'And' if I really truly love you I'll chunk my family, my home, and twenty-odd years of my life, and run away with you. Right?"

"If you're smart you will."

"Well, maybe I'm not so smart." Paula swayed unsteadily. Why doesn't he just take me in his arms the way he always does and forget about all this? She looked at Kurt pleadingly. "I want to."

Paula was surprised at the effect *those* three words had. Kurt straightened, took a step toward her, an animal poised for the kill. "Then do it, Paula." He closed the gap between them, the intensity in his eyes making her take a step back. "What do you really want?"

I want you to make love to me, she thought. Don't make it any more complicated than that. Just make love to me with that same fire we've always known before. I don't care about anything else. She threw her head back defiantly. "No, Kurt, what do *you* really want?"

"More. Of you."

Paula held out her arms. "This is all I've got." When he didn't respond, she said, "Put your arms around me, I'm cold."

Kurt placed his hands on her hips. She was trembling. He pushed his hands upward, over her stomach, cupping her breasts, flicking her nipples with his thumbs, clasping her shoulders as if he were going to crush them. Paula was both frightened and excited by the barely restrained power beneath those hands. Kurt brought his face very close to hers. The savagery in his eyes took her breath away. When he spoke, his voice was slightly more than a whisper, slightly less than a growl.

"I want you in my life all the time, Paula, or not at all. I don't care about your husband or your kid or your fucking house. I want you and you want me. That's all that matters. Everybody else can go straight to Hell."

He kissed her brutally, letting her feel his strength, his power over her. Paula heard herself whimper. Oh God, please. She was engulfed in his arms. His passion was an all-consuming inferno, driving every other thought from her mind. She wrapped her arms around him, clung to him desperately. Kurt had made her feel like a real woman for the first time in her life. She couldn't lose that. She wouldn't lose that. She pulled back, panting for breath. "All right."

Kurt stood rigid, clamped the cigarette between his teeth again. His face was lost in shadow. "All right what?"

"I'll do it. I'll run away with you. To hell with all of them. I don't care what they think. They don't need me anymore. Dammit, I have a right to be happy. If that makes me bad, then I'll just be bad."

Oh God, Kurt, if you don't make love to me right this minute . . .

As if reading her thoughts, Kurt ran his fingers through her hair, pulled her head back so she was looking up into his face. He let the cigarette dangle from his lips menacingly, yet there was a gentleness in his eyes that astonished her. "Running away with me isn't bad, Paula. It's honest."

A volatile mixture of anger and joy exploded within Paula. She pushed herself against him, forcing him to support her. She grabbed strands of his hair, clenched them in her fingers until she knew it hurt. She wanted him to see the full fury of the fire blazing inside her, the fire he had kindled.

"All this talk of honesty and love and devotion turn you on, Kurt? Okay, I love you, I honestly do. You want me, you got me. Whatever you say, 'darling'. I'll run away to Never Land with you, okay? I'll love you forever and ever, okay? Now let's do what we do best, okay?"

Kurt laughed and Paula sensed the genuine relief in it. What a night this had turned into. "Okay," he said simply.

"Okay," she echoed, then slid the shoulder straps of her leotard down and was about to peel it off when she noticed Kurt had turned away. He was headed for his Jeep again. "I've got something for you," he said over his shoulder.

"Yeah, well, I've got something for you too, but I'm beginning to think you don't want it."

"Come over here."

Paula sighed, pulled the leotard back up, and walked over to the Jeep. Kurt pulled something wrapped in paper from a cardboard box in the back. He offered it to her. She gazed at him questioningly, then removed the paper to reveal a porcelain egret taking flight.

It was about the last thing on earth Paula would have expected Kurt to give her. She didn't know what else to say other than a feeble, "Well, isn't that something?"

Being a bit of an artist herself, Paula was impressed by the sculpture's fine craftsmanship. The base was fashioned like the grassy water of the Everglades. The artist had captured the egret just as it leapt into flight, the splayed feathers of its wings biting the air, its long, graceful neck reaching toward the sky, an expression of sheer joy and abandon in its eyes. It was a breathtaking work. And enormous. It must stand eighteen inches, she guessed. It was surprisingly heavy.

"Kurt, I don't know what to say."

Kurt let his hand explore the thickness of her hair. "Your eyes have already said it."

Really? Paula thought. I wonder what they said. Her head was spinning. What was going on here? The only gifts she and Kurt had ever exchanged were their bodies. It had always been an intoxicating game where each played out their fantasies. But this was no game. Tonight Kurt was making a sincere effort to show his affection for her. She was somewhat embarrassed that all she had done in return was act like a bitch in heat. God, men are such strange creatures.

"Gosh, it's . . . it's wonderful . . . "

Kurt leaned back against the Jeep, folding his arms over his puffed up chest, as close to beaming as she'd ever seen. "It's you," he said.

"Me?"

"Flying away to be free."

Paula thought: my God, if he thinks this is who I am, we've got big problems. She shrugged it off, gave him a sly smile. "You were pretty sure of yourself."

Kurt returned the smile, his eyes mocking her. "I was damn sure of you."

Paula laughed. Kurt removed the cigarette from his mouth and took her into his arms. Paula held the egret by its neck and snuggled close, eager to soak up Kurt's warmth. He kissed her lips, her nose, her eyes. He said, "I love you, Paula. We're good for each other, you and me. We're gonna have one hell of a life together. I'm gonna see to it."

He kissed her again, giving this time instead of taking. Paula gave too, no longer trying to comprehend what was going on. Chalk it up to warm bodies, moonlight, and the temporary abandonment of rational behavior. Whatever it was, she didn't want it to stop. She was content now to let Kurt initiate the lovemaking. Feeling the warmth of his touch, listening to the soothing roll and splash of the surf, letting the salty breeze caress her face, nothing else mattered now. Could I run away with Kurt, she wondered. Not likely, but why let the truth spoil the dreamy atmosphere that now enveloped her. Let him have his fantasy. After they'd wrestled on the blanket for a while, he'd forget about it. Right now she'd just go with the flow.

Kurt released her, stretched his long arms toward the stars, then rested his hands on his hips. "All right, M'lady. Let's get the hell outta here."

It was uttered so casually it took Paula a moment to comprehend what he'd said. "I'm sorry, what?"

He gave her a gentle swat on the ass. "I said move it, gal. We gotta lot of living to do."

"Uh, whoa, wait a minute, cowboy. You mean now as in right this minute?"

He was gathering up his towel and cigarettes but stopped upon seeing her slack-jawed expression. "What's the matter?"

"Are you crazy? I can't just up and leave right this very minute."

"It's the best way, Paula. Commit. Act."

She grabbed her head to keep it from spinning. “Commit? Act? Mother of God, Kurt. You speaking from experience, are you? You got maybe a wife and a kid and a home somewhere you're walking out on? I mean, come on."

"Paula . . ."

She heard the growl in his voice and hastened to add, "Look, there's lots of strings. I've got to cut them one at a time. It'll take a while."

Kurt took a step toward her, his stance becoming wary. "How long?"

"I don't know, I don’t know. Not long."

Kurt's mood was growing dark, menacing. "How long?"

"Soon, Kurt. As soon as I can, I promise."

"When, Paula?"

"Soon, dammit. Aren't I worth the wait?"

In answer, Kurt jerked the cigarette from his mouth, turned abruptly and stormed away, throwing the glowing butt into the surf. Guess not, Paula thought. She stood there, stunned, watching the cigarette bobble in the shallow water until a breaker buried it. She clung to the porcelain egret, tried desperately to think of something to say, but before she could, Kurt whirled around, pointing a finger at her.

"I'll give you a week, Paula."

"A week? Come on, Kurt, that's not fair."

Kurt threw his beach paraphernalia into the back of the Jeep. "One week. Saturday the Seventeenth. I'll meet you here, just like always. I'll wait for you till eight."

Paula felt sick. "If I'm not here by then?"

"I'll know what your choice is. You won't hear from me again."

Paula stood paralyzed by his words. It had happened too fast, too quick to comprehend. Yet there he was climbing into the Jeep.

"Kurt, wait . . ."

The engine roared into life.

"Kurt, don't leave me here like this. Kurt . . ."

But he was already zigzagging onto the trail, not bothering to look back. Then he was gone, even the sound of the Jeep was gone. Now there was only the gentle roll of the surf, the clanging of the buoy, the whisper of the wind. She noticed a wave swelling up a few feet away. Floating in it was the sodden clump of Kurt's cigarette.

Paula plopped down on the bed of mangrove leaves that was supposed to be their passion pit. She pulled her knees tight up against her chest in an attempt to quell the throbbing ache deep within her.

"Well, shit."

4

Taking a cold shower didn't help at all. Paula wondered whose lamebrain idea that was anyway. If anything, her need had only sharpened in the half-hour or so since she'd been discarded in the mangroves like an empty beer bottle. Knowing it was Kurt -- KURT! -- who had done this to her put a cruel edge to her suffering.

Paula tossed her towel into the hamper. Her skin was tingling like the sunburn you don't realize you have till you step out of the shower, remedied easily enough by slapping on Noxzema. This was different. Kurt had fanned these flames and they were still roaring like a blast furnace. She didn't think Noxzema was going to help at all.

Thanks a lot, Kurt.

Two months she had waited for tonight's tryst. Eight interminably long weeks. Sixty excruciating nights, tossing restlessly beside the cold lump of flesh she was married to, her mind spinning with what she and Kurt would do to each other. She was primed and ready to blow. It didn't take much for Kurt to light her fuse. Just his touch was enough, the look in his eyes.

Then --

Damn you, Kurt!

Paula stood naked in her bedroom, trembling. Her flesh was hot, her mouth dry, her breasts sore, but that was nothing compared to what was happening deep inside her pelvis.

Bastard.

Paula pulled on panties. The girls were too sensitive to be loaded into a bra so she simply threw on a loose cotton shift. She wondered why life had to be so traumatic. Kurt had been her escape, Kurt and sleep. Now that Kurt was gone, she was sure she'd never sleep again. Tears stung Paula's eyes. And now I'm going to cry.

Great.

All right, such is life. Who said it was going to be fair? You make the best play you can with the cards you're dealt. Seldom do you get a chance to stack the deck. Kurt's gone. You knew it couldn't last forever. You'll just have to find yourself another lover.

Paula dug a pair of sandals out of her overnight bag and pulled them on. Yeah, right. I'll put an ad in the paper: lonely housewife has immediate opening for new lover -- so to speak. Must have eyes reckless as a summer squall, total disregard for anybody's rules but his own, and make love like a runaway locomotive. Send picture.

Paula buried her face in her hands. Find another lover? The idea was preposterous. Until Kurt came into her life, the thought of extramarital activity had never entered her mind. Well, it had entered her mind, but that was where it stayed. She'd never acted on it. It was Kurt who had chosen her, not the other way around. All she had done was let it happen. How would she ever find another Kurt? The answer was simple, she wouldn't. What a crock of shit that was.

Paula's thoughts were interrupted by the sound of Birdy moving about downstairs, her mother's devoted companion since long before Paula was born. As usual, Paula felt a twinge of guilt for using her mother's home as an alibi for her affair with Kurt, and as usual, she got over it. During the past, year no one suspected her trips to Key Largo were for any other purpose than attending her invalid mother. From now on that really would be the reason she came back.

The only reason.

Paula sat at her childhood vanity and stared into the mirror. Her coppery hair hung in wet clumps around her oval face, but she decided against drying it, knowing a hot blast of air directed against any part of her body right now would be all that was necessary to send her straight over the edge.

Paula jumped to her feet with a genuine desire to punch somebody. Damn! Damn! Double-damn! What a dirty, stinking trick you played on me, Kurt Younger. Why couldn't you have left me alone? Why did you have to open me up, show me what I really am? I had accepted my life. It wasn't great, but I'd accepted it. How will I ever be able to accept it again? You've ruined it for me.

5

Kurt slammed his fist against the steering wheel, yelled, "Son of a bitch," then swerved sharply to miss a tree.

All right, cool down big guy. Make your anger work for you, not against you.

Without slowing, Kurt forced the tires of his Jeep back onto the barely visible track. He drove mechanically, hurling through the thick forest of slash pine, his mind focused on the last image he had of Paula, standing there in the mangroves, stunned, her arms reaching out pleadingly, bouncing about crazily in his rearview mirror as he roared away.

Slow down. Get control.

Kurt took a deep breath and held it.

Stop acting like an asshole.

Kurt relaxed his grip on the wheel. His breath hissed out like steam escaping a locomotive.

Better.

He eased off the gas, settled back in the seat, made a conscious effort to let go of his rage. The Jeep seemed to sense his change in mood. It no longer screamed at the forest to get out of its way. Instead, it bounced almost playfully onto the rickety timbers of the bridge spanning the inlet.

Calmer now, Kurt replayed the events of the evening, trying to determine where he had screwed up. It didn't take long to spot the problem. He had completely misjudged the nature of his objective: Paula. How could he have thought she would shrug off bonds twenty years long and simply walk away with him tonight?

Because basically you're an asshole, he told himself. The anger came surging back, filling up his chest, his arms. Again he forced himself to let it go, wondering what had come over him. Since when had his emotions taken charge of his life? He had always relied on cold, hard facts. And gut instinct. It had kept him alive through the blood and bedlam of countless killing fields. So what had changed? Why was he acting like such a shithead of late?

The answer was simple. Paula.

In his mind he pictured her again, rising from the surf. The image shot through him like a jolt of electricity. His entire body had tensed again. No other woman had ever affected him like that. No other woman ever would, of that he was sure.

He squirmed in the seat thinking about her. The hardness pushing against his trunks was ample proof of where he'd gone wrong. He'd been thinking with the wrong head. Because of that he'd grossly overplayed his hand with Paula.

He'd purposely prolonged the period since their last rendezvous into eight agonizing weeks. True, he had been a tad busy during those eight weeks, especially the last two, but he could have made time for Paula.

She had called twice, all but begging to see him. Both times he'd fabricated excuses why she couldn't, an act akin to kicking himself in the balls. But it was all part of his plan. He was depending on Paula's overwhelming need for sexual satisfaction and gambling that no one else was providing it for her. He had to have Paula hot and pliable tonight. She had to be putty in his hands.

Well, she had been hot all right, but not quite as pliable as he had hoped.

Damage report. How bad is it? Be objective.

A condition red at least.

Can you buy a week?

Possibly.

Longer?

Not and live to tell about it.

What's your counter plan?

Kurt thought about that. He'd spent nearly three months setting this up, at considerable risk to his person, to accomplish one objective: Paula. Now he just might have blown the whole deal. There had to be a way to salvage the operation. As if on cue, his training came back to him.

What was the most basic rule of survival?

Take a bad situation and turn it around, make it work for you.

His mind now calm, analytical, Kurt picked the original plan apart. He examined each piece carefully, rearranged here, reshaped there, added new elements to shore up the gaps. Gradually a new plan emerged, a better plan, so much better Kurt wondered why he hadn't seen it before. His muscles relaxed. Maybe this evening's events were fortuitous after all.

He reached 905 then headed south toward Key Largo where his boat *Black Jack* was moored. But he did not go there. He had other business to attend to first. Instead, he hooked up with the Overseas Highway and turned north toward Miami.

6

Paula knew she was on the verge of tears again and was determined not to let it happen. Damn it, Kurt Younger, you succeeded very well at making me feel cheap and undesirable, but you're not going to make me cry. No sooner had she completed the thought than tears stung her eyes. Her nose turned red and wet. She was utterly humiliated by her inability to control her female emotions.

Shit, shit, shit!

Paula ran back into the bathroom, splashed cold water on her eyes, then patted them dry. She flicked off the bathroom light, then the overhead in the bedroom too. Its glare was just too intrusive. She plopped down at her dresser again, but her eyes wandered to the homey little surroundings she'd grown up in, ghostly now, bathed in moonlight.

Whatever happened to the little girl who grew up here? Paula searched for her in the gauzy shadows of the room. Was that her on the bed, a gangly girl ten or eleven years old, propped up against a stack of pillows, one knee cocked up, the other swinging lazily over it?

Yes, I recognize that girl.

Carrot-colored hair pulled back in pigtails. Face full of freckles. Green eyes wide with concentration as she shuffled through baseball cards, stopping on her favorite, Dizzy Dean. Bib overalls rolled up to her knees. Faded plaid shirt beneath. Her feet big and bare. Her battered gym shoes hooked over the bedposts. Chomping on a wad of Double Bubble yet humming a jazzy little song at the same time. Blowing a big pink bubble then popping it.

Not a care in the world.

Paula thought back to the hours spent in this room, giggling with her best friend Mary Lou Simmons, or studying late into the night for a test she knew she didn't have a chance in hell of passing, or just dreaming -- those long, lazy, sun-washed days when the surety that all things were possible buzzed in her head like a bee going from one blossom to another. It was all so sweet, so innocent. So carefree.

Where did it go wrong?

Twenty-one years had passed since she'd left this room to attend college. Her mother, with the complicity of Birdy, kept it pristine for her visits back home. Alzheimer's had sidelined her mother, but Birdy still kept up the charade. It was decidedly a girl's room, no trace of the tomboy she had been. There was lace on the curtains, bedspread, and lampshade. The woodwork was white, round, and conspicuously feminine.

The only hint of the room's coastal location was a ceramic lamp in the shape of a leaping dolphin. It had been given to Paula by her father who said dolphins meant good luck and she'd been the luckiest thing that had ever happened to her mom and him. Her dad had also built the bookshelf mounted on the wall. On it, two ballerinas of chipped porcelain still held upright her yearbooks, along with a few tattered Nancy Drew adventures.

It was all set dressing. A shrine to the 'Missy' that her mother and Birdy wanted to remember, but never was.

Gone were the jazz records, the aviator hat with goggles, the grass-stained baseballs. Conspicuously missing also were tennis racquets and basketballs (her height had paid off there). Those relics were boxed up in the garage somewhere, if they existed at all.

For perhaps the millionth time in her life she pondered the curious dichotomy between the Paula people wanted her to be as opposed to the Paula she really was.

Her mother and Birdy wanted her to be sugar and spice and everything nice in frilly dresses and ribbons. Never happened.

Bill wanted her to be Mrs. Taylor, the perfect subservient housewife and hostess. He lived daily with disappointment.

Mama Taylor wanted her to be the model of motherhood and Bill's devoted handmaiden. Well, she didn't give a damn about the handmaiden bit, but she had given her very best shot at motherhood. Somehow she failed. That one really hurt because all she ever wanted to be was a good mother.

Only Kurt accepted her for who she really was. Or so she thought.

Paula shook her head, trying to clear the muddle. It didn't help. She was so confused.

So alone.

She stepped over to the window, stooping because it was an attic room. It was also something of an art gallery. More than a dozen of her best watercolors were neatly displayed on the wall. Most were scenes of life in the Keys: leather-faced 'conches', their lines cast from the bridge, gulls circling fishing boats, old salts repairing their nets.

But there was also one of her dad at the helm, his head thrown back in a hardy laugh.

Another yet of her mom standing at the dock, holding on to her hat with one hand while waving to him.

And still another of Davy Jones Locker, that ramshackle structure of local fame which hung precariously over the water, seeming to defy both logic and gravity.

Scrutinizing them now from the vantage point of two decades, she had to admit little Paula Doherty had possessed a smidgen of talent.

A breeze billowed out the curtains, carried with it the rumble of traffic, the laughter and music of Saturday night, the relentless sighing of the ocean. Paula gazed out across the back lawn to the rocky shoreline. A long pier extended from it. Her father had moored his boats there but now a young couple was strolling down it, hands locked together, pausing occasionally to embrace in the dull silver moonlight. Not just embrace, they were devouring each other.

That's what she had planned for her and Kurt tonight. That's what she needed right now. What the hell happened? Was it really less than an hour ago?

Or had it happened at all?

Smoke. It's all smoke. Was it ever anything more?

"Missy," Birdy called out, "I'll be puttin' yore mama to bed directly."

"Okay, I'm coming," Paula said, then zippered shut her overnight bag. She was about to leave when she noticed the porcelain egret lying cockeyed on the bed where she had dumped it earlier. She snatched it up, reopened her bag, and shoved it in.

7

At the Eastern counter Kurt said, "My name is Jack Mendelson. I have two seats on tonight's flight to LaGuardia. I need to trade them for two on an afternoon flight, same destination, Monday the nineteenth."

The lady behind the counter was short, plump, and cheerful. "I'll be happy to do that, Mr. Mendelson, but you realize you'll have to pay a penalty charge for ..." Kurt paid little attention as she recited Eastern fare policies, focusing instead on being Jack Mendelson, 4750 S. Bayshore Dr., Miami, Florida.

He knew that some people traveling incognito preferred aliases with the same initials as their real names so monogrammed clothing and luggage could serve them in both lives. But Kurt knew cops were onto that old trick. They could cross-check passenger lists for similar initials faster than a pickpocket could work a carnival crowd. From that point on, zeroing in on the individual they were after was deadly quick.

Jack Mendelson actually existed. He really did live at 4750 S. Bayshore Dr. in Miami with his wife Bernice. There was nothing about Kurt's alias that when checked would throw up a red flag. Or Paula's.

Several months earlier Kurt had casually snapped a few pictures of Paula against a white beach towel draped over a limb. They were good enough for his old master forger buddy in Miami to generate a flawless passport and driver's license in the name of Bernice Mendelson. When he and Paula were abroad, they would exchange these for yet another set of identities.

Kurt was as adept at switching identities as he was at laying false trails. It was one of the reasons he was still alive.

The ticket agent finished her recitation, saying, "We have a nonstop departing 19 October, 4:45 PM, Lockheed Constellation service to LaGuardia arriving 10:05 PM. Will that work for you, Mr. Mendelson?"

"Perfect."

Kurt paid the fare difference, grabbed the new tickets, and made his way to the cafe, where he cheerfully addressed the disgruntled woman behind the counter.

"Two burgers, heavy on the grease. Fries, the kind that break when you bend them. And a PBR."

The woman said nothing. She pulled two precooked patties out of a tray of water, threw them on the grill to warm, then dumped a basket of frozen fries into grease the color and consistency of dog shit.

It made Kurt's mouth water.

"Oh, and Sunshine, try not to put too big a head on the beer when you draw it."

Miss Sunshine took a moment to glare at Kurt then pointed to a few dozen bottles of beer half buried in a bed of ice. Kurt nodded his thanks, grabbed a frosty Pabst Blue Ribbon, settled up at the register, and ignored the tip jar next to it. Miss Sunshine plopped back down on her stool, burying herself again in the latest issue of Modern Screen. When the food came, it was everything he expected. Men in his line of work by necessity had cast iron stomachs. They took pleasure in cuisine pilfered from a landfill.

As he ate, Kurt went over the details of the new plan once more. It had several advantages. Originally, he and Paula were just going to take the money and disappear. Kurt was certainly a master at disappearing, but there would've been those intent on finding him. The chances of them doing so would've been slim, but why invite trouble. Why live with a specter over your head?

The new plan was cleaner. Kurt Younger would be dead, as would be the man most interested in finding him. Mr. and Mrs. Mendelson, or whatever name they finally ended up with, would start a new life, one in which they'd never have to look back over their shoulders.

Kurt imagined how Paula's eyes would sparkle as they visited jolly old England, Paris, Rio, Sardinia, the Greek Isles, places he had always wanted to see, but his work kept him far away from. Places where the chance of someone recognizing his face was next to nil.

They would make the civilized world their own personal playground. Eventually they would decide where they wanted to settle. The thought brought a smile back to Kurt's face. He noticed Miss Sunshine watching him sullenly. He winked at her and took another swig of beer.

It was all going to work out perfectly. It always did, another reason he was still alive. The new plan also meant he and Paula would be able to enjoy a day together at Curiosity Cove before leaving. They would need that.

8

Paula descended the stairs to find a familiar scene. Her mother was sitting in her usual place by the big window, her eyes locked on the gently swaying palm outside.

Across from her sat Birdy, looking regal as always. Her caramel-colored arms were folded across a bosom so enormous it made Paula look flat-chested. Birdy had just finished shelling peas, the remnants of her work piled on a sheet of newspaper on the sofa beside her.

Birdy wasn't just her mother's faithful companion, she was an institution.

"Your mother and Birdy have known each other since childhood," Paula's father once told her. "Amazing how she always seems to know when your mom needs help. Just shows up. Never called her once. I tell you, Missy, I don't know what I'd do without her. You know how slight your mom's always been."

'Slight' was the term Paula's father always used to describe her mother. Not frail or sickly, which was more accurate. Just slight.

Paula's hardiness and Amazon proportions came from her father, a grizzly bear of a man. But Paula's beauty was a gift from her mother, a woman so beautiful it almost hurt to look at her. Even now.

"You're purdy, Missy, but you'll never be as purdy as yore mama," Birdy used to say. "Nobody could be. That woman is an angel set down here on earth."

Angel was what Birdy always called Paula's mother. There was something so ethereal about her that the nickname seemed appropriate. It was a nickname, however, Birdy never used when referring to Paula.

"Angel, that youngun of yore'n needs a good wallopin' for what she done. Now I know you're too tender hearted to do it, but I ain't gonna stand round an' see her deprived of the medicine she needs. No ma'am. I'm gonna snatch that girl up an' whack the everlovin' daylights outta her."

Which she had done many times, each time richly deserved. But justice dispensed at Birdy's hand had never hurt Paula as much as the sound of her mother's tears of disappointment from the other room.

Paula gazed at Birdy now: the freshly coifed hair, the pearl necklace and earrings, the suede house shoes, the expertly cut dress, lemony with big white collars, open at the neck revealing the deep cleavage of her truly awesome bosom.

How many times have I nuzzled into that bosom seeking comfort and refuge, Paula wondered, never to be turned away. It was a wondrous place filled with handkerchiefs and change purses and shopping lists. Paula was sure if she dug deep enough she'd probably find a Swiss Army knife in there too.

When Paula first started earning money it occurred to her that her father never paid Birdy for looking after her mother. She asked him why. Her father tossed his head back with that hearty laugh Paula loved. "Good Lord, Missy, Birdy could probably buy and sell both my charter boats two or three times over. She'd throw any money I gave her right back in my face. Likely as not, call me a few choice names to boot."

It confused Paula. Birdy was colored. Colored folks were supposed to be poor. At least most of the ones she knew were. "And diamonds are nothing but lumps of coal taking on airs," her father replied, which only confused Paula further.

"It's not what you've got, Missy, it's what you do with it. When your mom was just a toddler she wandered off to play on those rocks out on the point. When the tide came in she got trapped. Birdy swam out against the current and saved your mother's life. Your grandma never forgot it. When she died -- let's see, 1910, I think it was -- she left Birdy $1,500.00 -- a lot of money back then. Birdy turned that $1,500.00 into a small fortune."

When Paula asked how, her father grinned. "Invested it. Smart as a whip, that Birdy is. Even Mr. Johns down at the bank consults her before making an investment. Shrewd. Got a natural genius for it. Saw the crash coming and got out, then bought her way back in when prices were rock bottom. Put all three of her children through college, something we're still saving up to do for you."

Again her father had laughed, shaking his head in admiration. "Birdy made a deal with each one of them. Said she'd pay their way through college, but once they settled into their careers, they'd be obliged to pay her ten percent of whatever they made for as long as she was alive. It was only right, she told them. College education was a hefty chunk of money and she expected a return on her investment. Pretty smart move when you consider one's a lawyer, another's a doctor, and the third one owns a trucking company."

It wasn't until after her father disappeared that Paula learned just how much he had relied on Birdy. She had advised him on several investments whose earnings would more than provide for her mother. There were also insurance policies that paid off handsomely as well. Yes, Birdy was a Godsend.

Paula crossed the room and knelt beside her mother, choking at the lack of recognition in her eyes. Old Doc Hutchinson told her to be prepared for this, that it was inevitable. He told her father that too, but the first time the woman he worshipped looked into his eyes and didn't know him, he broke like a dry twig, took his boat out alone into an approaching storm and never returned. Lost at sea in more ways than one. That had been two years ago. That's when Birdy moved in for good.

Paula gazed into her mother's empty eyes. She remembered when they danced with laughter, sparkled with the sheer joy of being alive. Now there were only clouds.

"Oh Mama, you don't even know who I am, do you?" Paula pressed her mother's hand to her cheek. "Funny thing, I don't know who I am either. I just know I love you and I can't stand seeing you this way."

Her mother shifted her gaze back to the palm tree, dismissing Paula.

"Oh God," Paula said, then turned and threw herself into Birdy's arms. "Oh Birdy, Birdy, I've lost everything that's ever meant anything to me. Billy's gone off to college. Bill's so far removed from the man I married that I no longer recognize him. Daddy's gone and . . ." she had to swallow hard to say it, "Mama might as well be."

Birdy lifted Paula's face up by the chin and stared down at her with shrewd old eyes. "Uh-huh. An' now you done lost your lover boy too."

9

For the second time in little more than an hour Paula found herself reeling. "What?"

"Don't look at me like that with them big green eyes. Just how dumb you think I am?"

"What are you talking about?"

"Oh, chile, chile . . ." Birdy shook her head sadly then said, "Yon 'bout a year ago you all a sudden start takin' nighttime swims when you down here visitin'. An' when you come home, yore face is all rosy an' you go roun' singin' like Snow White when she's cleanin' house for dem little dwarfs. But tonight you come home with yore eyes all puffy and yore cheeks kinda white an' you seem ta lost yore singin' voice."

Paula's face burned. "If you knew about it, why didn't you say something?"

Birdy's eyes narrowed. "Didn't know fuh shore. Till now."

Paula was stunned, knew she was going down for the count. Stars seemed to spin before her eyes. Sobs rose up in her throat like vomit and she couldn't choke them back. Nor could she keep the floodgates shut. The torrent began in earnest, cascading down her cheeks and leaving its salty taste on her lips. This hurt. This really hurt. Under the circumstances, all she was able to say was, "Oh shit."

"Yeah," Birdy agreed, "Deep shit."

Just as Paula knew she would, Birdy pulled a handkerchief from her bosom, handed it to her, then continued talking. "How long you think you coulda kept it up 'fore Bill found out? I'll give ya he ain't no Rock Hudson, but he's kept a purdy nice roof over yore head. An' I notice yore clothes ain't too shabby."

But Paula wasn't listening. "Thank God Mama's beyond knowing what I've done. God, I'm so embarrassed."

"Oh stop yore snivelin'. Yore mama might be an angel, but she was a woman too. Just so happened she was married to a man who worshipped the air she breathed. All the years I knew him, he never strayed once. Yore Mama was all the woman he ever wanted. You thought Bill'd be that way. Well honey he ain't an' you jus' gotta accept that."

"I have accepted it. I know Bill isn't like Daddy. All Bill cares about is his business. I've learned to live with that, Birdy, believe me."

"Until lover boy came along."

Why don't you just jab a knife in my heart and twist it around a little, Paula thought. "God, you make it sound so cheap."

"Missy, I don't think it's cheap at all, considerin' what it could cost ya."

Paula buried her face in her hands, not wanting to see the scorn in Birdy's eyes. "I'm so sorry, Birdy. I know I've been a fool." Paula dried her eyes, then said, "I know you're disappointed in me. You have every right to be."

"Yes I am. But not 'cause you let some tomcat crawl up on yore back. Always knew you was hot blooded. Figgered it was just a mattera time."

"Hot blooded?"

"Well, I was right, wasn't I? No, Missy, I'm disappointed 'cause you had it given to ya on a silver platter an' all you done was sit back an' let it be taken away. Now you can't find nothin' better to do than whine an' moan about how unfair life's been instead of using that smart brain an' that strong body your mama an' daddy give ya to take back what b'longs to ya. My God, chile, where's yore spine? Just 'cause yore a woman don't mean ya gotta act like a pussy."

"Birdy!"

"Jus' take a look at that paintin' business of yore'n."

"It's hardly a business, just something I do to bring in a little extra spending money."

"There ya go. That's what I mean. You could turn that into a whale of a business. Give ol' Bill a run for his money. You do an' ya might be surprised at how Bill starts treatin' ya. But what do ya do instead? You throw in the towel, say you was mistreated, then spread yore legs for the first man that comes along an' scratches yore butt."

Birdy laughed scornfully. "Yeah, you gettin' screwed, all right -- in more ways'n one."

She grabbed Paula by the shoulders and shook her. "You fight for it, Missy. You take back what belongs to ya. You got the stuff in ya to do it. I know, I helped put it there. You gotta protect an' develop your assets, chile. You gotta keep your nose to the wind. You gotta invest yourself wisely. You do, an' it'll pay off for ya."

Birdy released her grip on Paula, but her voice remained stern. "You put lover boy behind ya an' get yo'self back home. You fight for what's yore'n. But first you go dry that hair."

Paula replaced the sting of humiliation with fires of indignation. Paula was tempted to lash out at Birdy, let her know she didn't need this, that she'd been punished enough tonight.

Instead, she took a deep breath and willed her mouth to stay shut. After all, Birdy was here with her mom every day. She couldn't be blamed for being a little testy after watching her best friend gradually wither away. Or for delivering sermons about things she didn't understand. Best thing to do was just get away from here.

Paula glanced at the clock. 10:30. Yes, time to go. She kissed Birdy's cheek, smiled, and said, "You're right. I'll be after 1:30 getting back as it is. You know how it upsets Mama Taylor when I come in late."

To Paula's surprise, Birdy didn't try to expand on her lecture. She merely grunted, then pushed to her feet with amazing agility. She accompanied Paula to the door, asking, "How is Bill's mother?"

Paula wanted to say Mama Taylor was her usual pain in the ass, but decided to keep it light. "Oh, she's doing fine. Has trouble getting around with her walker, especially if I'm in the room, but otherwise seems quite content."

They were silent for a moment as they continued toward the door, then Birdy said, "An' Billy's all settled in college, ya say?"

Paula scoffed. "That's one way of putting it. Stopped off to see him on my way down. He's a pledge with Pi Kappa and feeling very important about it."

"What's he majorin' in?"

"Female anatomy."

"Uh-huh. Hot blooded jus' like his mama."

"Yeah, well as I recall, Bill had quite a tiger in his tank too when he was Billy's age."

Birdy actually laughed, then said, "You oughta dry that hair 'fore you get out in the night air, honey."

There it was, the twinkle in Birdy's eyes she'd known since she was a girl. It melted her. She threw her arms around Birdy's neck. "I love you," she said. "I love you so much."

Birdy rocked her gently the way she'd always done. "Go on home, chile. I worry about you out drivin' this late."

Paula wiped her nose again with Birdy's handkerchief then handed it back to her. "Yes, I'm going." She picked up her bag, took one last look at her mother. "Does she ever change?"

"Only for the worse."

Paula nodded, forced a smile. "So how's your family?"

"Lewis' wife is 'spectin' again."

"Again?" Paula laughed. "How many does that make?"

"Be their sixth. Not all God's children got rhythm."

At the door Paula asked, "Then they're all healthy and happy?"

"They all eat a lot, so I 'spect they're healthy enough. Ain't you gonna dry that hair?"

"No."

"You need a good whackin'."

"I know." Paula kissed Birdy's cheek. "Thanks for putting up with me."

"Comes with the territory."

10

Kurt glanced at the clock on the café wall. 11:00 PM. Time to get moving. He gulped down the last of his beer and by 11:20 was back on Highway One heading south toward the town of Key Largo.

On the west side of town was Handsome Harry's Marina and Bait Shop, where Kurt tied up his boat *Black Jack* when in town. He also rented storage space for his Jeep there. Harry got his nickname because he was considered to be one of the ugliest men God had ever allowed to walk the earth. Despite that, Kurt considered him a damn good man and, what the hell, he couldn't help how he looked. Didn't stop him from getting hitched to a stick-of-dynamite little runt named Velma, who was so homely she was almost cute.

As Kurt pulled into Handsome Harry's he pondered the oddities of this love thing. I guess when it hits you there's not much you can do except go with it. Harry got Velma, I got Paula. Meant to be. He thought about that a moment, then said to himself, sure, has to be.

He stowed his Jeep then hopped on the *Black Jack*, fired it up and headed home, also known as Curiosity Cove. It was his own private island, a small coral outcropping only about fifty acres in size, covered in thick subtropical growth, and tucked in close to the Everglades' southern reaches. It was one of many tiny islands that peppered Florida Bay. The only way to get there was by boat.

The name came from a curious geological phenomenon that allowed fresh water to bubble up from the Florida Aquifer deep below, forming a spring approximately three-hundred feet in diameter near the center of the island. It poured out into a meandering channel that emptied into Florida Bay. Having access to fresh water meant Kurt didn't have to rely on cisterns to gather rainwater or to have water boated in. The primary reason most of the nearly 1700 islands in the Bay, originally called cays, were uninhabitable was because fresh water was unavailable.

At cruising speed, Curiosity Cove was twenty minutes in a northwesterly direction across the Bay from the town of Key Largo. As Kurt glided the *Black Jack* across its glass-like surface, he wondered what Paula would think of his little island paradise? He had told her about it, but never brought her here before. He wondered why.

What if she didn't like it?

He smirked at the absurd thought. Didn't matter if she liked it or not. They'd only be here for a day. After that the whole world would be their home. Curiosity Cove would be a relic of the past. It would belong to another life. A life he was putting behind him.

Kurt throttled back as he approached the entrance to the channel. The bow of the *Black Jack* laid down obediently and the wake swished and bubbled away into the calm waters of Florida Bay.

Home. Not just home, the perfect hide-away. But not any more. Not since Red found it.

11

Paula pushed north through downtown Miami. She had a Chesterfield fired up and was puffing away like a steam locomotive on a steep grade. Thank God for doctor-recommended cigarettes, she thought, one of the few pleasures left to her she didn't have to feel guilty about.

Which was good because so far, feeling guilty was what the evening had been all about. Kurt doing fun little things with all her fun little parts never entered the equation. Guilt sure as hell had. It made Paula burn with resentment, then frustration, then anger and she just had to vent it somehow, so she screamed out the window, "You can all just go straight to Hell!"

People on the sidewalk turned to stare at her. Some of them laughed. One woman yelled back, "You tell 'em, sister."

My God, Paula thought, I really am losing my mind. She laughed too, surprised it didn't make her feel better since laughter was supposed to be the best medicine. What's the matter with me?

She slumped in her seat, hands dangling over the top of the steering wheel. She flicked her cigarette butt out the window, then desperately fired up another one. She sucked the smoke deep into her lungs where it would do the most good.

Yes, better.

She became aware of her surroundings. Saturday night in Miami. Its festive air was reflected in wildly colored neon, pulsating Latino music, the thick traffic swirling around her. There was a sense of urgency to it. Paula found herself caught in its undertow, pushing hard to keep up. Everywhere she looked people were partying, dancing, laughing.

Embracing.

Paula stopped at a traffic light and noticed a raven-haired beauty looking her way. Her crimson-tipped fingers, studded with rings, were tucked possessively around the arm of a tall, lanky guy casually clad in a tropical shirt and porkpie hat. Her mascara-thick eyes sparkled knowingly.

Her generous lips glistened red, then parted ever so slightly in a confident smile. The coy downward tilt of her head tossed a wave of lustrous blue-black hair onto her pert breasts.

Paula knew what was going through the young woman's mind and the young woman knew that Paula knew. It was the secret language of women, no words necessary. As if to prove it, the young woman abruptly stopped the guy, stood on her toes and bestowed a sexy kiss, pressing her breasts and hips against him, feeling for the hardness that confirmed she was in total control, that the moment was hers. She winked at Paula as if to say: hope your night turns out good too.

The light changed and Paula pulled away. The young woman was soon lost in the rearview mirror. Paula pounded the steering wheel, screaming out in frustration. I had every intention of my night turning out good. Not just good, spectacular. Why didn't it? Kurt was there, I was there, we were alone, and we both wanted it. Why didn't it happen? Was it me?

She knew it wasn't. It was Kurt. His crazy demands. His refusal to listen to reason. His way or the highway. Well, here I am on the highway.

The Sunshine State Parkway, to be specific. New and beckoning. Paula opened up the throttle. Soon the speedometer was passing sixty-five. She eased off, wondering why she was in such a hurry to get home. Maybe that's not it at all, she reflected. Maybe I'm in a hurry to get away from Kurt. The two of them had such a good thing going. Why did he have to ruin it?

Damn you, Kurt. Damn! Damn! Double damn!

But did they really have a good thing going? Oh come on, Paula, who're you kidding? This past year with Kurt was definitely a good thing, a damn good thing. You went into it with your eyes wide open, so don't try conjuring up remorse now that it's over because you, God, and Birdy all know you don't have any, not even an ounce.

A horn blared behind her. Paula realized she'd swerved onto the grassy shoulder, distracted by the conflicting thoughts ping-ponging through her mind. She jerked back onto the road, gave the driver behind her a thank you wave, and fired up another Chesterfield.

Get your butt home, Paula, right now, fast as you can. Put this crazy little fling behind you. In a few months you'll be forty. Grow up.

But I did grow up, she reminded herself. I was a bona fide grown up American woman doing everything expected of her. I know all about being grown up. I just don't particularly like it. Kind of like turnip greens. Sure, they're supposed to be good for you, but I don't like them. They're bitter. Boring.

Then Kurt came along.

He didn't like turnip greens either.

12

When Red pushed open the screen door at a little past midnight, Kurt was ready for him. He put all his weight behind a left that broke Red's nose. It sent him crashing back through the door and out onto the verandah. Before Red got his sea legs, Kurt fired three quick jabs into his kidneys, then lifted a knee into his crotch. As Red doubled over, Kurt grabbed him by the shoulders, spun him against the railing, then heaved him over, letting him drop about four feet to the ground below.

Kurt knew the punishment he'd just administered would have left most men incapacitated with blinding pain. Not so with his old comrade-in-arms. Red merely coughed twice, jumped gingerly to his feet, put a handkerchief to his bleeding nose, and said, "Partner, before I hand you your ass, you wanna tell me what that was all about?"

He stood six-foot-seven and weighed 250 pounds, not an ounce of it fat. He had a chest like a bison's and a waist like Betty Boop's. Balloon-like muscles ran the length of his simian arms and phone pole legs. A shiny bald dome separated two clumps of iridescent red hair overhanging his jug-handle ears, giving him the appearance of a circus clown. But there was nothing funny about Michael J. Owllart. He had brutally earned the nickname Red Alert.

Among the various mercenary outfits Kurt and Red had served in, speculation was that Kurt could take Red. True, Red had three inches and twenty pounds on Kurt, but Kurt was quicker, better skilled, faster thinking, and wasn't afraid of a damn thing.

Kurt had no interest in putting that theory to the test at the moment. He was setting a plan in motion. The outcome of the next few minutes was critical to the plan's success. He assumed a command pose as he looked down at Red from the verandah. "You're lucky I didn't kill ya."

It all started ten weeks ago. The perimeter alarms on Curiosity Cove roused Kurt at 3:00 AM. A few minutes later an outboard came chugging into the lagoon under the watchful eye of Kurt's .30 caliber M1919 machine gun.

It was Red, waving his arms and yelling, "Stand down, partner. It's me." Kurt met him at the dock. He had never seen Red in such a huff. "They got Sonny Stewart," he said as he tied up. "We gotta move fast."

'They' were a gang of Colombian mercenaries involved in marauding, kidnapping, extortion, murder, and anything else that turned a quick buck. There was no negotiating with them. You paid up or people died. Sometimes, lots of people.

Kurt didn't hesitate. Sonny Stewart was a full metal jacket hound from Hell, but a righteous one. He only fought for the good guys. Unlike Kurt, Sonny was still naive enough to believe he knew who they were. Twice Sonny had saved Kurt's life. You don't turn your back on that kind of debt. He and Red were underway before daybreak.

Red had rustled up a pontoon plane and they puddle-jumped across the Caribbean, skipping above the waves and below radar, skimming the treetops as they entered Colombia. By nightfall they were deep in the jungle within miles of their target. Kurt wanted to enter surreptitiously and snatch Sonny, preferably without being detected and without spilling blood.

Red had different plans. Capitalizing on the element of surprise, he charged in with guns blazing. It was an all-out firefight and Kurt had no choice but to kill or be killed. By midnight the carnage was over. More than a dozen men lay dead.

Sonny Stewart was nowhere to be found.

"Guess he must've gotten away," Red said lamely, but Kurt smelled something foul in the air and it wasn't just rotting corpses. He watched Red frantically search the compound and a lump of ice lodged in his bowels. He knelt beside one of the bodies and read the insignia on the sleeve. Andean Mining Federation.

These men weren't mercenaries. They were merely a security unit. And he and Red had slaughtered them in cold blood. Why?

His answer came with Red's jubilant laughter as he dragged a strong box out of a tin shed. It had several big locks on it but bursts from Red's automatic opened them faster than any key could. "Well, looky here," he said, lifting out a leather bag and pouring a cascade of what appeared to be green rock candy onto a camp table. Raw, uncut emeralds.

Kurt wanted to pull the pin on a grenade and shove it down Red's throat. But Red obviously anticipated Kurt's reaction and kept his weapon at the ready.

Their escape route didn't leave much time for conversation, but once they were airborne Red spelled it out. All about the notorious South American crime lord Salvador Estrada and his plot to destroy the AMF. All about how this deal was going to set them up for life. Laughing at Kurt's rage over having been made an unwitting accomplice in what was nothing more than a jewelry heist, one that left his hands dripping with innocent blood.

"Now look here, partner, if I told you what was going down would you have gone along? Hell no. Why? 'Cause you've let yourself get soft, old buddy. You were turning into a pussy. I just handed you your balls back. And made you stinkin' rich. You oughta be thanking me."

By the time they got back to Curiosity Cove, Kurt had already worked out what he was going to do. Convincing Red to let him take over negotiations with Estrada had been easy. Red was a man of action, not finesse. Now the final hand was about to be dealt. Kurt was the dealer and he had stacked the deck with a joker so he'd come up all aces.

As for Red, he would get a dead man's hand.

A lot had happened in the ten weeks since then. Right now Red's face was full of thunder but his eyes were those of a lost puppy. Kurt shook his head disgustedly. He headed back into the house, saying, "I thought if there was one asshole in this slimy world I could trust it was you, you dripping sack of ape shit."

That did it. Red hurtled the rail and pushed through the door on Kurt's heels. He grabbed Kurt's arm, swung him around. His face hung inches above Kurt's, boring down with those paralyzing eyes of his. "Who says you can't trust me? What the fuck's going on?"

Red's eyes were his best weapon. They were large under hawk-like eyebrows and were completely devoid of color. The effect was almost hypnotic. By merely locking eyes with an adversary he immobilized him for that precious split second necessary to deliver the first thrust of fist or blade. For many of the world's best fighting men, Red's eyes were the last thing they ever saw.

But Kurt was immune to them and the nine-millimeter automatic now in his hand seemed to have materialized out of thin air. He jabbed it into Red's stomach. Red didn't have to look down to know what it was. He held his hands out, backed off. "Whoa, Kurt . . . Easy, boy . . ."

Kurt leveled the weapon at the bridge of Red's nose. "You really thought you could double-cross me and get away with it? Me, Red?"

"Double-cross? What the hell? No fucking way, partner. I'd never do that and you fucking know it."

"You fucking tried, 'partner'. Didn't work though, did it? Don't try to outsmart me, Red, you don't have the equipment."

Kurt could almost see the wheels spinning inside Red's head, groping for traction. It took a moment, then it dawned on him. "This about the emeralds?"

Kurt laughed scornfully. "Brilliant deduction, Sherlock. Give the big ugly shithead with the bloody nose a gold star."

"Partner, you really are starting to piss me off."

"Good. Now both of us are pissed off." Kurt made it clear he was a man barely able to contain his rage. He had to sell it, make Red believe he was about to lose control. He had to scare the shit out of a man who didn't know the meaning of fear. If he didn't, his plan was over before it even began.

Think of Paula, he told himself. Think of Paula being snatched away from you. By Red. That did it. Kurt bared his teeth. His eyes flashed unbridled rage. "I'd like to shove this nine in your ear and keep pulling the trigger till all the bullets are gone."

There it was. Red flinched. Kurt relaxed a little, let the insanity evaporate from his eyes, then added, "Only it would be a total waste of ammunition because I wouldn't hit anything."

"For fuck's sake, Kurt, what in blue-blazing hell are you talking about?"

"Two million bucks in uncut emeralds, Red, that's what I'm talking about. Remember those?"

"The ones we snatched from the Andean Mining Federation? Uh, fuck yeah, partner. I do seem to remember those."

Kurt ignored Red's sarcasm. He turned the heat up. "Do you also remember they're the most ruthless gang of cutthroats in the entire fucking southern hemisphere? They want those emeralds back, Red, like a seadog wants pussy. And they've got the heat turned up full blast."

"So what? We knew there'd be heat. We planned on it."

"Right, we planned on it. You didn't believe it."

"What?" Red shook his head as if trying to clear the fog. He was clearly losing his mental equilibrium, which was what Kurt had intended. "Partner, you just ain't making much sense."

"I warned you all it would take was one careless word, one sloppy move, and the whole shooting gallery would come down on us like maggots on a rotting corpse."

"I haven't said Jack shit about this to anyone. I've been holed up in the 'glades ever since we finished the job. You think I'm crazy, man?"

"I think you're stupid, Red. And greedy."

Kurt realized that Red was reaching the melting point. He still held the handkerchief to his nose, shifted his weight from one leg to the other, and puffed like a bull about to charge.

"You better tell me what's going down, partner, or I'm going to take that little pop gun away from you and shove it up your ass sideways."

"Well go ahead mother fucker, make your play. Excuse me if it should go off and give you a bad headache."

Red stayed where he was. Kurt said, "Yeah, that's what I mean. Stupid." He pressed the psychological advantage by letting the black eye of the nine's barrel stare Red down. Beads of sweat popped out on his forehead. It was an old trick. The longer you stared at the business end of a gun, the bigger it got. The darkness inside the barrel gave one pause to contemplate eternity. Red was aware of this gambit. But being aware of it did not lessen its effect.

13

It occurred to Paula that driving down a deserted arrow-straight pavement into unending darkness was a perfect metaphor for her life. She shivered, but not from the cool night air. Only one thing to do, she decided. She reached for her smokes.

She remembered something Birdy said earlier. It was time to take charge of her life. Paula knew women who'd made careers for themselves. Some even made money. A lot of it. But most of them weren't married, or if they were, didn't have kids. Which proved the old adage: if you can't get a man, get a job. Better yet, get a career.

A career.

Paula couldn't picture it. It's easy enough to talk about pursuing a career but how does one go about doing it? Not just a job -- Bill would never let her get one anyway. A career. Big difference.

The so-called painting business Birdy referred to was little more than an excuse to keep her artistic skills up. It allowed her to bring in a little mad money in a way that didn't threatened her lord and master. It was really more of a decorating service. Palm Beach was lousy with big yachts and the owners liked them adorned with soaring marlins, ghostly pirate ships and, most popular of all, buxom mermaids. A couple of trendy restaurants had even hired Paula to decorate their walls with seascapes.

Turn it into a real business? Paula didn't know about that. What she did know was that painting put her back in touch with the magic she'd always known, especially as a girl. The older she got, the more she needed that feeling of being in love with everybody and everything.

With her mom and dad who hugged frequently and laughed a lot.

With Birdy, nosing her out of danger like a faithful Shepherd, then guiding her down the right path.

With her white clapboard home and her screaming, giggling girlfriends.

With running and jumping and turning cartwheels and defying gravity at will.

With blue skies and puffy white clouds, whining gulls and Fluff her fat calico cat.

With mischievous gusts of wind that snatched away her cap and played chase with her.

With fishermen on their swaying boats, laughing amongst themselves as they worked.

With fishermen's wives who helped with the catch and brought hot meals in straw baskets.

With life.

And later with being beautiful. The magical, mystical process of becoming beautiful. No conceit. Mirrors don't lie. She didn't really work at it like so many of her girlfriends. It was just the way God made her. It was there in the way guys looked at her. The way some of the gals looked at her too. She was ripe and bursting and she knew they all wanted to taste her fruit. Several boys made it clear they wanted to do 'it' with her. She was itching to find out what 'it' was all about.

Paula questioned her mother about ‘it’. She just smiled sweetly, kissed her on the cheek and said this was the magic time, when it was all still a mystery and she could imagine it to be anything she liked. She said to savor the mystery, but save the fruit to prevent it from being spoiled before its time.

Somewhat confused by that, Paula turned to Birdy, who explained it in terms that were easier to understand. “It's real simple, Chile. All ya gotta do is concentrate on yore panties. You keep 'em pulled up tuh yore waist till the day yore daddy marches ya down th' isle an' gives ya away to Mr. Right an' you say 'I do' in frunna Gawd an' ev'rybody then ya can go ahead an' have yore fruit plucked an' ev'rythin'll be just fine an' dandy. Clear 'nuff for ya?”

Paula smiled at the memory. Nobody explained things as succinctly as Birdy. But her mother had been right too. It was a magical time for Paula. It bubbled up within her. A woman's magic. It affected almost every thought and everything she did. It was the life force and that was God's gift to women, a secret magical power that He shared only with them.

Magic.

What happened to my magic? I need to feel it again. I have to feel it again.

But how?

Trying to figure that one out ate up another sixty miles and four more Chesterfields until a sign indicating she was nearing Palm Beach flashed by. One thing was certain: she wasn't going to rediscover her magic here.

Where, then?

Paula thought back to what Kurt said earlier about the lie she had been living for the past twenty years. Dead-on accurate. Painfully so. Kurt had bared his soul to her but Paula hadn't been listening very well because it all seemed so absurd. He was offering her a way out and she couldn't see it, hell she couldn't even comprehend it.

He said he loved her. Her. Paula. For who she really was.

He said he wanted to devote his life to her. He said he wanted the two of them to live happily ever after. Have fun. Do just as they pleased. What was wrong with that?

Not a damn thing.

Kurt was right about Bill and Mama Taylor too. Paula knew she meant nothing to them, why pretend she did? They've never worried about her feelings. Why worry about theirs? In reality, she wasn't dependent on Bill. She had her own home, the one she was born and raised in, and long since paid for. It would be hers soon. The happiest times of her life were in that home. It was where she first found her magic. Maybe she'd find it there again.

As for Billy, Paula would always be his mother, nothing Bill could do about that. Billy might be hurt at first, perhaps even feel betrayed, but that would gradually subside as he came into adulthood. They'd build a new bond, just the two of them, without Mama Taylor's constant interference. That could be magical too.

Paula sucked in the sweet night air, filled her lungs with it. She glanced in the rearview mirror. She was smiling, not with vindictiveness but with joy.

It's my life, she declared to herself. It's the only one I get and nobody has the right to tell me how to live it.

Yes. I can do this. I *will* do this. That's how I'll find my magic again.

She tried to shake another Chesterfield loose but the pack was empty, which was fine because she didn't really want another one anyway. She wadded it up and tossed it out the window, then pushed back in her seat, happy, excited. The night sky was an explosion of stars, all winking at her. She winked back.

Yes, yes, yes. I can do this. I'm *going* to do this.

Kurt gave her a week to prepare. Okay, not much time. Lots of loose ends to tie up, but she'd get it done. She had to.

To hell with Bill. To hell with Mama Taylor. To hell with Palm Beach.

I'm Paula Taylor.

No, no, no, I'm Paula Doherty.

Starting now and for the rest of my life I'm going to do just as I damn well please.

14

The long look down the nine-millimeter's barrel worked its usual wonder. Seeing that Red was sufficiently humbled, Kurt said, "Somebody else is pissed at us besides our friends at AMF."

"As if I give a shit." Seeing Kurt's smoldering glare, he added, "Who?"

"Salvador Estrada. Remember him?" Kurt marveled at how expressive those lifeless eyes of Red's could be under the right circumstances.

"Estrada? Why the fuck should he be pissed? That asshole trying to back out of the deal?"

"Red, you give stupidity a bad name. Back out of the deal? When he's planning to wipe AMF's ass with those emeralds?" Kurt shook his head sadly. "It was so simple, Red. We deliver the emeralds to Estrada, he gives us a little gift for our trouble. Simple."

Despite his rather precarious position, Red guffawed. "Two mil worth of cocaine is hardly what I call a little gift, partner."

"Try eight-hundred large, Red. Won't be worth two mil till we cut and move it. Its forgetting little details like that, 'partner', that makes me worry about you."

"I haven't forgotten a goddamn thing."

"Well, I'm damned confused then. How 'bout you tell me your version since it's obviously different than mine."

"Cut the shit, man. Ain't never been but one version. Same as its always been."

"I'm not so sure. It's our asses at stake, in case you haven't noticed, and while you may not put much value on yours, I've grown real fond of mine. Go ahead, Red, let's hear it."

Red was a volcano about to erupt. "Nothing's changed, dammit. Estrada wants to even the score with AMF for the sucker play they pulled on him."

Red was dead-on accurate, of course. The Andean Mining Federation had run a near perfect scam. They had romanced Salvador Estrada into a joint venture on a new emerald mine. After months of digging, the Federation declared the mine a dud and closed it.

Estrada lost his investment. Not long afterwards the Federation had better luck with another mine, located in the same general area, but that Estrada was not a partner in. It was virtually spitting out emeralds, all of them high-grade stones.

It gave Estrada pause to think, and as he did, the distinct aroma of decaying fish came to mind. His spies learned that the new mine was nothing more than a cleverly routed shaft that joined the end of the original mine, which was where the emeralds were all along.

Now Estrada was out for blood. He was going to plant the emeralds Kurt and Red had stolen from the Federation in such a way as to make it appear as if AMF's president had stolen them. This would set up a sequence of three events.

First, the president's life expectancy would be reduced to a matter of hours, possibly minutes. Second, the vacuum left by the late president's demise would create a bloody power struggle, which would further eliminate some of the major players. Third, in the midst of the chaos, Estrada would step in and take control. Red was right. The original plan had not changed.

But Kurt's had.

His voice turned as deadly as his eyes. "Think very carefully before you answer my next question. You get it wrong and you'll still be going back to the 'glades tonight, but as gator food."

“Ask your fucking question.”

“If you understand Estrada's got a big hard on to get his hands on those emeralds. If you understand he'll stop at nothing to make it happen. If you understand the deal we made with him and how it works. Why the hell did you try to cut a deal with someone else?"

Red looked as if someone had grabbed his balls by reaching down his throat. "Say again?"

"Never occurred to you Estrada would find out?"

"What the fuck? I didn't try to strike a deal with anyone. That's fucking crazy."

"Crazy like a fox. According to Estrada you found a guy willing to pay you a cool mil for the emeralds, as much as you were gonna to make anyway after you split with me. And it'd be cold cash. You wouldn't have to fuck with the drugs."

"Man, who told you this shit?"

"Estrada. He heard about the deal through the grapevine. He's got a hell of a grapevine."

"I'll wrap that grapevine round the little sonuvabitch's neck. He's lying."

"You forget how well you stand out in a crowd. The guy described you perfectly. A big goon with a head like Clarabell the Clown."

Red was quiet for a moment. The silence in the room was so complete that the night sounds and the drone of the generator out back became deafening. "Somebody's trying to move in on us, partner. Gotta be."

Kurt used his other hand to steady his aim. "Try again."

Red ignored the gun. He was focused inward, trying to work it out. He was unwittingly following Kurt's script to the letter. His eyes sharpened. "Wait a minute. When did this go down?"

Bingo. The question Kurt was waiting for. "Thursday. Why?"

A menacing smile spread across Red's face. "I was hunting 'gators on Thursday."

"Bullshit."

"With Scooter and Ace. They'll vouch."

Kurt said nothing, just reached behind the bar and dialed his CB radio until he got the connection he wanted. But the call to Scooter was merely a ruse for Red's benefit. Kurt knew for certain that Scooter, Ace, and Red had been hunting alligators on Thursday. Floyd Ketchum told him so. Floyd was one of several swamp rats Kurt kept supplied with booze and cigarettes in exchange for updates on Red's movements.

"Scooter? Yeah, Kurt. Tried to reach you shitheads Thursday. Thought we'd get a game together, lighten the load in your back pocket a little." Kurt paused just long enough for dramatic effect. "Say what? No shit. Any luck? I'm impressed. Must've had your hands full being just the two of you."

Kurt displayed the best stunned look he could muster. "He was? All day? Shit. No, man, nothing's wrong. Over and out."

Kurt set the microphone down, turned the nine-millimeter away from Red, flicked on the safety, ejected the clip, and tossed the weapon onto the bar. Red relaxed noticeably, putting his hands on his hips. "You're right. Somebody's trying to cut in."

Red walked past Kurt toward the kitchen. "I oughta roast your nuts." He returned holding a washcloth full of ice cubes against his nose. "Okay, so what're we gonna do?"

Kurt shrugged. "What can we do?"

Red thought for a moment, then said, "Well, don't you think we gotta change our plans?"

It was like Red was reading the lines Kurt had written. Perfect. Scene one in the can. No need for another take. But still a lot of scenes to go. He gave Red his best brother-in-arms grin.

"Guess we do. Guess we better have a drink first."

"First sensible thing you've said all night, partner."

15

It was 1:28 AM when Paula pulled into the driveway of the horseshoe-shaped Casa Taylor. She coasted into the triple-wide carport then parked in her usual space between Bill's gold Caddy Eldorado and his new twenty-four foot Chris Craft Sportsman.

For the second time tonight Paula had arrived stealthily at a destination, although this one couldn't be more different than the first. Nothing wild here. Nothing lurking in the dark but snobbery, duplicity, and avarice.

Their home was almost identical to every other house in the upscale neighborhood. Sprawling brick ranches bordered with thick shrubs. Planters overflowing with colorful explosions of flowers. Large manicured lawns flat as putting greens with a splattering of royal palms here and there. Oversized flagstone patios around back complete with competition-size swimming pools. Upper middle class anywhere else in America. Entry level in Palm Beach.

Paula eased her way quietly through the kitchen then turned left toward the hallway leading to her bedroom. The light was on in the family room. Good. Bill had probably fallen asleep in there watching TV. He'd been doing that a lot of late. Fine with Paula. She'd have the bedroom to herself.

It was located at the end of the hallway. She passed Mama Taylor's room first, heard bedsprings squeak so hurried by, then continued past Billy's room, empty now, and crept into her and Bill's room. She shut the door soundlessly and sighed with relief. Made it.

Nothing seemed more appealing to her at the moment than diving into bed and pulling the covers over her head. She dropped her overnight bag near the closet. In one swift move she pulled the shift over her head then tossed it into the dirty clothes hamper.

"I've been waiting for you."

Paula screamed out and whirled to face Bill sitting in the chair by the sliding glass door. He was wearing a red bathrobe. He had one leg crossed casually over the other. She was very aware of being naked except for her panties. Reflexively she covered her breasts.

"I thought you were . . ."

Before she finished, Bill charged out of the chair, grabbed her panties, ripped them off, then shoved her backwards onto the bed.

"No, Bill, wait . . ."

He tossed off his robe and was on her, wedging his legs between hers.

"Bill stop."

She pushed at him, but he grabbed her wrists and pinned them over her head.

"NO!"

He spread her legs and shoved into her with one powerful thrust. Paula cried out, arched her back, and as he pounded away at her, was surprised to find her body responding.

Everything she wanted Kurt to do to her earlier Bill was doing to her now. Not the Bill of her long, empty marriage, but the Bill she'd fallen in love with all those years ago. The Bill of their wedding night. The Bill that couldn't get enough of her, that wanted to possess her completely and make her his own.

The Bill who wanted to make the two of them one.

She broke his grip and threw her arms around his neck, pulling him closer, kissing him.

"Oh God, Bill."

For an instant they were something they had not been in nearly twenty years. Lovers. It felt so good, so damn good. She realized she was crying, tasted the salty tears.

They fell into the perfect rhythm of old, their bodies familiar, working together to give each other maximum pleasure, their breaths coming in gasps and whimpers and growls. Their lovemaking reached its crescendo and they climaxed together, Bill bucking with each final thrust, hissing, grunting, Paula screaming out, her climax long and deep.

Bill rolled off her, spent, panting.

Paula was flushed, tingling. She wiped the tears from her eyes but that did not keep more from coming. What the hell just happened? she asked herself. They only made love on rare occasions and even then it wasn't love, it was just perfunctory sex. A bodily function. A marital duty. She looked over at Bill. He was staring at the ceiling, apparently as mystified at what just happened as she was.

"Bill . . ." She said it tenderly, her hand on his shoulder, a caress.

"Sorry," was all he said then turned onto his side with his back to her.

Paula pulled the sheet up to her neck and turned on her side too so that they were back to back. She folded her knees up to her stomach and sobbed uncontrollably until she blessedly, drifted off to sleep.

16

Mama Taylor remained deathly still in her bed for a few more minutes until she decided the wrestling match down the hall was finally over. She didn't think badly of her son for needing to do it. He was a man and he had his manly needs. She was grateful there was at least one thing that waste of a wife of his seemed to be good at.

She tossed the covers back and grunted her way out of bed, grabbing a pillow on the way and tucking it under her arm. She pushed her walker aside and stepped gingerly over to the window. She drew open the curtains, tossed the pillow on the floor beneath the window, and kneeled on it.

It was her favorite spot to pray because she was able to look up at the night sky with all its twinkling stars and know that God was up there watching her. She clasped her gnarled, arthritic fingers together beneath her chin and said, "Dear Heavenly Father, it's your humble servant Lucy Taylor again, down here in Palm Beach, Florida. Can you see me?"

She paused for a moment to give Him time to locate her, then smiled piously and continued. "Lord, I know you get tired of me bringing this up, but can't you do something to lighten the load on my precious son Bill? I mean, *your* son, Lord. I'm just the unworthy vessel you used to bring him into the world, glory be to you. I'm sure it hasn't escaped your notice how he works like a slave and never gets a bit of help from that whiny little wife he's stuck with."

Mama Taylor thought that might have sounded a bit harsh and added, "Just calling a spade a spade, Lord." Her voice dropped ominously. "You and I both know what she's been up to lately. I'm just everlastingly grateful my Bill doesn't know. It'd kill him. You know how proud he is."

If Bill really had any self-pride, she thought, he would have cut Paula free like an ingrown toenail years ago. But no need to bother God with that right now. Stay focused, Lucy.

"What my Bill needs is a helpmate, Lord. Oh, I do what I can but you see how old and feeble I am . . ."

To emphasize the point, Mama Taylor lapsed into a coughing fit. When it passed, she looked back up at the night sky sheepishly.

"Excuse me, Lord, you see what I mean. Not that I'm complaining about the infirmities you've visited upon me. You are as always merciful in your judgment and I deserve whatever punishment you deem necessary for my transgressions.

"But I'm not here tonight to talk about my problems, Lord. I'm asking you to bestow your blessings on my Bill. What he needs is someone who'll take an active interest in his business, help him realize his dreams, 'cause he's still got mighty big dreams, Lord. He needs someone to stand by him and believe in him and sacrifice for him.

"As for Paula, well, maybe you could show her there's fulfillment beyond the flesh that can be discovered only through devotion to the man she loves and service to your kingdom."

Mama Taylor took a deep breath and trembled. She was about to broach a subject she had never discussed with God before, but she was convinced she couldn't put it off any longer.

"I know you put Paula here to mock me for my own sins, Lord. And I also know the Bible speaks of the sins of the father being visited on the son."

She swallowed hard then said, "But I don't recall it saying anything about the sins of the mother. Why must Bill suffer for what I did? He is without fault. Punish me, Lord, not him. Punish me."

Mama Taylor reckoned she had already been punished enough, but you could never be too humble and submissive with God. She added her usual closer, "I ask this in your son Jesus' name. Amen."

She was still a moment, as if waiting for an answer, but when it didn't come, decided God heard her and she'd made her case the best she could. She pulled herself upright, tucked the pillow under her arm, closed the curtains, and made her way back to bed.

The alarm clock beneath the lamp read 2:15. She'd have to be up in less than four hours to rouse the household, prepare breakfast, and make sure everybody got to church on time. One thing was certain; Paula couldn't be counted on to do it. Mama Taylor turned off the lamp and curled up under the covers. Oh well, she thought, everybody's got their cross to bear. Mine is Paula.

17

Kurt yawned, pushed back in his chair and said, "Okay, let's run through it one last time."

If Red was tired he showed no signs of it. He paced the room, counted off each point on his fingers. "Okay, one: we change the meeting with Estrada from this Tuesday to Sunday the eighteenth. That's your job."

"Right," Kurt said.

"Two: that gives us a few extra days to find out who's trying to horn in on our deal. That's my job."

Kurt nodded and thought, good luck pal.

"Three: we meet here Friday at twenty one hundred," Red continued. "Any last minute snags will be dealt with. Then four: we divide the emeralds evenly between us."

In his mind Kurt said, yeah, asshole. That's how we keep each other honest. Only problem is, those are fake stones we'll be dividing up. I've already got the real ones cut, polished, and hidden away.

Not what you should be thinking about right now, he reminded himself. Concentrate. Stay in character. You're playing the role of your life. If you aren't completely believable, your life won't be worth a whore's promise of love.

Kurt adopted the cold, business-like tone that had been his trademark in countless briefings prior to a mission launch. "And then?"

Red seemed to be buying it. "We split, each taking different routes to Bogotá. We rendezvous at Plaza de Bolivar Sunday night, twenty-hundred."

Yeah, Kurt thought, you wait there for me in the middle of Bogotá looking like the big ape you are. Meanwhile, I'll be back here with Paula. Kurt had to suppress an urge to laugh maniacally as he listened to Red drone on about how they would meet with Estrada and attend to the myriad other details of a plan that would never be executed.

Red departed just after 5:00 AM. Kurt lit a storm lantern, shut down the generator, and made his way to the bar. It had been a long night. He grabbed a bottle of Jack Daniels Black, fired up a Camel, stepped out onto the verandah, and dropped into a sling chair. The breeze whispering across the lagoon was fresh and mixed nicely with the booze, the tobacco, and the exhaustion.

Red, you worthless piece of shit, you're finally going to get yours, Kurt thought as he settled into the chair. His only regret was he wouldn't be there to see it happen, to see the expression on Red's face when it dawned on him he'd bought it. And that his old 'partner' Kurt had written out the Bill of Sale.

Their history together went back to the early thirties as young leathernecks patrolling rivers in China, keeping them safe for U.S. Commerce. During World War Two they fought in many of the bloodiest Pacific campaigns: Iwo Jima, Peleliu, Okinawa.

Red and Kurt were known as the warriors elite that other Marines looked up to and wanted to emulate. Their combat exploits became legend. Nearly 20,000 of the Corps didn't make it back from the Pacific slaughterhouse. Red and Kurt did.

When the war was over, they had difficulty adjusting to a peacetime Marine Corps. They knew how to fight. They didn't know how to stand down. It was Red who came up with a solution. "There're lots of other bad guys out there, partner, just itching for us to kick their asses. Hell, Africa's full of 'em. One little country after another fighting off some hard-on trying to stick it in sideways. They need somebody to blow away the shitheads. That's us."

Red and Kurt left the Marines and were soon back in the ass-kicking business. Kurt still believed his was a necessary job, killing as a means to a better end. Red went beyond accepting to thoroughly enjoying. As the killing went on, Kurt noticed Red's eyes were not only devoid of color; they were devoid of life. Gazing into them was like peering into Hell.

On several occasions Red tried to involve Kurt in questionable missions in which they would clearly be the bad guys. Kurt always refused, but the lines separating right from wrong were becoming blurred, if they were ever clear at all.

He found himself overthrowing regimes he'd helped put in power only a short time earlier, regimes that had promised to bring freedom to their people, and food, and jobs, but had instead brought an even greater tyranny than existed before.

No matter how many of the 'bad guys' he killed, there seemed to be no respite from the suffering around him. And the carnage. Each passing day made him increasingly aware of that one bullet every warrior knows is out there, the one with his name on it. The longer he carried a gun, the better chance that bullet had of finding him. It was just a matter of time. The question was: how much time?

The turning point came a little over two years ago. They were all sitting around a jungle campfire getting royally smashed when Red showed up. He had a village girl with him wearing nothing but a loincloth and an expression of abject horror. No more than fifteen or sixteen, Kurt guessed. Red bragged about how he had trained the girl like a dog. She'd do anything he told her. He demonstrated this by commanding her to go down on Wally Smith, which she did without hesitation.

In their drunken stupor the guys didn't know quite how to react. But the expression on the girl's face broke through even their callused hearts. Her eyes, when she looked up, provided a glimpse of the nightmare she was living.

Wally pulled the girl off and said, "Nice trick, Red. Why don't you let her go home?" Sonny Stewart grabbed a stick and threw it toward the village saying, "Go fetch, girl," hoping she'd keep on running.

But the girl didn't move, and Red said, "See, she won't answer to anyone but me. That's how I got her trained. Watch this." And before anyone knew what was happening Red handed the girl his .357 magnum and said, "Here, girl. Put this in your mouth and pull the trigger."

All Kurt remembered was leaping over the fire, trying to stop her. He was in mid-air when the gun went off, blowing her brains out the back of her head. He fell on her limp body, landing badly and breaking his arm. It was all that had kept him from grabbing the gun and putting Red out of his misery.

The memory of that night still made Kurt flinch. That had been the end for Kurt. No more delusions. Killing was killing and he wanted out. He used the money he had stashed away to buy Curiosity Cove and the boat. His Jeep was Army surplus from years back. He didn't need much else.

But Red never gave up the game. He liked killing too much. Worst of all, he never gave up Kurt. "We're comrades in arms, partner. Nothing's ever gonna come between us."

Getting rid of Red posed several problems. You were either Red's friend or his enemy, that's the way his mind worked. Kurt wasn't prepared to be his enemy. It would mean retaining the jungle mentality and Kurt was through with the jungle. Or so he thought.

18

The kettle whistled and the bread popped up in the toaster. Mama Taylor got to her feet and, knowing she was the only one stirring this early, stepped lively over to the stove, leaving her walker beside the table. A few moments later her customary breakfast was spread out before her: farina, unbuttered toast, grapefruit, and Sanka. As she dug into the grapefruit, footsteps sounded in the hallway. She scooted her walker closer.

"Morning Mom," Bill said in the middle of a yawn. Mama Taylor looked up to see her son ambling in with the Sunday paper tucked under his arm.

Bill Taylor had ex-jock written all over him. He still had the same swagger, same cocky air, but the years of fighting Nazis, then barehandedly building a thriving printing business, were written on his weathered face. And in the trace of ruthlessness in his eyes. His six-two frame was still fit, but thicker in the middle, with the slightest stoop to his broad shoulders.

"Mornin', son," Mama Taylor said. She thought he looked particularly handsome in his dark brown three-piece suit, pinstripe shirt, and burgundy tie. "Sit down, I'll pour you some coffee."

She reached for her walker but Bill already had a hand on her shoulder. "I'll get it."

As he filled his cup she asked, "Sleep well, dear?"

He gave her a raised eyebrow, as if he thought her seemingly innocuous question might conceal a barb. He shrugged, "Like a rock." He sat across from her and opened the paper.

"Then I guess Paula didn't wake you when she came in?"

Now he was sure she was baiting him. He refused to take it. "Did she come in?" He gazed over the front page, discouraging further inquiry. It didn't work.

"Well, her car's here. Figured she came with it."

“Reasonable deduction,“ Bill said with a grin. He went back to his paper.

“Stayed up till midnight waiting for her but I had to put these tired old bones to bed. Oh if that child only knew how I worry about her."

Bill smiled at his mother, but there was a hint of impatience in his eyes. It stung her. "Mom, Paula’s made the trip to her mother’s a hundred times. She always finds her way back”

"You don't worry about her? Out there on the road all alone in the middle of the night?"

Without looking up from his paper, Bill said, “No.”

"Well, somebody needs to."

"Fine. That can be your job. My blessings."

Clearly miffed, Mama Taylor glanced at the clock then scooted her chair back and reached for her walker. "Dear me, it's after seven. If Paula doesn't get up and get a move on we'll be late for Sunday School." She noticed Bill shaking his head with a cynical grin. "What?"

"Do we really have to go through this charade every Sunday? Paula hasn't been to church in over a year."

"Well it's time she started back."

Before Bill protested, Mama Taylor threw open the sliding glass door and was gone.

Launching across the broad flagstone patio, Mama Taylor clump-clumped a direct diagonal course to the end of the wing where the bedrooms were located. Due to the darkness inside, the sliding glass door was virtually a mirror. As she paused there, the sun broke through, lighting up the bedroom and at the same time creating a rather jarring phenomenon: the grotesque specter of her own reflection superimposed over the sublimely beautiful form of Paula asleep. It was an image that mocked her.

The sculptured beauty of Paula's face against the Pekinese features of her own.

Paula's full, sensuous lips in contradiction to her own tight grimace.

The fiery cascade of Paula's hair opposed to the dingy white ringlets framing her own face.

The rhythmic flow of Paula's body compared to her own stooped, squatty form.

Paula's sleek, graceful legs contrasted with her own bowed, spindly limbs.

"I know I'm an ugly old woman," Mama Taylor said, not sure whether she was talking to her reflected image, Paula, or God. "But this isn't necessary."

She swallowed the lump in her throat. No, she resolved, tears are for the weak and I cannot be weak. She slid open the door and entered, quiet as a shadow in a cemetery.

Once inside, Mama Taylor paused again. If the sight of Paula through her own reflection had been unsettling, the vision of her lying only a few feet away, clearly naked, the sheet twisted about her providing only a modicum of modesty, made her catch her breath. The aura of Paula's raw sensuality was palpable. Mama Taylor's nostrils flared. She detected the scent of sex. She swallowed hard, her mouth dry.

Don't be a fool, she scolded herself, but when she closed her eyes, the image came back to her. Vividly. Paula, her head thrown back, crying out in wild ecstasy, clinging desperately to the bull-like man on top of her. A man that was not Bill, as he . . .

Mama Taylor jerked her eyes open. Her heart raced. Her face was clammy. No good, she told herself, you've got to stop it. Just wake her up, get on with it.

Mama Taylor moved closer until she was standing directly over Paula. Warmth radiated from her, a warmth that seemed to beckon her.

I was like her, she thought, and again she saw the intertwined bodies writhing beneath the moon. Only this time it wasn't Paula being ravished by the bull-like man, it was herself, head thrown back, crying out in ecstasy. Oh no, don't let it happen again.

Father, save me from this.

A breeze rushed in. Paula groaned, shifted to find warmth. The top of the sheet gaped open revealing the heavy roundness of a breast. Something stirred deep within Mama Taylor that was intensely frightening and she cried out, "Paula!"

Paula leapt up like an unleashed spring, yelping so loud that it elicited a similar shriek from Mama Taylor. Paula collapsed against the padded headboard, both hands pressing the sheet over her chest, as if searching for a heartbeat. It took both of them a moment to recover their composure. Mama Taylor said, "Sorry to startle you like that."

Paula brushed her hair back from her face and looked at Mama Taylor with undisguised loathing. The green in Paula's eyes shone even brighter when she was angry, Mama Taylor noticed. No matter. Let them turn pea green for all I care. I will not be intimidated. She cocked her head with an air of authority and said, "You need to get up, Paula. We'll be late for Sunday School."

Paula responded in a low growl that Mama Taylor couldn't decipher. "What did you say, child?"

This time Paula's voice rattled the windows. "Get out! And don't you ever come into this room again!"

It was like a physical blow to Mama Taylor and she actually staggered back a step. "Paula," she said, stunned, her face ashen. They had quarreled often but Paula had never spoken to her with such unconcealed enmity.

But before she voiced her outrage, Paula leapt out of bed, jerked on a nightgown and was out the door, running across the courtyard.

She burst through the open sliding glass door and commandeered the chair next to Bill. "She's got to go," she said without salutation or preamble. "Buy her an apartment in a retirement community, put her on a slow boat to China, do whatever you have to do, but get her the hell out of our house."

Bill calmly folded the paper, took a sip of coffee, and said, "Yes, I slept well, thank you. And you?"

"Don't play games with me, Bill. You've got to get her out of here. Billy's gone. We don't need her anymore. We never did."

Bill had never seen Paula this livid before. He wondered what had transpired between his wife and mother in the bedroom just now. "Are we talking about my mother?" clearly goading her.

"I want her out of here," she yelled and there was not the slightest hint of fear or contrition in her eyes. She was blatantly challenging Bill and the very audacity of that act made him grow dark with anger. "Lower your voice," he growled. "She's right behind you."

Before Paula responded, Mama Taylor entered, panting for breath. She stood indignantly for a moment, eyeing Bill and Paula. "Am I interrupting something?"

Bill got up and made his way to the coffee pot. He had the situation firmly in hand. "Of course not, Mom," he said. Paula was glaring at him. In turn, he merely smiled at her.

"Actually," Paula said to Mama Taylor with the barest semblance of cordiality, "Bill and I were just discussing Billy."

"Billy? What about Billy?"

"Now that he's gone, you need to go too."

Mama Taylor gasped.

Bill gulped down the scalding sip of coffee he had just taken and said, "Paula!" so loud it made her jump. "That's not what we were talking about at all."

"Oh yes it was," Paula snapped back. "Listen Bill, we need to talk to each other as husband and wife. We haven't done that for a long time, and believe me, it's really important that we do it right now." She was clearly trying to send him signals with her eyes. "I mean, really important," she added.

Damn, he thought. What's gotten into the woman? Give her a good roll in the hay and she starts thinking they mean something to each other. He instantly regretted the thought, even if it was true. They both knew it was true.

Fuck this, he thought, and was about to make a cutting response to Paula when Mama Taylor interrupted with an air of injured dignity, saying, "You two can talk all you want. I wouldn't dream of interfering. I'll just go to my room, son, and wait for you to call me."

Bill glowered at Paula. "You don't have to leave, Mom. Paula and I have no secrets from you, do we honey?"

It was a term of endearment that went back to their college days. It stuck in his mouth now, indicating how hollow their relationship had become. He was aware that Paula was gazing deep into his eyes, as if searching for something.

"No secrets, Bill, but possibly a few things that wouldn't interest her."

Bill folded his arms and looked at her with amusement. "Funny," he said, "I'm trying to recall the last time you said something that interested *me*."

For a moment Bill thought Paula was going to slap him. Instead, her voice was calm but insistent. "We need to talk, Bill."

"We need to get moving or we'll be late for church," Mama Taylor said.

Paula grabbed Bill's arm and said, "Don't go to church. Stay home so we can talk."

Mama Taylor was having none of that. "And what will I tell people when they ask why you could bring me to church but couldn't come yourselves?"

"Tell them to mind their own business."

Bill decided this was getting out of hand. He jerked his arm free. "All right that's enough . . ."

But neither woman was paying attention to him. His mother burst out with, "I most certainly will not."

Bill was really pissed now and was about to tell both of them to shut up when Paula slammed her fist down on the counter so hard that both he and Mama Taylor flinched. "Bill, damn it, we need to talk! Now!"

Bill's face was burning. He utilized the silence following Paula's outburst to give her his most withering look. "I think you'd better go back to bed," he said. "Sleep it off."

Paula was trembling, but whether from remorse or rage he couldn't tell. "Why can't we talk, Bill?"

"About what, Paula?" He let her see in his eyes the full measure of his disdain for her. It made her shudder and he took advantage of that small act of submission by again yelling, "About what?"

But instead of cowering as he expected her to, Paula whirled on him and said heatedly, "About beer and Chinese takeout and working together in the garage all night and screwing on the table next to that old press that broke down every fifteen minutes."

Bill's face flushed. It was as if she had opened a dusty file drawer and extracted a cherished photograph he had nearly forgotten. Those days came rushing back to him along with overpowering feelings of passion and joy and lightness. The two of them little more than newly weds, chunking every penny they had into a wheezy old press, using the garage of their small rental house for a shop, working all night, laughing, screwing, building a business. How many lifetimes ago was that? Whatever happened to those two kids in the picture?

He looked at Paula standing expectantly before him now, her eyes full of hope. The photo was shoved back into the file and the drawer slammed shut. She was the one who made it go wrong. She was the one who betrayed the dream. How stupid of her to dredge up memories of a happier but long dead time in an attempt to soften him.

"It might interest you to know that that old press is still kicking. Use it almost every day." He watched with satisfaction as Paula's mouth gaped open and her eyes filled with fire. "In fact, I don't know what I'd do without it."

Paula reaction was akin to a volcano erupting. "Damn it, Bill, you know I'm not talking about that fucking press!"

Mama Taylor reacted as if stung by a bee. "Well, maybe I had better leave. I won't have that kind of language ringing in my ears when I step into the Lord's house."

Bill calmly put his cup in the sink then turned back to confront Paula with the one tactic he knew would knock away her underpinnings. "I think we need to get you help, Paula."

It did the trick. "What?"

"I think you're going nuts."

It clearly unnerved her. He heard the quiver in her voice. "Why? Because I want to find out what happened to our marriage? That makes me nuts?"

Tears glistened in Paula's eyes and Bill knew he had won. He shook his head sadly and said, "Go back to bed, Paula."

They were interrupted by boisterous shouts, the clatter of shoes running in the hallway, and a shrill woman's voice yelling, "Now just slow down, you two." A second later Jimmy and Johnny, the two brats from next door, all decked out in their Sunday best, tore into the kitchen and skidded into the table. Mama Taylor's bowl of farina flipped over and crashed onto the floor.

The boys froze. Millie, their long-suffering mother, appeared and cocked her hands on her hips in an exasperated pose. She looked first at Bill, then at Paula, and shook her head in mock despair. "Children."

Paula pressed her hands against her forehead as if to keep her sanity from flying away. She knew what Millie was going to say next -- the same thing she'd said a hundred times before. Paula recited it for her now. "Yes, Millie. At least mine is in college. We don't know if you can survive that long."

She ran from the room.

19

Kurt was wakened from a deep sleep early Sunday afternoon by Wally's trilling whistle. He jerked up from the sling chair and almost knocked over what remained of the Jack Daniels. He righted the bottle then stood up and stretched, the cracking of his bones sounding like an Independence Day celebration.

Aw Kurt, he said to himself, you're not the man you used to be and probably never will be again. That's all right, he decided, he could still kick the asses of guys twenty years his junior. Well, fifteen, anyway.

Seeing that Kurt was up, Wally soared ten feet into the air and reentered the lagoon with hardly a ripple. He resurfaced and whistled again, bobbing his head up and down, clearly wanting to play.

"Okay, I'm coming, I'm coming," Kurt said, then stripped naked, ran down to the lagoon and dived in. Wally laughed and did a back flip. Like most bottlenose dolphins, he lived to play.

On the dock was a beach ball that had washed up onto the island a while ago. Kurt grabbed it and punched it toward Wally but wide to the right. No problem. Wally fielded it effortlessly then fired it back at Kurt as if it were shot from a cannon. They continued the game for a half-hour or so until Wally lost interest, bobbed his head goodbye, then flipped over and torpedoed out the channel to the Bay.

While Kurt lathered up in the shower he thought of all the tasks he had to accomplish in the next few days. It was a formidable list, but he knew the success of any mission was the result of meticulous preparatory work. Make a mistake there and the mission was doomed before it started.

Food came first, though. He was starving. After toweling off, he slipped into white Bermuda shorts, a polo shirt, and canvas deck shoes, then fired up the *Black Jack* and aimed her toward Key Largo.

The Pickled Pirate was Kurt's favorite Key Largo eatery. It had a dock where he could park the *Black Jack*, a big outdoor deck with a panoramic view of Florida Bay, and food that was just damn fine. As usual, Kurt ordered their Fishermen's Bounty and ate contentedly, watching the colorful array of boats parade across the Bay.

"You look terribly alone."

She was blonde, bronzed, and mid-twenties, dressed in high heel sandals, short-shorts and a loose blouse unbuttoned and knotted below her bursting breasts. Her bare stomach was rock hard. Her legs were three miles long.

"How can you say that?" Kurt replied. "I've got all my pals keeping me company." He gestured toward the lobster, scallops, stone crab claw, and a dozen shrimp spread before him."

She smiled, leaning forward enough for her blouse to gape open. "You can do better than that, don't you think? Mind if I sit down?"

She didn't wait for an answer. She sat across from Kurt and said, "You've got a big appetite."

"I'm a big boy."

She smiled, ran a finger along his arm. "Yes, you certainly are. And I suppose after a meal like this you're probably going to want something really sweet for dessert."

Kurt wanted to tell her she was coming on too strong, that he was familiar with the scenario. It seemed to him these scuba bunnies were all cast from the same mold. He glanced up. A short but tightly muscled young man in swim trunks, polo shirt, and sandals was striding purposefully toward his table. Yeah, he thought, that's the way I had it figured. "Here comes your boyfriend," he said to the girl.

"Barbara!"

Barbara gave the guy a drop-dead sneer, leaning back in her chair as if she had been with Kurt for hours. "Yes?"

The guy jerked another chair out and plopped down, inserting himself between Kurt and Barbara. "Won't you join us?" Kurt said, but the guy ignored him, turning instead to Barbara. "What's going on?" he demanded.

By way of reply she smiled knowingly at Kurt and fingered a shrimp. Kurt decided he'd enjoyed about as much of this as he could stand. He turned to the boyfriend and calmly said, "You mean you don't know?"

"Know what?" the boyfriend challenged.

It occurred to Kurt that someone should write a book on how to speak under duress. He thought it even funnier when Barbara winked at him, as if they were acting in harmony on this little charade. Time to burst some bubbles, he decided. He dabbed his mouth with his napkin, turned to the boyfriend, and held out his hand. "Hi, my name is Kurt Younger."

The guy didn't know how to respond, so he shook Kurt's hand and revealed that he was Jerry Statler.

"Well, Jer, it seems you haven't been showing Barbara the attention she thinks she deserves. So she decided to make you aware of just how great the demand for her charms are by throwing herself at me. Figured it would make you jealous, get you back in line."

Barbara's bronzed face appeared sunburned. Her mouth formed a large "O" and her eyes revealed the true nature of the beast within. "You bastard."

Kurt was undaunted. "What you need to do, Jer, is take Barbara back to wherever you're staying and treat her like a bitch in heat. It's what she wants."

Barbara flew out of her chair, outraged. Kurt smiled and said, "Now don't go into your righteous indignation act, Barb. All three of us know what I've just said is true."

She glared at Jerry and screamed, "Are you going to let him talk to me that way?"

Jerry, his face showing befuddlement, stared at Kurt, who simply shrugged. A faint smile spread across Jerry's face. "Yeah, I am."

Barbara looked as if someone had just bayoneted her through the heart. She spun on her heels and stormed out of the restaurant. Jerry rose unhurriedly and held out his hand to Kurt. "Thanks."

Kurt took his hand, smiled mischievously and said, "Don't thank me yet, Jer. But good luck, anyway."

Jerry smiled and departed, leaving Kurt to reflect on how much being in love with Paula had changed him. A year ago he would have taken Barbara for every ounce of pleasure she had to offer, then thrown the remaining husk back to Jerry.

He ached to have Paula sitting across the table from him now, the two of them enjoying the vast sweep of bay as the sky put on its grand finale, running through every shade of red and purple until giving way to the dark mystery of night.

He sighed. Six more days.

Paula. No, he didn't deserve her. But he was going to take her anyway. Because, number one, he could, and number two, for the first time in his life he was in love. And anybody who had a problem with that could go fuck himself.

20

Lester Jenkins jumped up as headlights played across the curtains. Peering out the window, he was disappointed to see it was just a neighbor pulling out of his driveway. Lester stepped back away from the window and gazed at the clock again.

"He said he'd be here at 9:00."

"Oh, relax," his wife Ruth said. "It's only 9:20. When was the last time you arrived any place on time?"

"Look, this guy's my last chance of selling that piece of junk. Ain't nobody else gonna buy it, that's for damn sure."

"He said he'd be here. Don't have a hernia."

"I won't, Ruth. You've already told me we can't afford it. Besides, I'm buying that new cabin cruiser. I don't care what you say."

"All I said is you can't buy it on credit. You got cash, then bon voyage for all I care."

He was about to tell her she didn't tell him what he could or couldn't do but was stopped by a car door slamming. He sat frozen, listening to the sound of approaching footsteps.

"Here comes Santy Claus," Ruth commented dryly.

Lester sprang to his feet. He was at the door even before the bell rang. He tried to appear blasé as he greeted his visitor. "Hello, hello. You Ames?"

Ames was tall, dumpy and, Ruth observed, had a terminal case of acne. He adjusted thick glasses under bushy eyebrows. "Sorry I'm late. Hope I didn't inconvenience you."

"'Course not, 'course not. Just sitting around watching a little TV. Come in, come in."

"Thanks, but if it's all the same to you I'd like to hitch up the boat and skedaddle. Told my wife I'd be back by 10:30."

You're damn right it's all right, Lester thought. Get the old carcass out of here. Just give me the money. What he said was, "Sure thing. I'll turn on the carport light so we can see better."

When Lester stepped into the carport he wished he hadn't made the offer. Under the raw truth of the naked bulb, the *Far Horizons* looked as if it should be named *Lost Horizons*. Every warp, chink, and crack in the woodwork was glaringly apparent, and the predominant color of the old fourteen horse Evinrude was rust. The boat reeked of gas and oil, fish and beer.

But much to Lester's relief, Mr. Ames lifted the trailer's tongue and pulled it toward the hitch on his old Chevy wagon. Really must be in a hurry, Lester thought. "Here, let me help."

"I can manage," said Mr. Ames. Indeed he made the task appear effortless. As he was fastening the tow chains, he turned to Lester. "You got the title?"

"Sure, sure." Lester turned to fetch it but found Ruth right behind him, smiling sweetly at Ames, waving the title in the air. "You got the money? You said you'd bring cash."

Mr. Ames drew an envelope from his back pocket and counted out crisp, new hundred dollar bills. "That do it?"

Lester couldn't keep the excitement from his voice. "Yes sir!" He scribbled his signature on the title, shook Mr. Ames' hand, and looked his last on the *Far Horizons*.

“See,” Ruth said. “Dreams can come true, even for a grumpy old fart like you.”

21

Betty picked up the receiver and dialed her own house. "Consuelo? Betty. Gotta work late again. Don't know. Late. You'll have to stay over. Hey, Connie, it's my job. I don't work, I don't get paid. I don't get paid, I can't afford you. Got it? Life's tough, so what? Let me speak to the kids."

She had placed that call at 5:37 PM, right after Bill left to have supper with his bitch wife and battleaxe mother. B and B, she called them. Her own supper had been packed before leaving for work this morning. It consisted of an egg salad sandwich and a tangerine. She drew a cup of coffee from the office urn and ate at her desk.

Afterwards she made her way to the ladies room. Time to check out the merchandise. She stood posture perfect before the mirror and turned in small increments to permit careful examination of front, profile, and rear views.

Betty knew she wouldn't stand a chance in swimsuit competition with the current Mrs. T, but she learned long ago that being a small woman worked to her advantage. Most men felt more heroic around a small woman. It prompted them to be protective, especially men like Bill. Accordingly, she wore clothes that emphasized her compact, trim figure in a feminine, old-fashioned way.

She also wore a lot of lace. Bill loved lace. "Makes a woman look like woman," he said once and she never forgot it. Today she was attired in a lacy blouse with a big bow at the neck. The principal attraction of lace, Betty knew, was all the little holes that revealed just enough of the woman beneath to thoroughly rev up a man's imagination. This particular blouse also buttoned up the front. That was important for tonight's schedule of events.

Betty's long, straight hair was honey-colored and completed the effect. It reached to her waist and was a pain in the ass to keep brushed and shiny, but she believed her mother's words of long ago: if you don't have boobies, have hair. She made the effort.

Betty unbuttoned her blouse enough to dab some perfume between her breasts, then added a smidgen behind her ears. She touched up her make-up then smoothed out her red skirt. In her experience men were like bulls. They were inclined to charge whenever they saw red. High on the agenda tonight was bringing out the raging bull in Bill. She took a step back to study the overall effect. Delicious, she decided. Strawberry shortcake with whipped creme. She turned confidently and left the room.

Betty had been waiting to make her move for over three years now. She'd come close to lift-off several times, but each time the mission got scrubbed at the last minute. Yesterday, for whatever reason, the moon and stars aligned in her favor.

It started when Bill had to fire two pressmen for stealing. Another pressman was on vacation way up North. When Hank, the chief press operator, took a double gainer off the service scaffold and busted his leg in three places, Betty knew her prayers had been answered and in the ensuing confusion she secretly pulled the little pin from the bottom of the big press. Amazing how removing a three inch steel cylinder so easily crippled several tons of machinery. And it was always the last thing the repairman looked for. Happily, he wasn't scheduled until the following morning.

That left only the smaller presses, but they weren't designed to do four-color printing, and TMP-1, which was. It meant she and Bill would have to work all night to meet several nonnegotiable deadlines. Devoted employee that she was, Betty was ready to do her duty.

She slipped on her work apron then pulled her hair back with a pink ribbon so it wouldn't get caught in the press. The apron did hide the merchandise, but seduction wouldn't occur until a few hours later, at which time the hair would come down and the apron would come off. What else came off depended on how well she played her hand.

At long last it was going to happen. She was about to put her tiny size four foot into the glass slipper, knowing it would be a perfect fit.

And then . . .

She would live happily ever after.

Naturally there were a few obstacles to overcome. First, that Amazon Bill was married to. Betty didn't think she'd present much of a problem. Bill and Paula's stars might have glittered brightly once upon a time, but it didn't take an astronomer to see they'd long since fallen into marriage's noxious atmosphere and burnt out. Mrs. T would have to hit the road. Too bad about that. War is Hell, there's bound to be casualties.

Second, Bill's son. The reason she'd waited so long to make her play. Bill was the kind of man who would cling to his marriage, no matter how empty it was, simply for the sake of his child. But now the boy was off at college. No longer a factor.

Last of all was mother dear. Again, no problem. That paragon of Plymouth Rock Puritanism was about to be brought kicking and screaming into the twentieth century. Betty would be her travel agent. Time the old gray mare was put out to pasture.

The way was clear for an all-out assault. If she handled tonight's events skillfully, there would soon be a new Mrs. William Elliot Taylor. The current Mrs. T would be . . .

History.

A buzzer sounded in the shop indicating the front door had just opened. Bill was back. Betty greeted him with her most radiant smile.

22

Paula sat alone at the wrought iron table near the swimming pool, her feet propped up in another chair, sipping a tall glass of water. It was actually tonic water laced with vodka, but that was information Mama Taylor didn't need to know.

Supper had been Southern fried chicken. It was Bill's favorite meal, served with mashed potatoes, gravy, and buttermilk biscuits. According to Bill, nobody made it quite like his devoted mother. Paula just couldn't seem to get it right. Which was fine with Paula. True Southern fried chicken and homemade biscuits were a pain in the ass to prepare. Anything that kept Mama Taylor out of her hair for an extended period of time was like manna from Heaven.

Watching Mama Taylor prepare the meal was always interesting. She never stopped moving from stove top to counter top to table top, her hands so full of pans and bowls and plates that she had to push the useless walker in front of her, grunting and groaning all the while as if being humped by a sailor who'd been too long at sea. The thought of Mama Taylor assuming the position made Paula laugh. It made her feel much better.

Bill had departed right after supper because of something urgent he had to attend to at the shop. Something that couldn't wait till morning. As for Mama Taylor, she was inside doing her evening devotionals before crawling into bed.

It was a quiet, starry night with a waxing moon. A wayward breeze stirred the wind chimes hanging from a nearby live oak and it played its haunting song. Paula savored the moment. It was good to be home alone.

She gazed up at the stars and her mind was flooded with memories of how her affair with Kurt began. Billy wanted to spend Labor Day weekend at Grandma Doherty's, saying that in her condition who knew how much longer she'd be around. Paula almost bought it until she found out about the blouse-busting blonde he'd met the last time they were down.

They all made the trip, including Mama Taylor. Birdy was away with her family, which was normal whenever the entire Taylor brood visited. To Paula's surprise, Mama Taylor volunteered to look after her mother, and did so with a gentleness and sensitivity that Paula thought her incapable of. It left Paula free to browse the craft shops in Tavernier and watch the mating dance between Billy and Christie, the incendiary blonde.

As for Bill, he was up before dawn each morning fishing, coming back late Sunday afternoon half-smashed, bringing with him a line of smelly fish for Paula to clean, and Kurt Younger. She never understood how they managed to meet. She only knew they'd been together all day fishing and drinking and generally having a high old time.

Seeing the two men side by side was jarring. Bill had become virtually asexual, the animal attractiveness that first aroused her long since gone. Kurt, in contrast, had a raw masculinity, untamed, uncompromised, mixed with the kind of reckless good looks that made Paula flush when their eyes first locked.

They stayed outdoors on the back deck, Paula cleaning and grilling the fish, Billy relentlessly teasing Christie, Mama Taylor helping with supper, Bill and Kurt continuing to drink. Bill did most of the talking. Very loudly. Kurt just grinned, added a comment occasionally, and watched Paula. She could feel his eyes on her. She liked how that made her feel. When was the last time Bill looked at her like that?

After the meal, Billy and Christie hurried off for a party somewhere above town. Mama Taylor put Paula's mother to bed, then retired herself. She hated to see Bill drunk.

He passed out in the chaise longue a little after one. Paula was still nursing a vodka-tonic, sitting on top of the picnic table, enjoying the ocean breeze in her face. Kurt walked over and stood before her, staring into her eyes. They had not spoken to each other beyond polite dinner conversation. He looked at her now, a man looking at a woman, his intention perfectly clear. Does he really think he's going to just . . ?

To her amazement, he did.

He took the drink from her hand and led her down to the water's edge. To her further amazement, she didn't resist. She didn't ask what he thought he was doing. She didn't say anything. Even when he unfastened her halter and slipped it off casually, as if he had undressed her a thousand times before. Even as he stood and looked at her brazenly, letting his eyes take their fill, cupping her breasts with his rough hands.

And still Paula didn't speak, couldn't speak. She was aware of the ocean spray against her bare skin, of Bill's snoring only a few yards away, of other people's laughter further down the reef, of Kurt's eyes devouring every inch of her.

He kissed her then, whisking her off her feet, setting her body on fire. Paula was bewildered by her own lack of morality but overwhelmed by the passion this stranger unleashed within her. He laid her down, threw her down was more like it, then stripped off his shirt and trunks.

She looked up at the tall, powerfully built man standing naked above her, moonlight gleaming on his muscular chest and shoulders and his . . . Staring at it made her go cross-eyed. He seemed to be aiming it at her, threatening her with it. She was vaguely aware of pulling off her shorts and panties and that in doing so she was brazenly inviting him to take her. Mostly she was aware of a force surging up within her that was savage and primal and would not, could not be denied.

Then he was on her and she was luxuriating in the wild abandon of their lust making, no longer asking how or why but simply succumbing to a hunger so feral it startled her. By the time it was over, Kurt had opened many doors, taken her to a pinnacle of overwhelming carnal joy she didn't know existed, revealed to her the depths of her womanhood.

Call it the awakening of Paula Taylor.

It had happened a little over a year ago.

She redirected her attention to the task at hand, tried to ignore the dampness between her legs. Enough, she told herself. Just get on with it. Do what you know you have to do.

Paula considered how best to approach Bill about leaving him and knew the best way was not to approach him at all. She was sure he'd try to stop her, hold her prisoner. Not because of any love he had for her but because of his monumental ego. She belonged to him, dammit.

No, a letter was best. It would defuse Bill. It would make it impossible for him to interfere. She would simply drop it in the mail on her way out of town Saturday. He wouldn't get it until Monday and by that time she would have made her peace with Billy and be long gone.

After a few months had passed, after she had some idea of the course her new life was going to take, after Bill had time to accept that she wasn't coming back, she'd file for divorce.

Paula went inside, sat at the small desk in the kitchen. She removed a sheet of personal stationary from its lilac-decorated box. She extracted the fountain pen from its holder and checked to make sure it had ink and that it flowed smoothly. She held the pen poised over the sheet of stationary and took a deep breath.

She began with a simple, bold “Bill --”.

23

Bill carried his forty-two years very well, Betty decided. Getting a little thin on top, but he's tall and I'm short so I don't see the top all that much. And the glasses are okay. Without them his eyes would look too beady. But that perpetual five o'clock shadow was a problem. Maybe he should just grow a beard. Yeah, he'd look good with a beard.

"Thanks for staying late," he said. "We've really got our work cut out for us."

Betty thought, you don't know the half of it.

Bill unbuttoned his cuffs and rolled up his sleeves. "Ready to get on with it?"

Betty thought, you bet, buster. But what she said was, "Aye, aye, Captain," while snapping a playful salute.

Bill laughed as he started toward the press room. "You're a good sport, Betty."

And you're dead meat, she thought, following him.

The print room was a lofty, cinder block structure housing messy work tables, refuse bins, shelves filled with printing supplies, and a number of small presses. The high ceiling allowed ink vapors to rise then get sucked out by an exhaust fan. That was the theory anyway, but the place reeked. The room's main attraction was the massive main press, currently crippled. It resembled a sleeping monster.

They took up positions at TMP#1; the ancient little press Bill started the business with two decades ago. He fired it up and let it idle while Betty handed him the first set of plates.

They worked steadily for a couple of hours, not speaking except about the job at hand. That was the way Betty wanted it. Let him savor my presence. Let the tension build second by second, minute by minute. She enhanced this by innocently brushing against him each time they passed, making sure her breast pushed against his arm, letting him get a whiff of her scented hair as she leaned over to inspect the work coming off the press.

It was just shy of blatant flirting, but done with an air of guileless innocence. It was clearly having the desired effect. Bill was having trouble keeping his mind on the job.

At 10:00 PM Betty excused herself to make a quick call. They continued working for another half-hour then the front door buzzer sounded. Bill looked up impatiently. "Who the hell can that be?" Betty flicked him a smile as she trotted out of the room. "Pizza man."

She paid the driver with petty cash, grabbed a couple of beers from the small fridge in the snack room, and returned to see Bill shutting down the press. She plopped the pizza and beer down on a work table. "One large with the works. Two tall Buds. Did I do good?"

"Naughty girl," he said cheerfully. They both removed their work aprons and plopped down on wooden stools so ink-stained they resembled modern art. Bill shook his head and said, "Can't resist pizza and beer, even if it means I'll have to loosen my belt a notch."

Betty's laugh indicated just how preposterous she thought that was. "Getting fat's one thing you'll never have to worry about, boss, not at the pace you go all day. I just thought the food might help. Still got a long night ahead."

Betty handed him a slice. Bill grinned at her and did his best John Wayne imitation, "Always looking after me, aren't you, little lady?" It wasn't a very good imitation.

"Well, somebody should." She cast her eyes downward, her face flushing, a trick she had learned as far back as junior high. "Sorry, I shouldn't have said that."

Bill was quiet for a moment, watching her. Was he going to take the bait? "You mean, you don't think I can look after myself?"

Oh shit. Might have known he'd take it like that. Remember you're dealing with the male ego here. "No, no. It's just that I . . . Oh gosh."

Bill cocked his head quizzically. "What?"

"You know." She said it shyly to the floor.

"Know what?"

"How much I . . ." She took a deep breath, as if working up her nerve, then turned and gazed directly at Bill. "How much I care. Not just about TaylorMade Printing, but about . . . you too, boss."

Bill had just chomped down on a mouthful of pepperoni, anchovies and green peppers but seemed to have forgotten how to chew. "You do?" It came out muffled.

Betty looked hurt. "Of course I do. Haven't I always been right in the thick of battle with you?" Betty thought of a more stimulating comparison. "Haven't I always cheered you on while you stormed the field and scored the touchdowns?"

Bill's jaw muscles started working again. Ferociously. He gulped down the pizza, then blurted, "You always have, Betty. Don't think it isn't appreciated."

Betty managed a little sparkle in her eyes. "Thanks boss, but I'm the one who's appreciative. You hiring me to work here. Letting me be just a small part in making the company grow. How often does a girl get an opportunity like that? It's all been very . . ." She feigned a loss for the right word, “Exciting."

Bill was tearing off another slice and Betty decided it was time for a little body language, saying, “Well, as long as the press is off.” She pulled the ribbon from her hair, letting it cascade around her shoulders, then brushed it back with her flattened hands. It made her small breasts push hard against the lace and her stomach disappear beneath her rib cage. It emphasized her tiny waist while her pelvis reached out invitingly. To complete the effect, she crossed one shapely leg over the other.

She noticed Bill's reaction out of the corner of her eye. He was frozen in place, the slice poised in front of his half-opened mouth.

“Delicious, isn't it?” she said, trying not to look too coy and almost succeeding. Bill continued his statue imitation. “The pizza,” she added.

He grinned wolfishly. “Better than I expected.” He chomped down.

Electricity was in the air. It made Betty’s scalp tingle. Now she had to think of a way to make sparks jump. But it was Bill who seized the moment.

"You think my wife's a bitch, don't you?"

There is a God, Betty thought. She looked shocked and did her blushing trick again. "My goodness. Whatever gave you that idea?"

"The bit about somebody should look after me. What you’re saying is, my wife's not doing a very good job of it."

Betty shifted her gaze to the floor again, sensing that sparks were about to fly after all. Three years of planting seeds had paid off. Harvest time was at hand. Her heartbeat quickened. Don't blow it, she told herself.

"I shouldn't have said anything, Bill. It's none of my business. I'm sorry."

"You can speak freely. There's no one here but the two of us."

Oh, that's finally occurred to you, has it? But what she said was, "If I start saying what I feel, I won't be able to stop. I'm afraid I'll say too much. I'm sorry I said anything at all."

Bill had that solemn, intense look men get just before a woman takes off her bra. "Am I hearing you right, Betty? I mean, it sounds to me like what you’re saying is . . ." He seemed to be at a loss for words, then said, “Okay, what *are* you saying?"

All right, she told herself, this is it. Give it your best shot. She faced him defiantly. "I do have very strong feelings for you, boss. I'm not ashamed to say it. I can't help how I feel. I'm just so sick of seeing you treated so unfairly."

He jerked forward as if by the line now firmly hooked in his mouth. "By who?"

"Your wife. I'm sorry, I really am sorry, but yes, yes, yes, she most definitely is a bitch." She sucked in her breath, threw her hands over her mouth. "Oh God. Now you'll hate me. Please, I don't want to say anymore." She managed a tear in the corner of her eye.

Bill steadied her by putting his hands on her shoulders in a gentle, fatherly way. Damn, she thought. I don't want to be his frigging daughter. I want to be his wife.

"I could never hate you, Betty. Just be honest with me. Tell me why you think Paula's treating me unfairly."

Betty took a deep breath, pretending to bolster her courage, then looked directly into Bill's eyes. "Because she's depriving you of your dreams."

"My dreams?"

"You think I don't know about your dreams? How could I work with you as closely as I do and not know? I want to see your dreams come true more than anything. Why doesn't your wife? I know you want to expand TaylorMade Printing. I know you want to open shops in every major city in the country. I know. I'm ready, willing and able to help you make that happen. Why isn't your wife? You can't do it alone. You've got to have somebody moving in the right social circles, making contacts behind the scenes, talking up your business, infecting people with your ideas, your dreams. You can't do that yourself because you're too busy running the company. I can't do it because I'm just your secretary and don't count. But your wife could do it. Why doesn't she?"

Betty wiped away a tear and glanced toward the ceiling as if afraid of the reproach she might see in Bill's eyes. When she decided her silence had lasted long enough for good dramatic effect, she said, "I'm sorry. I told you, once I got started I'd say too much, and I have."

Bill took her hands in his. "Look at me, Betty."

It was difficult, but she managed.

"You count, Betty, more than you'll ever know."

Betty reacted as if she'd just been crowned Miss America. "I do?"

Bill grabbed her arms. "Betty, I . . ." He leaned forward to kiss her but she pushed away, gasping.

"Oh no, Bill, we mustn't . . ." Betty knew that saying no to a man when he was about to kiss you was like trying to put out a smoldering fire with gasoline. Bill was no exception to the rule. When his lips were planted firmly on hers she knew the metal was hot and ready for the hammer. She threw her arms around his neck and returned his kiss with such force that he almost fell over backwards. He'll go for my breasts next, she predicted, and true to form he was almost ripping the buttons off her blouse.

"No, Bill," she said, kissing him again and again. Her blouse was being slipped over her shoulders and she caught a glimpse of her Maidenform Lycra bra sprinkled with little pink hearts. He tugged at it, then gave up and reached around back for the fastener. She tried to push his hands away. "No, boss. Not here. Not like this."

"Yes, Betty. Right here. Just like this."

"Someone might see us."

"There's nobody here but us."

"Oh boss."

"You've got me on fire."

"Please." Her bra popped open. "Okay, but just the bra."

Bill pulled it away greedily and grabbed her small breasts with both hands. She wondered which one he'd chow down on first. He opted for the right and Betty swooned, not having to fake it at all.

"Oh, boss. Oh, my darling. I've waited so long. Oh God." She grabbed his hair and lifted his face away, heard her nipple pop out of his mouth, then kissed him with all the heat she could muster -- which was considerable under the circumstances. She looked deep into his eyes and said, "Tell me it will always be like this. Tell me."

He looked as if he intended to devour her with a single bite. "It will, baby. Always. But you gotta quit calling me boss, okay?"

“Okay . . . my darling Bill,” she said, then pushed his head back down and let him nurse. Through the cascading tears she smiled triumphantly.

24

Ames pulled into the deserted park just before 10:00 PM. It was dark and heavily wooded, meaning there was little chance of being observed while he went about his business. He found a particularly secluded spot and cut the engine.

He'd spent most of the day answering ads for pro camera equipment, fishing rods, jerry cans, camping gear, supplies that would indicate a prolonged photo safari. The back of his 1954 Chevy wagon was full of it. All used stuff. He didn't want to be seen with an old boat full of new gear. People remembered things like that. He also stocked up on water, beer, canned goods, and ice. Now he transferred it all from the wagon to the boat.

It was just after 11:00 when Ames towed the *Far Horizons* into Homestead. He stopped for fuel, putting about twenty gallons total in his car and jerry cans, and paid for it with a five-spot. A buck and a quarter more got him burgers, fries, and a Coke at an all-night diner. He ate as he continued driving southwest a while, then turned onto a dirt road leading inland.

Signs of civilization soon vanished in the murky Everglades wilderness. The road grew narrower and rougher, eventually becoming nothing more than a couple of ruts cutting through thick saw grass. Twenty minutes later, lights danced through the shadowy foliage. He followed them to a weathered board-and-batten cabin near the water's edge. He parked and got out.

"Mr. Ames?"

Ames whirled to see a small, lean man standing behind him. He was quite old but in no way feeble. There was just the trace of a smile on his face and a double-barreled twelve gauge crooked in his arm. He held it casually, like a hunter, but his hand was where it needed to be to settle any disagreements that might arise. Ames didn't blame him for being cautious.

Anybody living alone in this desolate patch of wilderness damn well better practice caution.

"Yes, I'm Ames. You must be Joe."

"It's what most folks call me."

Ames grinned. "Sorry to keep you up so late. Thought I'd be able to get away sooner than I did. Is that coffee I smell?"

"Figured you might need a Thermos full. 'Course, I got something stronger if you need it." Ames was tempted, but he was already tired and there was much yet to do. Keeping a clear head was imperative. "I'll just go with the coffee."

Joe nodded. "It's in the cabin." Ames didn't have to be told to lead the way. He knew Joe would never let him get behind him. He retrieved a Thermos from the boat and headed inside.

Even though Joe's cabin was little more than a shack, it exuded warmth and hospitality. The interior consisted of one good-sized room. Ames was not surprised by how neatly kept the cabin was. He had met many Joes in his life. They all followed a pattern.

"Good coffee," Ames said, sampling it before filling his Thermos.

Joe smiled, his leathery face breaking into more wrinkles than a bloodhound's. It was an apt comparison. Joe made his living as a guide for sportsmen, photographers, and law enforcement officers. It was a well-known fact you couldn't hide from Joe in this swamp. He'd track you down regardless of the nearly 2,400 square miles it comprised. At least a dozen men who now resided behind bars could testify to this.

Back outside, Joe helped Ames slip the *Far Horizons* into the water. "This thing gonna float?" he asked with a twinkle in his eyes. Ames shrugged. "We're about to find out."

It did float. In fact, it sat in the water almost regally.

"Where can I park so I won't be in your way?"

Joe showed him then went back inside his cabin for a moment. He rejoined Ames by the boat and unfolded a chart. "I marked the places I figured you'd have the best chance of getting the pictures you're wanting."

Ames said, “Appreciate that.”

“Sure ya don't wanna wait till morning to shove off?”

Ames was aware of Joe's steely gaze, the kind a police interrogator might use. He knew if he didn't answer appropriately, alarm bells would go off in Joe's head. He didn't need that. “Wish I could,” he said with a wistful grin. “Gotta be in position when the sun comes up. Morning light, low in the sky, is what makes us nature photographers drool.”

Joe accepted the answer as logical, folded the chart, gave it to Ames, then added, "Here, better take some of these too." He handed him a lumpy foil package. Ames opened it to find a half dozen steaming biscuits. Joe was as famous for his biscuits as he was for his tracking.

"You're a damn good man, Joe."

Joe laughed. "Well, you can always use them for bait. One last thing. You're new to the swamp so I need to ask if ya got a compass and know how to use it. Many are the tale of some poor fool who spent days cutting circles in this floating desert."

Ames pulled a standard issue Army lensatic marching compass from his shirt pocket, showed it to Joe, then climbed into the boat. "Look for me sometime Monday afternoon, if a gator don't get me first."

"Good luck with your picture taking," Joe said and shoved the *Far Horizons* off. Surprisingly, the old Evinrude turned over with only two yanks on the cord. Ames waved to Joe. Soon the little shack was no more than a speck of light among the shadowy forms of the swamp. Ames checked his bearings and puttered deep into the wilderness.

He emerged just shy of 5:00 AM, finished off the last two biscuits, gulped down the remaining coffee, then settled in for the hour long trek across the northern edge of Florida Bay to Curiosity Cove. When Ames slid into its protected lagoon right at 6:00, there was a hint of grayish light through the thick subtropical foliage.

He steered the little cabin cruiser to the side of the boathouse that would hide it from view. The mangroves were thick there, perfect cover for the small boat. Once it was hidden, he tied it to the floating pier. He crossed the footbridge spanning the small secondary channel that flowed from the lagoon, then climbed the sandy hill to the house.

Half an hour later Mr. Ames had become Kurt Younger again. It had been a long, tedious day. What he needed now more than anything was a steaming hot shower to remove the swamp stench and unlock his overly taught muscles. Afterwards, he sat on the verandah sipping an icy PBR. The rising sun peeked through the forest. Tuesday morning. So far his plan was coming together nicely. The final leg of the escape route was now laid out.

Before daylight the previous morning he'd packed his Mr. Ames costume into a small duffel, tossed it into an inflatable he kept in the boathouse, then puttered over to Key Largo, landing on a deserted shore of Lake Surprise. By the time the sun was lighting up the horizon, Kurt had hidden the inflatable in a thick growth of mangroves, changed into his Mr. Ames costume, and was hiking into town, less than a mile away.

He took a Greyhound bus to Homestead, then hopped a cab to the secluded hovel of Stringbean Jones, the thoroughly nefarious old codger who had, several months ago, generated the Mr. and Mrs. Mendelson passports along with other IDs for Kurt and Paula. Stringbean also specialized in making false license plates, any state, any type of vehicle, a trade he learned while in prison. He got the nickname Stringbean because that's what he looked like. Jones was obviously not his real surname. Even Uncle Sam didn't know what that was.

Yesterday Kurt ordered two plates, one for a car, the other for a boat trailer. Both were legitimately registered to a man who lived in

Brunswick, Georgia. A middle aged insurance salesman named Harold P. Ames. They were waiting for Kurt when he arrived, along with a false Georgia driver's license. The loan of an old Chevy wagon was part of the package, forged plates already attached. Kurt spent the rest of the day chasing down the sundry items that would make him appear convincing to Joe. It all had gone off without a hitch.

Only one more little job to do before the escape route was fully prepared. It was a particularly nasty job, one requiring steady hands and nerves of steel. He'd leave it till later in the week. Lots of other stuff to take care of first. Right now, he just wanted to sip his beer and watch the world wake up.

And think of Paula.

The way she looked.

The way she looked at him.

Her scent.

He climbed the outside stairs to the second floor balcony and stepped through the French doors into the bedroom. Paula still lingered in his mind.

Nothing to worry about, he decided. She loves me as much as I love her.

It was a pleasant, reassuring thought, and still on his mind when he collapsed into bed.

25

It was a little before noon Wednesday when Mama Taylor clunk-clunked over to the bench in front of the library that encircled a stately royal palm. She plopped down, let out a prolonged groan, then said aloud, “Mercy me.” She was thoroughly exhausted by the short walk from the library's entrance. She glanced at the little watch pinned to her blouse and groaned again. The number seven bus that would take her home wouldn't be along for at least half an hour.

Paula made it clear at breakfast she'd be too busy running errands all day to take her to the library. She'd have to call a cab. Mama Taylor responded indignantly that while Paula had no problem squandering the money her poor son slaved to earn, she certainly would not do the same. She'd take the bus. But Paula had already left the room, leaving Mama Taylor thinking: someday you'll get your comeuppance, young Lady. Yes you will.

She folded her arms on top of her purse and in the warm sunshine started to nod off. A nearby movement caught her attention. She opened her eyes to see another elderly lady sitting nearby on the bench. Her twinkling eyes were glued to the latest Saturday Evening Post.

Mama Taylor took in the woman's heavily rouged cheeks, the fly swatter eyelashes, the freshly painted lips, the impossible color of her molded hair, the string of pearls, the dress suitable for dinner at the White House, and concluded she was probably dancing merrily on some poor clod's grave.

“Which bus you catching?” Mama Taylor inquired.

“The one to Worth Avenue,” the woman said cheerfully then giggled like a school girl. “Got oh so much shopping to do,” then giggled again.

“Probably run into my daughter-in-law while you're there. She keeps those shops in business.”

The woman thought this enormously amusing. "Well, things are a bit pricey on Worth but the exceptional quality makes it worth it.” The woman put her fingers to her O-shaped mouth and looked at Mama Taylor with merry little eyes. “Oh. I just made a funny.”

Mama Taylor forced a smile, although a painful one.

“Anyway,” the woman continued, “your daughter-in-law is probably just a very conscientious shopper. You should be proud of her." She patted Mama Taylor's hand to emphasize the point.

"I'd be even prouder if she exercised as much caution about a few other things in her life."

The woman giggled again, she seemed to be a chronic giggler, then asked, "What do you mean?"

Mama Taylor realized the woman was hoping for something juicy, so she simply said, "I mean raising children is a job that never ends."

This time the woman didn't giggle. "Oh. Well, at least you had children."

"You didn't?"

"Tried, but . . ." She shrugged her shoulders as if apologizing.

"That's too bad."

"Yes, especially when you consider that now I'll become extinct when I die. My husband's already dead, so he's extinct even as we speak."

Mama Taylor wondered what in God's name the woman was raving about. "How's that?"

"Well, I was just reading an article in here about how people who have children never really die because their blood and tissue live on in their children, and their children's children, and their children's children's children."

Mama Taylor was flabbergasted that this woman had to consult the Saturday Evening Post to discover what any high school biology student knew, but all she said was, "Uh-huh."

"Think about it. Inside you and me are bits and pieces of thousands of people going all the way back to Adam and Eve."

Right, Mama Taylor thought, suppressing a yawn, the Bible teaches us that. It's why Christians refer to each other as brothers and sisters.

"I mean, there might be an Egyptian queen inside me, or a Renaissance painter."

Or a court jester, Mama Taylor thought.

"But when someone dies who has never had a child, they don't just die, they become extinct."

It jarred Mama Taylor. "Extinct?"

"Yes, extinct. You know what extinct means, don't you, dear?"

Mama Taylor heard demons laughing deep within her soul. She cringed. No, this couldn't be. It was too obscene. She had to reject this profane notion. "Dinosaurs become extinct, not people."

The woman smiled patiently. "But don't you see, dear, when one has no children, one's essence ends with one's life, and, therefore, one most certainly does become extinct. Like Harry and me. We're extinct."

Extinct? It had never occurred to Mama Taylor before. Dear God, did I do that to Elliot? How utterly ghastly.

"Are you all right?"

"What?" The woman's voice was all but blotted out by Mama Taylor's thoughts of what she had done to Elliot. No woman could have asked for a more loving and devoted husband, yet infidelity and betrayal had been his reward. Certainly, she had paid a price for her treachery. The guilt she carried in her heart became an almost unbearable burden. It robbed her of the beauty and vitality her husband had cherished. It had literally crippled her. But the price she paid was nothing compared to the one paid unwittingly by Elliot.

"It's just that you went pale all of a sudden. You're not going to faint on me, are you?"

"No, I wouldn't do that," Mama Taylor said, still pondering her sin. She had not only allowed a card-carrying cad to impregnate her, she had let Elliot believe the cad's child belonged to him and thus was his link to immortality.

"That's good," the woman was saying. "How many children did you say you had?"

Mama Taylor wondered whether, beyond murder itself, there was an act so criminal as deceiving a man into believing his life force would continue after his death, when, in reality, the opposite was true.

"Did you hear me, dear? I asked how many children you had."

"Just one," Mama Taylor said, wishing the woman would go away.

"Boy? Girl?"

"A son."

The woman seemed to find this quite exciting. "Oh, then he's probably got children of his own."

Mama Taylor wanted to scream at the woman to shut up. "A boy. In college."

"Isn't that thrilling? You and your husband have already extended your life into two more generations."

Mama Taylor almost retched. Elliot, a kind, gentle and honorable man, was extinct, but the bloodline of the countless narcissistic and irresponsible reprobates who had spawned Jennings St. John was alive in Bill, who had already passed it on to Billy.

Mama Taylor was beginning to see the enormity of her sin, that it was being compounded with each new generation. She tasted the bile rising into her mouth. The sun seemed to disappear. Darkness gathered around her.

"Well, here's my ride," the woman said as a bus pulled up to the curb. "I hope you enjoyed our little chat as much as I did. Maybe we'll meet here again sometime." Stepping onto the bus, she added, "And may your grandson carry you and your husband into a thousand generations to come."

Mama Taylor buried her face in her hands, but the woman didn't see it. She tucked the Saturday Evening Post under her arm, settled into a seat, and was gone.

Mama Taylor pulled a handkerchief from her pocket and dabbed at her eyes. Dear God, she prayed silently, if the wages of sin are death, maybe it's time I drew my pay.

26

Kurt awoke Thursday morning drenched in sweat. His head pounded and his joints were in bad need of a lube job. He would have killed for two of Joe's biscuits.

A quick dip in the lagoon brought his muscles and joints back to life and an icy PBR chased away his headache, but he decided to postpone eating until he had finished the nasty job at hand. The general consensus among fighting men was that if you're going to die, it's better to do it on an empty stomach.

Clear-headed now and reasonably nimble, Kurt grabbed a second beer and made his way down to the boathouse. He had built it himself, making sure the roof was high enough to allow the *Black Jack* to be hoisted clear of the water. The result was a towering wooden structure with Gothic overtones. Once inside, he boarded the *Black Jack* and made damn sure its floodlight switch was in the "off" position.

Back on the dock, Kurt activated the winch, lowering a heavy-duty block and tackle with two big rubber stirrups hanging loose from it. He slid them under the hull then positioned one fore, one aft. A few minutes later the *Black Jack* was inching up out of the water until it hung precariously in mid-air. Kurt cut the winch motor, grateful for the silence, and reflected that there were few sights as jarring as a boat out of water.

Kurt had purchased the *Black Jack* at a police auction of expensive toys originally owned by bad little boys who had forfeited their right to play with them due to convictions for a garden variety of odious offenses.

The *Black Jack* was a very nice toy. It boasted a spacious cabin above deck complete with a fully outfitted galley, built-in bar, double bed, and a shower that accommodated a man of even Kurt's considerable size. The design resulted in a boat broad in the beam but with a very shallow draft, important when cruising the waters of Florida Bay.

The foredeck was broad enough for two adults to soak up copious quantities of sun. Located in the stern of the craft were plenty of compartments for coolers and fishing supplies. The cockpit was high and sheltered against stormy seas. A genuine teakwood-and-brass helm was the centerpiece of the stainless steel control panel. The big V8 inboard had the kind of muscle Kurt respected. Yeah, it guzzled gas, but so what? Gas was cheap.

Kurt mopped, then toweled the *Black Jack's* hull dry. He closed the big barn doors, which made it suffocating inside, but he couldn't chance being seen doing what he was about to do.

As a mercenary, working with explosives had been part of Kurt's job, a part he hated. When he held the stuff in his hands, he never forgot he was only a heartbeat away from oblivion. It made his skin crawl. He hated Primacord most of all.

Kurt thought back to his fighting days in the Pacific when, through a surprise attack, his patrol of only eight men captured twenty of the enemy. The problem of getting them back to camp was formidable. It would only be a matter of time before the prisoners realized the odds were in their favor and worked up the courage to turn on their captors.

That was when Kurt learned about the many uses of Primacord. It looked like common utility cord used to tie down tarps or perform any number of light duty jobs. In reality, it was a very deadly explosive. To demonstrate, his sergeant major wrapped a length of it around a good-sized tree and forced the prisoners to watch as it was detonated. The tree was cut in two as cleanly as if a chainsaw had been used. A longer length of Primacord was then wrapped around each prisoner's neck, stringing them together like Christmas tree lights. The end was attached to a hell box the sergeant major carried, keeping one hand poised on the detonator. On the long march back to camp, Kurt had never seen more compliant prisoners.

Now, in the sweltering gloom of the boat house, the *Black Jack* creaking and groaning above like a body hanging from a gallows, Kurt carefully measured out the length of Primacord he would need then, teeth clenched, cut it. He noticed that despite the oven-like conditions his skin was crawling with goose bumps.

Using a piece of chalk, Kurt drew a ragged outline near the *Black Jack's* keel resembling the kind of tear that might result from collision with a coral outcropping. On the other side of the hull was a fuel tank. In the center of the chalk outline he drilled a hole just large enough to accommodate the fuse. Kurt attached the Primacord to the chalk line with heavy marine glue, a tedious operation that seemed to take forever, then fed two minutes of waterproof fuse from the Primacord through the hole and spliced it to the electrical cable that provided juice to the powerful floodlights surrounding the craft. One flip of the floodlight switch in the *Black Jack's* cockpit and the fuse would be ignited. The explosion that followed would make the big boat go down faster than a whore in a backstreet alley.

Goodbye old friend.

Kurt lowered the *Black Jack* into the water, released the stirrups, and stepped out into the blinding sunshine. The air seemed particularly sweet to him, the way it always did just after he cheated death.

The escape was now set and Kurt was feeling euphoric. To Estrada and associates it would appear he had been killed in a boating accident while making a run for it.

So sorry, Mr. E.

27

Just as Mama Taylor suspected, Paula was indeed on Worth Avenue, armed and ready. Stowed away inside her purse was a relatively new gadget called an American Express card. Women everywhere immediately grasped its . . . usefulness.

Paula was flabbergasted when Bill gave her one without her even asking for it. “This way I can keep track of what you're spending my money on,” he said.

The only response Paula could think of was, “How very smart of you.”

The beauty of the magic little card was that Bill wouldn't get a statement until several weeks after it was used. He then had to pay for everything charged during the previous month. When he opened the next statement, Bill would be purple with rage.

Paula would be gone.

It brought a big smile to her face. I'm doing it. I'm really doing it. And this makes it official.

The Mermaid Boutique was not actually on Worth Avenue, the real estate was too pricey, but it was only a few blocks over. Paula stormed in carrying two Samsonite suitcases, one large, one small. Both were green, to go with her eyes. Both were empty, having just been purchased.

Mary, the owner of the shop, was speechless for a moment, then said, "Hi, Paula. You planning on moving in for a while?"

Mary was behind the counter unpacking a shipment of blouses. She had a purple silk scarf wrapped Gypsy-style around her platinum blonde hair, fashioned in what Mama Taylor would call ‘finger-in-the-light-socket’. But it suited Mary's zany, uninhibited personality. Her big eyes were always full of mischief. Today her pouty lips were painted neon red. Even though she was a short woman, she had a figure that would stop traffic.

Paula set the suitcases on the floor, took a moment to catch her breath, then asked, "How long you been indulging me, Mary?"

Mary laughed. "You better define indulging, honey. Sounds interesting."

Paula actually blushed. That made Mary laugh even harder. "No, I mean, how long have I been coming in here and trying on dresses and then never buying anything?"

"Oh, that. Lets see now. 'Bout a year, I'd guess."

Yeah, Paula thought, ever since I met Kurt. Then Mary said, "No, wait a minute. You did buy something once."

"Did I?"

"A pair of shorts. But you brought 'em back the next day. Your husband said they were too tight on your ass."

"Actually what he said was they showed too much of my ass."

Mary cackled. "Okay."

Mary's was not a place to shop for conventional women's clothing. Every item she carried reflected her own personality: fun, stylish, naughty, and forever youthful. Clothes with color and flair. Clothes for women who were confident in their womanhood.

Paula stopped by whenever possible to browse. She tried on different outfits; let her fantasies run away with her. But she knew if she ever wore one home, there would be no end to the chastisement from Bill and Mama Taylor. Today her fantasies were going to come true.

"Your patience has paid off, Mary," Paula said.

"Yeah?"

Paula set the two suitcases on the counter and opened them wide. "When I leave here, I want both of these filled."

Mary stared at Paula a moment, her mouth hanging open. "No shit?"

That's what Paula liked about Mary. No pretense.

"Yes shit," Paula confirmed. "Only the good stuff."

Mary stepped around the counter. Behind those big, zany eyes the wheels were turning at mach speed. She put her hands on her hips and stood before Paula, the top of her head only reaching Paula's shoulder. There was a twinkle in her eye. "Miss Paula. What are you doing?"

Paula burst out laughing. "I'm running away from my husband," she blurted.

Mary's mouth gaped open even wider. She grabbed Paula by the shoulders and shook her. "Good for you. I've met your husband. He's a real asshole."

"That's okay," Paula said, giggling, "You can tell me how you really feel."

They laughed a while over that. "Just tell me one thing," Mary said.

"What?"

"That you're running away with some tall, gorgeous hunk of man who makes wild, passionate love to you under the stars all night long."

"Couldn't have described him better myself."

"Oh my God," Mary screamed, jumping up and down.

"Not a word of this to anybody. Promise?"

"Cross my heart." She did. "May every piece of silk in this store turn to polyester if I should say anything."

"Good enough. Okay, let's start with this dress here."

It was the one Paula had been admiring for weeks. She darted into the dressing room, slipped it on, then stepped over to the mirrors. When she saw her reflection, only one word came to mind: Wow! The dress tamed her voluptuous proportions yet brought out her femininity, leaving her shoulders bare, and quite a bit of her chest.

"It was made for you," Mary was saying.

"I bet you say that to all the girls. I don't know, Mary. It's awfully low-cut."

"So what? If you got it, flaunt it. And honey, you definitely got it."

"Okay, if you're going to put it like that, wrap it up. No, wait. Cut all the tags off and pack it in the big suitcase. I'll use the smaller one for lingerie, shoes, things like that."

"You're the boss."

It went on all afternoon, more a party than a shopping spree. Other women came into the shop, saw what was happening, and immediately joined in the romp. Even a blue haired matron. She brought Paula one of the naughtiest pieces of lingerie in the store and said, "If you're doing what I think you're doing, you'll need this. My treat." The other women enthusiastically endorsed the selection. Giggles and sly comments ensued.

One item caught Paula's eye that was quite unusual and fanciful. She'd never seen anything like it before, but it was the perfect solution to a practical problem Paula had yet to address. She was glad that in a few days she'd need an item like this. Into the pile it went.

Mary raided the stock of champagne she kept in a small refrigerator in the back room. By the time Paula was finished, everyone in attendance was more than a little tipsy. One by one the other women departed, hugging Paula and dispensing good wishes.

The suitcases were bulging with every type of apparel from dresses, blouses and skirts to lingerie and swimsuits. There were also shoes, scarves, and handbags, along with an assortment of necklaces, earrings, and bracelets. The crowning touch was an assortment of perfume and other toiletries Mary said were so indecent she had to keep them in the back room.

She'd already closed the small suitcase and was practically standing on the large one to get it closed when she noticed Paula trying on one last outfit. "Forget it, honey. We'll never get it in here."

"Wanna bet?"

It was a cool, cream-colored linen dress with a wide macramé belt. The skirt had several slits in it and allowed unlimited leg movement. The top buttoned up the front but flopped open so that it always left a shoulder bare. Paula studied the effect in the mirror and said, "Kurt, you lucky dog, you'll never know what hit you."

"That's his name, Kurt?"

"You didn't hear me say that."

"Say what?"

Paula glanced at the clock. 3:30. "Gotta go."

"Gotta pay."

"Right."

She whipped out the shiny green card with a "Tah-dah."

Mary clapped her hands together and said, "God I just love these little things."

She helped Paula carry the suitcases to the car. "Just remember, young lady. These clothes are magical. Wear them and you'll never marry a jerk again."

"Mary, you're drunk."

"Paula, you're right." She threw the suitcases in the cargo area behind the back seat then stepped back and shook her head.

"What's the matter?" Paula asked.

"This station wagon. It hardly goes with your new image."

"Yeah, well, I'm going to take care of that."

28

Kurt's stomach roared like an angry grizzly bear. Time to do something about that, he decided. He loaded up his Webber kettle grill with hardwood charcoal and got it blazing. Kurt considered the Webber grill undoubtedly mankind's greatest achievement. There were certain foods that should not be cooked any other way than outdoors over a fire. Went back to cave man days. Hadn't been improved since.

This was especially true of steaks, as Kurt was about to prove. First he took a large ear of shucked corn along with a man-sized baking potato, slathered them both with butter, then wrapped them in foil, and placed them on the grill, since they would take longer to cook than the steak. He added a small frying pan filled with butter, dumped in a softball-sized Spanish onion all chopped up. And while he loved his Jack Daniels Black, ice-cold beer was the only beverage suitable to accompany a steak. Anything else was a slap in the face to the cow.

When the coals settled into that pale white glow tinged with reddish highlights that said, go ahead, bring on the beef, Kurt didn't hesitate. He threw down an inch-and-a-half thick, nicely marbled, slab of rib eye about the size of a hubcap, splashed on Lea and Perrins Worcestershire sauce, added a generous layer of sea salt, garlic powder, freshly ground black pepper, then topped it off with big dabs of butter.

As the steak sizzled, Kurt understood why God wanted the Hebrews to make burnt offerings. There was no aroma on earth so savory and mouthwatering as meat roasting. Pleasing unto God indeed. Before he turned the steak, he dribbled Jack Daniels on it, let it soak in a minute or so, then flipped it over. He did the same on the other side.

He devoured his feast on the veranda, leaving nary a scrap for the local critters. When done, he decreed the meal pleasing unto Kurt. He propped his feet on the railing and belched from the very bottom of his soul. While nursing another icy PBR, he went over the escape plan in his mind once again.

Before dawn Monday he would slip into his Mr. Ames getup, run a tow line from the *Far Horizons* to the *Black Jack*, and cruise out to 'Shipwreck Alley', a hundred yards or so of shallow coral reef that abruptly nose-dived into a deep trench.

Once in position, Kurt would take the few uncut emeralds he'd saved back and throw them out to sea. He would then radio a Mayday to the Coast Guard saying he had just knocked the bottom out of his boat and ruptured a fuel tank; that he was on fire and sinking fast.

Next, he would flip on the *Black Jack's* floodlights, scurry onto the *Far Horizons*, putter a safe distance away, then watch as the explosion blew a hole in the hull. It would also ignite the fuel tank, set the *Black Jack* on fire, and sink it to a depth of about 100 feet on the edge of the trench. Because of the swift Florida Straits, nobody would be surprised that his body was missing. Even though the *Black Jack* would still be visible (he was counting on that), the scorching from the fire would disguise the Primacord's burn marks.

Sure, Estrada would send divers down to scour the *Black Jack's* carcass for the emeralds. They would find them, too. At least a few of them, scattered along the ocean floor. They would assume the rest were with Kurt, who was now probably in the belly of some deep-sea predator.

The only part of the plan he didn't like was that Paula would be with him the entire time.

But she wouldn't know it. She'd be unconscious. Knocked out cold.

By Kurt.

He took several deep breaths and managed to keep his dinner down, but the bile still swirled in his throat. Come on, we've been through this, he reminded himself. There's no other way. No matter how many times he'd thought it through, a better alternative did not present itself.

He considered just coming clean with her, tell her step by step what he was going to do and why. But every time he played that scenario in his mind it ended with her looking at him as if he were a monster, then running for the hills.

No, this was way over Paula's head. She was an everyday housewife. Her world was the safe, predictable confines of Palm Beach where people at least pretended to be civilized. He marveled again that a woman from that kind of background was able to capture his heart. Hell, make him aware he even had one.

Not once had she asked who he was, where he came from, what he did for a living. She clearly didn't want to know. It would spoil her fantasy. Paula thought of him as a modern day pirate who plundered her treasure from time to time. Best leave it that way.

His plan called for them to have Saturday night and all day Sunday together at Curiosity Cove. Just thinking about what Saturday night would be like brought life to Kurt's loins. Sunday would be a day to relax and play, to fill her mind with images of Paris, Rome, Rio, Tahiti, any damn place that caught their fancy. He couldn't wait to see the excitement of it dancing in her emerald eyes.

His cover story was all worked out. It was essential they got away early Monday morning in order to make their flight. That's what he would tell her. While they were packing, he would add a little something to her coffee. When she passed out, he'd make sure she stayed out. He sure as hell knew how.

Inside the *Far Horizon's* tiny cabin was a bunk. Kurt had already removed the rotting mattress, replaced it with a new one, and fitted it with clean sheets, a big fluffy pillow, and a thick, warm blanket to make sure she didn't get chilled. Sleeping Beauty, that's who she'd be.

It made his skin crawl to think about it, but it was for her own good.

After sinking the *Black Jack*, he would guide the *Far Horizons* back through the swamp, taking a few moments to change into his Mr. Ames getup before arriving at Joe's cabin in the afternoon as expected. Joe would help him winch the *Far Horizons* onto its trailer, unaware of the beautiful stowaway aboard, and hitch it to the Chevy wagon. When Kurt was far enough away from Joe's to avoid being seen, he would transfer the sleeping Paula to the Chevy's front seat, then head for Miami.

Once there, he'd find a side street in the seamier side of town and drop the boat there. He knew it wouldn't stay there long. Since there was nothing in the boat that identified him, whoever stole it had his blessing. After that he would pull into the same secluded park he'd used last Monday night when he was stocking up the *Far Horizons*.

The next part would be the trickiest: reviving Paula, telling her she'd scared the shit out of him passing out like that, saying he was about to take her to a hospital but that she started coming around, asking her if she felt well enough for them to start their grand adventure together.

He knew Paula would be confused at first as she emerged from the fog of the drugs. Kurt expected that. He'd keep talking her down as they drove to the airport, fresh air in her face, and before she got it all sorted out they'd be wining and dining in New York prior to departure for Europe. She'd soon forget all about her curious 'dizzy spell'.

Kurt was confident he would be able to lie his way out of any questions she'd have.

Lie.

The word stuck in his throat. Was that really how he wanted to start his life with Paula? Everything Kurt had planned, from his duplicity toward Red to deceiving Paula, was a lie. He scooped up his plate and hurled it against the house with such force that it exploded into tiny shards.

Shit. Fuck.

He trembled with rage. All right, cool down soldier. Get your emotions under control. Think clearly. Think of the greater good, asshole. Remember that rule? You gotta break a few eggs to make an omelet. Trite but true.

He calmed down. He thought it through yet again. Yes, he decided, it was a sound plan. No Red. No drug deals. No cutthroats trying to track him down. His days of blood and treachery behind him. Just Paula. A clean start. The world as their yo-yo. Enough money to live comfortably for a very long time.

Yes, it was a perfect plan. The only plausible plan.

Then who was that laughing at him? It was a high-pitched, mocking laugh that unnerved Kurt. Was it in his head?

No, it was Wally splashing around in the lagoon. Good ol' Wally. The ultimate party animal. All he did was eat, play and cavort with lady dolphins. And now he was telling Kurt it was time to play again. Kurt laughed, stripped off his T-shirt, ran down the white sand hill to the lagoon and dove in.

29

Friday morning found Mama Taylor at Wilson's Super Market dodging shopping carts. It seemed to her that women today equated grocery shopping to a contest of territorial rights. She'd lost count of how many times someone had slammed into her walker without offering even a hint of apology. Get out of the way you old bag, they seemed to be saying, this is war. Whatever happened to respect for your elders? she wondered.

Mama Taylor clunk-clunked toward the checkout counter. She caught sight of Paula down aisle three. She looked so pretty that Mama Taylor wanted to throw up. Her hair was freshly washed, luxuriantly thick, and glistened with fiery highlights. Her shirtwaist sundress lived up to its name. Lots of sun exposure; not much dress. Bare arms, bare shoulders, bare chest. Thin straps struggled to hold up enough fabric to maintain a modicum of decency.

“Dear God,” she muttered to herself, “Where does she get the nerve?” If Bill knew she was displaying herself like this in public he'd be mortified. Then there were those big eyes of hers, dazzlingly green. Somehow they were lighter, more carefree.

Mama Taylor wondered about that. Both Bill and Paula seemed to have developed a little extra pep in their step this week. For Bill the change became apparent Tuesday when he arrived home after working all night. He was like a stranger to her. Something had happened. Mama Taylor had a pretty good idea what. Or at least who.

Betty. The mouse that roared. Dynamite wrapped in a small but very lethal package.

Evidently her fuse had run out and she'd gone off with a big bang. Now Bill went around whistling all the time. She hadn't heard him whistle since he found out Paula was pregnant.

"Did you want something?"

Mama Taylor realized with a start that Paula was staring back at her. "No," she answered. "I was just seeing how far along you are."

Paula glanced down at her nearly empty cart. "I'll be a while," she said.

"Yes, I have no doubt you will. I'll be waiting outside." Mama Taylor turned away from Paula's insolent stare and continued on toward the cashier. I wonder how insolent she'd be if she knew I was watching out the upstairs window that night while that beast ravished her and know just what a shameless little tramp she is? All I'd have to do is tell Bill. She'd soon find out what being human refuse was all about.

But while thoughts of vengeance brought temporary satisfaction, Mama Taylor knew she'd choke on her own hypocrisy if she ever tried to act on them. After all, she was no better than Paula. Worse, in fact. Paula's infidelity had not resulted in an illegitimate child. All she had bred was deceit. Mama Taylor's infidelity resulted in Bill, a secret she would carry to her grave, deceiving her son just as she had her husband. But had she?

Elliot was kind, considerate, and loving. But not stupid. Bill resembled him not at all and only faintly resembled Mama Taylor. How many times did Elliot search Bill's face, then hers, the question hanging darkly in the air?

No, it was the face of the libertine who impregnated her that was stamped indelibly on Bill's face, a constant reminder of her sin. It mocked her every time she looked at him.

Elliot never gave voice to his suspicions. Not once. Even on his deathbed as pancreatic cancer was bringing his life to an early end. His last words, barely a whisper, were for Bill's ears, not hers. “I love you, son.”

The memory of it made Mama Taylor cry out, as if from a sharp pain. A nearby clerk turned to her and said, “You all right, ma'am?”

“Yes, yes, just leave me alone,” she snapped.

She paid for her tangelos and grapefruit, made her way outside, found a bench under the store's awning, and plopped down. “Dear God,” she muttered again, but God seemed to be incommunicado. She was so lonely and despondent that she had to bite back tears.

She had always believed in a merciful, forgiving God. It was pounded into her from childhood. And God had forgiven her, as Jesus had the adulterous woman. “Go and sin no more.” Casting off her yoke of guilt had not been as easy. The devil himself had put it there then weighted it down with every sinful act she'd ever committed. Most of them against Paula.

She hated Paula from the beginning, convinced she was the devil's handmaiden tasked with taking Bill away from her. Indeed the vixen with the big, bouncing bosoms, and sinfully long legs, proved to be a formidable foe. She was only eighteen, a college freshman, but she effortlessly pried Bill away without him offering so much as a backward glance.

The speed with which Paula Doherty became the young and beautiful Mrs. William Taylor made the elder Mrs. Taylor dizzy. Now there were two Mrs. Taylors, but Bill reserved his affections for only one of them.

And it wasn't me, Mama Taylor recalled bitterly. She was abandoned, left alone with nothing but an all-consuming hatred of Paula, and a firm resolve to get Bill back. Her sins laughed maniacally at her in the night. She bided her time, waited for the right moment.

It came with Paula's pregnancy, the worst Mama Taylor had ever witnessed. Hyperemesis gravidarum. Incessant nausea. Violent vomiting. Dehydration. Insomnia. Paula was confined to bed. Somebody had to take care of her while Bill was at work. In moved Mama Taylor. And while there was little to be done for Paula beyond prepare meals, sponge her off, change bed linens, and give her the medicine the doctor prescribed, there was a lot she could do for Bill. She could teach him to hate Paula.

She did so with a relentless onslaught of venom injected daily into Bill's heart, his mind, his very soul. It gradually took its toll. Especially after insinuating that the child Paula was carrying did not belong to him.

As Paula neared her delivery date, Mama Taylor was determined to keep it from happening again. Having her sin propagated once was one time too many. She convinced Bill to 'take the precautions all men must take' to prevent another pregnancy. She warned him if it did happen, both Paula and the child would most certainly die. And even if she lived, how would he ever know for sure that the child was his?

She needn't have bothered. Although Billy was born healthy in every way, he ripped a path of destruction on his way out. Paula had a big, carrot-headed baby boy. What she didn't have was a uterus. It devastated Paula. She'd always dreamed of having a houseful of children.

She slid into a deep depression. Just as she was coming out of it, the United States was swept into a second world war. Bill was gone for over two years, half a world away. Yet it was nothing compared to the distance between him and Paula when he got back. Theirs was a marriage in name only.

In the end Mama Taylor won. Bill belonged to her again. For the coup de grace, Mama Taylor tried to make Billy hate Paula too, but with little success. She had to be satisfied with simply spoiling him to the point of obnoxiousness. Whenever Billy got in trouble, Mama Taylor convinced him Paula was to blame for being a bad, uncaring mother.

Which she never was. She was never a bad woman. She was never a bad wife either. She most assuredly was never the devil's handmaiden. Convincing Bill, Billy, and anybody else within hearing range, that she was had been Mama Taylor's second great sin. She wasn't sure God had forgiven her for that one. Or should.

But the damage had long since been done. The pattern of their lives was now set in concrete. Unchangeable. Had she killed Bill and Paula's marriage? Unquestionably. Had she tried to stifle Paula's enormous capacity for love, her infectious charm, her natural determination to be happy, and her indomitable spirit? She'd certainly given it her best shot.

Was it any wonder Paula sought affection in the arms of another man? Or that Bill was doing likewise with Betty? All because of me, she reflected. I am an abomination to God.

"Mama Taylor?"

Paula was standing in front of her with a cart piled high with groceries and a look of genuine concern that caught Mama Taylor off-guard.

"Well are you ready to go?" she said gruffly, because she had forgotten how to speak otherwise to Paula. She grabbed her bag of fruit, reached for her walker, and got to her feet. It was like moving in a vacuum. Nothing around her seemed real. The late morning sun couldn't penetrate the shroud of darkness that enveloped her.

"Why don't you put that in my cart?" Paula said as they approached the curb.

"Because there's not any room left. My word, girl, you've bought enough to feed a small army. How you do love to spend Bill's money."

Her voice sounded strange to her, as if coming from somewhere outside her head.

"Don't start in on me, Mama Taylor," Paula was saying, but she also sounded funny. "I'm in no mood for it. There's plenty of room in the cart."

"I can manage just fine without your help."

Paula reached for the sack impatiently. "Let's not make a big deal out of this, all right?"

"Just leave me alone." Mama Taylor jerked away, stepping directly into the path of an oncoming delivery truck. She saw the look of horror on the driver's face, heard Paula's shrill scream, then every bone in her body exploded.

And she was flying, flying . . . into oblivion.

30

For the uninitiated, stepping into Davy Jones' Locker was a test of nerves. Key Largo's most famous landmark at first sight seemed to be suspended in mid-air. Probably because it was built high on a forest of stilts rising from the Key Largo limestone beneath. The front of the building was on the island's western shore, but the rest hung over the Bay.

The walls and roof of the boxy clapboard structure sagged so severely it looked more like a cartoonist's caricature than a real building. The stilts supporting it were rife with dry rot, spliced here and there with rusty metal plates. It was generally conceded that if a cat walked across the roof at the same time a pelican sneezed against the side wall, the whole thing would collapse like a house of cards.

Those who did muster the courage to enter developed jelly legs upon seeing the store's proprietor. George "Pappy" Delaney stood just shy of the seven-foot mark and weighed in at a fifth of a ton. His usual method of greeting new customers was to squeeze around the counter and thud-thud across the drooping floor, holding out a big slab of hand. An ugly groan emanated from below, the building swayed, and the Bay's horizon tilted in relationship to the window frames. That usually did it. The newcomer ran for the door, convinced that Davy Jones' Locker was headed for the place it was named after.

But even if that eventually happened, the old landmark would live forever in countless drawings, paintings, and photographs. Artists had been making pilgrimages to the village since the mid-thirties for the purpose of capturing their own personal vision of the structure. In fact, it was not unusual to drive by the store on a sunny afternoon and see a half-dozen easels set up.

On this particular day there was only one. It belonged to a snowy-haired wisp of a woman. She worked with quick, deft strokes, pausing occasionally to take a sip of wine from a plastic tumbler, or a drag from her cigarillo. She was applying the finishing touches to her work when a shadow fell across her canvas. She gazed up at the big man who was creating it. "You block out a lot of sun."

"Sorry," Kurt said. He stepped to the side but continued to gaze at the painting. He thought it captured Davy Jones' Locker perfectly. The fishing nets draped across the walls. The antique gas pump with the glass reservoir on top. The rusting RC Cola thermometer nailed to the center post. The 'Colonial is good bread' screen door. "Only one thing wrong," he said.

"What?" the woman asked patiently, not taking her eyes from her work.

"None of those other things are anywhere near the store."

"What other things?"

"Fishing boats in the harbor. Waves splashing against the rocks."

"You're right, they're not."

Kurt grinned. He liked this eccentric old bird. "Okay."

"I paint things the way I choose to see them."

The woman created a gull with quick flicks of her brush, then said, "It's the way we live, isn't it? We see things the way we want to see them, not the way they really are. That's particularly true when it comes to people, don't you think?"

It was Friday. Paula would be here tomorrow. "In that case, why not add a beautiful naked woman sunning on the rocks?"

The woman lowered her brush. She peered at Kurt over her glasses. His big, roguish grin was infectious. She smiled too, somewhat saucily, Kurt thought. "If I do, will you buy it?"

"Yes ma'am."

"What does she look like?"

"Red hair, big chest, long legs."

"Give me half an hour."

Kurt winked at her, slung a small canvas bag over his shoulder, and crossed to the rickety stairs that led up to the store's entrance. When he stepped inside he almost collided with a big black woman on her way out. He pressed back against the wall to let her pass, but she stopped right in front of him, making him hold his pose while she hiked a bulging sack of shrimp up under her arm. "Be back tomorrow for them stone crabs, Pappy."

"I'll have 'em dressed and ready, Birdy. Thanks for coming by, now."

Kurt watched the woman waddle out, feeling the floor shift beneath him. He peeled himself from the wall and turned to Pappy with a grin. "Do the Giants know about her?"

"Hiya Kurt, good to see ya." Pappy extended the side of beef he called a hand and Kurt watched his own disappear within it. When he regained use of it, Kurt laid his canvas bag on the counter. "Little something for your collection."

He pulled out three bottles, one blue, one amber, one green. Pappy didn't bother to hide his excitement, but then Pappy never bothered to conceal any particular emotion he was feeling at the time. "Say, those are real beauties."

"Found ‘em while I was out diving this morning," Kurt said. He didn't bother to add that he hadn't been treasure hunting; he’d been trying to work off some of the anxiety of waiting for Paula. He hadn't been successful.

Pappy pushed his Greek fisherman's hat back into the explosion of sandy hair. "Looks Spanish to me. How old you think they are, Kurt? Four, five hundred years?"

Kurt shrugged, but knew what was coming.

"Yeah," Pappy continued, his voice full of awe, "these look just like the kind of bottles used on Spanish ships around Columbus' time. Why, I wouldn't be surprised . . ."

"Right, hang that story on 'em and they'll fetch a good price. Just be sure to hide the 'made in Japan' marks stamped on the bottom."

"Sure, I'll hide . . . Hey, wait a minute. There ain't nothing stamped on the bottom. Oh, I get it. Having fun with Pappy, eh?” He chuckled. So did the building. “That's okay, I don't mind. Say, where'd you find these?"

"Uh-uh. My secret."

"Sure it's your secret, Kurt. What do I care where you found them? None of my business. I'm just glad to have 'em in my collection."

Pappy nodded toward the display in the big window facing the parking lot. It contained a collection of 'treasures' scooped up in fishing nets or brought in by other divers like Kurt. There were also heirlooms indigenous to the area. Locals called them white elephants. Tourists called them 'real finds'.

Residents of the Keys gladly donated to Pappy's collection, knowing he'd use the money he clipped from tourists for his other collection: a rag-tag gang of youngsters in all shapes, sizes and colors. Kids who'd been either abandoned, abused, or suffered from poverty and neglect. To them, Pappy was akin to Santa Claus (he played that role at Christmas, too) making sure each of them had food, clothing, a school to attend, and a home where they were treated right. Because of this, Pappy was known as the gentle giant.

"So, what can I get ya, Kurt?"

"Case of champagne. Best you got."

"Whole case, eh? Boy-o-boy, must be expecting company. Lots of company. Of the female persuasion, too, I bet ya. Little hideaway you got out there is perfect for . . ."

"You gonna sell me champagne or are you gonna talk me to death?"

"I'm going to sell you champagne, Kurt. I make a whole lot more off champagne than talk." Pappy disappeared, returning with a case of champagne tucked under his arm. He dropped it on the counter. Kurt braced himself for the inevitable swaying of the building. He glanced out the window. The Bay's horizon was now running downhill. He decided to ignore it. He stepped gently over to a tank filled with spiny lobsters. "Better let me have Larry, Curly and Moe, here."

"You'll be wanting garlic butter and lemon-pepper, too."

"Guess so."

"'Course, if you're planning on entertaining ladies . . ."

"The bubbly's for some folks upstate celebrating their golden anniversary. The lobster's for me, okay?"

"Sure, Kurt. Why, I never thought . . . Say, that's awfully nice of ya. I mean about the champagne, ya know."

"Butter and lemons, Pappy. I'll need a few other things, too." Kurt read off his list and Pappy kept the building groaning and swaying as he filled the order. When he had everything bagged up, he said, "All righty now, everything but dessert. Got some super New York cheesecake just in."

Kurt picked up the bag and said, "Thanks, Pappy, dessert's taken care of."

Kurt loaded the groceries in the back of the Jeep. When he turned around, his artist friend was standing there holding up the painting for his inspection. There was Paula, naked, stretched out sensuously on the rocks, her hands tucked behind her head. How'd she do that?

"Perfect." he said in awe. "How much I owe you?"

She leaned forward, kissed him warmly on the lips, and said, "Not a thing." She turned and strolled away, a slight swing to her hips.

31

11:57:27. 11:57:28. 11:57:29.

It was one of those enormously large, black and white institutional clocks with big bold sans serif numerals. It dominated the room. It didn't just give you the time, it yelled it at you as if to say: what are you going to do about it? It did everything but flick you off. Paula hated it. She hated the chrome-and-foam furniture too, and the plastic flowers. So modern. So cold. Most of all she hated the clock. It was loud. Obnoxiously so. The second hand didn't sweep, it jumped belligerently from one second to the next with a nerve grating thunk-thunk that echoed off the hard, blindingly white walls of the Intensive Care waiting room.

It made Paula want to scream.

11:59:57. Thunk. 11:59:58. Thunk. 11:59:59. Thunk.

Midnight.

Saturday the seventeenth.

Kurt day. Liberation day.

Not likely. Damn! Damn! Double-damn! Why in hell had she agreed to take Mama Taylor to the store this morning -- yesterday morning? It was unfathomably stupid considering she was planning on leaving the next day. Why? Why? Why?

Now Mama Taylor was fighting for her life just a few feet away. Paula realized her fists were clenched, her fingernails digging into her palms.

She took a deep breath, stood up, stretched, extended her arms and legs to their fullest. With her physique, this was normally a provocative pose, but she was the room's only occupant and she didn't care anyway. She was lonely, frightened, confused, and bone tired. This had been the longest day of her life.

For lack of anything better to do, she walked over to the window and gazed out at the parking lot. It was mostly empty now. A young Negro man was pushing a cart of dirty linen toward the laundry room, dancing to a beat only he heard. A slim young nurse wearing a blood-splattered uniform walked confidently out into the lot, a fashionable purse slung over her shoulder. A mangy dog was scratching at the garbage overflowing the big metal bin.

And there was Kurt.

He was walking toward a car at the back of the lot, moving in that lion-like stalk she knew so well, the muscles rippling in his back and shoulders. Her hands frantically searched the window frame, tried to find a catch, a lever, a crank. There was nothing. She pounded on the glass, but Kurt just kept walking.

"Oh no," she cried. She wondered if she could make it outside before he reached his car. She had to try. She turned, was about to run, when it struck her.

His car.

Kurt didn't drive a car. He had a Jeep. She watched as the man stopped, turned. He had a mustache and a long, droopy nose. He wore glasses. The nurse ran up to him, took his arm. They drove off together.

Paula pressed her head against the window. Its coolness brought a welcome relief to her fevered brow. Oh, Kurt, why can't you see what's happening to me? Why don't you come screeching up in your Jeep and rescue me? If ever a woman needed it, I do. Come on, Kurt, be my hero. Sweep me off to your castle.

Paula pushed away from the window. She folded her arms against the artificially chilled air, the sundress making her feel exposed, vulnerable. With a start, she realized Bill was standing before her. His posture, the expression said it all, but still she asked, "Any change?"

He merely shook his head, then plopped down into a chair. The air whooshed out of the cushion. After that, all was silent again. Except the damn clock. Bill was trembling. She had never seen him tremble before. He clasped his hands tightly together as if trying to make himself stop, but he kept on trembling. “Just thinking,” he said. There was a tremble in his voice too.

Paula sensed he had more to say, that he was waiting to be prompted. “About what?”

“Dad.”

That surprised her. “Elliot?”

“He said this would happen. Or something like it. He was right. He was always right. I hate him for it. I hated him then and I hate him even more now.”

Paula was puzzled by the comment. Bill rarely mentioned his father, who had died years before she and Bill met. “Sorry honey, I’m not following you.”

Did I really just say honey? Slip of the tongue. A very old habit dredged up by fatigue.

Bill took a deep breath, held it. Paula hated it when he did that. It made her want to breathe for him. He looked up at Paula, glared at her.

She realized it was rage he was trembling with. "Dad said mom would pay a high price for her sins."

Paula wasn't sure how to respond. "Your mother can certainly be very difficult to get along with, Bill . . ."

"For you, maybe," he snarled.

"Okay, for me. Fine. But she lives by every word in the Bible," Paula said, and couldn't refrain from adding, "according to her interpretation. What sin was your father referring to?"

"Adultery."

Paula knew that laughing hysterically would probably be inappropriate right now, but it was hard to contain herself. Instead she squawked incredulously, "Mama Taylor?"

Bill ignored her. "Dad was not really my dad."

"Oh Bill, that's crazy. Who told you that?"

"Dad."

Bill stood up, paced restlessly. The room now seemed very small, too small for the both of them.

"He told you he wasn't your father?" Paula's head was spinning. "Why would he do that? He loved you, Bill. At least, that's what you've always said."

"But he hated Mom. Ever seen a picture of Dad?"

"Of course I have. It's on the mantle."

"Right. Well, look at me. Is there even the slightest resemblance? A couple of inches shorter and Dad would have met the physical requirements for a jockey, while I look like Attila the Hun."

Paula was about to say that was an apt comparison, but remained silent. Pieces of a puzzle were forcing their way up from the recesses of her mind, trying to form a picture. She tried to ignore it, tried to focus on what Bill was saying. She added lamely, "You can't always go by that. Lots of kids don't resemble their parents."

Bill wheeled on her. "Yeah, kinda gives you an idea how pervasive this is, doesn't it?"

It jolted Paula. A few more puzzle pieces appeared. She wanted to keep Bill talking while she tried to fit them together. "When did Elliot tell you he wasn't your father?"

"When he knew he was dying. He wanted me to know the truth about Mom. About women."

"Oh." There it was. Picture complete. Paula felt sick. "About women."

Bill glared at her accusingly. "Yeah. Women."

Paula sat down heavily, closed her eyes, leaned her head back against the wall. "Well, go ahead, Bill. Let's hear the rest of it."

Bill stared out the window, arms folded, still trembling. "Dad never let Mom know that he knew. Said he was so angry he wanted to kill her. But he never said anything."

“Why not?” But Paula already knew where this was going.

“To confront her with it would have left him only two options. He didn’t like either one. Option one would be to divorce her. But he knew if he did, the facts of the case would come out then everybody would know he'd been cuckolded. His pride wouldn’t allow that.”

“Option number two?”

“Forgive her. But if he did, he’d be relieving her of guilt, in effect sanctioning what she’d done. That wasn’t acceptable either.”

“What about option number three? Love and devotion.”

Bill scoffed at her. “According to Dad, that had been Mom’s option, but she threw it away.”

“That’s pretty harsh,” Paula said.

“Being a woman, you would think that. Try playing father to a child your wife conceived by another man. Raising him like he was your own son. Teaching him to throw a baseball, shoot a basket.” He looked pointedly at Paula. “Teaching him right from wrong.”

Bill paused for a moment, gazed back out at the parking lot. “There was another reason Dad never brought it up. The real reason.”

Paula waited. She had already guessed his father’s motives, but it was difficult to imagine anyone being so diabolical, being so filled with hate.

“Dad realized what a powerful force guilt was, especially for a Bible-beater like Mom. It was making her old before her time. It stripped her of her youth. Her beauty. It eventually crippled her. Dad decided it was punishment far beyond anything he was capable of. He could think of no reason to deprive her of it."

Tears burned Paula’s cheeks. She searched in her purse for Kleenex but to no avail. To her surprise, Bill offered his handkerchief.

“It’s clean,” he said, tossing it into her lap then sitting in the chair across from her.

“Ever seen pictures of Mom when she was a young woman?”

Paula shook her head, daubed her tears.

“She was beautiful. There’s a picture of her on the beach. Probably taken right after they were married. Maybe when they were dating. She’s running. He caught her in mid-air, her head tossed back, laughing, carefree, her arms out like wings, like she was trying to fly.” His voice became coarse, strained. “She was so damn beautiful.”

Paula composed herself. She looked Bill straight in the eyes. “All right, I want you to listen to me, Bill. You always brag about what a good judge of character you are, how you can look into someone’s eyes and tell immediately if they’re lying. Look into my eyes right now and pay close attention to what I'm saying.”

Bill did. Her green eyes flared, not with warmth, or love, or charm, or even beauty. They were intensely earnest. “Billy is your son. From your body. Granted he doesn’t look like you physically. He looks like me. That’s the way it happens sometimes. But on the inside he’s all you and you know it." She leaned forward, bringing her face closer to his. "Am I lying, Bill?"

The fierceness in Paula's eyes caught him off guard.

"Am I lying?" she asked again.

Bill was unnerved. When had she learned to be so confrontational? He did the only thing he knew to do, the thing that always put his wife in her place. He turned away, dismissing her, then leaned back casually in his chair.

Paula's mouth gaped open. How many times over the years had he done that, dismissing her as if she were totally insignificant, not only to him but to the world in general? Paula wanted to ball up her fist and throw a roundhouse punch into his sneering face.

She stood up, tall, towered over him. "Take a good look, Bill. My back's straight. My head's high. I don't need a walker because my legs work just fine. What's missing here?"

"You tell me." It was said sarcastically. And with scorn.

"Guilt. After all these years, that never occurred to you? I was never crippled by guilt. But our marriage sure as hell was." She burst into tears, angry tears. "Oh God, Bill. Why couldn't you have at least given me the benefit of the doubt? Why couldn't you have talked to me? Why did you let this happen?" She crossed the room to the window, choked on more tears. "You fucking bastard."

Bill merely shrugged. "Like father, like son."

They were both quiet while the ringing of their voices evaporated, leaving only the thunk, thunk, thunk of the clock.

Paula shook her head, mystified. "How did I ever let myself get drawn into this . . . sickness?"

Bill's sneer had a menacing edge to it. "The better question is, *why* did you?"

Paula looked him directly in the eyes. "I was in love with you."

Bill was clearly not expecting that response, but dismissed it with a sneer. "Anyway, it's a moot point. Looks like you're going to get what you want."

Paula flushed. Did he know about Kurt? How? "Excuse me?"

"Sunday morning, Paula. Have you forgotten what happened last Sunday morning?"

Her shoulders sagged with relief. It wasn't about Kurt. "Under the circumstances, yes."

"She's got to go, isn't that what you said? Buy her an apartment in a retirement community, put her on a slow boat to China, do whatever you have to, but get her the hell out of our house." He paused. "I think I'm quoting verbatim."

Paula walked across the room and knelt before him. "Bill," she said gently, "We've just uncovered some big misunderstandings that go back a lot further than Sunday morning. Maybe now's not a good time to bring them up. Maybe now we should just focus on your mother pulling through this."

Bill scoffed at her. "Oh, so now you're concerned about her well being? How nice. Let's not be quite so hypocritical, Paula. We both know you hate her guts."

Paula plopped down in the chair next to Bill, her anger rising to the surface again. "Look, I feel bad enough about what happened today. Yesterday. But I can't change it, okay?"

"No you can't, Paula. Like Mom, the time to have changed it was before it happened."

"Meaning what?"

"Hey, don't you dare look at me like that. You know damn well what I mean."

"No, Bill, I don't."

His hands were trembling. He wanted to slap that insolent look right off Paula's face. "You were arguing with Mom outside the store, right? You tried to grab a bag away from her, right? That's why she stepped in front of that truck, right?"

"Shut up, Bill. Don't say another goddamn word."

"Those are the facts, Paula. Face it. If it hadn't been for you, Mom wouldn't be lying in there on a hospital bed in a coma."

Something snapped in Paula's eyes. Her hand swung out, cracked against his jaw. He hadn't been prepared for that. He looked at her, stunned. He shook from the inside out. He couldn't control it. He realized with horror what was about to happen and knew he couldn't stop it. It was the ultimate humiliation. He bent over, put his face in his hands and bawled.

To Paula, all sensation of time and place seemed to shatter into small, deadly shards. She found herself in the elevator. She didn't remember leaving the waiting room or walking down the hall or pushing the button for the car. She was only aware she was descending too damn fast.

The doors opened to a sterile lobby. Except for a stooped old man in coveralls slinging a mop back and forth, the place was deserted. Paula hurried outside and filled her lungs with fresh night air. It helped. But it was the Chesterfield she fired up once inside her car that saved her from screaming lunacy.

She sat there for three cigarettes, staring at the hospital, at the window on the fifth floor in particular. What gods have I crossed, she wondered. Why am I always stepping into piles of shit? Paula flicked the butt out the window and immediately lit a fourth, but broke down, sobbing.

Oh Kurt, where are you? Save me, quick. She banged the steering wheel with both fists. Somewhere behind the hard, racking sobs a voice screamed at her.

Leave. Now. Crank up the damn car and just drive away. Do it now. Don't think about it. Don't wait another second. Just go. Go to Kurt. Make it real. Now. Do it.

The urge to heed the voice was overwhelming, but she knew she couldn't. There still remained a few small, hidden places in her heart tender to the touch. Paula knew if she drove away now those places would turn to stone. And if that happened, she wouldn't be able to live with herself, much less Kurt.

Paula used the rearview mirror to repair her makeup and hair. She rolled the window up and got out of the car. The hospital stood before her, beckoning.

She slung her handbag over her shoulder and walked resolutely toward it.

32

Mama Taylor was flying through a dark tunnel. Amazingly, she was able to keep pace with Paula. Ahead of them the tunnel filled with golden light. It made her heart sing.

They shot out of the tunnel and flew high over a crystal lake, seemingly endless. Purple mountains rose straight up from the water. Their towering peaks were frosted with snow. Tiny islands were sprinkled throughout the lake too. On each of them was a small temple, nestled among willows, flowering bushes, and jewel-like rocks.

Paula let out a loud whoop, clapped her hands together overhead and dove straight down. Mama Taylor followed suit. As they skimmed over one of the islands, she said, "I never thought I'd be able to fly like this."

Paula looked at her curiously. "But you've always been able to fly."

Mama Taylor swooped low enough to snatch up a handful of wildflowers then settled next to Paula on a rock overhanging the water. Paula pointed to the water. "Look."

Mama Taylor gazed down and was surprised at what she saw in the mirror-like surface. "Who's that?"

A young and stunningly beautiful woman stared back at her. Long, golden hair. Eyes large and blue. Limbs gracefully slender. Mama Taylor leaned closer. Dear God, that's me. Then she noticed something else and caught her breath again.

"What's wrong?" Paula asked.

"We're naked!"

Paula looked at her quizzically. "Of course we are," then shifted her gaze toward the sky. Her face broke into a bright smile. Mama Taylor followed her gaze and saw people emerging from the tunnel, flying in formation. "Good grief! Who are they?"

"A pack of men," Paula said excitedly. "And they're looking for us." She grabbed Mama Taylor's hand. "Come on."

Paula darted skyward with lightning speed, almost pulling Mama Taylor's arm out of its socket. "Paula, you're taking my breath away!"

A bronzed body whisked by. And another. Within seconds men were all around them, flashing golden smiles. One of them swooped down below Mama Taylor and kept pace. "Grab my shoulders," he called to her.

Mama Taylor reached down, firmly gripping his hard, muscular shoulders. She was jerked forward. With his strength he flew much faster than her.

"Where shall I take you?" he asked.

With a shock, Mama Taylor realized that the man whose shoulder she was griping was Jennings St. John. He was still so incredibly beautiful it made her stomach quiver when she looked at him. Those dark eyes of his still taunted her. He still had that same reckless laugh. She was overcome with joy. "Where to?" he asked again.

Mama Taylor giggled like a child chasing soap bubbles. "I don't care, just take me."

Which he did. While they were flying, no less. Paula and the others laughed approvingly at Mama Taylor's screams of ecstasy, but she paid them no heed.

Two men were flying with Paula, each holding onto one of her hands. In front of her, two more were performing acrobatics for her amusement. Mama Taylor laughed. That Paula.

"Where to now?" Jennings asked.

Mama Taylor threw her head back and gazed into the heavens. Above the blue of the sky was a mysterious purple that gradually tapered into rich, velvety black. In that blackness were millions of twinkling stars.

"Take me to the stars," she commanded.

"We're heading for the stars," Jennings called to the others. They all signaled in the affirmative, arched their backs and shot upwards. Jennings shot upward too, so abruptly that Mama Taylor lost her grip. He was far above her now, not even bothering to look back as she fell. She thought she heard his laughter mocking her. Paula called to her. She was little more than a pink speck in the vastness of the sky. "Come on, Mama Taylor. Spread your arms out. Fly."

Mama Taylor made an effort to straighten herself into a flying position, but hot needles of pain jabbed through her arms and legs when she tried to move them. She continued to fall, faster and faster. "Oh, no," she cried out. "Help me, Paula!" But she'd lost all sight or sound of Paula. Below her the gaping mouth of the tunnel opened to receive her. "No!"

And then she was hurling through it. The warm, golden light grew dimmer until it became a chilling darkness. Her hands were once again wrinkled with age, her legs bowed and spindly. She cried out in despair. At the other end of the tunnel someone was waiting for her. Elliot. A malevolent grin on his face. In his hand was her walker. He was brandishing it.

"Oh, God, no!"

She tried to scream, but something was jammed in her throat, choking her. She struggled with it, tried to tear it out before it strangled her, but she couldn't move her arms. They were tied down for some reason. Panic swept over her. She was going to suffocate. She was going to die.

The obstruction was removed and she sucked in great lungfuls of air. She opened her eyes to see a fuzzy image of Bill and Paula hovering above her, along with a couple of nurses working nearby. Paula was saying, "I think she's coming out of it." But her voice had an odd echo to it.

Bill leaned over so his face was only inches from hers. Or was it Jennings St. John? "Can you hear me, Mom?" No, it was Bill. Her son. His hand grasped hers. "Can you squeeze my hand, Mom?"

Paula leaned closer, too. Such a sweet smile. But why the tears? "Don't worry, Mama Taylor. You're going to be fine."

"What time is it?" Mama Taylor whispered.

"One-thirty." Bill saw the confusion in her eyes. "In the morning. Saturday. You've been out all day."

"I didn't want to come back," she said, but was touched that Paula had abandoned all those golden men to be with her. She had gotten dressed, too. "What was it like?"

Paula leaned closer. "What was what like?"

"The stars," Mama Taylor said. "What were they like?"

One of the nurses gave Paula an encouraging smile. "Just go along with her."

Paula put her hand on Mama Taylor's cheek and said, "They were beautiful, Mama Taylor. They were just beautiful."

"I knew they would be," Mama Taylor sighed.

33

It was nearly 2:00 AM Saturday when Red appeared at Kurt's screen door. He hesitated before entering. Kurt said, "What's the matter?"

"Last time I opened this door I got my nose broken."

Kurt motioned him to a seat at the bar and said, "What're you drinking?"

"A little of your Black Jack, if you can spare it. Leave off the ice."

Kurt cocked an eyebrow quizzically at Red as he topped off a rocks glass with whiskey, then handed it to him. His former partner threw back half of it in a single gulp. He sat there quietly for a moment, staring down at the bar, drumming his fingers. "I couldn't find out who's trying to cut in on us, partner."

Kurt tried to appear as if he was having difficulty controlling his anger. It had the right effect on Red. He shifted his weight in the chair, appeared decidedly uncomfortable.

"This is bullshit, Red. We had a smooth campaign up till now. I don't like operating under this kind of vulnerability."

"Fuck, me neither. Man I've searched under every rock and bush from here to Colombia and back. Whoever's trying to cut in has done a damn fine job of covering their tracks."

"It's not the Federation?"

"First place I looked. No dice. They're still walking around in a fog." Red leaned close to Kurt. "Maybe we should push back the meeting with Estrada one more week so we can both have a go at it."

Kurt didn't miss the sarcasm in Red's voice. He answered it with a sneer of his own. "And get ourselves a Colombian necktie? Remember how pissed Estrada was about the last postponement. We do it again, he's gonna send a welcoming party. He wants those emeralds in the worst kind of way, Red. And he doesn't give a flying fuck about our problems."

Red leaned back, properly chastised. He punched his fist into his palm repeatedly. "Sonovafuckinbitch."

Kurt folded his arms and paced back and forth behind the bar, his head down as if in deep thought. When he felt the tension had built to a sufficient level, he faced Red again, hands on hips in a gesture of having made a major decision. "Okay, here's what we do."

Red became a statue. Kurt had his full attention.

"The original idea of splitting the stones up is no good. If either one of us is taken out, the deal is blown. Estrada won't settle for half. Our chances are better if only one of us carries the emeralds."

Red's lifeless eyes turned wary. "Say, why's that, partner?"

"Because if the guy without the jewels gets taken out, the deal can still go through."

"Uh-huh, yeah, okay," Red said, bobbing his head up and down. Then he said, "But what if the guy who has the jewels gets taken out?"

Kurt shrugged. "Gotta make sure that doesn't happen, don't we?"

"Sure, sure, sure, but uh, see, I guess the question is, which one of us carries the stones?"

"That's easy. The one they'd least expect."

Red's eyes locked on Kurt, his face expressionless as marble. "Right. So who would that be, partner?"

Kurt was enjoying himself. "We can safely assume whoever's trying to horn in knows we're aware of their intentions. Think, my friend. They tried to make it look like you were setting up a double-cross, obviously trying to discredit you. They might even have hoped I'd take you out. What does that tell you?"

"They want me out of the picture."

"There you go. But why you instead of me?"

Red looked like he was trying to solve Einstein's theory of relativity. Beads of sweat popped out on his brow. Kurt said, "Because they think you're more of a threat. That it would be easier to take the emeralds from me."

Red relaxed. He liked that reasoning. "Okay, makes sense. So what should we do? Who, uh, carries the emeralds?"

Kurt waited just long enough to twist a few more knots in Red's stomach, then said, "You do."

Red made a miserable attempt to appear cool. "Well, you're the brains in the outfit, partner. Whatever you think's best."

"Let's use a little judo on 'em. Instead of trying to resist when they lean on us, we'll just go with them and knock them on their asses. They think you've been discredited, that I won't trust you now. My bet is they're going to focus their attention on me."

"Maybe we oughta head south together, work as a team."

Kurt knew Red only suggested it because he was sure Kurt would dismiss the idea, so he pretended to give it serious consideration before saying, "No, if we split up, it splits them up, too. And since even you and I don't know how the other is going to get to Colombia, it forces them to cover a lot of possibilities. That'll spread them even thinner." He shook loose a Camel and fired it up. He didn't offer Red one. Oddly enough, Red found smoking a disgusting habit.

Red said, "Okay partner, makes sense to me." He popped his knuckles. "So now, where are those beautiful emeralds?"

Kurt smiled to himself. Can't wait to get your hands on them, can you, Red old boy? He grabbed a magnum-sized bottle of creme de menthe from the shelf behind the bar. "Might I interest you in a glass of liqueur?"

Red scoffed. "Liqueur my ass." He threw back the rest of his whiskey and slammed the glass down for more. "Let's get down to some serious drinking. Fill'er up."

"That's where we differ, Red. I find liqueur a richly . . . rewarding drink."

Kurt poured the syrupy green fluid into two small glasses. Within seconds the bottle was empty. He feigned a puzzled expression, saying, "How can this be?" He withdrew a stiletto from a drawer. He held it up for Red to observe. "Still haven't got the point?"

A crafty grin spread across Red's face. "Yeah, okay." He jabbed the blade into the throat of the bottle. A plug of wax fell out, followed by a steady stream of uncut emeralds. They looked more like green rock candy than jewels. Red scooped them up, rolled them from hand to hand. "Good to see you girls again."

Kurt spent the next half hour showing Red a number of devices he had crafted to safely and secretly carry the emeralds. Red was duly impressed. Afterwards he gathered his gear, ready to leave. He paused at the door, holding out his hand to Kurt.

"No," Kurt said. "Bad luck. We'll shake hands Sunday night at Plaza de Bolivar."

Red grinned. "All right, then. Plaza de Bolivar." He turned and was gone. Kurt stepped out onto the verandah and watched Red's battered runabout glide out of the lagoon.

End of an era. End of Red.

Kurt plopped down in the sling chair feeling pounds lighter and years younger.

At last I'm free of that piece of shit.

Without knowing he was going to do it, he let out a whoop of joy, something he had never done before. It flew across the lagoon, echoed through the tunnel, and out into the Bay.

34

Paula had never seen a man look as tired as Dr. Abrams did. The bags under his eyes had bags of their own and were purplish, as if bruised. He was the Senior Resident. Bill and Paula were glued to his every word. Both of them.

"She'll live." While he waited for a response, he took a drag off his Lucky. His head bobbed as if he were having trouble balancing its weight.

Paula smiled up at Bill and patted his arm encouragingly. Bill asked, "Any brain damage."

"None we can see. So far."

Bill waited for Dr. Abrams to elaborate, but after several awkward seconds passed, said, "Any idea how long she'll have to stay here?"

Dr. Abrams took a sip of coffee, grimacing as he swallowed it, then said, "Long time."

Paula was beginning to wonder if the good doctor charged by the word. "Why is that?"

"Severe concussion. Multiple contusions and lacerations. Broken bones in all four limbs. Broken ribs."

Bill looked like he was going to be sick. "Oh my God. Any good news?"

"Her hip isn't broken."

Paula asked, "Will she walk again?"

Dr Abrams made an expression as if he'd bitten into a lemon and shook his head.

Bill and Paula took a moment to consider the implications.

"She'll need lots of care." Abrams looked directly at Paula, as if she were a nurse to whom he was giving orders. "Round the clock." He paused a second. "From now on."

Bill folded his arms and nodded. "Won't be a problem. My wife'll look after her."

Paula reeled. She almost said, "The hell I will." Instead, she gave Bill a frigid smile and tried to remain composed.

The doctor gave them a pasted-on smile. "Well, then." He didn't offer to shake hands because both were occupied, so he simply turned and loped away.

Through the nearby floor-length window, the sun was visible peeking over the horizon, red and bursting with energy. Full of promise.

Reprieve.

She was bursting too. All she thought about was bolting. Kurt would be waiting for her tonight. She would damn well be there. But there was still lots to do. Time to get moving.

Bill turned to Paula, took a deep breath then hissed it out. He placed his hands on his hips, chuckled, and shook his head as if they'd just escaped a close call. "Well, dear, guess things are going to be a lot different now."

Paula wanted to say: you have no idea. But now wasn't the time. Keep it short and sweet, she told herself. Just say goodbye and get the hell out of here.

"Bill, darling," she began, surprised she'd so easily used that term of affection as automatically as he had just used 'dear'. He looked at her expectantly, his eyes like a puppy just wanting to be loved. Paula was overcome by a feeling of deep sorrow.

"Bill, I'm sorry. I'm just . . . so damn sorry."

"No, Paula." He put his hands on her shoulders, looked deeply at her with eyes full affection. That it was genuine was somehow more jarring than a slap in the face. "I'm the one who's sorry. I said some pretty awful things to you last night. I don't know why I said them. You had every right to slap me."

She wanted to slap him now. It was the first time he had apologized to her since before Billy was born. Why now, when she was about to walk out the door forever? Why couldn't he be his usual asshole self? Why couldn't he make it easier for her?

Forget it, she told herself. Give him a peck on the cheek, say goodbye, and get the hell out of here. But instead she threw her arms around him, held him tight, and said, "I'm really, really glad your mom's going to be all right."

He returned her embrace, enveloping her in his arms, crushing her to him the way he did so long ago, in a way that said he needed her; that he depended on her.

Oh, no, Paula thought, please don't. Not now.

"Oops, guess this isn't a good time."

Bill and Paula sprung apart. Betty stood before them on the elevator, a shopping bag in her hand. Paula wiped away a tear. "Oh, hi Betty. Who's minding the store?"

"Nobody, Mrs. T. It's Saturday. We're not open on Saturdays, dear." She turned to Bill and laughed as if the two of them shared a secret joke that Paula was the butt of it. "I just had to stop by. I was so worried about your mom."

"She's going to be okay," Bill informed her.

"Oh Boss, that's wonderful." She gave him a big hug, kicking one leg up. The hint of intimacy did not escape Paula's notice.

"Isn't it sweet of you to be so concerned?" she said icily.

Betty opened the shopping bag. "Anyway, I picked up some necessaries for you. Razor and blades, shaving cream, toothbrush and toothpaste . . ." Then in a whisper, "Deodorant."

Bill looked into the bag and grinned. "No Crackerjacks?"

Betty laughed like a donkey braying. She grabbed Paula's elbow and leaned so close that her forehead was almost on Paula's shoulder. "Isn't he the funniest thing? And at a time like this too." She turned an adoring gaze on Bill while still commandeering Paula's arm.

Paula jerked it free, thinking: you'll never know how close you came to being cold-cocked, sister. Bill was decidedly uncomfortable and Paula wondered what that was all about. For the second time in this painfully long night, puzzle pieces came together.

Bill said, "Thank you, Betty. Very thoughtful of you."

She slapped him on the shoulder. "Don't be silly. It's my job." She turned to Paula again with a smile that would crack a mirror. "He does need looking after and, well, I know how busy you always are. I just wanted to make it easier for you."

Bill turned crimson. Paula sucked in her breath. Well, son of a bitch. The puzzle pieces came together. Bill and Betty. Right under my nose. Never had an inkling. And I was so worried Bill would find out about me and Kurt . . .

She laughed at the absurdity of it. Unable to stop herself, she laughed so hard she grabbed her stomach and had to sit down. Bill was looking at her oddly. "You okay?"

"Yes. Fine. Just . . . relieved," she said, honestly, then laughed harder. Even she heard the hysteria in it. She forced herself to stop. She looked over at Betty. "Oh yes, dear, you've made it very, very easy for me. Thank you."

Betty winked at Bill. "That's why he keeps me around. To make things a little easier."

"I bet," Paula said. She got to her feet, fully composed now. She straightened her dress. "All right, then." She stood tall, confident, and formidable, her shoulders back, head high, breasts prominent. She knew it didn't matter now, but she wanted Bill to get a good look at what he was losing. She towered over Betty, who now resembled a little girl still developing. "Guess I'd better get going."

Bill looked puzzled. "Going? Where?"

"Did you forget I had to help my mom again this weekend? Birdy asked me to. We talked about it Tuesday morning, remember?"

Bill nodded his head with far more enthusiasm than was necessary. “Sure, right, right.”

“You'd just come home from working all night.” She looked pointedly at Betty and smiled sweetly. “I was expecting him to be cranky. I was so surprised at what a good mood he was in. ”

Panic flashed in Betty's eyes. Bill stepped in with, “Sorry. You’re right. My mind’s scrambling for traction right now. Yes, by all means, go look after your mom. There's nothing more for you to do here."

How true, Paula thought. Then Betty chimed in with, “That's right, Mrs. T, you run along now. Don't worry, I'll take good care of him.” Her face was beaming.

Paula struggled to keep from bursting out laughing again. Instead, she wiggled her fingers at them. “Tah-tah.”

Then she looked her last at Bill. Her husband. The father of her child. Her one-time lover. She smiled at him, fondly, wanting to remember the best about him.

It only took a second.

She turned and got the hell out of there.

35

Paula jumped into the wagon and sped out of the parking lot. The clock on the dash read 7:02. She wanted to be at the bank by 9:00. There was a lot to do before tonight's fireworks with Kurt began and it all took money.

At 7:30 precisely she backed her station wagon down the driveway, parking so the tailgate was only a few steps from the kitchen door. The Chris Craft on one side and the house on the other provided cover. It also shielded her from Millie's prying eyes. She spun out of the car and ran inside.

Few homes in Palm Beach had basements but most had shallow attics used primarily for storage. Paula knew Bill would never look there and Mama Taylor wasn't able to, so that's where she'd stashed her Mermaid Boutique treasure. She grabbed the two suitcases and trotted down the hall to her bedroom.

She showered, shaved her underarms, but skipped her legs, having shaved them yesterday morning before going to the store. She whipped off the shower cap she'd worn because of the hair appointment scheduled for later, then toweled off. She slipped on a pair of sexy black panties but was otherwise naked as she plopped down at her vanity.

Not how she normally applied makeup, but she wanted to see herself now the way Kurt would see her tonight, so the dressing gown she usually wore stayed in the closet. She gazed at herself sitting there, blatantly female.

My God, I'm really doing this.

She laughed out loud and liked the way the woman in the mirror laughed back at her, especially liked the sparkle in her eyes. She had to admit she looked pretty damn good for a thirty-nine year old broad. Her face had a healthy glow. The girls were tight and standing proud, nipples snapped to attention. Her heart was going giddy-up. Years of coitus deprivus were over. The wild woman in her nether regions was starting to growl. The thought triggered delicious stirrings in her port of entry.

Good. Let the sexual tension build all day then explode tonight when Kurt has his way with me.

She finished her makeup, studied it from all angles then puckered her lips to make sure they were irresistibly plump and creamy. They were. Eat your heart out Marilyn Monroe.

She stood, pumped the bulb on her perfume bottle several times to spray the scent into the air, then walked through it, waving it toward her in the process.

Perfect. Next, she scooped all her makeup into a large travel bag with an exotic floral design, then zipped it shut. Wonderful sound zippers.

Now for the fun part.

She popped open the two suitcases and one-by-one hung the different outfits over her bamboo dressing screen, closet doors, even the gooseneck of a floor lamp. The sight of them was delightful to her eye. Her mind was swimming with possibilities, some nice, some naughty.

Next she laid out her new shoes in a neat row, each pair suitable for a specific activity. Clearly she was expecting an active life. There was also a new pair of sandals. Sexy sandals, no less. How silly. It brought a smile to her face. Fun, fun, fun.

All that remained was lingerie, bracelets, necklaces, earrings, watches, and other fanciful female accoutrements. She pulled out a lacy black bra the girls instantly fell in love with. When she looked in the mirror and saw how boldly it displayed her assets, she almost blushed. She liked that it fastened in the front. Kurt would like it even more.

Paula glanced at the bedside clock. 8:05. Gotta get moving. But what would her getaway outfit be, the one she would put on now?

It only took a moment to decide. It was the last one she bought, the cream-colored linen dress with the slit skirt and wide macramé belt. She slipped it on and one glance in the mirror told her she'd made the right choice.

Except for the bra, black wouldn't do with this dress. She whipped it off and found an identical one in white. She had to change out the panties too. She stepped into the sexy sandals then added a bracelet, necklace, and earrings all made of tiny seashells. The last item was a heart-shaped wristwatch with an elastic silver band. Voila. The new Paula.

By 8:42 Paula was exiting the kitchen door. She opened the tailgate and laid her suitcases flat in the cargo area. She slammed the tailgate shut and was about to lock up the house, but stopped abruptly.

The letter. Damn.

She ran back inside. Her letter to Bill was in the drawer with her lingerie, her old lingerie from her old life. That's why she hadn't seen it. She'd only packed her new stuff. She rummaged through the drawer and found it hidden next to the figurine Kurt had given her. Damn, she had forgotten that too. That would have been disastrous. Come on, Paula, she scolded herself, now is the time to be cool, calm, and collected. No mistakes.

At 8:50 precisely she pulled straight out of her driveway. Millie was next door purportedly trimming her shrubs, but her eyes were locked on Paula's carport. She waved frantically. Actually, she almost fell over sideways trying to get Paula's attention. Paula smiled sweetly, wiggled her fingers, and never slowed down.

36

At 9:05 Paula was sitting at the desk of Thurston Kingsley III, managing director of Fidelity Federal Savings Bank. "Sorry to do this to you, Mr. Kingsley, but something's come up. I'm going to need to withdraw quite a bit of money."

Paula was expecting Kingsley to flinch, or at least display a pained expression. Instead he was the model of decorum. "Of course, Mrs. Taylor. We've been informed of your mother-in-law's unfortunate accident. All of us here at Fidelity Federal have been so concerned. Tell me, how is the poor lady faring?"

Paula hadn't even thought of that angle. She entered the bank a few minutes ago prepared for a fight, knowing how fond financial institutions become of your money. "Well, she's out of the coma, but beyond that . . ." She dropped her head as if it was difficult to talk about.

Kingsley flushed and hurried around his desk to pat Paula on the shoulder. "Of course, of course. So sorry." He called out his door, "Mrs. Carter? Would you step in here, please?"

Phyllis Carter did so quite briskly. She was wearing a stylish gray suit, conservative black heels, an impressively filled-out scoop neck blouse in a pale pink tone, a faux pearl necklace and matching earrings. Only the feline glasses hinted at what she might be like away from the office. She stood at attention, notepad and fountain pen at the ready. "Yes sir?"

Kingsley addressed Paula again. "Mrs. Taylor, may I introduce my assistant, Mrs. Carter."

"Please call me Phyllis," Mrs. Carter interposed. "So very sorry to hear of your misfortune."

Paula smiled bravely, caught her breath then said, "Thank you, Phyllis." She was about to ask for a Kleenex, but decided it was best not to overdo it.

Kingsley informed Paula that Mrs. Carter would attend to her needs and they should feel free to use the privacy of his office as long as was necessary. He made a little bow and exited.

"Don't worry about a thing, Mrs. Taylor," Phyllis said as she settled into Kingsley's big, leather chair. She was the model of decorum and efficiency, but Paula's instincts told her it was a well-crafted act. Another woman lived directly beneath the surface. It was easy for Paula to spot another caged lioness.

"We'll have you out of here in no time," Phyllis said. She pulled forms out of a bottom drawer and jotted down account information. "Now, Mrs. Taylor, how much did you need to withdraw today?"

Paula smiled ever so slightly. "$24,876.52."

Phyllis stopped writing and simply stared at the form for a moment. She looked up at Paula. Their eyes locked. Yes, there it was. Each recognized the other woman for who she really was. Both smiled almost imperceptibly. Phyllis said, "Why not just make it twenty-four-nine? Or an even twenty-five?"

Paula had carefully done the math and half of their checking and savings accounts came to $24,876.52. Not a penny more. Not a penny less. It did not factor in money from TaylorMade Printing's accounts. She pushed the withdrawal slip she'd already filled out across the desk and said, "If you could get me that exact amount, please, Phyllis."

"You got it," Phyllis said, and the Cheshire grin on her face revealed she was adding up more than bank account figures. "And how do you want it?"

"Cash."

"All of it?"

"Yes."

"Wow." Phyllis kept her head down but looked up at Paula over her cat-like glasses. Her grin widened and there was a mischievous glint in her eyes. "Sure you don't want some of this in cashier's checks?

"I don't think that would be a good idea."

"You're right, Mrs. Taylor, it wouldn't."

"Please call me Paula."

Phyllis laid down her pen and pushed back in Kingsley's big-boss chair. She rocked for a moment then said, "Nice dress, Paula."

"Mermaid Boutique."

Phyllis nodded. "Been by there." She pointedly glanced at her unadorned ring finger. "Maybe I should buy something there." She wiggled her eyebrows at Paula. They both burst out laughing.

Kingsley stuck his head through the doorway looking very serious. "Is everything quite all right?"

"Yes sir. We're almost done." He waited for further explanation, and Phyllis said, "I accidentally dropped a paper clip down the front of my dress. It made us both laugh."

Kingsley's face turned an iridescent red before he disappeared. Phyllis said, "Okay, I'm betting you've already worked out what denominations you want this in?"

"I have." Paula consulted her figures again. "Twenty thousand in hundred dollar bills. Four thousand in fifties. The rest in twenties and whatever."

Phyllis wrote it all down then winked at Paula. "Be right back."

When she returned, Phyllis had a large envelope in her hand. She closed and locked the door, then closed the Venetian blinds on both the interior and exterior windows. She counted the cash out for Paula's inspection, then had her sign a receipt. Paula looked at all the cash spread across the desk and said, "God almighty."

"Amen to that," Phyllis said.

They both laughed like teenyboppers smoking in the girl's room, then Paula said, "One more thing. While I'm here I'd like to pay off the loan on the Country Squire."

Phyllis cocked her hands on her hips and shook her head playfully. "No problem, Paula. How about the house loan while we're at it?"

Paula grinned. "Oh, I think just the car today."

They owed a little over a thousand on it. Paula paid with the cash in front of her, then stuffed the title in her purse along with a handful of cash. The rest of the money went into the special item she bought at Mermaid Boutique. It was a girdle of sorts. It fastened around her waist under her skirt and hung down to just above her knees. Built into it were a number of money-sized pockets that zipped close.

Phyllis gawked and said, "Wow. I've heard of cash-and-carry, but . . . Let me guess, Mermaid Boutique?"

Paula adjusted the load, lowered her skirt and said, "A gal's gotta protect her assets."

It was 10:17 when Phyllis escorted her to the door. They shook hands and Paula said, "Thanks, Phyllis. You've made this very easy."

"That's what I'm here for." Phyllis started back through the door, then stopped and said, "Oh, Paula . . ." The meaning behind her smile was unmistakable. "Send me a postcard, huh?"

A rush of affection for Phyllis made Paula hug her warmly, hoping someday she too would find her Kurt.

Tears glistened in Phyllis' eyes. "Good luck, honey." She pulled the door shut.

37

Among Palm Beach's salons de coiffure, Lenny Frank's was all the rage, even if he was a bit 'light in the loafers', which incidentally was his standard footwear. Along with a Marcel Marceau-like outfit consisting of an open-neck black and white striped pullover tucked into form-fitting white pants.

When Paula walked in at 10:30 the place was hopping. Lenny was working miracles on a stoic society matron, his scissors flying around her head in a mesmerizing dance. He moved more like a ballet dancer than a hair stylist, Paula thought. He caught sight of her and his face lit up. "Hi Ginger." Then he noticed her outfit. "My, My. Are we in style or are we in trouble?"

Paula did a mock curtsey while the other women tittered. "Trying for a little of both. I'll need your help."

She took a seat across from a row of women whose heads were half-devoured by drying-hoods. She grabbed the latest issue of Photoplay from a table beside her. A picture inside of Marilyn Monroe immediately caught Paula's attention. Her hair was cut relatively short; nape of the neck, but it was full of wild, swirling curls that seemed to have a life of their own. It reflected Marilyn's sexy, untamed persona perfectly. When Lenny called her back, she showed him the photo. "That's what I want."

Lenny gazed at it thoughtfully, chin resting in his palm, little finger tucked on his bottom lip, muttering, "Yes, um-hum, um-hum," then waved the photo aside, saying, "Leave it to me, Liebchen. By the time you walk out of here, we'll have poor Marilyn weeping with envy."

Lenny ran his fingers through Paula's hair, like Michelangelo searching a block of marble for the statue hidden within, then stopped. "Please tell me you don't want to go blonde."

Paula laughed. "No, no, I like my red hair."

Lenny sighed with relief. "Darling, I love your red hair. I just want to fondle it and cherish it." He leaned close so his forehead was resting against hers, lowering his voice leeringly. "Probably not first on the list of what your men like to fondle."

It broke Paula up. "No, they usually aim a little lower. But I'm flattered you think I've got 'men'.

Lenny scoffed at that. He put his lips to her ear, whispering huskily. "Honey, you've probably been fantasy-fucked by more men than any other female in Palm Beach County."

"Lenny! Boy, you're in a randy mood today."

"Every day. Now tell Uncle Lenny all about him."

Paula looked at Lenny with a wide-eyed innocence that would make Miss Monroe proud. "About who?"

"Please. I want length, breadth *and* width."

Paula motioned with her eyes at the other women. "Can't. Not here."

"Sure you can. They've all got their heads buried in extremely noisy hairdryers. Or up their butts. They can't hear a thing." When she didn't respond, he held up his scissors and made snipping sounds. "No talky, no cutty."

"Okay, okay. Just start working your magic. I've got things to do and places to go."

"I bet."

Lenny began by washing her hair. It felt so damn sensual that Paula had no trouble spilling about Kurt. It was like gossiping with a trusted girlfriend. Lenny listened intensely, made occasional yummy sounds, then prodded her with, "Yes, then what?" or added a particularly naughty quip that cracked Paula up.

They continued bantering playfully throughout the session until Paula's favorite part drew near -- the big reveal. Lenny completed a few final brush strokes, going for perfection as usual. Satisfied at last, he threw his brush down and spun her around to face the mirror.

Paula gaped at Lenny's stunning vision of her. He had created a masterpiece. "Oh my God, Lenny, you're a genius."

A chorus of women called out, "Let's see, let's see." Paula willingly obliged. When she heard the oohs and ahhs, along with a smattering of applause, she thought, forget Kurt, I'll run away with Lenny.

Lenny threw his arms out like a world famous magician then bowed so low his head almost hit the floor. When he straightened, Paula was surprised to see a tear in his eye.

"Why Lenny, what's the matter?"

He stepped very close, gazed deeply into her eyes. He folded her hands into his. "I'm not going to see you again, am I?"

Paula realized he was probably right. It brought a lump to her throat and sprung a few tears of her own. "Oh Lenny . . . Damn."

"Yeah, big ol' damn."

Paula took his face in her hands and planted a warm, lingering kiss on his lips to the accompaniment of woos and snickering from the outer room.

Lenny actually blushed, then said, “You'd better get out of here before my reputation is shot completely to hell.”

But before Paula left, Lenny's assistant, Judy, ran up saying, “Wait a minute, wait a minute, picture time.” She had a Polaroid camera and motioned for Paula and Lenny to move closer together. “We gotta have a shot of this for the scrapbook.” As she framed up the picture she added, “Wow boss, you really outdid yourself. Okay, say cheese.”

Later, after the picture dried, Judy wrote on the bottom, “Lenny and Paula Taylor. October 17, 1959.”

38

For Paula it was love at first sight. Judging by the swaggering grin on the fire engine red '56 T-Bird, the feeling was mutual. It sat low on its wire-spoke whitewalls, ready to pounce.

She liked its headlamps, with their inquisitive upper lids. They seemed to track her as she sashayed in front of it. She heartily approved the way its shiny chrome bumpers reflected how sexy she looked.

Yeah, we're going to get along just fine, she decided.

Like all T-Birds, it was a convertible. Its white top folded down behind the sporty leather seat, also white but trimmed with red. Its speedometer was see-through. How clever, Paula thought. It made her smile.

She studied the big hood. Every self-respecting car-buyer was supposed to lift it to take a gander at the engine. Well, men anyway. To men, it was like unbuttoning a woman's blouse to see what was underneath. She also knew no matter how long she stared at the engine, it wouldn't mean a thing to her. But this was an expected ritual when buying a car, so she reached for the release. And couldn't find it.

"Careful now. You got 235 horses under that hood just raring to bust loose." It was a man's voice coming from somewhere behind her. Paula was too busy wondering how to get the hood open to register his presence.

"Loaded to the gills and cleaner'n the Pope in a bubble bath. Only one thing missing far as I can see."

Paula chose that moment to turn and face the man with feigned wide-eyed innocence. "Me?"

She really wasn't expecting him to go slack-jawed or for his eyes to bug out, but that's what happened. His lips went rubbery. He seemed unable to verbalize a word. Paula thought he was having a seizure. She put her hand on his arm. "You okay? Should I get help?"

He recovered his wits somewhat. Although still reeling, he mustered up his best Bogart imitation. "Of all the car joints in all the towns in all the world, you walk into mine."

Paula had no response to that. The man smiled warmly, his eyes glistening. "Hello, Paula Doherty. Don't you remember me? Bob Ballentine."

Recognition hit Paula. "Bob! Oh my God!" She threw her arms around him in a big hug. They had dated in college before she met Bill. She remembered him as being sweet and a lot of fun and about a hundred pounds thinner with a full head of hair. "This is your place?"

He gestured toward the towering Ballentine Ford sign overhead saying, "Yep. Originally Dad's, but he retired a coupla years ago. I moved up from Miami to take over."

Paula was genuinely happy for him. "Good for you, Bob."

"It's a living. By the way, the hood release is under the dash. Did you want to see the engine?"

Paula laughed. "No, no. Gosh, Bob, it's so wonderful to see you."

"And you. Wow, you haven't changed a bit. I know people say that all the time, but you really haven't. Whereas I . . ." He patted his rather prominent belly.

Paula gave him a big smile. "You look great, Bob." But seeing his stomach made her realize she hadn't eaten since yesterday afternoon in the hospital cafeteria.

She hooked her arm in Bob's. "I've got an idea. Lets grab some lunch and fill each other in on all we've been up to since the good ol' days at UM. Then we can come back here and I'll buy this T-Bird from you. Deal?"

"And a half. Just a sec while I tell my number two."

They walked to Bernardo's, two blocks away. It was Paula's favorite Italian restaurant. Great food. Comfy booths. Stylish decor. During the walk, Paula noticed Bob had a pronounced limp and his left arm hung straight down. She had a good idea what that meant.

When they entered Bernardo's, a congress of Palm Beach biddies was already gathered. As Paula and Bob were shown to their booth, she sensed daggers flying her way. She smiled inwardly. Damn, I must look really good.

Once seated and the small talk over, Bob confirmed Paula's suspicions. "Anzio. Got hit three times going in. Real quick, like I was the only guy they were shooting at. Spent the rest of the war in an Army hospital recuperating."

Paula laid her hand sympathetically on his. His face colored slightly, then he shrugged. "Hey, I made it out alive. Lot of my buddies didn't."

"Thank God you did, Bob. What an awful thing to go through." She knew most guys didn't like to talk about their war experiences, even Bill. Those like Bob who were visibly wounded usually wanted to get it out up front, get it over with; forestall the questions. Paula understood. She didn't say any more about it.

"Yeah, so I heard you and big, bad Bill got hitched," Bob said, to change the subject. "Any kids?"

"One. Billy. He's just started at our old alma mater."

Bob looked surprised. "No kidding? My little girl just started there too. Jill."

"Too funny. What's she taking?"

"Cheerleading." Paula laughed. Bob added, "Actually, she's studying to be a teacher."

"Good for her."

As they talked, Paula learned that after college Bob married a girl from up north by the name of Ellen. When he was discharged from the Army he got a job at a big insurance firm that liked to hire war vets. Gradually he worked his way up to district manager.

"So how's Ellen dealing with the empty nest?"

Bob looked down at the table for a moment before responding. "Yeah, well, thing is, we lost Ellen. Little over six years ago. Cancer."

This time Paula used both her hands to grip his. "Oh Bob . . . You've had such a hard time of it. I'm so, so sorry."

He looked up at her with a smile full of conviction. "Don't be, Paula. I've had a truly wonderful life. Yes, I'd give anything if Ellen was still with me, but our years together were the best of the best. Can't remember us ever having a cross word. She loved life and for reasons I'll never understand, loved me. Totally. Completely. That's all I ever wanted. All I ever hoped for. It was more than I deserved."

Tears welled up in Paula's eyes. With his one good hand, Bob whipped a hanky from his back pocket. "It's clean."

Paula grabbed it. "Thank you." She dabbed at her eyes. "Sorry, Bob, don't mean to be such a cry baby."

"It's 'cause you got such a big heart. Ellen was like that. Way I see it, God put women like you two on this cruddy ol' earth to show guys like me what we're fighting for. Even before the war. That's why I fell head over heels for you back in college. That and those big honkers of yours."

"Bob!" Paula laughed and slapped him on the arm.

They chatted on. Paula was happy to let him take the lead. All his stories were either funny adventures he and Ellen had experienced or fond remembrances that were never maudlin. Paula struggled to find upbeat stories about her and Bill. Nothing came to mind. She found herself envying what Bob and Ellen had. It was all she'd ever wanted.

He grew serious, looked earnestly at Paula. "Listen to me, old friend. Your job is happiness. When you're happy you bring happiness to others. You brighten their day. You lift their heart. It's a big job but if you're still the Paula Doherty I knew from way back, you're up to the task."

Paula felt a rush of affection for Bob. She leaned forward so that her sparkling green eyes were only inches from him. "I'm still her. And you can count on me to do my job." She took his face in her hands and kissed him warmly on the lips. It thrilled her to see his eyes light up and his face flush.

Back at the lot, Bob gave the Country Squire a once-over then led Paula to his office. "She's been kept in good shape. Should get full value. So how's about this: even swap."

Paula gawked. "What?"

"You sign over the title to the wagon, I'll sign over the title to the Bird. I'll even throw in a free set of keys." He chuckled at his little joke.

"But Bob, that's not right. The T-Bird's got to be worth a lot more than the wagon, even if it is a year older. I don't feel right about it."

"Yeah, so you gonna tell me how to run my business? Don't worry, I'm not losing anything. You don't understand how the car business works. I do."

"But Bob . . ."

"Look, you want that T-Bird?"

"Of course I do."

"Then that's my deal, take it or leave it. It would make me happy if you take it. Remember, that's your job, dispensing happiness."

Paula laughed, shaking her head in disbelief. "I'll take it!" She dug into her handbag for the wagon's title, then an idea struck her and she also pulled out a pair of hundred dollar bills. "But part of my deal is that you take these."

Bob looked at her quizzically. "But why?"

"I want you to buy a nice necklace or bracelet or some other piece of jewelry, something Ellen would have liked. Put it with her things and when it comes time to pass it all to Jill, it will make me happy to know a piece of it is from me, in memory of a sweet woman who loved a very sweet man. Will you do that?"

Now it was Bob's turn to well up. "I will." Paula handed him back his hanky. He dried his eyes, then, musing out loud, said, "Yeah, maybe something with emeralds. She loved emeralds."

The deal was completed in minutes. Bob walked her out to the T-Bird, then motioned to a young worker in oil stained coveralls. "Yes sir?"

"Tommy, transfer Miss Doherty's things from that Country Squire over there into this T-Bird."

Tommy said, "Yes sir," again and got busy.

Paula smiled at Bob. "Miss Doherty?"

"Paula, if you're doing what I think you're doing, then good for you and God bless you. Bill always was an asshole."

Paula wondered how many times she'd hear that today. But Bob wasn't through.

"He doesn't deserve someone like you and it doesn't bother me a bit to say so." He held out his hand. "So long, Paula."

She ignored his hand and gave him a big hug. "Goodbye, Bob. Thank you."

Bob winked at her, turned, and walked away to a waiting customer.

Paula looked down at the T-Bird. Her T-Bird now. She tingled all over, took a deep breath, patted her chest to calm her racing heart, then glanced at her watch. 1:42. Time to climb into this tiger and hit the road. One last order of business to take care of though: posting the letter to Bill. There was a drop box halfway down the street and Paula covered the distance in seconds. She jerked the lid open, then froze.

This was it. The final act. After the letter left her fingers and descended into the box there was no turning back. She caught a glimpse of herself in a nearby store window. The woman staring back was stylish, sexy and carefree. A woman whose life was ahead of her, not behind her. Paula liked the woman in the store window. She opened her fingers. Twenty years of her life dropped into the void.

While her hand was still poised over the box, she noticed something that gave her a jolt. Her rings. Bill's brand was right there on her finger. If she truly was running away to be free, they had to go. They were symbols of another life. She slipped them off and dropped them in her handbag. But the white circles on her skin still marked her as a married woman. Paula shrugged. The good ol' Florida sun would take care of that soon enough.

She hurried back to the T-Bird, double-checked to make sure all her things were there, surprised at how spacious the trunk was, then slid behind the wheel and settled into the warm leather. It seemed to fit the contours of her body perfectly. She inserted the key, turned it. The engine growled at her gently. Her skin vibrated in rhythm with it.

She whipped out her scarf, tied it on, then extracted the silver cigarette case and matching lighter she'd bought at Mary's. She balanced a Chesterfield on her bottom lip and fired it up. The savory smoke reached deep into her lungs, then into her brain, tickling it. She engaged the clutch, grasped the shift knob firmly, slipped it into first. Ready to go. She pulled out into traffic.

Leapt out was more like it. Easy now girl. You're not used to driving something this powerful. Get the feel of the gears, the steering, test the brakes. Watch it. Red light.

Paula sat at the traffic signal, waiting impatiently. She was aware of people in nearby cars glancing at her, admiring her car, admiring her. She liked that. She liked the feel of the T-Bird too. It was alive in her hands, a well muscled animal pulling at the reins she held, obedient to her alone, but wanting to break loose, to run with the wind.

The side panels of the traffic signal turned amber. Paula downshifted, felt the Bird crouch, ready to charge. Her stomach fluttered. Easy, Paula. Don't act like a child. She sucked more cigarette smoke into her lungs. It only added to her sense of excitement.

The signal turned green. Paula heard the scream of tires clawing hot pavement, the growl of an animal lunging for the kill. It was coming from her car. Now she knew why it was called a Thunderbird, because that's the sound the engine made. Rolling thunder.

She was astounded to find herself halfway down the next block. She passed a park, heard music coming from a pavilion. Kids were dancing the Madison.

Yes, music.

Paula flipped on the radio, found the beat, turned it up loud. What a great sounding radio. The sensuous thump of drums pounded in her veins. The wind tried to push her scarf back, wanted to run its fingers through her hair.

She shifted into third. The car wanted more, more . . . Paula whipped around a woman in a station wagon and laughed. Don't you wish you were me? The entrance ramp to the Parkway was a block away.

The Parkway.

Escape.

Paula charged up the ramp only to be blocked by a guy in a shiny black Caddy pretending not to see her, refusing to yield space to her. Going to make her slow down, fall in behind him.

Paula downshifted. Her tires barked and she lunged forward. The guy in the Caddy sped up too, but Paula was already around him, surprised at how fast the Caddy became a small, black speck in her mirror.

Open road lay ahead. Paula turned up the music even louder, moved her body to the beat, pushed her shoulders back and forth, stretched her arms out in wild thrusts because that's what she felt like doing.

She was aware of a big truck beside her. A tanned face behind sunglasses grinned down at her. He gave her a thumb's up.

Paula laughed, stuck her thumb up too, and pushed the accelerator to the floor. The truck slid away behind her, giving her a couple of toots with his horn. The T-Bird seemed to take flight. No stopping her now. She was into the wind.

39

It was Kurt's whoop of joy that did it. Red was already out in the Bay but he was still able to hear it. It struck him as odd. He'd never before heard Kurt let out a whoop like that, whether he was very, very happy or very, very drunk. He usually kept a lid on his emotions.

He pondered it as he crossed the Bay back to the edge of the Everglades, tying up at his hidey-hole a little before 5:00 AM Saturday. His hidey-hole was a dilapidated fishing shack near one of the piers that lined the water's edge, half of which had collapsed leaving only the pilings. Pelicans and seagulls used them for roosts.

After a breakfast of tortillas and beans, he assembled his kit in preparation for the arduous trip south. But Kurt's whoop kept nagging at him. What did it mean?

He opened up the package of uncut emeralds and rolled them from one palm to the other. Beautiful. Yeah, these were the genuine articles. These were perfect. No way they weren't.

But what did that whoop mean?

He kept fondling the emeralds, not liking what he was thinking. He got angry at himself for even having such thoughts. What the fuck? This was Kurt he was having these twisted thoughts about.

Kurt Younger.

His best buddy. His one true friend. Fuck, his only friend. Kurt and Red. Red and Kurt. Brothers in blood.

But still, that whoop. It meant something.

What?

It kept banging around in his head, getting bigger, darker. "Shit! Son of a bitch!" He yelled it out, full of rage. Not fucking possible. Kurt would never do this to me. Not Kurt.

But he had to know for sure. A mistake here would cost him his life. He knew when Estrada extracted payment in blood, it was slow, humiliating, and gave a new definition to pain and suffering.

By 7:00 he was in South Miami behind a small jewelry store named Rothschild's. In his pocket were a handful of the uncut emeralds. In the shoulder holster beneath his field vest was a Colt Python .357 magnum with an eight-inch barrel. He slipped on gloves and jimmied the back door lock. Inside was a well-ordered work desk set against the wall adjoining the showroom. It had a magnifier lamp on a swing arm along with several other instruments of the trade. Red found a dark corner and waited, considering what it would mean if the emeralds were fake.

It meant Kurt had deliberately set him up to be killed. It meant the plan for the two of them to meet Estrada in Bogota was nothing more than an elaborate ruse for the purpose of eliminating Red while keeping the real emeralds for himself. It meant Kurt had no intention of going to Bogotá.

Why?

Red didn't like having to think this hard. He was a man of action. He left the thinking to Kurt. But he knew he'd better think now until it hurt. It made him break out in a cold sweat. The answer didn't require that much brain power. Kurt wanted Red out of the way, so he was sending him on a deadly wild goose chase.

Okay.

Kurt wasn't going to Bogotá, never intended to.

Okay.

Kurt had other plans.

Okay. What were they?

Best way to figure that out was to review Kurt's actions these last few months. Red had been keeping tabs on him. It was only prudent to do so. Not all the time. Kurt was too good at detecting surveillance for that. Just general movements, when Kurt was otherwise distracted. Like when he was fucking that redheaded bombshell from up Palm Beach way.

Red snickered to himself. Yeah, Mrs. Paula Taylor. Wouldn't Kurt shit a brick if he knew I had Mrs. Taylor's home phone number? Nice piece of trim. Wouldn't mind plowing that field myself.

So was she part of Kurt's plan? Was he going to take the real emeralds and run away with her, knowing I was dead and unable to stop him?

He shook with rage, then forced himself to calm down, to think it all through. The rage dissipated. In its place came remorse. He was thinking all these awful thoughts about Kurt yet he didn't even know if the emeralds were fake.

What if they were real? What if everything Kurt said was true?

He shook his head, disgusted with himself. Of course the emeralds were real. Kurt said they were. Kurt had never lied to him. Why would he start now? They'd been through too much together. They were brothers in blood.

What's the matter with me? What am I doing here? We're on a mission, the biggest one of our lives. I gotta get moving. Kurt's counting on me. His life depends on it. First thing I gotta to do is get my head out of my ass. Then I gotta get the fuck out of here.

He was in the process of doing just that when he heard a car pull into the parking space behind the store. A door slammed. A moment later keys jingled in the lock.

Too late. Gotta go through with it now. Red ducked back into the shadows. He drew his pistol, held it ready.

A wisp of a man entered; old, stooped, and using a cane. He turned on the overhead fluorescents and crossed the room with shaky baby steps. Red assumed it was Mr. Rothschild himself. God, he looked older than Noah's grandpa. In his free hand was a paper sack. Lunch. A finger was crooked through the lid of a Thermos. Despite being in South Florida, he wore a cardigan sweater, unbuttoned. Dumb old fart.

Rothschild puttered around a few minutes, completely unaware of Red's presence, then took a seat on the stool at the work table. Red gave him a minute to get settled, then stepped silently up behind him, placed the barrel of the .357 against the back of Rothschild's wrinkled old head, and cocked the hammer. Rothschild jumped as if stuck with a cattle prod.

Red used the barrel to push the old man's head down so it was only a few inches above the table. "Just keep looking straight down, asshole. You look back, you die."

"I won't, I won't," Rothschild said. "I don't want to die."

"Smart man." Red noticed that the old man was relatively calm. He's been held up before, he decided. Good. He wouldn't have to worry about him doing something stupid. He tossed the emeralds on the work table directly in front of the old man. "Know what these are?"

"Well, they appear to be uncut emeralds."

"Right. That's what they appear to be."

"But you want to know if they're genuine?"

"Right again."

"I can do that."

"Then do it now."

"Yes sir. But I'm going to have to raise my head in order to properly examine them. I won't look back, I promise."

"I promise if you do I'll blow your brains all over this table." Red pulled the barrel back a few inches to give the old man more freedom of movement. "All right, get busy."

"Yes sir."

Rothschild switched on the magnifying lamp then picked up a loupe and carefully examined each of the stones. He rotated them in his fingers to better evaluate their color and clarity, grunting occasionally. Red wondered what the grunts meant. Rothschild laid down the last piece and sighed.

Red was about to explode. "Well? Are they genuine?"

Rothschild took a deep breath. "Yes."

Red felt as if he had just shrugged off a seventy-pound field back. He knew it. Kurt would never double cross him. “They are? They're genuine?”

“Yes,” Rothschild said. “Genuine fakes. They're worthless.”

Red pictured Kurt's head blowing apart as he pumped bullet after magnum bullet into it. Kurt Younger. His brother in arms. The only man in the world he trusted. The only man he would lay down his life for. Now his mortal enemy. The pain was more than he could bear. He screamed out in agony. He pulled the trigger and blew Rothschild's brains all over the work table.

That had been almost six hours ago. It was now 2:00 PM. Red was back in his shack working out his plans to disembowel Kurt before taking possession of the real emeralds.

And Mrs. Taylor. AKA Big Red.

He wanted to keep Kurt alive just long enough for him to watch how she reacted to being pounded by a real man. Then, lights out, Kurt old buddy. Lights out forever.

By tomorrow night all that had been Kurt's would be his. Including Big Red and the house at Curiosity Cove. Kurt damn sure wouldn’t need that anymore. It was the perfect pirate's hideaway. He was undeniably the perfect pirate. But there was a lot of planning to be done to make that happen. Help would be necessary.

40

As soon as Paula entered the University of Miami campus she noticed guys were stopping whatever activity they were presently engaged in and staring at her. Yeah, hot chick in a hot car. That's me. She waved playfully at two jocks rolling on the ground, howling like wolves. She loved it.

The clock on the dash showed a few minutes past three. Right on schedule. She'd be away from here by 4:00, 4:30. At her mom's by 6:00. She'd give Birdy the lowdown on what she was doing, listen respectfully to her speech about why this was the worst mistake of her life, and still make her 8:00 rendezvous with Kurt.

Pi Kappa was midway down the street on Fraternity Row. She focused on the meeting she was about to have with Billy. She had written, rewritten, rehearsed and rehearsed again what she was going to say to him. She was ready. She was confident.

She'd take his insults, knew he'd react angrily at first. She'd let him get it all out, his rage, his hurt. Then she'd wrap her arms around him, reclaim him.

Billy was an extension of her own body and spirit. She was going to make him glad of that. She was determined to bury the mother-son relationship. They would become friends. Someone he relied on, came to for advice. Or comfort when he was troubled. Her son. The boy Mama Taylor had taken from her so long ago. Time to take him back.

Paula parked and to her surprise, Billy bounded out the door and ran toward her, whooping and hollering. Ed and Linden, two of his frat brothers, accompanied him, less verbally.

"Oh wow! Oh Mom, wow!"

Paula laughed. "I'm glad to see you, too."

Billy grabbed his head as if trying to keep it from exploding. "Man, I can't believe this."

Paula was dazed. "Gosh, Billy, I wasn't expecting such an enthusiastic reception." Maybe being away from home for the first time made him appreciate her more. Maybe this was going to be easier than she thought. Right now she just wanted to sweep him up in her arms and hug him, rather ridiculous considering his whopping six-five size.

Which was three inches taller than Bill but without his father's athletic build or ability. Instead he was a towering, lanky klutz. Paula never understood that since both she and Bill were very athletic. From the neck up he was all Paula. He even had Paula's disarming green eyes, along with her red hair, cut in its requisite flat top. As usual he'd used too much butch wax.

She opened her arms for him but he was still acting like a wild chimpanzee. Ed and Linden laughed at his antics. Paula laughed, too. "Okay, what've you guys been drinking?"

"Drinking? You kidding? I mean, look at this. I don't believe it. Dad said he was going to get me a new car, but, man, this is too much."

It took Paula's breath away more completely than if she had been gut-punched. "What?"

Billy caressed a chrome fender as if it were a woman's breast. It made Paula queasy.

"Whoa, hold on, Billy . . ." But he had already shouldered past her, opened the door, and sat behind the wheel. Ed slid into the passenger seat, shoving Paula's purse to the floor. Billy cranked up. Ed swooned with approval. "Sounds like a panther in heat."

Billy and Linden thought this uproariously funny. Paula did not. "Billy . . ."

"Proof once again that Dad never lets me down. Said he'd get me a new car, but like, wow, I never expected anything like this."

Paula tried to focus on why she was here. "Billy, please get out of the car. I don't have much time, okay? We've got some talking to do. I need you to turn the engine off . . ."

Billy looked at her with those same insolent eyes that had first attracted her to Bill. "Hey, Mom, wha'd ya do to your hair? Looks kinda sexy." Ed and Linden laughed.

Paula's face flushed hot. In one swift move, she reached inside, turned off the ignition and removed the keys. "Get out." She glared at Ed. "You too, please."

They climbed out, big, gangly boys, all arms and legs. Even though Paula was tall for a woman, they made her feel like a little girl. Ed decided it was exit time. "Hey, catch you later, Billy." As he and Linden ambled off, Paula heard one of them mutter, "Bitch."

Yes, she thought, and not the hot chick variety. Just a bitch. The motherly kind. She felt twenty years older. Billy stood in front of her, folding and unfolding his arms, shoving his hands in and out of his pockets, shifting his weight from one foot to the other. Paula tried to remember her opening line, but her head was in too much of a spin. "Billy, I, uh . . ."

But Billy grabbed her, pinned her arms with his big hands, and leaned down so she could see how earnest he was. "I gotta say something, Mom. I gotta tell ya what this means to me."

"Billy . . ."

"Just listen, okay? I just wanna say I've learned a lot living here on campus, ya know? I mean, it's a lot different than what I expected. It's like, ya gotta do things right. Like clothes, for instance. You wear the wrong threads, you're nobody . . ."

Clothes, Paula thought. How did we get on clothes? "Billy, if you needed more clothes . . ."

"No, Mom, no, no, you're not following. The clothes situation is cool, okay? No, listen, just making a point. Like parties. Same thing. I mean, there's cool parties and there's uncool parties, follow?"

Paula wanted to say she wasn't following at all, but instead said, "I can't believe you're having a problem with that."

"Not a problem per se, no. Mix and mingle real well, you know that. You've seen me in action. I make all the right party scenes, okay. Definitely not a problem. Same with the chicks."

"I don't think I want to hear about the chicks."

"Chicks dig me. Cool with that. Dance card's filled to the brim." A cocky laugh. "I mean, look at me. Do you blame 'em?"

He's just like Bill, Paula thought. She wanted to scream.

"And, 'course, gotta belong to a frat. I belong to the best, right? So there ya go, Mom. What's left?"

Well done, Paula thought. "Could it be a car?"

"Right, Mom, good. Yeah, wheels." He threw his arms out as if to emphasize his point. "Wheels. That's how come I been buggin' Dad about it. Without wheels, I mean, not just any wheels but the right kinda wheels, you don't rate. You don't rate big time."

"Billy, you already have a car."

"The Pukemobile?" Billy looked at her incredulously. "Are we talking about the Pukemobile, Mom?"

It was parked two spaces over. A vintage '48 Ford Coupe. Windshield cracked. Rear fender missing. Left side caved in. Chipped paint. Exhaust pipe held on with a clothes hanger.

"Yeah, it was great for high school and stuff, but, hey, this is the big league, Mom. Which is why Dad got me this T-Bird. Definitely major league wheels. I just want you and Dad to know I appreciate it and my grades are gonna come up, okay. I mean, I don't just like take this for granted and all. I'm gonna earn this car, okay? Promise."

"Billy . . ." Paula put her fists to her head. "Please shut up."

Billy said, “Okay,” then threw his arms around Paula in a bear hug, pressing her face against his shoulder and lifting her off the ground. "Thanks, Mom. I love you. I love you so much. I love you, I love you."

"Hey Billy, who's your new squeeze?"

Billy spun away from Paula so abruptly she had to stagger a few steps to regain her balance. Standing before her were two girls in cheerleader outfits. Billy leaned casually on the T-Bird. "Oh, hi Cindy. Hi Jill. Squeeze? Ha, you crazy? She’s no squeeze. She’s my mom."

Jill's eyes grew large. "No way. You’re not old enough to be Billy's mom. Impossible." She turned to Cindy. "Look at the way she does her hair. Don't you dig it?"

"Gorgeous," Cindy agreed. "I wish my mom could see you. I mean, she dresses so matronly and everything. Kills me, really."

They paused and waited expectantly. "Thank you." Paula was about to add, “I think,” but refrained.

"Cindy and Jill are cheerleaders, Mom."

Cindy hit Billy over the head with her pom-pom. "Bet she already figured that one out, Silly Billy. Usually when girls go around wearing funny little skirts and carry pom-poms it means they're cheerleaders."

Both girls laughed. They laughed a lot, Paula noticed. She also noticed they were hardly girls. These were women, young, ripe and voluptuous. The kind you find in the center of Playboy. Both were confidently aware of it.

Cindy moved close to Billy, making sure he was aware of it, too. "This your car, Billy? Looks brand new."

"Yeah, Mom just drove it down for me. Neat, eh?"

"You know, Billy," Cindy purred, "I think this would look real good on me." She winked at Paula, who was aware her mouth was gaping open but was incapable of closing it.

"Hey, there's one way to find out," Billy was saying.

"Yes there is,” Cindy said, flicking her hair back. “Give me a lift to practice?"

"You got it."

"Cool. I'll be back in a few.”

"I'll be here waiting."

Cindy gave Billy a peck on the cheek that seemed to lift him about a foot off the ground. Both girls giggled, then Cindy winked again at Paula. She rustled her pom-pom in Billy's face.

Paula watched helplessly as the girls strolled away. "Bye, Mrs. Taylor," Jill called over her shoulder in a lilting, teasing voice. "You sure have a sweet son." Both girls burst into laughter and ran off down the sidewalk.

As soon as they were out of earshot, Billy said, "See Mom, that right there is what I'm talking about. I've been trying to get on Cindy's radar screen for weeks now, but, like, to her I was the invisible man. Then she sees the T-Bird and, well, you saw what happened."

Paula was mesmerized by Billy; smothered by his force of personality. She studied his beaming face, tried to see herself there, didn't. He looked like her but he was Bill incarnate. No, she wouldn't accept that. Billy was hers too, part of her body, part of her spirit. Wasn't he?

Paula forced herself to look into his eyes, tried to appear stern. "Billy, I need you to be quiet a moment, okay? I need you to listen to what I've got to say."

"Sure, Mom, sure, sure. You bet."

"You shouldn't have told those girls this was your car."

Billy laughed that same cocky, dismissive laugh she'd heard from Bill countless times before. "Why not?"

"Because it's not your car, Billy. It's my car."

Billy thought this was uproariously funny. "No, no, Mom, you drive the wagon. By the way, how's Maw-Maw?"

Once again Paula found her head spinning. "Maw-Maw?"

"Isn't she in the hospital? Dad called last night, said she'd been hurt or something."

Maw-Maw. Mama Taylor. It was what Billy had always called her. God, I'm losing it, Paula thought. "Uh, she's going to be all right, they think. But she'll be in the hospital for a long time. Now look, Billy . . ."

"Geez, I really hate that." Billy hooked his thumbs in his pockets and gazed at something over Paula's shoulder. "Good ol' Maw-Maw. Remember how she'd play catch with me in the back yard? Her with that 'ol walker chasing the ball all over the place. God, she was so funny. And at night she'd sneak me in cookies when I was in bed. Didn't know about that, did ya? I mean, nobody made chocolate chip cookies like Maw-Maw. Nobody."

A tear rolled down Billy's cheek. It was like a knife slicing through Paula's heart. "I . . . I'm sorry, Billy, I didn't know she meant that much to you."

"I mean, come on, she raised me." He wiped the tear away, looked at the ground. "I don't want to think of her being hurt, Mom, okay? I want her to be well and everything."

Paula's throat was raw. There was an ache from deep within her womb. She folded her arms over stomach; bit her lip.

"Maw-Maw was always there for me," Billy was saying. "No matter how bad I was, she was always there. Always, man."

Paula wanted to scream at him that she was there too. Why didn't he remember that? She looked at her son and wondered who he was. She remembered being given the little pink bundle that had just emerged from her body. His large, liquid eyes gazed up at her as she rocked him, singing softly to him. What happened to the little boy in blue jeans playing in a rain puddle, drawing on the wall with his crayons, singing in a school play

-- a hundred different moments, each one a tiny, startlingly vivid tile in a mosaic that somehow didn't resemble at all the young man standing before her.

"Oh God, Billy, do you have any idea how much I love you?" She threw her arms around him, held him close, never wanted to let him go again. But Billy pulled loose, embarrassed.

"Hey, Mom . . ."

This wasn't going right at all. Why was she here? What had she planned to say to Billy? Her mind was a blank.

"Hey, Mom, you okay? I mean, you're kinda weirding me out, ya know?"

"I'm just tired, Billy." And she was, painfully so.

Billy laughed derisively. "I mean, look at how you're dressed. Look at how your hair's fixed. I don't get it. It's kind of embarrassing. I mean, you're my mother."

The sun was low in the sky, right over Billy's shoulder. It made her squint. "There's so much I have to tell you, Billy."

"Okay, so tell me."

But now that the moment had arrived, Paula didn't know where to begin. She tried to conjure up the little speech she'd prepared, but her mind was a blank. Billy was waiting, his eyes drilling into her impatiently the way Bill's always did.

"First of all, Billy, this is my car. I bought it for me, not you. I got tired of driving the wagon; it's as simple as that. And I got tired of the way I dressed and the way I wore my hair and a lot of other things. Can you understand that?"

He was silent for so long that she thought he wasn't going to respond. "If you're telling me this isn't my car, then no, I can't understand that at all."

The hostility was there, the anger. She had expected it. But because she was leaving his dad, not because of a damned car.

"I tried to tell you, Billy."

"You didn't try very hard, did you?"

"Yes, I did. You just wouldn't listen. But you're going to listen now."

He looked at her with such undisguised loathing that it took her breath away. "Some other time, Mom. I gotta split right now. Cindy's gonna be back in a few minutes and I don't want to be anywhere around when she does."

"Billy, wait . . ."

But he was already sprinting away. "I'm outta here."

Paula chased after him, grabbed his arm. "Billy . . ."

"Let go, Mom."

"We're going to talk," Paula insisted.

"No, we're not." He'd become a brick wall. Just like Bill.

"I'm your mother and you will do what I say."

He whirled on her then, as if he were going to attack her. "Whadya you gonna do, give me a spanking or something? Huh? I mean, wha'd ya do, drive all the way down here just to give me some shit? Save it for Dad, okay?"

Paula sucked in her breath, unable to believe what he'd just said. She knew tears were coming, but fought them back. "Billy, I just want you to love me."

"Then why'd you do that to me?"

"Do what?"

"The car. You think I can face any of my friends again? I mean, I'll probably have to switch colleges."

I say love, he says car, Paula thought. "Is a new car really that important, Billy?"

"Come on, Mom, I already told you how important it is, okay? It's the most important thing in the world."

Paula realized she was trembling. She tried to keep her voice steady. "No, Billy, the love we have for each other is the most important thing in the world."

He looked at her belligerently. "Oh yeah?"

Paula grabbed his hand and slammed the T-Bird's keys into it. "Yeah."

41

“I know who you're talking about.”

This caught Red off guard. Not easy to do. “Oh yeah?”

“Kurt Younger, right?”

“Yeah. How the hell you know him?”

“Congo. Four years ago.”

“Whoa,” Red guffawed. “Man, that was fucked up before it even got started.”

“To be sure. Lotta good dogs hit the dirt.”

His name was Gator. At least that's what he was known by. His alligator boots, belt, vest, and campaign hat made it easy to understand why. Even the sheaf for his Bowie knife with its twelve-inch blade was made of alligator hide.

Now that Red’s mission had been changed from an expedition to Bogotá to a raid on Kurt’s place in Curiosity Cove, he needed to put together an assault team. When he learned that Gator, a true dog of war, was available, he didn't hesitate to come knocking.

A battle-hardened vet, he’d be able to hold his own alongside Red and Kurt. Physically he was similar to Kurt. Six-four. Hard as a rock. Quick on his feet. Not afraid of a damn thing. His head was shaved. His light-blue eyes glowed from within. They never missed a thing.

“All right,” Red said. “Lets get down to it. Why do you want on the team?”

Gator stepped up so that he was facing Red, no more than a foot away. The look in his eyes was so intense even Red was a little unnerved. “Two reasons. Money. I'm expecting a big pay out.”

“Son, that ain't a problem. Second reason?”

“The chance to take out Kurt Younger.”

Red leaned in, bearing down on Gator with those lifeless eyes of his. He stared fiercely into Gator's as if trying to see what was going on in his mind. “Explain.”

“It's personal.”

“Fuck that. It's personal for me too. I told you why up front. Now you tell me why it's personal with you. This is a mission. You know the drill. No secrets.”

Gator took a deep breath then relocked eyes with Red. “Kurt Younger stole something from me. My most valuable possession. My most irreplaceable possession.”

“Which was?”

“My girl.”

Red laughed scornfully. “My God. Your girl? You fucking pussy. Hell, just get another one, you dumb shit. They're all over the damn place.”

Gator was unfazed by Red's response. “Told you. She was irreplaceable.”

Red sighed, scratched one of his clumps of red hair. “Okay, give me the whole story.”

“He fucked her.”

“So?”

“Right in front of me.”

“How'd he pull that off? Tie you down or something?” He tried to keep the laughter out of his voice.

“He didn't know I was there. Didn't know I was watching them. Problem was . . .”

“Yeah?”

“She knew I was watching. Wanted me to watch. Wanted me to see her fucking him. It was her way of getting back at me.”

“For what?”

“For fucking her sister.”

“Well, okay then. That sounds to me like justifiable fucking. Kurt was only doing his manly duty.”

“You don't fuck a fellow dog's girl.”

Red thought about that a moment. “Yeah, you're right. I think that's in the manual somewhere.” He shook his head again, baffled by the importance so many seemingly smart guys put in a piece of ass. “So after Kurt got through doing her, you teach her the error of her ways?”

Gator smiled. It was the deadliest smile he had ever seen. “She paid the price.”

Red was impressed. “No shit?”

Gator held Red's gaze. Said nothing. Red considered everything that had been revealed by Gator, then held up his hand. Gator clasped it. For a moment it looked like they were going to arm wrestle. Instead, Red said, “Welcome aboard, brother.”

They held the clasp for a moment then Red said, “I got a deal sweetener for you. And man I mean sweet. Kurt's not alone. He's got his play-pretty with him. And let me tell you, mister, she's prime cut.”

Red didn't think it was possible but Gator's eyes glowed even brighter. “You saying what I think you're saying?”

“That's right, soldier. You get to fuck her while Kurt watches. Hell, we're all gonna fuck her. And Kurt ain't gonna have any choice but to watch.”

42

Billy simply stood there staring at the keys. "Oh, wow."

"But you listen to me and you listen good," Paula said.

"Yeah, okay Mom." But his eyes were fixed on the keys.

"This car is from me. Just me. Not your Dad. Understand?"

"Sure, Mom."

"Your Dad doesn't even know I bought it."

"Yeah, okay."

"It's a gift from me. To you. Because . . ." She found herself choking on what she was about to say. "Because I need you to know how much I love you."

He raised his eyes, looked into hers. "Okay, I get it. It's cool."

Was that love in his eyes? For Billy it probably was. Maybe it was the only kind of love they'd ever taught him. Paula was overcome with a sense of failure, a sense of utter worthlessness to a degree she'd never experienced. "Come on, Billy, put your arms around me."

"Sure, Mom." He did as he was told, holding her lightly. Paula squeezed him, clung to him. The tears came now, unchecked, and she buried her face in Billy's shoulder to hide them. But the racking of her body gave her away.

Billy jerked free of her embrace. "Hey, what're you doing? Come on, Mom, stop it."

Paula tried, but failed. "I'm sorry."

"Just don't cry, okay? Oh God, Mom, stop it."

"I'm all right, Billy."

He turned his back to her saying, "Oh shit, oh shit . . ."

Paula desperately wiped away the tears with her fingers, smearing her mascara in the process. "I'm okay, Billy. Really. You know how moms can be sometimes."

"Just don't cry, okay? I can't stand that."

"I won't. I'm through, I promise. Oh look, here's Cindy."

Cindy came bouncing up looking like a gumdrop on a whipped cream pie. When she saw Paula, her playful demeanor turned to concern. She ran over and threw her arms around her. "What's wrong, Mrs. Taylor? Billy, did you say something mean to her?" She drew Paula's head down onto her shoulder, patted it as if she were a child. "Oh, you poor thing." Then she looked sternly at Billy.

He threw his hands out in exasperation. "I didn't say anything. Honest."

Paula found herself laughing at the absurdity of the situation. Could this have possibly gone more wrong? She pulled away, saying, "I'm fine, Cindy. Thank you for your concern. You're very sweet. I'm just being a silly ol' mom. I've missed my boy."

Cindy put her hands on her hips and struck a cheerleader pose. "Well, there's nothing silly about that, now is there?" Then she turned a smile on Billy so dazzling it made the sun pale by comparison. "So, do I get that ride?"

"You bet. Hop in."

Billy actually held the door open for Cindy. Paula wondered where he'd learned that. Once she was comfortably seated, he jumped in. The T-Bird roared to life. Paula stopped him before he drove off. "Purse, please. Got some repair work to do." Cindy happily passed Paula's purse to her. "Thanks. Please don't be long, okay? I'm on a tight schedule."

"Don't worry, Miz Taylor. Be back in a jiff," Cindy called, waving her pom-poms overhead. Billy left about twenty yards of rubber on the pavement as they peeled off.

Paula moistened a wad of Kleenex in a nearby fountain, then sat at a masonry bench while she repaired her makeup. Thirty minutes passed. Paula wondered if cheerleader practice was being held in the next county over. She glanced at her watch. 4:15. Come on, Billy. She decided to give him another fifteen minutes then leave a message with Ed or Linden and get out of there.

Then it dawned on her. Shit! All her belongings were in the T-Bird. And Billy had the keys to the Pukemobile. She wasn't going anywhere. Damn. She forced herself to take a deep breath. Don't panic. He'll be back any moment now.

But he wasn't. Not at 4:30. Not at a 4:45. Not at 5:00. Oh Billy . . . Then she heard Billy's laugh, saw him about two blocks over, the T-Bird loaded with at least a dozen kids. Paula waved her arms, jumped up and down, and called his name. Then he was gone.

He pulled up at 5:30. All alone, but there were scuff marks everywhere. "Billy, where have you been?"

Billy laughed and looked at the clock on the dash. "Oh wow, is it really 5:30? Geez, sorry, Mom. Cindy wanted me to stay and watch her and I wanted to do that too 'cause there was a lotta interesting stuff to watch, let me tell ya." He made bug eyes and shook his hand as if he'd just touched something hot. “Then the gang wanted me to take 'em over to the Silver Moon to grab a shake, so, wow, guess the time just got away from me. Anyway, I'm back now, so what was it you wanted to talk about?”

Paula was fuming. “It'll have to wait. Get my things out of the T-Bird and put them in your car.”

“Okay, okay, don't get so pissy. I said I'm sorry.”

While he was doing it, Paula signed over the title to him then slammed it into his hand. ”That's the title. Don't lose it. Give me your keys. I've got to go.”

She shouldered the sprung door open, slid in, inserted the key, and turned it. Again. And again. It wouldn't crank. Paula wanted to scream.

Billy unlatched the hood and lifted it up. “Relax, Mom. Geez. Does this all the time.” He jiggled something then said, “Try it now.” The engine roared to life.

When Paula pulled out of the University, it was well after 6:00. She wanted to bawl but that wasn’t an option. She was all out of Kleenex.

43

By 6:00 PM Kurt declared the scalloped oysters dish he'd just prepared a work of art. He slipped it into his propane-powered refrigerator and at the same time extracted a chilled PBR. He popped the cap off, took a swig then surveyed the kitchen. It was a wreck. Kurt shrugged. Who gives a shit?

He was ready for Paula. When they got back here tonight, he'd throw the scalloped oysters in the oven and let them cook for thirty or forty minutes. That would give him plenty of time to cut and clean the spiny lobsters, throw them on the grill, melt the garlic butter, and pour the champagne.

Kurt elbowed his way through the kitchen door then climbed the steps to the balcony two at a time. The object of the exercise was to check tonight's field of operation one last time to make sure the mission was a go.

He 'd chosen the far corner of the second story verandah, which was as big as the one below. Due to the house sitting somewhat cater-cornered, it provided a clear view of the lagoon. He knew Paula's reaction to the outrageous centerpiece of the setting would be priceless. It made him chuckle to think about it.

To serve as a table for tonight's feast, he'd nailed to the top of the railing about four feet of ship's planking salvaged from a long ago wreck. Several hurricane lanterns hung above it. Intermingled among them were colored bottles, strings of coins, and a few other trinkets he'd found while snorkeling, a homemade wind chime. The final touch was a genuine ship's bell.

The table was already loaded with two sets of dishes, silverware, an ice bucket for the champagne, flutes, real cloth napkins, a pack of Chesterfields for Paula, and matches. He fired up a Camel himself, then stepped back to survey the overall effect. He was satisfied it was worthy of the fair maiden he was about to rescue. He double-checked the grill, which he had brought up earlier. He made sure it was loaded with charcoal and ready to be fired up.

But something was missing. What was it? Flowers. Damn, he forgot the flowers. No time to buy some in Largo before meeting Paula. He pondered the problem a moment then realized the solution was all around him. The island was lousy with exotic flora. Kurt even knew a few of them by name: frangipani, lignum, and several types of orchids.

His favorite was frangipani with its white and yellow blossom and a scent so sexy it got his blood up. He pictured Paula with one tucked behind her ear giving him that 'come hither' look. His crotch tightened.

He grabbed a bucket and made quick work of filling it. While doing so he noticed a gathering breeze. Trees and bushes were starting to dance sensuously. The water in the lagoon was working into a slight chop. A blustery night was ahead. Good.

Back upstairs Kurt stuffed the flowers into a dozen empty beer bottles. He pictured Paula in the middle of them. Perfect! Not far away, palm fronds swayed lazily. The wind was definitely picking up. Maybe I should move the feast inside, he thought then shrugged. So what if Ma Nature gets a little feisty? It'll just add to the atmosphere. He clapped his hand together. Okay, time to go get his woman.

He shut the generator down. The *Black Jack* lug-lugged out of the boathouse at 7:00 PM on the dot. Even though it was already dusk, he made damn sure he didn't touch the floodlight switch. He crossed Curiosity Cove's lagoon then glided gently through the tunnel-like corridor that meandered out to the Bay. Once in the open, the *Black Jack* tugged at its rein, wanting to run fast, run hard. Yeah, I know, Kurt thought. So do I. So do I. A sizable wave slapped at the boat, made it lurch angrily.

"All right, big fella. Let's go get her." He pushed the throttle full forward. The *Black Jack* roared, lifted up out of the water, and hurled into the darkness.

44

"Damn it, Billy, why didn't you tell me the gas gauge was broken?" Paula yelled it out loud, but there was no one to hear her. She was stranded on the shoulder of the highway on what was turning out to be a breezy night.

She stood beside the car with the hood raised hoping someone might stop and help her. Someone did. Two young guys in a hot rod. One of them leaned out a window and gave a wolf whistle. "Hey, mama, you need some help?"

"I got all the help she needs," she heard the other one say.

Paula turned toward the nearby woods, yelling, "Honey! You and Max come here quick!"

"Aw hell," one of the boys said, followed by peeling rubber.

Paula hopped back in the Pukemobile, rolled the windows up, locked the doors, and sat trembling. She looked down at the way she was dressed. In the mirror she caught a glimpse of her wild locks, her sexy makeup. All that was lacking was a sign saying, 'Come and get it'.

Any thoughts of hiking to the nearest phone were gone. She wasn't leaving the relative safety of the car. She turned on the dome light, checked her watch. 7:12. Damn! Damn! Double damn! The inside of the car lit up. She glanced back. Somebody pulled up behind her and rolled to a stop. Their headlights blinded her.

Oh my God, Paula thought, I'm trapped. The locks on these doors won't keep anybody out. They'll just break a window. She was pretty sure she knew what would happen next. Please God, no, no, no.

Wait. A red flashing light. Highway patrol. It was the most beautiful sight she'd ever seen. Paula jumped out of her car at about the same instant the officer was getting out of his. He shined his flashlight on her. "You okay, ma'am?"

He was a regular Marshall Dillon type, except no vest. Instead of a big Stetson he wore a flat-brimmed trooper hat. Paula fought to hold down her skirt in the stiffening breeze. "Yes, I'm fine, I'm fine. Oh, God, am I glad to see you."

"What's the problem?" He had a kind, concerned voice.

Paula heard the hysteria in her trilling laughter. "I'm out of gas, can you believe it?" She noticed the way he looked at her, then at her car. She knew what he was thinking: they don't fit. "Oh, it's not my car, Officer. It's my son's. The gas gauge doesn't work, only he didn't bother to tell me."

He grinned. "Yeah, I got one of those at home. His life expectancy gets shorter every day. And it's Trooper, not Officer. Trooper Madigan."

"Thank you so much for stopping, Trooper Madigan."

He motioned to his car. "Well come on, lets get you some gas. There's a station 'bout a quarter mile back."

Paula threw her hands out with a laugh. "In other words, in easy walking distance."

"Not out here. Not after dark." He flashed her a big teasing grin. "Not in that dress." Paula blushed and they both laughed. He's got a little sister, Paula thought. She had always envied her girlfriends who had protective big brothers.

As they rolled into the station Paula was cheered by the bright lights. Trooper Madigan said, "Be right back." He went into the store and returned a few minutes later carrying a five-gallon can filled with gas. She offered to pay but he said the can belonged to the owner. When she returned it she could add its cost to the fill-up she would undoubtedly be wanting due to the gas gauge being broken. He gave her a stern big brother look. "Right?"

Paula made big eyes to emphasize her point. "You bet."

When they got back to the Pukemobile, Trooper Madigan put the gas in, then added a little to the carburetor, and helped her get it cranked. Paula thanked him for his help.

"It's what I get paid for, ma'am."

"I know, but I still appreciate it." She gave him her most heartfelt smile. To her surprise he blushed.

"Well, I guess you're good to go. Be careful now."

Paula shook his hand. "I will. Thank you."

Paula pulled into the station a few minutes later and while the attendant filled her tank and serviced the engine, she thought how lucky she was that Trooper Madigan came along. No doubt his high school sweetheart was waiting supper for him, along with two or three rambunctious brats. Trooper Madigan's a vet, she figured. War hero probably. Lots of them around. Good guys.

God bless the good guys.

The attendant closed the hood. He was stooped and wiry and wore blue coveralls that some good woman kept clean and pressed for him. He stepped up to her window. His friendly, twinkling eyes looked out over wire-rimmed glasses.

“All righty then. Comes to $4.25. Had to put some oil in."

“Not surprised.” Paula gave him a five. “Keep the change. Oh, and thank you so much for letting me borrow your gas can."

The old man's smile broadened. "Glad to help, daughter. Your tank's filled to the brim so it oughta get you where you need to go. And 'case you're ever this way again, folks call me Pops. It'd make me feel mighty good if you did too.” He held out his wrinkled old hand, webbed with thick blue veins.

Paula shook it. “Sure, Pops. My name's Paula.”

He patted her hand and let it go. “You be careful Paula."

"I will, Pops." She wiggled her fingers as she pulled out of the station and back onto the highway. She glanced at her watch. 7:30. Thirty minutes till I'm supposed to meet Kurt. Damn. She’d have to step on it if she was going to make it.

As Paula sped into the darkness she thought about Trooper Madigan and Pops, Bob Ballentine and Lenny, Phyllis and Mary. All good people. All wanting to help. Real, everyday people. Raising kids. Building businesses. Doing their duty. These were the kind of people she had grown up with, had known all her life. Like her mom and dad. Like Birdy.

She understood them. How they thought. Because she was one of them. And the sexy clothes and the Marilyn Monroe hairdo didn't change that. Billy made that painfully clear. She was his mother. Bill's housewife. Nothing more. The realization chilled her and she rolled up the window.

My God, what am I doing? This is insane.

The turn-off was just ahead. She had two choices. Take it and keep her rendezvous with Kurt, or go past it to her home in Key Largo. Either way, the road was dark and lonely.

Kurt. He was not like anybody she had ever known. Two things she knew for sure. She was not like him. Never would be. And he was dangerous.

A voice deep in her mind screamed: “Go home, Paula. Home to your mother and Birdy. Home where you grew up. Where you belong. Where you'll be safe. Now. Before it's too late.”

45

By 7:30 Kurt had anchored the *Black Jack* about thirty yards out and was starting his second circuit of their usual meeting place. No passion pit tonight. More comfortable accommodations awaited them at Curiosity Cove.

He wore a terrycloth jersey over his trunks, more than adequate with temperatures in the mid-seventies. But the blustery night, thanks to Tropical Storm Judith approaching the Fort Myers area, made the air feel cooler. His body heat, at fever pitch in anticipation of Paula's arrival, nullified the effect.

By 7:40 Kurt had made eight circuits of the area. Guard duty, really, checking the perimeter. Old habits die hard, he reflected. What did you expect to find? Think Red might jump out of the shadows like the bogeyman?

Not likely. Right now Red was making his way to Bogotá. Maybe he was already there, waiting for him. It was going to be a long wait.

By 7:50 Kurt knew if he didn't do something to work off tension he was going to blow like the Primacord on the *Black Jack's* hull. He slipped off his jersey, waded out until he was waist deep, then dove in. He swam hard, pushing his muscles to the limit. They quit on him about two hundred yards out, but he felt much better. He let the incoming tide carry him back to the mangroves, fully expecting Paula to be waiting for him.

She wasn't.

Kurt checked his watch. 8:05. He shrugged it off. She might have run into heavy traffic on the way down. Or maybe she had trouble getting away from Bill. Nothing to worry about. She'd show up in a few minutes.

By 8:15 Kurt was feeling uneasy. Something was wrong. Unlike most women he'd known, Paula was always punctual. His ears throbbed from the strain of listening for her car engine. But all he heard was the roll of the surf, the whipping of the wind, the persistent clanging of the buoy in the channel. Damn, where was she?

8:30.

Kurt wrestled with a tempest of emotions. Confusion. Anger. Hurt. Frustration. He scanned the woods, willed them to light up, to tell him her big Country Squire was approaching. Didn't happen.

Kurt thought of Red pacing on a beach somewhere in Colombia, preparing for tomorrow's trek inland to Bogotá. Both of them were standing in the dark, fifteen hundred miles apart, waiting for their dreams to be fulfilled like children listening for the clatter of reindeer hooves on the roof.

By 8:45 he knew Paula wasn't coming.

He'd blown it.

He'd abandoned her at this very spot a week ago, his last sight of her in his rearview mirror, her arms reaching out to him, pleading. Now she had abandoned him. All during the past week he'd been cock sure she was scrambling to shut down her Palm Beach life to start a new life with him. Instead, she was . . . What? Buying groceries? Cleaning house? Playing tennis? He didn't know. He only knew she wasn't here. With him.

The world around him dissolved away. He stood in a complete void, no sound, no physical sensation. He stepped into the surf and headed for the *Black Jack*, simply because he didn't know what else to do. Except get away. Far away. He'd leave first thing tomorrow.

Hell, he'd leave tonight. Now.

Kurt climbed aboard, pulled in the anchor, fired up the engine, let it idle just enough to keep the tide from carrying her in.

Where to?

He didn't really give a damn. He had a sudden, overpowering urge to set a course for the open sea and just go until the fuel ran out. Then drift, just drift, alone with memories of Paula. The intoxicating fragrance of her body. The green fire that danced in her eyes. The heat of her womanhood as he penetrated her.

The more he thought about it, the more he liked it.

Kurt pushed the throttle full forward, spun the wheel and made a wide sweep. He took one last look back at the secluded place where he'd discovered it was possible to love somebody more than his own life.

That's when he saw her.

She was running down from the woods, a suitcase in each hand. Even over the roar of the engines Kurt heard her calling his name. He turned the wheel sharply. The *Black Jack* shuddered, rolled over on its side, threatened to capsize. Kurt didn't care.

Paula tripped and fell flat on her face. One of the suitcases broke open. Clothes spilled out and were scattered by the wind, snagged by the mangroves.

Kurt cut the engines, leapt onto the bow, then sprung into the air. He swam to her, his arms like steam pistons in the water. She was in the water too. Her wet dress clung to her. Her arms reached out for him. Just like Saturday night a week ago. When he abandoned her.

Not tonight. Not ever again.

He tackled her. They both went under, arms and legs intertwined. Kurt picked Paula up and carried her up to their special spot, the place where they had gorged on each other's passions so many times before. He smothered her with kisses, singed her with the fire blazing within him.

He was aware that she was pounding on his shoulders with her fists, but not in a loving way. He pulled her loose. She took a big gulp of air. "You're suffocating me." They gazed at each other, panting, laughing at the wildness in each other's eyes. Kurt grabbed Paula's arms, shook her. "You're a fucking hour late!"

Madness jumped in Paula's eyes. Her slap had the weight of her entire body behind it. His head snapped to the side. The bones in his neck popped. The stars he saw were not in the sky. They both dropped to their knees, limp, purged. Paula fell into Kurt's arms, still gasping for breath, sobbing. "My car . . ."

Kurt looked up into the woods. "Yeah, where is your car?"

"In the inlet."

Kurt stared at her, unable to comprehend. "Say again."

"That's why I'm late." She was still panting for breath. "It went right off the bridge into the . . ." She threw her hands up, shook her head incredulously, as if that explained everything.

"The wagon?"

"The Pukemobile."

"The what?"

"Billy's car. His old beat-up coup. The windshield was so cracked I could hardly see out it and when I crossed that rickety old bridge, I ran right off the side somehow . . ."

Kurt actually gawked, something Paula had never seen him do. "You ran off the bridge?"

"Yes, well, over the side but not completely over. It snagged on something. So I pulled on the hand brake and jumped out. Managed to get my suitcases out too. Then I thought if I got here to you, you'd help me get it back on the bridge. That was kind of a dumb thought, wasn't it?"

Kurt shook his head, bewildered. "Yeah."

"Then there was this awful creaking sound and the car pitched over and now it's lying upside down on the bottom of the inlet under about six feet of water."

Kurt just stared at her, unable to speak. Paula shrugged and said, "No kidding."

Kurt's uncontrollable laughter earned him a punch on the shoulder. "It's not funny, dammit."

But Kurt only laughed harder.

"Oh, shut up."

“Sorry, sorry . . .” But he kept laughing.

“There I was standing on the bridge looking down at the car under all that water and thinking I'll never get here in time. It was already after eight and I still had a mile to go and I didn't even know if you'd still be here. I hoped you'd still be here. I prayed you'd still be here."

"Easy, Paula, easy. I'm here. I'm here."

But the torrent continued unabated. "I ran as hard as I could but the suitcases got so damn heavy and my sides were killing me and I couldn't run anymore and I knew you'd think I wasn't coming, I knew you'd be gone, and then when I got here and saw you pulling away . . . Oh God, Kurt."

She threw herself at him, knocking him flat on his back. She lay on top of him, clinging to him, trembling, crying.

"It's okay, baby. We're here. We made it."

Kurt rolled her off, sat her up. He gathered up her clothes strewn everywhere, the egret figurine among them, and stuffed them all back into her suitcase. Now Paula was laughing, saying, “Could I have possibly made a worse mess of things?” Kurt was about to respond and she said, “Don't answer that.” Kurt pulled Paula to her feet, held her face so she was forced to look into his eyes. “I've never been more afraid in my life.”

The simple, earnest way he said it astonished her. “Oh, Kurt. It's okay. I'm here.” She kissed him, again and again. “I'm here.”

He scooped her up and carried her out to the *Black Jack*, waiting for him like a faithful steed. He hurried back for the suitcases, threw them in.

Paula waited in the bow, propped up on her knees, arms held out for him. Several buttons on her dress had torn off, baring a soft shoulder to the moonlight, revealing a breast bulging from a satiny bra. The wind whipped out her hair, her skirt.

Kurt climbed aboard, gathered Paula into his arms and carried her up to the cockpit. He planted a kiss on her that sent shockwaves through her body. She reciprocated with equal ferocity, locking her legs around his waist, pushing against the hardness in his trunks, urging him to do his manly duty. He clearly had other plans. He peeled her off and displayed the roguish grin that appeared so often in her dreams, and said, “Lets go home, Miss Doherty.”

“Lets do, Mr. Younger,” she said, excited at the thought of seeing where Kurt lived.

He fired up the engine and shoved the throttle full forward. The *Black Jack* growled, reared up like a stallion. Paula screamed out in delight and held onto Kurt.

He spun the wheel. The *Black Jack* galloped off into the night, the glorious night, with a million twinkling stars.

46

The nearly-full moon over Florida Bay was unusually bright due to the crisp, clear air. The *Black Jack* seemed to be flying, an effect the Bay was famous for due to its shallow, crystal clear water. It created for Paula a sense of enchantment and she was swept up in its spell.

Kurt was casting a spell of his own. He held Paula close. The dynamo humming just beneath his skin made her flush hotly. She looked up at him. Etched by moonlight, the lines of his face were even more rugged than usual. Wind rippled through his sandy hair, adding to his wild and reckless look.

"You really are a pirate," she said, voicing her thoughts.

Kurt looked at her quizzically. "Pirate?"

"They say that once upon a time this place swarmed with pirates."

"So they say." He struck a Captain Kidd pose, fists on hips. "Avast ye landlubbers."

Paula laughed. "Don't call me a landlubber, mister. I was raised on big boats."

"Yeah?"

She detected the challenge in Kurt's voice. "Yeah." She hipped him out of the way, and took the *Black Jack's* reins. She pushed the powerful cruiser to its limits, maneuvering it through the channel like a champion quarter horse cutting out cattle. Her touch was light and sure. The *Black Jack* did as she told it.

Paula turned the controls back over to Kurt then gave a little curtsy in response to his admiring grin. "I think she likes you," he said.

They were silent for a while, caught up in the magic of the moment. It ended when Kurt heard a sniffle then jerked Paula's head up. Tears were running down her cheek. "Hey . . ."

"It's okay, darling, they're happy tears."

Kurt shook his head, exasperated. "Guess I'm never gonna understand that one."

"You don't have to. Just accept it."

They stayed like that for a while, rocking gently with the boat, neither speaking. Paula pulled away and took a deep breath. "I'm all right now."

"You are?"

She lifted up the bottom of his jersey and used it to finish drying her face. "Yes, thanks."

"Okay then." He stared off toward the horizon as if trying to solve one of the great mysteries of the universe. He ran a hand through his hair. "Happy tears. Jesus."

Paula spontaneously burst out laughing. She covered her mouth, trying to muffle it.

Kurt spun around as if stung. Paula held out her hands apologetically. "Sorry," she said. "I get a little emotional sometimes."

"A *little* emotional?"

Paula laughed harder, stumbling back against the side of the cockpit. Kurt regarded her in befuddlement for a moment, then also broke into laughter. "You're really losing it, aren't you?"

Paula nodded her head vigorously. "Got a hanky? You're supposed to have a hanky."

"In swimming trunks?" Kurt pulled off his jersey and handed it to her. "Here, you can finish ruining this."

Seeing his magnificent bared chest was too much for Paula. She gave Kurt a mischievous grin then shoved her hand inside his trunks and grabbed his penis. He jolted as if struck by lightning. "Holy shit!"

Paula felt it grow hard in her hand. Rock hard. She squeezed it and he growled like a rutting stag. "Whoa, Paula . . ."

She loved it. She wiped the sticky moisture from the tip of his penis, then withdrew her hand and licked it from her finger. Judging by the fierceness in Kurt's eyes she was sure he was going to rip her to shreds. She smiled tauntingly. Go ahead, Kurt. Rip away.

Instead he displayed amazing restraint. Experience and a vivid imagination left no doubt in Paula's mind about what he wanted to do to her, but he obviously had an agenda all worked out for the night and was biding his time. Okay, Paula thought, I can be patient.

But not for long.

"We're getting close," Kurt said. "Grab yourself a front row seat on the foredeck. First time in, I want you to have an unobstructed view."

Paula made her way down from the cockpit then treaded carefully along the narrow gangway to the foredeck. Bench seats lined both sides and joined at the bow. That's where she took up position. She jumped as Kurt's voice boomed from behind her. "Don't face forward till I tell you. Turn around and face me."

She complied, saying, "I like facing you," but her words were inaudible over the grumble of the engines. She leaned back against the bow, hooked her arms over the railing, and let the empty expanse of the Bay, with its canopy of sparkling stardust overhead, claim her. To her it seemed they were inside a giant snow globe. The *Black Jack* was at the bottom. The stars were at the top, drifting down on them like snowflakes. Were they really the only two people in the world?

Kurt pulled back on the throttle and the *Black Jack* sat down obediently in the water. With the roar of the engines reduced to an impatient whicker, he no longer had to yell to be heard. He simply said, "Welcome to Curiosity Cove."

Paula wheeled around to see a shadowy knob of land suspended in the Bay, clearly an island. The narrow beach that ringed it ended abruptly in a wall of subtropical growth so thick it seemed impenetrable. Kurt steered toward a break in the wall. As they drew near, the break opened gradually to reveal a channel leading into the island's interior. It was overhung with dense foliage, giving it the appearance of a tunnel. Kurt eased the *Black Jack* into it.

It was dim inside but Paula was able to identify strangler fig, poison wood, mastic, and pigeon plum. Virgin growth, no doubt, and all indigenous to the Keys. The channel meandered snake-like through it and was just wide enough to accommodate the *Black Jack.*

Eventually they approached a bend in the channel, rimmed with moonlight. Paula sensed that just beyond it something wonderful was about to be revealed. Kurt grinned at her the way her father did just before she opened her presents on Christmas morning. She smiled happily in return and directed her vision forward again just as they rounded the bend.

The tunnel opened up like a first act curtain, revealing a broad lagoon of crystal water ringed by palms and flowering bushes. No mangroves -- they didn't grow well in fresh water. On the other side of the lagoon, center stage, was Kurt's house. It sat friendly and welcoming atop a small hill of unblemished white sand, undoubtedly the island's highest point -- eight, maybe ten feet. It was not as Paula had imagined it at all. It was much better.

"Oh Kurt, it's wonderful."

The two-story clapboard house might have belonged to Hemingway himself. A wide verandah ran all the way around it, bathed in the warm light of hurricane lanterns strung out like Christmas tree lights, creating a festive air. The verandah was topped by another identical one providing access to rooms on the upper level, each accessible through French doors. Behind the house a windmill's blades were turning briskly.

It was all very masculine, very Kurt, and pure Key West, even though it was located a hundred miles northeast of the Keys' southern tip. Paula looked back at Kurt admiringly. "It's got you stamped all over it."

Kurt beamed proudly. Paula had never seen him do that before. She was beginning to realize there was a depth to him she hadn't imagined.

Palms swayed lazily, casting soft shadows on a pier of weathered planks and on the slat-backed chairs and shipping crate tables scattered about it. Lashed to the pier's pilings were poles hung with yet more hurricane lanterns. There were also the requisite fenders in the form of old tires and a large propane gas tank, easily accessible to service boats.

It was a setting rich with mysterious shadows and pregnant with romance. The moon danced wickedly on the lagoon's waters, a lovers' call to arms. Paula heard the call loud and clear. She looked up at Kurt. Did he?

Kurt thought Paula had never looked more enticing. As she gazed up at him, her coppery hair fell back from her face, making the angles more prominent. Every star in the night sky sparkled in her green eyes. Her skirt gaped open just the way it was supposed to, revealing her long, sinfully shaped legs. Her bounteous breasts, round, fleshy and frosted with moonlight, spilled from their satiny retainer. Kurt wanted to lick that moonlight right off.

Not yet, he cautioned himself. You've carefully laid out the evening's events. You wanted this to be special for Paula. Don't spoil it.

The night is still young and full of promise.

On the far side of the lagoon stood a slender two-story boathouse with a sharply peaked tin roof and a welcoming hurricane lantern hanging over its open barn doors. The *Black Jack*'s home, Paula guessed, verified when Kurt glided his noble steed toward it.

47

As Paula and Kurt exited the boathouse he held her larger suitcase by the handle and tucked the smaller one under his arm. "Hey, I can take one of those," Paula said.

"All part of the service, ma'am. Please remember to tip generously."

He circled her waist with his free arm as they crossed the footbridge over the smaller channel that wound through the back of the island. As they ascended the sandy slope to the house, Paula draped an arm over his shoulder and tried to match his long strides.

She was giddy and completely beguiled by Curiosity Cove. Since meeting Kurt she had often wondered what his home would be like. She never imagined anything like this. It reminded her of a scene from a jungle adventure movie. In her mind she heard the thumping of wooden drums, the chanting of restless natives, the tooting of the African Queen as it rounded the bend.

Kurt asked, "What are you thinking?"

"That I'm Katharine Hepburn to your Bogie."

He laughed. "In her wildest dreams Miss Hepburn wishes she looked like you. As for me and Bogie, you kidding? Guy was a runt. Wad him up and put him in my field pack."

They climbed the steps to the wide verandah then stopped at the front door. Kurt put the suitcases down and looked at Paula with such affection in his eyes, such warmth in his smile, that Paula thought she was going to melt into a puddle right there on the verandah. Just mop me up into a bucket and I'll be fine.

"Home," Kurt said.

Paula took in the house, warm and inviting, yet sturdy and confident. Much like the man who owned it. "You never fail to surprise me, Kurt Younger. I thought you lived in a pup tent or something."

"Really?"

"Maybe a bamboo hut."

"No kidding?" Kurt considered it a moment. "I'm very impressed."

"Why?

"To think you'd run away with me to live in a pup tent. You're some gutsy broad."

Paula wrapped her arms around his neck. "I'd run away with you to live in a refrigerator box." She inclined her head toward the house. "But we'll make do with this."

She kissed him, then turned around and used his body as a leaning post. She wrapped his arms around her and sighed as she gazed out at her new world. "Just look at this. Come Monday you'll have to run me over to Tavernier so I can buy some paints and brushes. Got to capture this on canvas."

She gestured toward the lagoon. "I've never seen water so clear, even in the Bay. It's just so . . ." She threw her arms out expansively. "Perfect." She laughed with delight. "And that spooky-looking old boathouse. Really. Like something Charles Addams might've drawn."

"Who's Charles Addams?"

Paula gave him a look. "One of my many lovers."

"Oh. Him."

Paula slapped him on the shoulder then settled back against him again. "Yes, I can see me spending many happy weeks here just painting, painting, painting."

She glanced up at Kurt in time to see him look as if someone had just walked over his grave. "What's wrong?"

Kurt shrugged it off. "Just wondered if you wanted to see inside."

"Of course I want to see inside, you idiot. I'm dying to."

He bowed slightly. "Then you shall, m'lady. Back in a second." He disappeared around the verandah.

Nearby were two oversized rattan chairs, beautifully crafted with a palm frond design woven into their backs. They were white with a chipped paint motif. The seat cushions were slightly mottled with mildew. Between them was a matching table. There was also makeshift shelving, a hammock, a rack full of fishing gear, and an old fashioned swing in sad need of repair.

To Paula's artistic eye it was a visual feast. The background score was equally rousing: hurricane lanterns squeaking in the blustery wind, trees groaning, palm fronds clattering softly like applause from a ghostly audience. She heard night hawks yipping from the woods and the gawk-gawk-gawk of mangrove cuckoos out near the Bay. Tree frogs and crickets completed the ensemble. Their spontaneous harmony always fascinated Paula.

Her scrutiny was interrupted by a metallic cough then a low whine. Lights blazed from every window. Paula was familiar with the set up. A propane gas generator provided electricity. Propane also fueled the hot water heater, stove, and refrigerator. The windmill behind the house drew fresh water from the lagoon to a storage tank above the roof. Gravity took it from there. Curiosity Cove was completely self-reliant. Just like the man who owned it.

Kurt jerked open the front door, scooped Paula up in his arms and carried her over the threshold. She was a little jarred by the gesture but then his lips found hers. His raging hunger overwhelmed her, driving every other thought from her mind except that she was pretty hungry too. Let the fireworks begin.

Much to her chagrin, Kurt stood her up inside and said, "Follow me, Miz Taylor."

Paula held up a warning finger. "No, no, enough of that. Miz Doherty, if you please. I'm going back to my maiden name. Mrs. Taylor is in a hospital bed in Palm Beach." Kurt cocked his head quizzically. Paula said, "More on that later."

He said, "Do I look like I give a shit?" He grabbed Paula's suitcases and led her through a narrow foyer lined with pegs for foul weather gear, shelves for footwear and other personal items, and a small bench. The opening at the end framed a tantalizing view of the rest of the house, which seemed to expand up and out as she drew nearer.

She took two steps down from the foyer, entering an immense, lofty room that reached all the way up to the two-story high vaulted ceiling. Hanging from rough-hewn beams were clusters of ship lanterns mounted on spoked helms. They bathed the room in a soft, romantic glow. The walls were made from broad planks of Dade County pine, telling Paula the house was probably built seventy or eighty years ago.

"Gotta put something in the oven," Kurt said, then trotted off toward the kitchen. Like Pavlov's dog, Paula's stomach grumbled at the mention of cooking. Yes, food would be most welcome. While Kurt was gone, she continued to study the room.

Most eye-catching of all were the wall decorations, an eclectic assortment of paintings, curios from far away places, and objects d'art, all dating back to before Kurt's time.

Among them were a number of trophy fish, the most impressive being a marlin that must have tipped the scales at a thousand pounds. It all stirred her imagination and provided a revealing glimpse into a part of Kurt's life she knew nothing about.

Paula assumed the staircase directly to her left gave access to a second floor walkway. Bedrooms? Please God, yes. At the far end, separated from the main room only by a ship's railing, was a cozy dining room. Next to it was a narrow hallway, with a glimpse of the kitchen at its end. In the wall across from the dining room were a couple of doors. Bathroom and some kind of closet, she guessed.

The wall to her right was a procession of French doors opening out to the verandah. Directly above them in perfect symmetry was a row of tall windows that tilted out to provide maximum air flow.

The result was a big, airy room that during the day would be filled with light. But pretty damned nice at night too. The same style of rattan furniture from outside was scattered throughout the room, overflowing with wildly colored cushions.

Very comfortable. Very masculine.

Especially the massive bar located mid-room, lined with a half dozen stools. It was all exquisitely crafted in dark bamboo. Paula especially liked how well stocked the bar was. She faced Kurt as he returned. "Is it happy hour yet?"

"Baby, it's happy hour for the rest of our lives."

"Good answer." She flicked her eyes toward the top of the stairs inquisitively. "And what may I ask is up there?"

"The answer to a maiden's dreams. Follow me."

He picked up her suitcases and started up the stairs but Paula stopped him. "Wait, show me what's behind this big door here first." She referred to a heavy mahogany door set imposingly in the wall to the left of the great room.

Kurt gave her a crafty smile. "All in good time, my sweet. All in good time." He led her upstairs to the master bedroom, located directly above the mystery room below. It was a big room with a big bed, an arrangement she heartily endorsed in her current frame of mind. French doors were open to the upper verandah. Sheer curtains danced lazily in the breeze.

Paula noticed that one set of doors was closed, a heavy curtain drawn across them. Intriguing, she thought. There was also lots of closet space and a bathroom next door. Nice. This would do just fine. In her mind's eye she pictured her and Kurt making that big bed bounce across the room.

Kurt set her bags down then motioned for Paula to join him on the balcony, which she gladly did. She placed her hand on his arm affectionately and he whirled to face her, his eyes flaring. Once again he seemed poised for the kill, ready to pounce.

So why doesn't he? she wondered. What's holding him back? She thought of how he resisted her last Saturday night. Now he seemed to be doing it again. What was wrong with him? Or was there something wrong with her? She took a step away, giving him a fuller view. No, his expression confirmed she was okay in that department. What then? Did he need prompting?

She lifted her hands to her hair, ruffling it as if trying to shake out the salt and sand, her breasts almost popping out of her bra. "I need a shower. Care to join me?"

The words were barely out of her mouth before her back was slammed against the wall, her arms pinned above her head. His tongue was in her mouth. His hardness was pressing against her pelvis. The wetness she felt now had nothing to do with their tumble in the surf. Paula broke free of his grip, wrapped her arms around his neck. She pulled him back through the French doors toward the bed.

She panted heavily, burned as if running a scalding fever. "Come on, Kurt. Come on, come on . . ."

But he simply straightened up, lifting her off the floor effortlessly. She wrapped her legs around him and threw her weight backward trying to topple him onto the bed. It was like trying to topple a giant redwood. "Kurt!"

"Not yet."

She leapt out of his embrace. Her anger surged to the surface, flashed in her green eyes. "Don't do this to me, Kurt. It's been nine weeks, dammit. Haven't I done everything you asked? What more do you want? Are you waiting for me to tell you I love you?"

"Do you?"

"Right now I could kill you."

He smiled then, not recklessly or wickedly, but with genuine warmth and affection. "God, you're incredible," he said. "If I had a picture of the way you look right now, I'd get arrested."

Okay, that was a different approach. "Really?"

She stepped over to the dresser, peered into the mirror and immediately saw what Kurt was referring to. "Yeah, and you'd probably get life."

Kurt laughed and headed toward the verandah, swatting her on the behind as he passed. "Put your things away. I'll call for you in a few minutes."

She pulled her skirt out and did a formal curtsey. "Oui, monsieur." He wheeled on her and raised his finger in warning. "Do not leave this room until you hear the ship's bell and do not, for any reason, open that curtain. Why are you smirking like that?"

"It's kind of like God telling Eve not to eat that apple."

Kurt smiled wickedly. "Yeah, but I'm a lot meaner than God." He was halfway out the door, then stopped. "Do not take a shower just yet."

"Okay, but what's with all the 'thou shalt nots?'"

"You'll like it," he said with a wicked grin. "Promise." Then he was gone.

The bed frame was also fashioned from bamboo and held an honest-to-God feather mattress. Paula plopped down on it expecting to hear squeaky springs. When she didn't, she dropped to her knees and discovered that a rope web supported the mattress. Clever. She immediately thought about the uses a fine bed like this might be put to.

Paula opened the large suitcase. Among her clothes was the egret Kurt had given her. She placed it on the dresser then finished unpacking. She heard the generator shut down. The overhead light went out but there was plenty of light from the hurricane lanterns hanging just outside the French doors, soft and warm and very romantic. She took a deep breath, elated.

She had escaped. She was with Kurt, hidden away from the world. Completely safe.

48

Paula had just slipped off her 'cash-and-carry' girdle when she heard the ship's bell clang twice. She stuffed it in one of the empty suitcases then stowed them both in the closet. She stepped out onto the balcony, but it was empty.

"Where are you?"

"Around here."

Paula followed the balcony around to the backside of the house then stopped in her tracks. A smile lit up her face.

Who but Kurt Younger would think of installing a tub outside on the balcony? And a brass one at that. It was grandly ornate with big-clawed feet. A scene of naked Roman ladies at their toilette was etched in the side. Hanging around the gaudy fixture were hurricane lanterns, gilding it with a golden glow. Without question it had been designed for double occupancy. Paula wondered what cathouse Kurt had stolen it from.

He was already in the tub, a Camel dangling from his bottom lip, his head cocked back recklessly, his eyes challenging hers. He held up a glass of champagne as if offering a toast. "Princess Paula, I believe."

It was a scene she would someday commit to canvas: Kurt in all his glory, that shit eating grin on his face, that roguish glint in his eye. Shadowy palms swayed behind him. The moon's reflection bobbed in the lagoon. She bowed regally and said, "In the flesh, m'lord."

He took a drag on his cigarette. "Yeah, counting on that."

Paula sat on the rim of the tub. She let her eyes feast on his broad shoulders, muscled chest, washboard stomach, and all those other parts that made her stomach flutter. She ran her hand through the thick mat of his chest hair. "Would it embarrass you if I said you're beautiful?"

"Damn right it would."

Paula laughed. He gave her a testy look and hooked a finger in the sleeve of her dress.

"You said you wanted to get out of that wet dress. Now would be a good time."

Paula knew Kurt wasn't asking her to get undressed. He was asking her to strip. She knew the difference. In their previous encounters it had always amazed her how fast he got her naked and on her back. But tonight Kurt seemed to favor a more leisurely seduction. That was fine with her. She took Kurt's face in her hands, kissed him, said "Yes sir," then stood and gave him a silly smile, wriggling her eyebrows up and down.

The macramé belt came off first. She tossed it aside with a bump of her hips then took her time unbuttoning her dress, holding it together with one hand.

"You're the first man who's known what to do with this," she said, then opened her dress to show him what she was talking about. The look in his eyes made her skin tingle. It's one thing to believe you're beautiful, another to have that belief confirmed in your lover's eyes.

Paula shrugged the dress off then took Kurt's hand and placed it on her stomach. It was wet and warm and made her tremble. He slid it down into her panties and managed to hit the button first try. She gasped, grabbed the rim of the tub to steady herself. "Careful, that thing's loaded."

In reply, Kurt ripped her panties off. Paula staggered back a few steps; naked now except for her bra and high heel sandals. She put her hands on her hips and said, "Keep those. I've got another pair."

Kurt tossed them over the railing. "How 'bout I buy you a whole dresser full of 'em. All silk and lace and embroidered with 'Property of Kurt Younger' on the front?"

Paula had a flash of herself in the emergency room surrounded by doctors and nurses, her dress being cut away to reveal panties with 'Property of Kurt Younger' on the front.

Paula peeled the bra straps over her shoulders one at a time, trying to make the movement as provocative as possible. It seemed to have the right effect. Kurt was gazing at her as if she were a steak sizzling on a grill. Now for the coup de grace. She reached between her breasts and unhooked the bra. Gravity did the rest.

She let Kurt feast on the sight of them for a moment, loving the look of reverence in his eyes, then asked, "Room in there for one more?"

"Only if you board now."

Paula was about to step in when she heard someone laughing. It came from the lagoon, high pitched and obnoxious. Paula said, "Well shit," and ducked down beside the tub.

Kurt seemed to find the situation highly amusing. "Relax. It's just my friend Wally."

"Wally? My God, Kurt, you might have told me you invited someone over."

Kurt gave her a gruff look. "Hey, Wally's welcome here anytime. You'll just have to get used to it."

"Kurt, I . . ."

Paula saw the intruder then, splashing about playfully in the lagoon. She stood back up, her eyes filled with wonder. "A dolphin?"

"Yep. We're pals. Hang out. Play catch. Shoot baskets."

Paula remembered the dolphin shaped lamp her father had given her. "Dolphins are lucky," he'd told her. Magical too, she thought, especially this one, cutting graceful figure eights in the silvery moonlight. She waved at him. He stopped then bobbed his head at her, laughing again.

"He likes you," Kurt said.

"How do you know it's a he?"

"The way he's looking at you."

Paula laughed. Kurt held his hand out for her.

"Enter, Lady Paula."

She did a mock curtsy then stepped out of her sandals and into the tub. "Oh God!"

"Too hot?"

"No, no, just needs a few potatoes and carrots." She slid down until only her head was above water, letting the fiery liquid draw the tension from her neck, shoulders and back, aware of the physical toll the events of late had exacted. She groaned and said, "I feel muscles unwinding I didn't even know I had."

A wide shelf of ship's planking bordered the tub. A checkered tablecloth concealed its contents, but couldn't conceal the wonderful aroma emanating from it. Paula found herself salivating. "Pray tell, m'lord, what's under there?"

With a theatrical flourish Kurt whipped the tablecloth away to reveal two plates piled high with scalloped oysters and wild rice. He lifted the grill's cover to reveal spiny lobsters simmering. There was also a bucket of ice nearby with two bottles of champagne chilling, a pack of Chesterfields for Paula, a pack of Camels for Kurt. There also was soap, shampoo, and long handled brushes.

Paula was duly impressed. "You made this?"

"No, there's a takeout joint right around the corner." He splashed water in her face.

She threw her arms around his neck, slopping water over the rim of the tub. When she leaned back, he was surprised to see tears running down her cheeks. "Hey, what's wrong?"

"I never realized until now just how much you really love me." She put one hand over her heart and the other over her mouth, stifling a sob.

Exasperated, Kurt said, "More of those happy tears?"

Paula nodded. "You don't know what it means to me that you went to all this trouble. It's wonderful, Kurt. You're wonderful."

Kurt fired up another Camel, gave her a cocky grin. "Well you know what they say: the way to a woman's heart . . ."

49

The lovemaking began during the meal, playfully feeding each other tasty morsels, kissing, fondling, gulping champagne, and teasing while building up the fire gradually. Kurt's makeshift wind chimes along with a few wild birdcalls provided exotic background music that followed no rhythmic patterns other than whimsy. Swaying hurricane lanterns added to the atmosphere, casting grotesque shadows that undulated like pagan dancers around a bonfire.

In Paula's opinion, the food Kurt had prepared was nothing less than oral sex. It was succulent, boldly seasoned the way only a man would do it, wickedly delicious, and perfectly cooked. She was raised on spiny lobsters. In her estimation, nobody cooked them better than Birdy. Kurt just proved her wrong.

Paula gorged herself. It was so damn good and she was so damn hungry. Kurt laughed at her as she shoveled it in. "Nice to see a girl with a healthy appetite." She was too busy eating to respond.

When the meal was finished, Paula groaned with satisfaction. She laid back so her head once again rested on the rim. "What's the point of sex after that?" Her arms dangled over the edge and her nipples floated on the surface like rose blossoms.

"That was just the appetizer. Wait'll you get to the main coarse."

Paula laughed and splashed water in his face.

"Want to play rough, huh?"

Kurt grabbed the shampoo, stepped out of the tub, and kneeled down behind her. My God, Paula thought, is he really going to wash my hair?

He did, working the shampoo in thoroughly, massaging her scalp at the same time. "This is hard work," he said. "Light me a Camel."

She knocked one loose, fired it up then inhaled deeply. "Yuck. How do you stand these things?"

"Smoke your own, then," he said, snatching the cigarette from her lips, clamping it in his. He shoved her head underwater. She broke free of his hold, but stayed under, working the soap out of her hair.

When she surfaced, Kurt applied another treatment, but slower this time. The way his strong fingers massaged her scalp made her say, "Oh, that's heavenly. I'm not even going to ask were you learned to do it."

"Good." This time when he was finished Paula lurched away, dunked her head underwater. She rinsed the soap out, making a thorough job of it.

When she came up for air, Kurt was back in the tub topping off their glasses with champagne. He threw his back in one big gulp. Paula followed suit, laughing. "Okay, now I get to wash your hair."

Instead of getting out of the tub, she rose up on her knees and instructed Kurt to lean down. Paula was about to apply shampoo when she immediately realized the strategic error she'd made. Kurt's face was virtually in her groin. He did not hesitate to exploit the situation.

"Kurt! Kurt! KURT!"

Using both hands, she shoved his head under, held it there a moment then pulled him back up. "You going to behave?"

"Nope." He dive-bombed her and they wrestled for a while until Paula screamed, "Okay, okay, I give."

"Good." Picking up one of the long handled brushes, he said, "I take."

Wally chimed in with his obnoxious laughter. Paula said, "No fair. Two against one."

"Told you he was a guy." Kurt lathered up the brush. Using slow, sensuous strokes, he scrubbed Paula down. She threw her arms over her head, arched her back, let the bristles work their magic on her. What luxury. She was sure she heard a cat purring and equally sure it was her.

Then in a lightning move Kurt was out of the tub again, poised directly behind her. He grabbed both of her wrists in just one of his big hands and pulled her toward him until her back was arched over the rim, half out of the tub, her arms stretched over her head.

Paula laughed then said, "Okay. If I understand this right, my job here is to be completely submissive."

"You don't have a choice."

"Wanna bet?" She tried her best to break loose but to no avail. After a few moments she stopped struggling. "Okay, how about this for an idea. I'll just stay like this and meanwhile you can have your way with me."

"Brilliant idea, Miss Doherty." Kurt kept his end of the bargain with lion-like agility, using his free hand to leisurely explore her body. Paula was helpless to do anything but let him. Which she gladly did. He kissed her then, making a feast of it, nibbling at her lips, caressing her tongue with his.

Even though it was not the most comfortable position she'd ever been kissed in, there was something highly erotic about it. She did not struggle with much vigor.

Kurt rubbed a soapy finger around the tip of first one nipple then the other, making lazy circles that drove her mad until both nipples were hard as pebbles and tingling.

Waves of ecstasy washed through her veins, her muscles, her mind, possessing them. It was a force that obliterated all resistance. Paula let the waves take her where they wanted. She didn't care where that was.

God, it was good to be a woman.

Kurt's lips wandered over to her ear, his tongue flicking inside it. His hand slid down her belly, stretched taut and flat. It quivered obediently. Her breath quickened. She groaned with pleasure. The power of her womanhood wakened within her, raw, lusty and unfettered.

Kurt massaged her thick coppery bush. In a husky voice he said, “Look at me, Paula.”

She opened her eyes to find him only inches away, his eyes intense, searching. There was something else too, something unexpected, a look that spoke of his overwhelming need to love her. It filled Paula with joy and made her feel immensely sexy.

Kurt's fingers wandered down her bush, stroked her other lips, slowly, tenderly at first, then with increasing urgency, spreading them open, giving him clear access to . . .

Despite Kurt’s iron grip on her, Paula almost jumped out of the tub. The stirring in her groin pushed aside all other sensation. It was a stirring she had no desire to resist, a stirring deep and primal, spreading into her womb.

She wanted to close her eyes. Let it take her.

Kurt wasn't going to let that happen. “No, no, keep your eyes open,” he demanded. “Keep looking at me.”

She did as ordered. What she saw made Paula catch her breath. Through some unexplainable visual transfer she found herself looking out of Kurt's eyes. She saw herself as he saw her, through the eyes of his passion. She saw the flush of her face, the simmering green of her eyes, her wanton desire. It both fascinated and frightened her. Is that really me? Am I really that sensuous? That beautiful?

She saw through Kurt's eyes that she was.

He continued his clitoral caress. Faster. She saw herself respond. Twisting. Groaning. Crying out helplessly. Gasping in anticipation of what was about to happen.

“Keep your eyes open. Look at me.”

Then it did happen and she couldn't see Kurt. She couldn't see anything. She screamed and Kurt wasn’t sure whether it was in pain or pleasure.

He guessed pleasure.

He released his grip and let her slide back down into the steamy, soapy water, a limp rag.

She found herself floating weightlessly in a world where only physical sensation existed, where thought and logic did not.

Then she was being lifted from the tub.

50

"A sunken living room. I just love sunken living rooms."

Bill tossed his keys on the credenza. "It's okay, I guess. We hardly ever use it."

Betty put her hands on her hips. She looked up at Bill with mock scorn. "Well, shame on you, Mr. Bill Taylor. A room as beautiful and spacious as this should be used often."

Bill shrugged. "It was. Up till about a year ago."

"Why? What happened?"

"Paula's mother. Her dementia reached the point where she needed lots of attention. Paula had to be down in Key Largo every other weekend or so to help out."

"How sad."

"What's sad was how much we didn't mind being apart."

"Because you realized you didn't love each other anymore. You poor baby. How lonely you've been."

Betty stood on her tiptoes, pulled Bill's face down and kissed him warmly on the lips. "That's over now, sweetie. You'll never be lonely again. What you will be is happy, happy, happy. 'Cause, my darling, making you happy makes me happy." She gave him her most coy look. "Anything I can do to make that happen, I'm gonna do."

"Anything?"

"Anything." Her little speech opened up Bill's throttle. She darted out of his reach, then wagged a finger at him, giggling girlishly. "Uh-uh, Fireball. There's plenty of time for Captain Jolly to get his workout. Continue the grand tour first."

Bill looked like a lion sizing up a gazelle before pouncing. "Well anyway, this has kinda become Mom's room. She reads in here a lot, watches soaps."

"What about Paula?"

"She's either out by the pool or in the bedroom. Or doing whatever it is women do during the day. Hell if I know."

"In other words, living the life of a thoroughly pampered, spoiled little Palm Bitch wife."

"Look Betty, if you don't like Paula, just say so." It was delivered so deadpan Betty wondered if she had somehow just stepped in it. Then Bill winked at her and Betty collapsed in laughter. But even she heard the artifice in it. She slapped him on the arm. "Oh you."

"So the bedroom is Paula's digs. I sleep there, yeah, but otherwise it's her private boudoir."

Betty took a step closer, looked into his eyes meaningfully. "Bill sweetheart. Sleeping is about to take on a whole new meaning for you."

Another coal added to the fire. Bill's temperature was definitely rising.

But it wasn't hot enough to throw on the steak yet. "What about your son?" she asked.

"Billy lives on campus now. When he lived here, the rec room was his place. Now that he's gone, that's kind of where I hang out. You know, watch a little TV, read the paper."

"Awful. Just awful. When I think of everything Paula could've done to make your evenings more enjoyable, well, it just makes me want to slap her."

Bill thought, better not try that one, baby. Paula would turn you into pineapple puree. Instead, he chuckled. "Hey, take it easy. I thought we weren't going to talk about Paula anymore."

Betty wrapped her arms around Bill's waist and laid her head against his chest. "You're right, we're not."

Betty skipped over to the sliding glass door and looked out across the courtyard. "It's such a big house. You never told me it was so big. Kind of place you expect to hear children running around, wrestling and playing."

"Yeah, well, Billy ended up being an only child. Something wrong with Paula's plumbing."

"Well, sweetie, nothing's wrong with my plumbing. I can drop babies faster than most women can drop their pants."

Bill grinned sardonically. "Just what a man wants to hear."

Betty laughed, kissed Bill on the nose. "Don't worry, silly. The door to the baby making room is barricaded. For tonight anyway."

Bill slapped her on the rump. "Good girl." He shoved the glass door open, held his hand out. "Ladies first."

As they stepped out into the courtyard, Betty sucked in the blustery night air along with the fragrance of Mama Taylor's flower garden. Yes indeed, she thought, I can get used to this so fast it'll break the sound barrier.

A chair scraped on the flagstone. Betty turned to see Bill sitting down in front of the patio table, draping one leg casually over the other. A cigar appeared from somewhere. He fired it up, never taking his eyes off her.

"A little while ago you said you'd do anything to make me happy."

Okay, here's where we get kinky, she thought. All right, I can be kinky. "Yes I did."

"Lets start by getting you out of those clothes?"

Betty knew Bill wasn't asking her to get undressed. He was asking her to strip. She knew the difference. Theoretically. She leaned down so she was eye-level with Bill. She took his face in her hands then kissed him lingeringly. "Yes sir, anything you say, sir." She gave him her sauciest, most seductive smile.

But there was something in Bill's eyes that chilled her blood. He had never looked at her like that before. She forced herself to keep the smile she wasn't feeling. The big umbrella over the table clanged in the angry wind, echoing her own jangled nerves.

Come on, she told herself, don't blow it now. Be his little Tinker Toy. Think of your kids splashing around happily in this pool. You're here tonight to close the deal. Do it.

But how? She'd never done a striptease before. Never even been to a strip club.

"What's the matter?" There was a hint of impatience in his voice.

"Nothing, dear. Just getting in the mood."

"Maybe this will help."

There was a record player on the table she hadn't noticed before. Bill turned it on and dropped the needle. A drum roll. A cymbal crash. A boom-dum-dum-boom-dum-dum-boom backed by brassy horns. Betty recognized it immediately as the lead-in to that new musical *Gypsy* about the famous stripper. Ethel Merman belted out, "Let me entertain you."

Bill called out, "Come on baby, start dancing around a little." The cigar clamped in his teeth muffled his words. "You said you wanted to please me."

Betty swiveled her hips, got into the rhythm of the music. She high-stepped it across the courtyard, kicking off first one shoe then the other, right on the cymbal hits. Bill seemed to approve. Okay, this isn't so hard, she thought. I can do this.

Making the moves as provocative as possible, Betty inched her blouse out of her waistband. She worked on the top button while strutting up to Bill, kicking a leg out with each step. She was right in front of Bill by the time she was working on the second button. His hands flashed out, grabbed her blouse and ripped it off.

The violence of the gesture startled Betty. She jerked back with a little scream that had no artifice in it at all. The blouse hung on her in tatters, resembling a shabby boa whipping around in the gusty wind. She went with that concept, wiggled out of it with maximum shoulder shimmy, twirled it around overhead, matching the music's bumps and grinds, then slung it toward Bill.

It landed on his head, caught fire from the cigar, and with help from the wind, exploded into flames.

51

Kurt carried Paula dripping down to the lagoon, holding her gently as if she were a vial of nitro. Paula was aware of her volatile condition too, knew the explosion she'd just experienced in the tub was just a tremor. The main quake was yet to come.

Best of all she knew that Kurt knew it too, knew what she was capable of, more importantly, knew how to get her there. He'd amply demonstrated that ability many times before. Played her like a cathedral pipe organ with all the stops pulled out. Had her singing *Ode to Joy* at the top of her lungs. Metaphorically speaking.

When they reached the pier, Wally was already in attendance. He watched them curiously, sensing they hadn't come to play with him. Kurt stood Paula up then encircled her with big, beefy, hairy arms that completely engulfed her, even though she was a tall buxom woman. When he held her like this, Paula felt intensely safe and comforted in a way she hadn't known since she was a little girl bundled up in her father's arms.

The smell of Kurt overwhelmed her, a gritty musk tinged with acrid tobacco and a whiff of ocean salt from a billion years ago. It notched up her desire for him to a level that made her head swim. His lips drew close to her ear and whispered, "Look at the stars, Paula."

When she did, the effect was mesmerizing. The black velvet sky splotched with deep purple was bursting with them; so profuse in places they seemed like clouds of glitter dust.

"Try to touch them," Kurt said.

Paula laughed. The champagne danced giddily in her head. She said, "No problem." She reached up, stretching until she was on her toes. Her fingers reached for the star farthest away.

It felt good to stretch. Lounging in a steamy bath had reduced her muscles to tapioca pudding. Now every muscle in her body sang out to her, reclaiming the harmony destroyed by a week of tension and turmoil. Music stirred within her, a chorus of pulsating blood, pounding heart, and nerves vibrating like a tuning fork. She laughed and said, “I’ve almost got them.”

“Keep reaching.”

She did.

Standing naked outside on the pier was erotic as hell. It made the girls stand out proudly with nipples once more at full attention and saluting toward Heaven. Well, in the general direction anyway. The wind mussed her hair. Paula liked the rough masculine feel of it. She realized she was primed once again and her fuse was short. The slightest spark would be sufficient to set her off.

Kurt provided the spark.

He produced a towel from somewhere and dried her. The rough touch of it became his hands, the bite of the wind became his teeth nibbling on her neck, her ears, her breasts.

Paula moaned. “If you stop I'll kill you.”

He didn't, but he was doing different things to her now, incredibly gentle things with those big powerful hands of his. Paula wondered if the sighing she heard was the wind tossing palm fronds or her own quavering breath. Were those tiny sparks fireflies or the residue of her passion dancing around in her head?

She glanced up at the moon with just a sliver lopped off. She gave it her most winning smile. In return it drew the tide across the Bay. The sound of its roll and splash echoed through the secret tunnel. The cadence of it mimicked the rhythms within her body. She moved with it, had to.

She smiled at Kurt dreamily, let the music of her body control her, a song of primal seduction so natural, she was singing it eons before she was born. She waved her arms sensuously, imitating the swaying palms. Her hips undulated from side to side, her shoulders rolled in counter tempo, her head rocked to the beat of jungle drums only she heard.

Kurt stood spellbound. Paula’s movements were like watching dancing flames. Even though he was several feet away, he sensed the heat emanating from her. And like a fire, she glowed, especially her eyes, burning green emeralds that challenged him, beckoned him.

The gyrations of her body became more pronounced, more aggressive, challenging him, daring him. She laughed, taunting him. It singed every hair on his body.

The way Kurt was looking at her made Paula feel like Eve, Cleopatra, Scheherazade, and Helen of Troy all wrapped into one. They were all inside her. They were inside other women, too, but usually dormant, waiting. Not so with Paula. Not tonight, anyway. She reveled in her power of seduction, was lost in the carnality of it. No man could deny her. Definitely not Kurt.

He was the only man capable of bringing her to this point. Her desire for him was exhilarating and liberating of both mind and body. She was a dam about to burst. She wanted Kurt to open the floodgates.

She folded her arms behind her head, arched her back, offering her breasts to him. It worked. Kurt's hands were on her, but instead of kneading her breasts roughly like he often did, his touch was gentle, almost worshipful. She covered his hands with hers, letting him know she liked what he was doing.

She also liked the contrast between the milky smoothness of her breasts and Kurt's gorilla-like hands, the way her breasts overflowed his massive grip. She hissed and groaned, twisted and turned. She held his hands tighter while Kurt dropped to his knees and buried his face in her groin. His tongue penetrated her with quick, hard stabs.

She gasped and cried out, "Oh God!" and "Yes! Yes!"

He plunged deeper, then grabbed her ass with both hands and pushed her pelvis against him so he could reach deeper yet. Paula jolted, grabbed the back of Kurt's head and shoved it against her so hard that she wondered for one brief flash if he could breathe. Then decided she didn't care. If he did suffocate, what a way to go. All that was important now was this wild, uncontrollable force bursting from her womb, surging through her breasts. It must not be stopped from reaching her brain.

It wasn't.

The eruption rocked Paula. She screamed out so savagely that birds leapt into flight. It was too much for Wally. He flipped over backwards and disappeared from view. It was indeed a quake of epic proportion. She shrieked, shuddered, bucked, wondered if it would ever stop and prayed it wouldn't.

When it did, it was only because of sheer exhaustion. Paula was dizzy. Her focus was fuzzy. Her ears rang. She was panting like a racehorse that had just won the Triple Crown. She was once again tapioca pudding, very warm tapioca pudding. She grabbed Kurt, clung desperately to him, afraid she would ooze off the pier and into the lagoon.

She laid her head on Kurt's big chest. "Oh Kurt, I'm so, so sorry, baby."

Kurt was clearly puzzled. "For what?"

"That men can't experience a climax like that."

He laughed a deep hearty laugh then shook his head in wonder. "Was ever there a wench your equal, Paula Doherty?"

She gave Kurt her most beguiling look. "Never." She spun out of his arms, jumped on top of one the shipping crate tables and executed a perfect swan dive into the lagoon.

Kurt took a running leap from the pier, pulled his knees up to his chest and bombed her.

52

Bill whipped off the flaming blouse remnant, threw it on the tiles, and stomped it out.

Betty was frozen in horror, hands over mouth. But Bill was laughing, slapping his knee, relighting his cigar.

"That was pretty good. But you didn't have to go that far to get me all hot and bothered. Come on, baby, keep it going."

Betty perked up. Everything was okay. She put her hands on her hips, bumping them left, then right in perfect time to bass drum hits, knowing how sexy she looked in nothing but skirt and bra. Bill looked like a little boy in a toy store.

She raised her right hand over her head then her left, performing high kicks, then reached her right hand across with an exaggerated movement to unzip her skirt. But the fastener stuck and she was forced to use both hands to get it loose, looking more than slightly ridiculous. Bill jumped up. "Need some help?"

Betty backed away. "No, no, I've got it. Just sit down and . . . let me entertain you." She tore the fastener loose then wiggled her hips until the skirt succumbed to gravity. She kicked it off. The rowdy wind sailed it over to the big live oak, where it snagged on a limb. Betty did a couple of pirouettes in her bra and panties. It made her dizzy enough that she almost fell over sideways into the pool, catching herself at the last moment. Bill laughed, applauded, said, "That's my baby." His approval was evident in the way he was hot-boxing his cigar.

Betty had purposefully worn the only bra she owned that fastened in the front. Still dancing, she whipped down one strap, rolled her shoulder provocatively, then pulled down the other strap and repeated the act.

She slithered her arms free, knew this was it. Make it tantalizing, she told herself. Make it heart stopping. A big gust hit her. It whipped her hair out like a wild woman. She took advantage of the moment to charge Bill like a jungle cat, her eyes fierce, feral. She stopped with her breasts inches from his face. She unfastened the bra and let it hang there, flashing an inch of flesh. "Do what you gotta do, big guy," she purred.

Bill didn't hesitate. He ripped the bra open to reveal her small breasts with their small nipples, very hard, very erect. Betty shrugged her shoulders. The bra magically flew away. Thank you, Mr. Wind.

Bill used both hands to fondle her. Betty was somewhat disturbed that he still had the cigar crooked between his fingers. The wind made the ashes spark. Then in a lightning quick move he tore off her panties and threw them aside. Betty had never felt more naked or vulnerable in her life.

And frightened.

Bill turned off the record player. He picked Betty up effortlessly, carried her over to a spot in the middle of the courtyard, set her down, then moved back a couple of steps to take her all in. "You want to do whatever it takes to please Daddy, right?"

Betty shivered. She smiled at him, alluringly she hoped. "Of course, darling. I told you that already."

"That's Daddy's girl. Now raise your arms over your head and keep them there. You can sway around a little if you want."

Betty did as she was told, watching Bill's reaction carefully. Something wasn't quite right here. She tried to see herself through his eyes.

And then with a stab of panic she did. With her arms raised over her head her breasts all but disappeared, became prepubescent mounds.

Like those of a twelve year old girl.

Now he was behind her, his big hands on her pelvis, reaching around, scratching through her narrow patch of bush. "Call me Daddy."

"Okay . . . Daddy."

His hands wandered up her torso, groping savagely, then stopped on her almost nonexistent breasts. He put his lips close to her ears. "You want to make Daddy happy?"

"Yes . . . Daddy. I already told you."

"Anything?"

"Anything." She heard her voice quaver.

He kneaded her breasts but not in a pleasurable way. His thumbs rubbed roughly over her nipples. Betty tried to act as if she was becoming aroused, but the opposite was true.

He took his time, enjoying himself, then stepped away, clamped the cigar between his teeth again. "Doesn't seem right you're the only one who's naked," he said.

Yes, Betty thought, get him naked. Get to the main event. Let him get his load off. Maybe he'll calm down then. She cocked an eyebrow at him. "I can take care of that."

She stripped him down to his drawers then slid them down. His penis snapped to attention as if it was spring-loaded, aimed right between her eyes.

"Like it?"

This was better. This was natural. She was becoming aroused. "I like it a lot." Betty kissed the tip of it, ran her tongue over it. "So big, Daddy."

"Think a little girl like you can handle it?"

The alarm bells went off so loudly inside Betty's head she was hardly aware of Bill grabbing her, flipping her over, setting her down on her hands and knees. Oh, we're going to do it doggy style. Okay. I like doggy style.

Bill grabbed her hands, forced her to hold onto the tabletop. She had to stretch to do so and it did the same trick as before, made her breasts all but disappear. He was on his knees behind her now, his hands fondling her breast mounds.

She felt the pressure of his penis against her, positioning for entry. Just do it, she thought. Then he penetrated her.

But not her vagina.

She screamed out. "Oh God Bill!" She had never had this kind of sex before. It was extremely uncomfortable, not at all pleasurable. The raw wind slapping her face made it worse. Tears burst from her eyes. "Bill, please! It hurts!"

"You said anything. Did you mean it?"

In her mind Betty pictured her kids playing in the pool, having separate bedrooms of their own, going to the finest schools, the best colleges, wearing the most fashionable clothes, having the best of everything. "Yes. I meant it." She was about to throw up.

"Anything?"

"Anything . . . Daddy." She sobbed uncontrollably.

53

The water in the lagoon was fed by an underground spring and it was bracing to say the least. In plainer terminology, it was teeth chattering cold.

Paula and Kurt played like a couple of kids, splashing and dunking, laughing and chasing. Paula did flips off Kurt's shoulders, then when submerged played grab the weenie. She loved the way it snaked around underwater like it had a life of its own. Kurt was equally fascinated by what happened to Paula's breasts when they achieved buoyancy. He wondered how she managed to stay under with those big flotation devices attached to her chest.

This was the sorbet before the main course. A chance to recalibrate their body heat to some semblance of normalcy before resuming their exhilaratingly intimate exploration not just of body parts, but of their souls.

Realization of this escalated their feelings for each other to a depth and intensity neither thought was possible. Often they would spontaneously throw their arms around each other and just hug with all their strength, which combined was considerable, then laugh from sheer joy at discovering this uninhibited, unconditional friendship. This union.

For Paula, finding herself deeply, overwhelmingly in love with Kurt was completely unexpected. She was here to run away from a life she hated, to unleash her full womanly powers, to live her life now and forever more just as she pleased.

As for Kurt, he was determined to let Paula know this wasn't just about sex, that he truly loved her. Clearly he wanted her to believe it. It was there in his eyes. Paula found herself responding in kind.

Kurt was highly impressed with Paula's abilities as a swimmer. She was comfortable in the water, had no fear of it, even at night. She was able to hold her breath for minutes at a time even while performing acrobatic maneuvers. She was as athletic as any man and darted through liquid space like a torpedo.

Having a woman to play with -- outside of the sack -- was a new experience for Kurt. He liked it. Of course, Paula was no match for his physical prowess but then neither were most men. Yet despite her strength and agility, Paula was never less than one hundred percent woman. Kurt liked that too.

The wild antics wore down after a while. They circled each other, treaded water, moved closer. Paula threw her arms around Kurt's neck. He felt her full weight. She no longer made an effort to stay afloat. They kissed, gentle exploratory nibbles. Paula dropped her arms into the water, making herself dead weight.

"Hold me up, Kurt, or I'll drown."

Kurt grinned that wonderful swashbuckling smile of his. "Forget it. Ain't gonna happen. I got you." He pulled her over to the dock and effortlessly tossed her onto it, then heaved himself out. He sprawled out on his back, hands pillowing his head.

"Stay just like that," Paula said, her voice a husky whisper. She licked his lips ever so gently, a feathery touch. She ran her hand through his thick matte of chest hair. Then she raised her head enough so that she had a clear view of his crotch as she pinched a nipple. Her eyes lit up in wonder as she watched his penis grow hard, lift up from the dock. It was such an erotic sight, especially knowing she was the one who made it happen. "Good boy."

"Yeah, so what are you going to do about it?"

"Whatever I damn well please." Paula knew from past experience that once she took control of Kurt's joystick he was pretty easy to control. Tonight was no exception. And once she took control, she wasn't going to relinquish it.

It belonged to her now. Each time Kurt tried to reclaim it she was as vicious as a mother bear protecting her cubs. He growled, hissed, and pulled at her hair, but it didn't work. She was operating on her own rules. He'd just have to deal with it.

She straddled Kurt and slid him into her inch by glorious inch. He grunted, groaned, bucked, and was about to squeeze her breasts off, but Paula was not about to be thrown. She wished she had a cowgirl hat to wave over her head.

She laughed. The laugh gradually changed to a scream as the Climax Express raced to points north and beyond, faster, hotter. She screwed her eyes shut, clenched her teeth together. Her body quaked. Here it comes.

HERE IT COMES . . .

The explosion shot white-hot sparks to the tips of her fingers and toes. It seared her brain and electrified every pore in her skin. She lay on the dock tingling.

But the fire was still smoldering. She knew there was another eruption yet to come, bigger even than this one.

Kurt knew it too.

54

"Holy shit," Earl said as he lowered his camera.

Red clamped a hand over Earl's mouth and snarled, "Shut up," in a barely audible tone. He glared at Earl a moment then snapped his head around to give Gator a fierce warning too. He put his lips close to Earl's ear. "You get all that?"

Not daring to speak, Earl held up the camera with one hand and gave thumbs up with the other, accompanied by a nervous smile. He was scared witless of Red, but who wasn't. The look Red had just given them would instantly loosen the bowels of braver men than them.

Earl had taken a full roll of Kurt and Paula having the wildest sex he'd ever witnessed. He used a 35mm surveillance camera specially adapted to be soundproof. It was loaded with extremely high-speed film. The lens attached to it was the fastest available. Appropriate, Earl thought, since he was shooting a very fast woman.

God, the tits on her. And legs and ass to match. That fucking Kurt. Always got the cream of the crop. But this one was something special times two. He prayed Red would keep his promise to let him fuck her. Before they opened Kurt's guts and let them spill on the floor. 'Course Red would get his turn first. That was okay, long as he got his.

Red had come bursting into Earl's rusty old house trailer earlier in the day, around 3:30. Earl was a big, overgrown, hulking slob and seemed to be proud of it. He'd been on a two-day bender, which was not a problem for Red. It only took him a couple of minutes to slap Earl sober. Earl thanked him and said he felt much better now.

Red laid out the mission for him, explaining that it would be very dangerous, but the rewards would more than compensate the risk. And not just monetarily. As a bonus, he would get to have quality time with Kurt's current playmate, a woman who gave bombshell an entirely new meaning.

Red also said there would be killing involved. Earl asked if the person who was going to get killed deserved it, to which Red answered, "Hell, we all do." That made plenty of sense to Earl. He swatted at a fly circling his greasy hair. As always, Red explained that Earl's involvement in the job was entirely voluntary. Either he joined the team or Red would kill him on the spot. Earl signed on without further comment.

By 6:00 PM Red, Gator and Earl had accumulated all the gear they'd need and packed it into a stolen Jon boat. They'd also confiscated outboard motors from some unfortunate civilian -- one gas powered, the other an electric troller. Silent running as they approached Curiosity Cove was essential.

It took them almost two hours to wind their way out of the Glades, then cross a mile of Florida Bay to reach Kurt's hideaway. They dropped anchor a little after 8:00 PM at what Red knew was the only safe landing spot on the island, the place where the back channel from the lagoon poured into the Bay.

The normal approach to the island was through the main channel. That was also where Kurt had rigged most of his alarm devices.

Most, but not all.

Because Red and Kurt had been combat partners for many years, Red knew how Kurt's mind worked. He was confident there would be other trip devices hidden at strategic locations on the backside of the island. When triggered they would set off alarms. He was also confident he could find and disable them. Every trick Kurt knew, Red knew. That's what came of being best buddies. Kurt had been his very best buddy.

Now he was going to kill him. The thought of that made him very angry.

Sensing Red's mood, Earl tried to be as invisible as possible after anchoring the boat then wading ashore. It didn't work. Red turned his heart-constricting gaze on Earl. "When's the last time you took a fucking bath? You smell like a dead polecat. Hell, we won't have to worry about tripping alarms. Kurt'll smell you long before we get near the place."

Earl was afraid to contradict Red, so he kept his mouth shut. Gator chuckled and said, "Yeah man, you do smell like the shit I took yesterday."

Red whipped out his monster knife. "Alright, knock it off. From here on in, no more talking. Hand signals only. Remember, tonight is for surveillance and mission prep only. We're gonna do this right. Questions?"

Neither of them spoke. Red said, "Move out."

Red knew he had two big advantages going for him. First, the blustery weather. It rattled trees and created a sorrowful moan as it rushed over immoveable objects. Secondly, Red knew Kurt's attention would be entirely focused on bushy red crotch candy, not on fending off intruders.

They reached the house about 8:30. It didn't take long to realize the place was deserted. To make doubly sure, Red checked the boathouse. No *Black Jack.* Gazing around the compound he noticed quite a few hurricane lanterns were lit, swinging in the wind. Obviously Kurt wouldn't be gone long.

Red was right. Kurt glided into the lagoon with his playmate sitting in the bow, while Red, Earl, and Gator watched from the woods. Earl fired off two rolls of film while Kurt and Paula were playing in the tub. He had the panties Kurt had thrown over the railing. They smelled good. They smelled of woman. He stuffed them inside his shirt

When Kurt carried Paula down to the dock, Red had them change to a new position, one that gave them a clearer view. While Earl took more pictures, Gator took mental notes on what Kurt was doing to the woman that made her go crazy the way she did. He wanted to try some of the same moves when it was his turn.

They watched as Kurt picked Paula up again, then carried her toward the house. Earl couldn't restrain himself. "Can't that woman walk for herself?"

Red emitted a growly chuckle. "After what he just did to her, probably not. Okay, my guess is they're coming up on the final act."

Earl gawked. "You mean they're gonna do it again?"

"Shut up. Not another sound from either of you. We gotta change positions now. Be very damn quiet about it."

55

Kurt carried Paula upstairs. She felt queenly being carried from one part of her realm to another. Big girl that she was, most men couldn't manage the task. Kurt did so effortlessly. He stood her up just outside the French doors leading into the bedroom. He kissed her then said, “Wait a minute.” Before entering the room, he grabbed two of the hurricane lanterns swaying in the wind. He hung them from strategically placed ceiling hooks above the bed.

Their warm glow was in striking contrast to the sapphire moonlight filtering in through the French doors. The gusty breeze billowed out the sheer curtains making them whisper and pop. In the middle of it all stood Kurt, naked, hands on hips. He turned down the bedspread revealing crisp cotton sheets. He rolled back the top one, said, “Dive in,” then disappeared down the hall.

Paula didn’t have to be asked twice. She spread out on the bed, luxuriating in the feel of its cool sheets against her simmering skin. She drank in the invigorating salt air then stretched until her toes touched the bamboo rods at the foot of the bed. Queen indeed. Maybe Queen of Sheba. Why not?

Kurt returned with two basins, one filled with hot soapy water, the other with warm scented oil. He bathed her, making it a sensuous act, kissing every inch of her body as he did so. The oil rub down came next. Yeah, Paula thought. I really *am* the Queen of Sheba.

By the time he got to her thighs, Paula didn’t care who she was as long as Kurt kept doing what he was doing. His touch was expert, gentle, loving. And like all master craftsmen, he took his time.

Soon it was her turn to bathe and oil Kurt. She started by trying to soothe the injuries she’d inflicted earlier. The expression on Kurt’s face indicated she was succeeding.

She rubbed oil on his chest, turning the thick mat of hair into silver strands glistening in the moonlight. His heart pounded under her touch, his skin grew hot. He was primed. Time to put away the oil. She did, then took his face in her hands, kissed him, said, "You need to get out of bed for a second."

He did. Paula got on her knees, leaned forward and grabbed the bamboo headboard. She knew it was like dangling red meat in front of a starving lion. Kurt pounced back into bed and mounted her, doing it the way she liked, entering her a little bit at a time, driving her mad.

His hunger for her was manifested in his every move. He cradled her dangling breasts in his hands, massaging them roughly. Paula let him have what he wanted. She rode his passion, used it to stoke the flames of her own inferno.

He stopped. Tension built within him until he was shaking from it. His breath hissed out insistently like steam escaping from a pressure cooker. Paula tightened her grip on the headboard, knowing what was coming.

But she was wrong.

Kurt turned her over on her back and remounted her.

Face to face.

For Paula, the missionary position was not the most stimulating. But it was the most romantic.

And Kurt was clearly out for romance tonight. He would not be denied. He moved in and out of her with long, slow strokes. When she closed her eyes in ecstasy, he kissed her eyelids. He moved his lips to her ear, flicked his tongue inside. "I love you, Paula. God how I love you."

Paula opened her eyes. "I know." Tears rolled down her cheeks.

He kissed her tears away. At the same time he increased the rhythm of his strokes.

Paula sucked in her breath, moaned, moved her hips to match his rhythm. He was trembling, holding back, trying to bring her to maximum pleasure.

She went with it, gave herself completely to what was building inside her. She was not aware of anything else, only the pleasure between her legs. She didn't know where she was. Another country. Another planet. She didn't care.

Her heart raced. Perspiration made her skin glow, despite the wind whistling through the room. It made the hurricane lanterns creak musically. The pressure of her blood engorged lips as he drove in and out of her was so intense she got lost in the eroticism of it. She had no control over her motions.

She reached up, grabbed the headboard, and arched her back. In a voice raw wild with desire she said, "Let it loose, Kurt," then held her breath.

He did.

The beast roared out of the cage, mauling her savagely, pounding her so fiercely that she had to lock her arms to keep from being slammed against the headboard. Whenever their lovemaking reached this stage Paula often wondered if she could physically take it.

Tonight she didn't care. She was beyond any semblance of control. If she died, she died. Her screams were somewhere between abject terror and indescribable ecstasy.

Blinding white flashes filled her brain. She had no thoughts, no awareness other than the deep climax bursting from her groin, surging through her womb, up into her belly, drawing her breasts tight. She felt powerful yet helpless at the same time.

For Kurt, he had never known such release. His testicles seemed to be in a vise grip and the only relief was to keep pumping. Which he did, thrusting harder, deeper, pounding brutally against Paula's pelvis, hard blows he was incapable of stopping. The feel of her hot flesh pressing against his own just inflamed him further. He yelled out savagely. Adrenalin surged into his muscles, powering them.

They both collapsed from sheer exhaustion, panting like thoroughbreds. Paula wrapped her legs around Kurt to keep him inside her. She held on to him for his heat, for the touch of his skin against hers. She couldn't lose that.

Her muscles relaxed involuntarily. She was vaguely aware of the wind trying to steal her warmth, of the sighing of the Bay, the clatter of palm fronds. She fell into a velvety blue-black nothingness, floating happily somewhere above the bed, free of form and weight. She settled softly, delicately, into the sweet embrace of oblivion.

She was soon followed by Kurt. His last sensation was of his limp penis, ready for sleep, cradled in Paula's warm, moist vagina. Her exotic fragrance of sweat and oil and woman filled his nostrils and tickled his brain.

For a fleeting second, just before losing consciousness, Kurt thought he heard men's voices whispering.

Probably just a trick of the wind, he decided.

Then he was gone.

56

Paula's first conscious thought was: I want to lay here like this for the rest of my life. She was vaguely aware of sunlight flooding the room, beckoning her to open her eyes. But if she did, this delicious, fuzzy, coma-like state would be broken and she would be officially awake. She wasn't about to let that happen. She took refuge again in her slumber, letting it take her to its bosom the way a mother did a newborn.

She burrowed deeper into the pillows, seeking their cool darkness. The brightness on the other side of her eyelids subsided, replaced by a deep purple which gradually faded to a velvety black. The lazy, buzzing sound of sleep drifted into her brain once again, filling it up.

The buzzing stopped abruptly. Something feathery was playing with her leg. It was a pleasantly taunting sensation but it forced her mind to probe, to try to determine what it was. Not good. That kind of gray cell activity was the enemy of slumber. Who cares what it is, she decided, as long as it feels good.

Paula sighed and pulled the sheet tight around her. The sun on her shoulder felt good, sensuously so. The breeze coming through the windows carried with it the lullaby of the surf. It was as if angels were blowing softly on her hair, her face. Paula filled her lungs with the salty air, inhaling deeply, letting the warm cocoon of sleep reclaim her, falling willingly into its soft caress.

God, what luxury.

She reached out for Kurt, wanting the comfort of his warm, hairy body. Instead she found cool empty sheets. Her eyes popped open.

Dammit!

What a dirty trick. Now I'm awake.

Paula rolled over onto her back and playfully kicked the sheet off, stretching her arms and legs until she was sure her spine would snap. She wondered where Kurt was then decided somewhat giddily she didn't really care.

A strong gust pushed the curtains out over the bed. She tried to catch the flimsy material with her toes but was distracted by the aroma of bacon frying. Making us breakfast, is he? She heard him downstairs clanging pans together and whistling off-key.

Paula realized she was ravenous, then wondered how was that possible after the feast they had last night. Kurt’s feast. It occurred to her that except for a restaurant chef, never in her adult life had a man prepared a meal for her.

Paula laughed out loud. Now what does that mean, laughing out loud? Maybe it's just an involuntary expression of the joy and happiness I'm feeling, mixed in with this wonderful sensation of freedom.

Childhood emotions. We lose them as a penalty for growing up. Well, I've found them again and I'm not ever going to grow up. I feel like I've just turned sixteen and ready to start life. Only this time I'm going to do it right.

Sixteen.

When Paula sat up she was aware of Kurt's scent on her, mingled with her own. The sweat of their lovemaking had dried into a sticky film that covered her body, matted her hair. Well, maybe not sixteen.

But it felt good. Damn good.

Paula headed toward the shower then stopped to gaze out the open French doors. It was a sparkling day, fresh and clean. She grabbed her pack of Chesterfields, knocked one loose, then lit up. What an intoxicating combination salt air and cigarette smoke was. To hell with a shower, she decided, and stepped out onto the balcony.

She stood leaning against the railing, smoking contentedly, contemplating the gorgeous view spread out before her. Then it occurred to Paula she was out in the open in broad daylight, butt naked.

Well, so what? It was a good feeling. Liberating. Natural.

She was happy to see the Cove was just as friendly by daylight as it had been enchanting by moonlight. She watched a pelican glide in over the lagoon, then settle down on a post at the end of the pier.

She wondered where Wally was this morning. Probably out in the Bay stirring up bubbles with some dolphin cutie. The thought brought a grin to Paula’s face. Carefree and sensuous, that‘s the way life should always be.

Glancing down at the sand, Paula was struck by how it was swept clean of even the smallest rock, a straight, unspoiled run from the house down to the lagoon. Not only was it pristine but it was blindingly white. It would be a good place to spread out on a beach blanket, soak up some rays, just be lazy. She needed to be lazy for a while. Life had been way too intense for way too long.

Paula descended the outside stairs and across the verandah. She kicked her feet through the silky sand, then just stood still for a moment, eyes closed, and let the sun work its fingers down into her muscles, charging them up, making her want to move. Before her, the lagoon spread out like crystal, shimmering gently, beckoning her.

Paula tossed her cigarette, found herself running, laughing, leaping off the end of the pier into space. She broke the surface with hardly a splash then dove for the bottom. The water still held the evening's chill but it was glorious against her skin. This is my baptism, she thought. My old life is being washed away. When I surface I will be someone new.

Paula shot up out of the water. Her hands reached for the white, puffy clouds above. Then she arched backwards, throwing her arms out wide to make a big splash when she hit. She did and the droplets flying up glittered like diamonds. She surfaced again, filled her lungs with air and ducked back under.

She stretched out beneath the surface thinking: I *have* been reborn. I *am* a new woman. I have no past, only a future.

She found herself gliding torpedo-like through liquid space, exhilarated by her power. She stayed under until her lungs were on fire, then willed herself to stay down a few seconds longer, a test of her vibrant strength. When she surfaced, Paula laughed out loud again.

57

Breakfast for Kurt usually consisted of coffee and cigarettes, but today he was cooking enough to feed a small regiment.

He grabbed a handful of spuds, sliced them into tiny chunks -- to hell with peeling them -- then tossed them into a pan with onions and half a stick of butter. He threw bacon on next, a full pound of it soaked in Lea and Perrins Worcestershire and sprinkled with garlic and freshly ground pepper. He filled an enameled percolator with cold water, dumped coffee in until the basket was overflowing and placed it on the back burner to brew.

Gotta have toast too, he decided. He dipped eight slices of bread into a saucer of melted butter, laid the sopping slices on a pan and shoved them in the oven. He remembered the cantaloupe he'd purchased yesterday from a roadside vender, retrieved it from the fridge, and cut it into thick slices.

Yeah, breakfast was shaping up nicely.

While the bacon sizzled, Kurt used his fork to beat out a rhythm on the side of the frying pan. Then he heard something that froze him in place. Paula screamed from the direction of the lagoon. He almost tore the back door off running out onto the verandah.

There she was, butt naked, splashing about, laughing like a five year old.

Kurt simply stared. Her carefree, childlike romping was the most beautiful sight he had ever witnessed. The sound of her laughter was like gentle fingers massaging his mind, filling it with happiness more intense than he had ever known, a happiness that settled as a tight knot in his throat.

Back in the kitchen he took up the bacon and while it drained on a wad of paper towels, cracked open a dozen eggs into the grease and then scrambled them. While they were still soft, he scooped them onto a platter. With the dexterity of a professional acrobat, he conveyed the entire feast to the table on the verandah. Paula was nowhere to be seen. He decided she was probably upstairs and called out, "Chow's on. Get your ass out here."

He heard her descend the side stairs. She appeared around the corner a few seconds later wearing a flowery silk dressing gown. She stopped upon seeing the lavish meal spread out on the table. Her mouth dropped open. "Unbelievable." In a bud vase next to her plate was a single pink frangipani blossom. "Oh Kurt . . ."

"What?"

"You know what."

He pulled a chair out for her and bowed. "Madam."

Paula took Kurt's face in her hands and kissed him with warm, moist lips. She gazed into his eyes a moment to make sure he could see how much she adored him. The message was clearly received. She sat. The aroma wafting up from the table soon had her stomach growling like a lioness smelling prey. "How did you sleep?"

"Dreaming of you."

She gave him a saucy smile. "Explains the wet spot."

"Just one?" He reached down and ripped open her gown to expose her breasts. "Mornin' girls." He kissed each of them in a way that left no doubt of his affection for them. Paula looked down approvingly, joggled them, while in a little girl's voice she said, "Mornin' Kurt." She closed her gown, wiggled her eyebrows at Kurt then redirected her focus to the steaming platters of food before her. "Yum and double-yum."

They both dug in.

The bacon was slightly burnt, the hash browns were crunchy, the toast actually squirted butter when bit into, the eggs were greasy, and the coffee was strong enough to hold up railroad spikes. All in all, Paula thought it was probably the best meal she had ever eaten since last night. As she raked another helping of eggs into her plate she asked Kurt, "Do you like making love to fat women?"

"If the room's dark enough, who cares?"

"Hmm. Perhaps we'd better buy some black-out curtains."

Paula savored every bite. She wondered if life with Kurt would always be this sensual. They talked easily, teasing sometimes, but mainly just enjoying each other's company. The wind was still brisk, but not unpleasant. Kurt explained that it was Hurricane Judith moving across the peninsula even as they spoke.

Paula threw her hands up in surrender. "I give," she said and slumped back in her chair. "That was truly wonderful, my love. I probably won't eat again for at least a week."

"So glad madam approves."

"Madam most definitely approves. Madam is most definitely stuffed to the gills."

In a seemingly effortless movement, Kurt picked Paula up, chair and all, and moved her closer to the railing. He slid his chair next to her, grabbed a bottle of champagne, filled two glasses and gave one to her. “Hope you saved room for this.”

Paula took the glass. “Well, okay.”

Kurt clanged his to hers then lifted it in a toast. “To Pauline and Paulette.” Seeing Paula's quizzical look, he added, “That's what I've named them.”

Paula looked down at her chest. “I always wondered what their names were.” She gave Kurt a mischievous smile. “Which is which?”

“That's Pauline on the right, uh, your left.”

They propped their feet up on the railing. Oddly, the icy champagne was the perfect compliment to the farmyard feast. They were quiet for a while, listening to water lap in the lagoon, wind rustle through the forest, gulls crying like hungry puppies. It was very pleasant and utterly relaxing.

“This truly is paradise,” Paula said. She made a gagging sound. “I can't believe how much I ate.”

“Yeah, me too.” Kurt raised his leg and let loose a thunderous fart.

“KURT!” She turned sunburn red, threw her hands over her mouth and collapsed in involuntary laughter.

He laughed too. “Good thing there's a strong wind, huh?”

“God, you're such a . . . a . . . man!”

“Gotta relieve the pressure. Try it.”

“No!” She slapped him hard on the arm. “I can't.”

“Sure you can.” Before Paula knew what was happening, Kurt was out of his chair, leaning over her, tickling her mercilessly. “Oh no! Kurt! Stop! Stop!”

She tried to wiggle away from him, to hop out of her chair, but Kurt had her blocked. He proved to be a master tickler. “No! Please stop! Kurt! Stop! STOP!”

It ripped out of her, uncontrollably, not nearly as resplendent as Kurt's, but impressive just the same. She turned crimson and buried her face in her hands. Then she used both of them to beat Kurt.

He batted them away easily, laughing. “Well come on, don't you feel better?”

She was wiping away tears of laughter. “I feel mortified.”

“I don't even know what that means.”

“It means you're a horse's ass for making me do that. How humiliating.”

“That the first time you ever farted?”

“It's the first time I . . . did it in front of a man.”

“Really? What about around women?”

“We don't do that around each other.”

“No shit?”

“Stop it.” She giggled despite herself.

“Okay, so women don't fart, they don't belch, and they don't spit. How do they keep from blowing up?”

She tapped out a smoke and lit up. “Can we change the subject please?”

“Sure, but if you're honest with yourself, you'll admit you feel a lot better now.”

“Sounds like the same subject to me.”

“Okay, okay, what do you want to talk about?”

Paula threw her arms out expansively. “This. Curiosity Cove. You need to tell me how you managed to find this place, Mr. Younger."

"County had it up for auction."

"Foreclosure?"

"Kinda. Back taxes hadn't been paid. I was the only one to make a bid. Got it for a song."

"You make a habit of doing that?"

"What?"

"Capitalizing on other people's misfortune."

He grabbed his labels and a mimicked a backroom dandy. "I takes me gains where I finds ‘em, girly-o."

"Like me?"

"Damn right."

Paula considered that, wondering if she was just another bargain Kurt managed to pick up because the previous owner defaulted. She decided his motives didn’t matter. She belonged to herself now. Nobody owns me anymore. Not Bill. Not Kurt.

She drained her glass, then stuck it out rather defiantly. "More, please."

Kurt topped her off then draped an arm across her shoulder. “I think you like it here, Miss Doherty,” he said.

“I’ll say this, Mr. Younger, you sure know how to show a girl a good time. Whisk her off to your own private island resort. Stuff her with fattening food. Drown her in vintage champagne. And make love to her like a wild stallion."

Kurt smiled magnanimously. “My motto is, you gotta take the good with the good.”

Paula giggled and gave him a good-natured punch on the arm. “You just keep on being a rascal. That's really working for me right now.” She stood up, stretched. “Oh God, I’m stuffed. I’ve got to work some of this off. Care to join me for a swim?”

Kurt took the glass from her hand, encircled her in his arms. “No, but you can join me.” Paula looked at him quizzically. He said, “You like to snorkel?”

58

Paula helped Kurt clear the table. It required several trips straight through the house and each time they had to pass the closed door at the bottom of the stairs. When everything was put away and the dishes soaking, Paula said, "Okay Mr. Younger, it's time you showed me what's behind that closed door."

"You want to see what's behind the closed door?"

"My female curiosity demands it."

"You might not like it."

"I'll take my chances."

"Even though what you see might change your life forever?"

Paula guffawed. "In case you missed it, my life was changed forever last night, big guy."

"Point taken."

Kurt opened the door to a darkly paneled room almost as big as the main room but without its lofty ceiling due to the bedrooms directly overhead. Paula's wide-eyed expression revealed both surprise and disbelief.

The room was actually a private museum filled with countless military related treasures going back well over a thousand years, she was sure. There were displays of battle dress, including suits of armor. There were dioramas of famous military campaigns and paintings of warfare both on land and sea. There was every type of weaponry imaginable and so many other items that Paula couldn't take it all in with a single glance. "I'm . . . speechless."

"Bullshit. No woman is ever speechless."

She slapped him on the shoulder. "But . . . it doesn't make sense."

"Does it have to?"

"Yes, Kurt, it does. Out here on a secluded island? Hidden away from the world? Explain, please."

Kurt shrugged. "Can't. What you see here came with the house, like just about everything else. Before I bought the place, I checked courthouse records, talked to a few old-timers, and found out an Army General named Silas Winter built it in 1878. When he died it went to his estranged daughter who had never seen it and refused to pay taxes on it. After years of sitting here abandoned, the county got it. That's about all I know, except the General was a bit of a fanatic on military history."

Paula gawked. "Yeah, a bit. What an incredible collection." She regularly volunteered at several of Palm Beach's finest museums, including the one housing the Flagler collection. She had an appreciation for the quality and variety of the items spread out around her. She also appreciated its value. "This stuff must have cost a fortune, even back in the late 1800s. Could you get that rich in the military back then?"

"Doubt it. Probably built his fortune the only honorable way an officer could at the time. From his stinking rich family."

Paula noticed several busts of famous generals, works of art unto themselves. There was also an extensive library filled with a hundred or more leather-bound volumes. Among the artifacts were instruments used for punishment and torture. Cat o' nine tails. Bludgeons. Even a fully operational rack.

Paula smiled suggestively at Kurt. "Sure this room didn't have another use?"

Kurt ran his hand over the rack. "Why, want to try it out?"

"Sure. Hop on."

"Clever girl, you."

Paula laughed. "Do you have any idea what all this is worth?"

Kurt shrugged. "Not a clue."

"Two million dollars at least. Maybe more."

"Aw come on."

Paula shook her head in amazement. "Believe me, you're sitting on a gold mine. So what do you do in here?"

"See that nice leather armchair over there?"

Paula had already noticed it, along with the accompanying footstool, the side table, and the Tiffany reading lamp. "Yes. The lamp alone must be worth a couple of thousand."

"Okay, okay, put away your adding machine. See, I share the General's fascination with all things military." He plopped down in the chair, propped his feet on the footstool, ankles crossed. "So I hunker down in here from time to time, pull out one of those books over there, pour a healthy glass of Mr. Daniel's exceptional whiskey, fire up one of Cuba's finest, and read all about great battles and the strategies behind them. Never know when it might come in handy."

Paula walked over, sat in Kurt's lap. She draped her arms around his shoulders. "Kurt, honey, these are rare and important artifacts. They shouldn't be hidden away here. Let me see about placing them where they can be studied and properly displayed, you know, so everybody can enjoy them. Believe me, you'll be well compensated."

"Okay, my sweet. Whatever you think best. Its just stuff to me." He gave her his trademark roguish grin. "But not today. We got other things to do today."

59

Kurt had just finished stocking the *Black Jack's* cooler when Paula stepped into the boathouse dressed to kill. The scarf wrapped around her hair, the sunglasses, the high-heeled sandals, were all designer. They reeked of having just been purchased. The sleeveless cover-up was white with big splashes of color. It was gathered at the waist with a sash and gaped open to reveal a lot of Paula underneath.

Kurt grinned, thinking that with her long, slender legs rising up from those ridiculously high-heeled sandals, she looked like a filly prancing into a show arena.

Once outside the Cove, Kurt steered the craft southwest toward the Gulf, heading for a reef about twenty-five miles away. The picture postcard morning had given way to heat and glare and a milky white sky. They would have foul weather tonight. But his spirits were not dampened. His arm was wrapped around Paula's waist and they both were puffing on cigarettes. Something about salt air made tobacco especially heady. Kurt said, "I need a drink. Here, take the wheel."

Paula did and said, "Whatever you're fixing, make me one too." Kurt watched her check the heading, turning the wheel slightly to correct their course. She knew what she was doing. He mixed Bloody Marys, brought them topside, and was content to leave her in command all the way to the reef. When they arrived, Paula said, "Want to stay on this side of the reef, right?"

"Right. Water will be calmer. Find a spot about midway."

The coral mound was long and narrow. At some point it had acquired a crown of thin soil from which sprouted every imaginable variety of scrub brush. The water around it was so clear the boat seemed to be floating in space. Kurt moved to the bow, found a grassy spot of bottom where his anchor would be clear of the coral, and said, “This is good. Cut the engines."

"Roger dodger."

Kurt dropped anchor and made his way aft where Paula was waiting for him. The scarf, sunglasses, cover-up, and sandals had all disappeared. In their place were a few patches of cloth arranged strategically about her body

"Will that thing stay on in the water?"

Paula tossed him a snorkel mask. "Do you care?"

"No Ma'am," he said, and flipped backward into the water.

Paula found herself staring into startled eyes and large protuberant lips. She flicked her net out, but her reflexes were no match for the Nassau grouper, who simply changed color and darted away. She surfaced and pushed up her mask, trying to get her bearings.

"Hey."

Paula whirled around to see Kurt and the *Black Jack* bobbing within easy swimming distance. He glided over to her, a big grin on his face, looking like the overgrown boy that he was. She put her arms around his neck. "Thanks for bringing me here. It's wonderful."

"Caught anything yet?"

"Yeah, my swimsuit, on a piece of coral. How about you?"

"Nothing worth keeping. Tired?"

"Not at all."

"Good. Follow me, I want to show you something."

And he was gone.

Paula repositioned her mask then dropped back underwater. In doing so, she was magically traversed from one universe to another. Spread out below her was an exotic, gently swaying jungle of electric colors.

A school of herring passed beneath. Paula took a deep breath and dove down into them. The shimmering silver curtain opened gracefully, allowing her passage. Neat. She threw her arms out and soared through liquid space, watching in fascination as her shadow weaved through a big anemone then danced over coral castles. She arched up, gliding near enough to the surface to use her snorkel again. Kurt was not far away, beckoning her to follow.

This was a Kurt she had never seen before. He was the quintessential boy-man, brave, resourceful, protective. He was Peter Pan flying off to foil Captain Hook. Paula felt like a little girl again. Go ahead, Kurt, you be Peter Pan. I'll be your faithful Wendy.

She lunged toward him. But as she drew near, Kurt filled his lungs then dropped out of sight behind a coral ridge. Beyond the ridge was a dark blue void into which all the wiggling sea creatures faded away. Paula filled her lungs and pushed downward, jack-knifing over the ridge to find a steep wall of coral descending to the ocean floor a good fifty feet below.

Now where the hell did Kurt go? She was about to head back up when Kurt darted out of nowhere, took her hand, and led her to a cave cut deep in the coral.

So this was what Peter Pan wanted to show her. Captain Hook's ship buried down here in Davy Jones' locker. Well, a ship anyway, a small schooner lodged inside the cave. It was broken nearly in half.

Judging by the quantity of marine life that now claimed it as home, Paula guessed the vessel had been there for quite some time. It had an eerie feeling about it, like an old abandoned house on a moonless night, except spookier. Leave it to Kurt to find something like this. She watched him give the helm a turn. Amazingly, the rudder flopped back and forth. She fully expected Kurt to sail it right out of the cave, up out of the water, and into the clouds.

They surfaced gasping and laughing then Kurt played tour guide to other underwater wonders, hoping to find treasure for Pappy's collection, but coming up empty handed. Later they picnicked on the boat, guzzled more champagne, took turns slathering each other with suntan lotion, but mostly they just talked.

It was easy, random conversation, not really about anything in particular, just whatever came to their minds. Paula was surprised that Kurt seemed genuinely interested in her tales of motherhood and domesticity. He laughed freely and often, clearly enjoyed hearing about a part of life he had never experienced. They snorkeled a little more then headed back to Curiosity Cove. Paula considered it one of the most enjoyable days she'd spent in a very long time.

As they made their way back across the Gulf, towering blue-black thunderheads gathered and the wind stiffened until the water was choppy. Kurt knew they were in for a pretty bad storm and was glad when the entrance to Curiosity Cove was in sight. He throttled back, then noticed something leap from the water directly in front of the bow.

"Look, it's Wally," said Paula, laughing. "He's going to lead us in."

Soon they were in the dark, winding channel. Kurt visibly relaxed.

Home.

Safe.

60

While Kurt and Paula were cruising down the main channel, Red and his team were tying up near the back channel where it poured out into the Bay. The sky was getting dark and angry and the wind was spoiling for a fight.

Good, Red thought. Wind and rain -- only minutes away at best -- would provide excellent cover for their advance. His ears pricked when he heard the lug-lug-lug of the *Black Jack* crossing the lagoon.

“Okay, that's them just gettin' in,” he said to Gator and Earl in a very loud whisper. “It'll take 'em a few minutes to secure the boat then head up to the house. They won’t be staying outside with this storm whipping up.” He checked his watch. “We'll hold here another ten minutes then start our advance.”

The dynamic of the group was not what Earl had imagined. It was clear Red was the head honcho and Gator was his second in command. Earl was relegated to little more than lackey. When he pointed this out to Red, all he got in response was, “Just do your fucking job. You still get the payout and you still get your turn with the girl.”

Gator couldn’t resist needling Earl. “Being a lackey's okay. Being a clown ain’t. Being a clown’ll get you killed.”

Earl thought about that a moment, then asked, “How?”

Gator locked eyes with him. “Because I'll kill you.”

“Oh.”

Gator was confident he wouldn't have to do that. He knew Red would do it for him. As soon as the mission was completed and they had the loot, Red would slit the big oaf's throat, then dump his body in the Bay to start a new coral reef.

He was confident Red would try to do the same thing to him, not being a great believer in share and share alike. The difference was, Earl wasn't expecting it. Gator was. The more he thought about it, the more he was absolutely convinced only one of them would leave the island alive this afternoon. He was determined to be that person.

Red raised a fist. “Okay, move in. Now remember, stay behind me. I've got to neutralize the alarm triggers as we go. I know where they are. So stay behind me. And stay alert.”

Fine, Gator thought. Behind you is where I intend to stay. As he followed Red footfall for footfall, he devised a plan for taking the big goon out. His plans for Kurt and his girlfriend were a bit different than Red's. Yes, he'd make Kurt watch him do her, just like he had to watch Kurt do his girl. But Red and Earl wouldn't get their turns. They'd already be dead.

But that wasn't even the best part. When he had finished taking his pleasure, he would say to Kurt that he had to go now and that he was taking the girl with him. From now on she’d belong to him, be his sex slave, do his every bidding.

He would even let her kiss Kurt goodbye, give them all the time they wanted to cry and say their farewells. Then he would make her step aside while he unsheathed his Bowie knife and cut Kurt in such a way that he would bleed out. Very slowly.

He’d snap to attention, give Kurt a smart salute, throw his head back, and laugh uproariously. Then he would tie the girl's wrists behind her, loop a leash around her neck and lead her away. That would be the last thing Kurt Younger would ever see.

Rain came thundering down in buckets. It was like standing under a waterfall. They heard the woman yell out playfully, “Oh great. Now you’ve made it rain. You happy? And it’s cold rain, dammit.”

It was, too. Loud, like a timpani roll. That was to their advantage. They could do a pratfall worthy of Charlie Chaplain and nobody would be able to hear them. Which was good because that's just what Earl did.

Red and Gator immediately squatted low, weapons at the ready. Embarrassed, Earl tried to scramble up but Gator put an arm against his back and held him flat. He put his lips to Earl's ear. “Easy. Just stay low.”

Earl nodded, then glanced over at Red, who was giving him the kind of look that would make a cobra run for its life.

From the cover of wind-whipped foliage, they watched Kurt and his woman make out in the rain like a couple of teenagers. Lightning flashed, then thunder shook the ground, much like a tank round. The woman squealed and ran for the verandah, Kurt close on her heels. Once they were there, Kurt magically removed the top of her swimming suit, what little there was of it.

Seeing the gorgeous red head standing there topless made Gator's mouth drop open. “Holy mother of God.”

Red grinned at him and said, “Wha'd I tell ya?”

“Seein' is believin'.”

“You a believer now?”

"Makes me want to get on my knees and give thanks."

"Later. Right now we gotta keep them in sight. Move out, slow and easy." To Earl he said, "Think you can manage to stay on your feet?"

"Yes sir."

"Lets go."

61

As Kurt and Paula walked up from the boathouse, thunder rolled across the bay, echoed through the channel, then played out over the lagoon. The deteriorating weather didn't seem to bother Wally. He performed a series of back flips, wanting to play.

Paula was in high spirits too. She veered away from Kurt and walked out onto the pier. Kurt followed. Wally was waiting, chattering incessantly. He nodded at them to join him in the water. Paula kneeled down and laughed at his antics. "You can stop showing off, you clown."

Wally got close enough for Paula to hug him. "Sorry fella, we're not getting back in the water today. Come back tomorrow."

Tomorrow. It made Kurt cringe. This time tomorrow Red would be dead and Kurt knew it wouldn't be a pleasant death. This time tomorrow Curiosity Cove would be history. They would never again see this place that Paula had fallen in love with, the place she thought would be her new home. This time tomorrow she would be unconscious, drugged by Kurt's hand. He looked at her happy, carefree face, her sparkling eyes, and wanted to throw up.

Paula noticed his reaction. She draped her arms around his neck. Motioning toward the sky she said, "Hey, you know where these dark clouds are coming from?"

Kurt did his best to appear carefree and happy, too. He missed it by a mile. "I give up. Where?"

"You." She took his hand and led him toward the house. "Come on, loosen up. Everything's great. You should be happy about that." She made big eyes and touched the tip of her nose to the tip of his. "Look at me, I'm happy about that. How about you, Wally? You happy about that?" Wally chattered at them, bobbing his head up and down. Paula bobbed hers up and down in imitation. "See, Wally's happy."

It started to rain, not sporadically but a deluge. Paula pushed away from Kurt, threw her arms out in mock exasperation. "Oh great. Now you've made it rain. You happy?" She shivered. "And it's cold rain, dammit."

It seemed to do the trick. Kurt transformed back into the rascal she loved. Once again he was looking at her like a lion ready to rip her apart. His lips found hers and all the fiery passion was back. Yeah, that's more like it, she thought. She drew him tighter against her.

Lightning flashed, followed by a sharp clap of thunder. Paula jumped, said, "Whoops," and rolled free of Kurt. The two of them ran onto the verandah, laughing.

Kurt grabbed Paula and spun her around. By the time she caught her balance, her top was dangling from his hand. "Boy, you're really good at that."

"Lots of practice."

"I'll bet. Here, you might as well have the rest." She slipped off her bottoms, tossed them at him. She stood with hands on hips. "Happy?"

"Awestruck."

"I'll settle for that. Now come with me. Make yourself useful."

"Let me crank up the generator first."

When Kurt returned she led him up to the tub on the balcony. "Lots of hot water, please."

Kurt nodded and turned on the taps.

Paula jerked his trunks down. "Won't need these." She tossed them on the railing. "Wow. That thing ever go down?"

"Not when you're around."

"Amazing apparatus." She put her hands together under her chin like a little girl saying her evening prayers. "Thank you dear God for making penises." She glanced down at his and said, "Especially great big ones like that. Amen."

She reached down, grabbed his erect penis, and shook it. "Hi. I'm Paula. Glad to make your acquaintance."

A few minutes later they were both immersed up to their chins in steamy water, smoking leisurely. Paula inhaled deeply then said, "See. All better now."

Above them, rain drummed on the tin roof, accompanied occasionally by kettle drums of thunder. Wind rushed through the surrounding foliage, slapping leaves together, making a sound like distant applause. The water in the lagoon appeared to have kicked into wash cycle. Wally had taken his leave.

Paula's eyes were closed, her head laid back against the rim of the tub. She groaned, lost in the sensuousness of the moment. "What luxury." She stretched like a pampered feline, then folded her arms on the edge of the tub, and rested her chin on them. She gazed lazily out at the lagoon. "I'm crazy about your kingdom, Mr. Younger. Even in the rain."

It was the opening Kurt was waiting for. "Yeah, kinda gotten attached to the place myself." He added casually, "Gonna miss it."

Paula sat upright. "Miss it? What do you mean?"

"Sorry, my love, but as of tomorrow Curiosity Cove will no longer be mine. I've sold it."

Kurt was surprised by the look in Paula's eyes, as if he had betrayed her.

"Oh Kurt, why? It's so perfect. It's so you." She was momentarily at a loss for words, then added, "Where will you live?"

"You mean, where will *we* live."

Paula's only response was a puzzled expression.

"Have you forgotten the promise I made you last Saturday night? I said we were going to have one hell of a life together. I meant it. It starts tomorrow. Our new life together. Our new home."

Paula shook her head in bewilderment. "New home?"

"Spain. The Greek Isles. The south of France. North of France too, if you prefer."

The response of joy and excitement Kurt was expecting from Paula did not materialize. Instead, she lowered her head thoughtfully and settled back in the tub. "Oh, I see."

They were quiet for a while. The rain thickened until the lagoon was no longer visible, except during brief flashes of lightning. The roar of the downpour combined with its density, made Kurt feel claustrophobic. The fact that it was getting darker didn't help.

Paula shifted around in the tub and leaned back against Kurt. "Hold me," she said. Kurt wrapped his arms around her. She laid her head back against his shoulder. "Feels good to be in your arms."

Kurt kissed her cheek. "It's where you belong."

Paula turned her face up to him so he could kiss her properly. "I love you, Kurt. I wasn't sure of that a week ago. You wanted to hear me say it. I did, hoping you'd make love to me. But I wasn't sure I really loved you. Now I know I do love you. I've loved you for a long time. Only, for a long time I had to convince myself it was all about sex and nothing else. Because that was the only way I could justify what I was doing."

Kurt wasn't expecting that. "Justify?"

"I mean, if I didn't love you, I wasn't betraying my husband or breaking my vows. No, don't try to understand it, it's a female logic thing."

"Female logic. Isn't that an oxy . . . Whadya call it?"

"Oxymoron. Probably." She took another drag on her cigarette. "Jerk." She kissed him before continuing. "Anyway, I got to thinking about what that said about me. I knew it was all wrong because I'm not like that. I'm not a sex craved hussy."

Kurt raised an eyebrow. "No, I'm really not, Kurt. But I most definitely am a sucker for love. I love to love. I love being in love. I love making love. To you, I mean. You make it so damn sexy. You just get inside me and . . ."

Paula threw her arms out and made an explosion sound. "Lets just say you make me glad I'm a woman."

Kurt laughed. He squeezed her tighter, saying, "I'm pretty happy about that too."

"I know you are, sweetheart, but you're going to have to put that hand someplace else or I'm not going to be able to finish saying what I've got to say."

"A thousand pardons, your highness. Please continue."

Paula took a deep breath. She turned slightly to look Kurt straight in the eyes. "I'm not going to live with you in Europe."

62

"That fucking Kurt." Red's voice was slightly above a whisper as he watched through high-power binoculars. "Got a tub up on the top deck. Both of 'em are in it." He snickered. "Here, take a look." He handed the binoculars to Gator.

They were positioned about sixty yards behind the house in thick foliage. The torrential downpour made visibility sketchy but it also provided cover for them. They still had to stay concealed behind trees knowing a blast of lightning could occur any moment. When it did, it'd pick them out like a spotlight in a prison yard.

Gator took the binoculars and had to restrain himself from gasping. This woman was movie star gorgeous and not the least bit self-conscious lounging naked in the tub with Kurt. Gator ducked when she turned toward him, but not before seeing those incredible eyes of hers, sparkling like polished jewels. No doubt about it, she was prime cut. Knowing she would soon belong to him made Gator hard.

Come on, baby, sit up a little. Let me see those big mamas of yours. As if hearing him, the woman sat up, then reached her hands behind her head to fuss with her hair. It was everything Gator had hoped for. "Unfuckingbelievable."

"Okay, okay, that's enough," Red said, taking the binoculars back.

"Can I see?" Earl said.

"Shut up," Red said as he stowed the binoculars in his pack.

"Sorry sir."

"Looks like they'll be busy for a while so lets get moving. Lots to do."

They took a wide route to the front of the house where they would be out of view, then eased onto the verandah. Red put his arms on Gator and Earl like a quarterback in a huddle. "Alright men, we start upstairs in the bedroom then work our way down."

He slapped them on the back and the three split apart. Red noticed that Earl not only looked like a walrus, he moved like one, with the attendant rolling blubber. He had turned out to be a bad choice. Too late to do anything about that.

Red grabbed Earl by his chins and forced him to look into his nightmare inducing eyes. "Now you listen closely to what I say. Walk forward only. Look where you're going. Make damn sure you know what's in front of you before you take a step. You knock over a chair or lamp and the element of surprise will be gone. You clear on that?"

The scornful looks on Red and Gator's faces made Earl's face burn. "I been on a mission before. I know what to do."

Red put his face so close to Earl's that their noses were touching. "Are you clear on that?"

Earl instinctively backed away. He bumped into Gator, who was standing directly behind him, smirking. "Yes sir," he mumbled.

They removed their boots and climbed the outside stairs on stockinged feet. Even with the noise of the storm, they heard Kurt and the woman talking. She was doing most of the talking.

Earl was so terrified he almost pissed himself. He wished he had never met Red, that he had never agreed to do this job. God, how'd he get into this mess? Most of all he was dreading when it was his turn with the woman. He'd never had much success with women. Despite the bluster, the truth was, they scared the shit out of him. They usually laughed at him and made fun of his awkward ways. When it was his turn, what if . . .

Red slapped him hard and he forgot all about women.

"You need to snap out of it or I swear to God I'll slit your throat right where you're standing." Red turned to address both of them. "Each of you knows your job. Lets do it."

Red's warning still echoed in Earl's head. Yeah, you're gonna slit my throat anyway, he thought. That was your game plan all along. How stupid you think I am? He thought about that a moment then said, pretty damn stupid. Or else I wouldn't be here. A chill ran through him. His muscles went limp, his throat dry. He told himself he better quit being scared and figure a way out of this mess. If he didn't he'd be dead.

But how could he take out both Red and Gator? He needed some kind of advantage over them. But what? They were both bigger, meaner, smarter, and more experienced than him. He tried to focus on his job but he knew he had to think of something fast or he was a dead man.

Then it hit him. The one advantage he had. It wasn't much, but it might save his life. He breathed easier. It was going to be okay. He smiled to himself. Red and Gator were the idiots and didn't even know it. They were dead men walking.

As for Kurt, if he handed over the emeralds, Earl would let him live. He had nothing against Kurt except resentment for being everything he'd never be. He'd let Kurt keep the woman, too. Earl gazed at the picture of her he was holding. In it she was naked and had a wanton look in her eyes. And oh my God those tits. What he wouldn't give to just touch them; see how she reacted when he did. That's all he wanted from her. Surely Kurt would understand.

Red interrupted his thoughts by yelling at him in a hoarse whisper. "Come on shithead, get movin' or I'll cut your balls off and stuff 'em down your throat."

Earl said, "Yes sir," then turned away from Red so he couldn't see his devilish smile.

63

It was stated simply and unemotionally, but to Kurt it was like a mortar round to the heart. He tried to recover, but the only reply he was capable of was a feeble, "Say again?"

"I'm not going to live with you in Europe, Kurt."

Kurt said nothing. Paula studied his reaction carefully. He wasn't angry, just hurt. And confused. The look on his face broke her heart, which made her own face contort into sobs. Tears sprung loose and cascaded down her cheeks.

She threw her arms around his neck and hugged him, "Oh Kurt. Dammit Kurt, I love you so much. You own all the love I'm capable of giving to any man. Do you understand?"

Kurt held her tight and said, "Baby, my head is spinning like a cyclone. I don't understand a damn thing." He took her by the shoulders, moved her back to look into her eyes, "Except I love you, Paula, like I've never loved another human being. Whatever this is, we can deal with it. But you gotta explain it to me."

She kissed him warmly on the lips and there were salty tears mixed in with it. "Okay, okay, I'll try." She sniffed, swallowed hard. "Last Saturday you told me the life I had been living was a lie. You were right. I ran away from that lie and into your arms because I'm a woman who has to have love in my life. Last Saturday when you told me you loved me, I was shocked, Kurt. I really was."

"You thought it was just a line." He fired up another Camel.

"I thought you wanted one thing only from me and . . ." She gave a little self-deprecating chuckle. "That was okay with me. Or so I thought. Later in the week I realized you and I had been living a lie, too. We loved each other but pretended it was all about sex. I was getting screwed over in my marriage and pretending it was about love. Funny, isn't it?"

"Not at all."

Paula took his hand in both of hers. “Kurt I’m not going to marry you because I’ve done that and I don’t want to do it anymore. I'm not going to have any more children. I don’t need your financial support. So what's the point? I’m not going to live with you either or be dependent on you because I’ve got to know I can depend on myself. I’m not going to live in Europe or anywhere else because I’m going to live in my mother’s house in Key Largo, the house I grew up in. Does that make sense?”

Kurt laughed mirthlessly. “That's the problem, baby. It makes too much sense.”

“My mother won’t be around much longer. That's just a fact and it can't be changed. What little time she has left, I’m going to be there for her. Even though she doesn’t know who I am. Birdy, the woman who looks after her, is getting pretty old herself and needs my help. But even if she didn’t, it’s my mother. My responsibility.”

“I understand.”

“When she passes, the house will be mine. I’ll be happy there and I’ll be happy in Key Largo too, because I love the Keys. I love the way people live in the Keys. I love their free spirits. From now on I’m going to be a free spirit, too.”

“Never known you to be otherwise.”

She was struck by what that said about how Kurt perceived her. She knew her face glowed with pride, she could feel it. She laughed. “No, I guess you haven't. Neat.” She gave him his hand back then wiped a tear from her cheek. “There's something else, too.”

Kurt had already figured out the path she was going down. “Your son?”

“Yes. Billy. Yesterday I did something that made him love and adore me . . . For a few minutes, anyway. That'll vanish quicker than a co-eds panties when he finds out I've left his father. So I've got a lot of work to do there. I can't do it if I'm not close by. Certainly can't do it if I'm in Europe or somewhere far away.”

“No, of course not. If you could abandon your son, you wouldn't be the woman I love. Forgive me for being so self-centered not to consider that.”

“Thank you, Kurt. So . . .” She took a deep breath, gave Kurt her most radiant smile. “I lifted enough money out of my and Bill's joint account to make a start for myself.”

“A start? At what?”

“I’m going to take the little boat decorating business I started back in Palm Beach and make it into a big business here in the Keys. That’s what I do, for your information. I dress up people’s boats with pictures of swaying palms and game fish leaping out of the water and mermaids playing with sea creatures -- things like that. My mermaids are quite popular. I make sure they’re very well endowed.”

“Like you?”

She laughed. “Yep. Just like me. You’d like them. I've already decided how I'm going to decorate your boat. It's very, very naughty.”

“Do I get a special rate?”

“I bet we can work something out in trade.” She paused, then said, “Kurt, this is my chance to see what I’m made of and I’m pretty excited about that. Maybe you don’t understand those feelings, but your whole life you’ve done whatever you damn well pleased. I admire you for that. It’s you being you. For me, well, I’m going to have to make it up as I go along.”

Kurt chuckled, ran a hand through her hair. “My bet's on you. You'll do okay.”

“Yes, I will. So I’m not going to marry you and I’m not going to shack up with you either. Besides, you and I both know it wouldn’t work. You’re not the settling down type.”

Paula took his big hands and placed them firmly on her breasts. “You’re a rogue, Kurt Younger, and I love you for being a rogue. Don't you ever stop being a rogue. But a rogue can’t be tied down. I don’t want you to be tied down. I don’t want either of us to be tied down. Especially to each other. I don’t want there ever to be any ties between us but love.”

She kissed him again, a lingering kiss that was warm and moist. “And when you need to leave to do whatever it is you do -- and I hope you’ll never tell me what that is -- that’ll be okay, too. You’ll come back to me in Key Largo. To my home. And when you do, you can have your way with me all you want as long as I can have my way with you. And we’ll play together and we’ll laugh together and we’ll make wild, passionate love. Okay?”

Paula’s smile was so dazzling that he had to swallow the lump in his throat. Never before in his life had anybody, man or woman, put a lump in his throat. “If that’s the way you want it, my love.”

Rain roared, wind howled, darkness closed in around them. But in the darkness, Paula’s eyes were smoldering emeralds that penetrated deep into Kurt’s newly discovered soul.

“That’s the way I want it. Is that the way you want it?” This time when she kissed him she leaned in tight to make maximum skin contact. “I hope it is, lover.” He was hard between her legs. “Come on, say it.” Her voice was husky, feral.

Kurt felt helpless, a feeling he wasn’t accustomed to. This raw, primal force within Paula was something he had no defense against, no training to combat. That she was applying it instinctively, guilelessly, made it all the more potent. His voice was coarse, almost a growl. “What do you want me to say?”

“You know.” She smiled shrewdly. Kurt brought his cigarette up, but Paula snatched it from his fingers and tossed it out into the rain. “Say you love me.”

Kurt combed Paula's hair with his fingers. She purred like a cat being stroked. She kissed his lips, his nose, his eyes. "Say it."

"Already have."

"Say it again."

"I love you."

"Damn right you do."

She rose up on her knees, arched her back, brushed her breasts against his face, saying, "You go live in Europe if that's what you want. But if what you want is me . . ." She lowered onto him, said, "Oh God," and grabbed his shoulders to brace herself. Her breath hissed out like steam from a kettle. "If what you want is me, I'll be in Key Largo."

She rocked up and down on Kurt, crying out and taking him deeper with each stroke. "Am I what you want, Kurt?"

Kurt was searching desperately to find a way to regain control but the passion she was stirring within him was blotting out all other thoughts, all reason.

"Am I what you want?" Paula said again, the urgency in her voice intensifying as her motions quickened. "Say you want me."

Kurt was puffing like a bull about to charge.

"Say you want me."

"I want you, dammit." He kneaded her breasts roughly and she took his hands away, pinned them behind his head.

"Yes you damn well do." Her breathing was labored, her voice almost a scream. "Yes you do, Kurt. Yes you do."

Kurt growled, felt the eruption building.

"Say it again," Paula screamed.

"I want you," he snarled.

"Yes, yes, say it again."

"I want you."

And the eruption came, for both of them.

Paula collapsed against Kurt and he wrapped his arms around her. They stayed that way for a while, catching their breaths. Paula raised her head and gazed at him starry-eyed. "God Kurt, you really ring my bell."

64

Paula and Kurt were wrapped in the extra big, extra fluffy towels he kept stacked near the tub as they walked round the balcony to the bedroom. For Kurt, it was one of the longest journeys of his life. Time slipped out of gear while he pondered the implications of Paula's 'declaration of independence'.

The most difficult part to accept was the rationality behind it. It was reasoned. It was honest. It was bullet proof. It was totally unexpected. Paula had brilliantly left no room for argument. She did it while displaying devotion, love, and passion for him. At the same time, she used his overwhelming love for her to render him virtually impotent. It was a strategy built around human emotional components he had little experience with. She used them more effectively than he had ever used a machine gun or grenade. And she did it while she was naked. It was all the weaponry she needed.

But that didn't change the fact that he now found himself in one hell of a dilemma. Without making Paula aware of it, much less consulting with her about it, he'd set a plan in motion that couldn't be stopped. A fatal plan. Now, not only was his life in danger, so was Paula's.

God, how did he let this happen? Kurt Younger. The master planner. Leader of men. Not just men, but dogs of war. Vicious, ruthless men. Kurt Younger. The man other men trusted to flawlessly orchestrate a mission then bring them back alive.

Now, his carefully planned operation was collapsing like a trapping pit cover and he was falling helplessly into the deadly darkness below. For the first time in his life, Kurt was staring into the face of eminent failure. The fact that the face had green eyes and flaming red hair made it even more mind numbing.

As they entered the bedroom through the French doors, Kurt was trying desperately to think of a way out of the mess he'd created. Paula looked at him with love and trust. What would she think of him if she knew what he'd planned?

Outside, the storm raged on unabated, but storms were a part of life in the Keys. This one was not nearly as bad as some they had experienced. It was nowhere near hurricane force. But it echoed the dark turmoil he was feeling inside himself.

He was determined to keep Paula from seeing it.

She sat on the edge of the bed, humming happily as she used the towel she'd just peeled off to dry her hair. Kurt snatched the towel away and took over the job, somewhat more rigorously than she would have done it. That was okay with Paula. Anything less wouldn't have been Kurt. She closed her eyes and just enjoyed being pampered.

Once again Kurt had proven himself to be the man she'd always believed him capable of being. She had just given herself to him without reservation, without conditions, without strings. Herself being the operative word. Who she was. Not who he thought she should be. He was man enough to accept her on those terms and to realize she was doing the same for him.

It made her happy to a degree she hadn't experienced since childhood. A warm glow grew in her heart then spread outward. She was completely at peace with herself, with Kurt, with the entire world. It made her somewhat giddy.

It was in that mood that she blurted, "Can't decide what I'll wear tonight."

Kurt tossed the towel on a chair. "Why wear anything?"

"Because, Kurt darling, 'familiarity breeds contempt, while rarity wins admiration'."

"Yeah?" Kurt nuzzled his face between her breasts. "If having the finest caviar and most expensive champagne every day breeds contempt, call me contemptible. Wow, what an echo."

Paula pushed him away. "Uh-uh, don't get my motor started." She stepped over to the closet, retrieved one of her suitcases, and opened it on the bed. "Besides, I bought this whole new wardrobe the other day," she said playfully. "I'm dying to start dazzling you with it." She glanced around the room. "How very neat that you have a dressing screen in here."

"Like everything else, it came with the house."

Paula grabbed a few items from the suitcase then disappeared behind the screen. Kurt asked, "Why the modesty all of a sudden?"

"Undressing in front of you is very sexy, Kurt Younger. But watching me getting dressed is like watching sausage being made. Better you don't see that."

Better you don't see what's going through my mind, he thought. It was like a Chinese tangram puzzle. Theoretically solvable, but in reality the solution was inexplicable.

A few minutes later Paula stepped from behind the screen, striking a Suzy Parker pose. “Tah-dah.” She wore pedal pushers trimmed with gold fringe at the bottom. The design was very festive -- seashells, starfish, sailboats -- all rendered in a splashy, modern style.

Rubber-soled canvas loafers adorned her feet. Topside she wore a loose beige pullover with a white slash that started wide at her shoulder then diminished to a point at her waist. The neck gaped open enough to bare a shoulder, a black bra strap, and just a hint of cleavage.

She added earrings made of miniature pieces of fruit, all strung together on a gold chain. When she saw them at Mermaid Boutique, they made her laugh. They were the perfect finishing touch. She put her fists on her hips saucily. “Say it. You're thoroughly dazzled.”

Kurt laughed. “Lady, you definitely got style.”

“I'll settle for that. And excuse me mister, but you need to don some duds yourself. I need to remember what you look like with clothes on.”

“Fair enough.” He threw on khaki Bermuda shorts, leather moccasins, and a floral print island shirt. He let the shirt hang open, exposing a great expanse of hairy chest.

While he dressed, Paula said, “I do believe that wherever the sun is, it's well over the yardarm. Cocktail time, Mr. Younger. Why don't I go downstairs and rustle us up some drinks. Black Daniels on the rocks for you, right?”

“Make it stiff.”

“Yes sir.”

She pranced out of the bedroom then slammed to a halt at the head of the stairs. Everywhere she looked were large photographs of her and Kurt making love the previous night. Sickeningly explicit photographs.

Her heart caught. It took her a moment to find her voice.

“KURT!”

65

She was penetrated repeatedly, violently, and in ways she never imagined possible. Now she was having trouble even standing up. She was naked. Her breasts ached. Her nipples felt as if wasps had stung them. She was sure her vagina was a bloody pulp.

As she stood there, no longer feeling beautiful, no longer feeling sexy, just painfully naked, she knew there was probably more to come. Worse, she was incapable of stopping it. She'd just have to take it if she was going to get through this.

The thought of that made her tremble. How did this happen? This was not part of her carefully devised scenario. She thought she was completely in control. But now . . .

Why had he done this to her?

To make matters worse, the biggest gun she had ever seen was pointed right at her face. There was a couple of metallic clicks. The cylinder rotated a notch.

"Beaut, ain't it? Exact replica of Wyatt Earp's Buntline Special. Called the Peacemaker. As in eternal peace."

Betty gasped. "Bill, sweetie, is that thing loaded?"

He threw his head back, laughing. "Would I be pointing at you if it was?" He lowered the weapon to his side. "Naw, just wanted you to see what the outlaws saw just before their heads were blown off."

"I don't much care for guns. And with my kids moving in soon -- they will be moving in soon, right darling?"

Bill returned the gun to its case. "Sure they will. Won't be long at all. Told you that already."

"I know, I know, but with the kids here, we'll need to make real sure your guns are locked away safely, won't we? I never knew you had so many of them."

"Any man who's been through war knows a gun is his best friend. It's a bad old world out there, Betty. But don't you worry. I'll make sure your kids are protected."

Yes, Betty thought, but who'll protect me?

Outside, Tropical Storm Judith was howling, pushing patio furniture around. It had been like that all day, forcing them to stay inside. It was an unpleasant situation for Betty. Bill was only interested in one indoor activity.

She never dreamed Bill had such a voracious sexual appetite. All night. All day. And after they finished a session, experimenting with yet another new position, he would get hard again in a matter of minutes. Ready to go. It was unnatural.

They'd had anal sex three times now. She guessed she was going to have to learn to like it. They'd had sex missionary style, doggy style, tied up spread-eagle in bed style. They'd had joint oral sex, which she kind of liked. They'd done it sideways, upside down, him on top, her on top. Variety was the name of the game. Now he had that look in his eyes again, moving toward her, his intentions clear.

Betty backed away, cringing. "Ding, ding, ding, ding."

Bill stopped in his tracks, puzzled.

She made a referee's signal with her hands. "Time out, baby. I gotta put an ice pack on my you-know-what, you sadistic brute." She said it with a twinkle in her eye, wagging her finger at him like a mother scolding an errant child.

Bill was clearly disappointed. "But you said anything . . ."

"I know, honey, I know, but haven't we done everything you wanted? Many, many times? I mean, even that big old printing press has to be shut down occasionally so it can rest and be oiled and everything. And it's a whole lot bigger and tougher than I am."

Bill laughed at that. "Okay, so you need a lube job?"

"I need to eat, Bill. We haven't eaten all day."

"Great idea. Why don't we trying doing it while we're eating?"

"Because you'd just make me have another great big 'O' and I'd probably choke to death."

"Well, we can't have that." He slapped her on the rump. "You still got a lotta good miles in ya yet."

She kissed him on the nose. "You betcha and I want to make sure I perform my best for you. All right?"

"Okay, okay." He slapped his belly. "Come to think of it, I'm kinda hungry myself. I think there're steaks in the fridge. Lets see what kind of cook you are."

"Not till I throw on some clothes. I don't want hot grease splattering on my bare skin. Damage the merchandise."

Bill yawned and plopped down on a nearby chair. “God, women are complicated. All right, you go throw something on. I'll fix drinks. What would you like?”

Betty headed toward the bedroom, saying, “I think beer goes best with steaks.”

“Good idea. Beer it is. And bring my robe when you come back, will ya?”

“Sure, honey.”

When she got to the bedroom she fell on her knees and indulged in a sob-fest from the depths of her soul. It's worth it, she kept telling herself. Its just sex. Toughen up. You can take it. Then all this will be yours. He's already done things to you that you can have him locked up for. It won't be long now. Get the rock on your finger. Get the preacher to make him say 'I do'. Get the kids situated in this house. Get everything set in place. Wait for the right moment.

Then strike.

66

From the instant Kurt saw the photographs, it took him less than a second to comprehend what was happening, then only a half-second to react. He immediately grabbed Paula's wrist and almost yanked her off her feet. He ran with her back to the bedroom.

Gator was waiting for them.

Paula screamed but Kurt didn't flinch, much less slow down. He plowed into Gator with all the force of a defensive tackle, lifting him off his feet, driving him out the French door, across the balcony, then hefting him over the railing. He didn't linger to see how Gator landed. He yelled at a wide-eyed Paula, “Stay with me.”

The two of them scurried down the outside stairs to the verandah then rounded the corner to the front of the house just in time to see Earl burst through the door, submachine gun in hand. Paula screamed, “Oh God,” but again Kurt didn't hesitate. He slammed his fist into Earl's face with the force of a pile driver, stripping the M2 from his hands as he was thrown back against a porch post, cracking it.

Paula had never seen anybody hit that hard before. She had never seen blood explode like a watermelon hit with a Louisville Slugger. The angry wind caught the blood and splattered it onto her new pullover. And her face.

Everything was happening too fast for Paula. She didn’t know what to do other than keep yelling, “Oh God, oh God, oh God . . .”

Just when Kurt was about to hit the man again, yet another man appeared behind him, one of the biggest, meanest looking men Paula had ever seen. He spun Kurt around and threw a vicious punch right into his jaw.

Kurt stumbled back; dropping the gun, then fell backward against the railing. Before he recovered, the big man grabbed Kurt and shoved him over. He fell about four feet to the ground below. Paula screamed, then scrambled down the steps to his side. She was instantly drenched in the deluge. Kurt struggled to regain consciousness. They both heard the snickering laughter from above.

The big goon with the clumps of red hair leaned casually over the railing. “I owed you that one, partner.”

Paula helped Kurt, still woozy, to his feet, saying, “Honey, you okay?”

The rain was effective in washing the blood from Kurt's nose. His eyes were filled with deep remorse. “I am so damn sorry, Paula. I never wanted you to know about this. I never wanted you to be involved.”

“Know about what?” Paula's head was spinning. This all had to be a nightmare. She'd wake up in a moment. Her thoughts were interrupted by the man Kurt had thrown off the balcony limping around the side of the house, holding his shoulder with one hand. In his other was a very big knife. His boots and vest were made of alligator skin. He was not a happy man.

Paula looked from one man to the other, then to Kurt. This was all too crazy. In a near-hysterical voice, she said, “Kurt, I don't understand what's going on here.”

Again the big man on the verandah snickered. “Well honey, we're gonna see if we can't straighten things out for you.”

The man in alligator boots stopped face to face with Kurt. Their eyes locked and the naked hatred that consumed both men was so fierce it made Paula flinch.

Kurt said, “Gator, you steaming pile of shit. What're you doing here?”

Gator put his face even closer to Kurt. “I'm gonna do to you what you did to me.” His eyes ran over Paula from head to toe, then he grinned maliciously. In a lightning move, he lashed out with his knife, slicing Kurt across the chest.

Paula screamed, “Stop it! Oh my God!” She pulled him out of Gator's reach. “Okay stop it. Everybody just stop it. What's the matter with all of you?”

Gator just sneered then climbed the steps to stand beside the big goon. The other guy, the one Kurt had slammed into the porch post was staggering to his feet.

Earl's head lolled toward Red. “He hit me really, really hard, Red.”

Red looked at Earl with mock concern. “I know, buddy. Sometimes that's what happens when you play with the big boys. I'm sure Kurt didn't mean anything by it.” He gave Kurt his best shit-eating grin. “Did ya, partner?”

Kurt shrugged, said, “I was just saying hello. What's your name, asshole?”

“No, Earl.”

“No offense, Earl.”

Red patted Earl on the shoulder. “See?”

Earl smiled sheepishly. "Yeah, no problem, pleased to meet ya . . ." That's all he got out before Red backhanded him against the post again. After he recovered he said, "Sorry sir."

"Dumb fucking shit," Red said.

The blatant brutality made Paula feel sick. Who were these men? What connection did they have to Kurt? She took his face in her hands, looked pleadingly in his eyes. "For God's sake, Kurt, tell me what's going on. Please."

But it was the big goon who answered. "We're about to have a long discussion about that. So Kurt, why don't you and your cunt come on out of the rain and . . ."

Paula's face turned as red as her hair. "What did you just call me?"

Kurt put a hand on her shoulder. "Easy . . ."

She shrugged his hand off. "My name is Paula Doherty, mister. And just who the hell do you think you are?"

Red leaned over the railing to give Paula a full measure of his eyes. They were completely devoid of life. Paula shuddered.

"You can cut the crap, honey. Your name is Mrs. William Taylor, recently of Palm Beach, Florida. Who I am, Paula fucking cunt, is your worst nightmare come true."

67

As Kurt and Paula were marched into the main room at gunpoint, Paula was trying desperately to process the events of the past few minutes into something that was comprehensible, but her brain was incapable of getting traction. All she knew for sure was the trouble they were in was so deep their chances of surviving were minimal.

This triggered a flight response in Paula. She was a gazelle reacting to a stalking leopard. Every molecule in her body screamed run.

Anywhere.

Just run.

But she knew the predator was swifter, would outrun her, pounce on her. Take her down. Rip her body apart with blade or bullet. Her life meaningless to him. Just a kill.

The thought of eminent violent death paralyzed her brain, rendered her reasoning ability inoperable. She was helpless. Couldn't think. Couldn't move. It was humiliating. Demeaning.

Clearly the intended effect.

Paula gripped Kurt's left forearm with both her hands and pulled close to him. Power coursed through his arm, yet calmness too. How could that be? She tightened her grip. He looked down at her.

And smiled.

It was not the cavalier, roguish smile so familiar to her. It was a smile that said: everything's going to be all right. It said: be brave. It said: I'm going to get us through this.

But how?

He was gazing at the photographs hanging everywhere. She forced herself to look at them too. There were dozens of them. The image quality was like the fuzzy, black-and-white photos found in supermarket tabloids. But far more explicit.

Her skin crawled at the thought of these men watching them, photographing them, during her and Kurt's most intimate exchanges of passion. Memories of how she felt the instant each exposure was made flooded her mind. Every position, every expression of ecstasy, was still vivid, captured just as vividly in glossy eight-by-ten photos.

She looked more closely at the pictures then understood why Kurt wanted her to do so. Examining them brought about a surprising transformation within her. The terror that had gripped her heart, the fear that had eliminated her ability to think coherently, was melting away, replaced by a growing sense of outrage.

She realized the men were purposefully remaining silent; letting the tension, and the fear, grow. They gathered as a group in the center of the room, near the bar. Gator had sheathed his knife but held a submachine gun at the ready. Earl's Vigneron M2 was leveled at Kurt.

The big goon wasn't holding a weapon but had the biggest pistol she'd ever seen strapped to his leg gunslinger style. He also had what appeared to be a shotgun slung over his shoulder along with a couple of knives strategically placed.

The rain lashed the room's many French doors as well as the big windows above. The wind howled, became a giant's hand and pushed against the house, making it groan.

Paula let go of Kurt's arm, stood tall beside him, chin up, confident, defiant. The big goon saw this too and clearly didn't like it. Now we'll get down to business, she thought.

Kurt folded his arms across his chest, planted his feet firmly in a wide stance. “Thought you were in Bogotá, Red.”

So that was the big goon's name, Red. That figured, considering the red clumps of hair over his ears.

Red guffawed. “No partner, you thought I was dead.”

Unfazed, Kurt shook his head. “No 'partner', I thought we had a plan. I thought I could trust you to carry it out. Guess I was wrong.”

“All right, lets cut the shit. The plan was for you to meet me there.” He glanced at his watch. “About three hours from now. Looks like neither of us is gonna make it.”

Paula was listening closely to what was being said. Like yesterday morning at the hospital with Bill and Betty, each word spoken by Kurt and Red became a piece in a picture puzzle, but she did not have enough pieces yet for an image to form.

Kurt shrugged. “You've got all the goods, Red. Remember? You didn't need me to complete the deal. I decided I didn't want to risk my life being your decoy. Sorry if you can't understand that, but then, hell, you've never been very good at thinking.”

Okay, that was deliberately provocative, Paula thought. Was that the best-defense-is-a-strong-offense strategy? She tried to read the subtext in Kurt's vocal tone, his body language, so she'd be ready to follow his lead.

Red was getting visibly agitated. There was a noticeable hiss in his voice. He jerked a leather pouch from a pocket inside his field jacket and held it up in front of Kurt. "Yeah, partner, I've got the goods alright." He ripped open the pouch, turned it upside down. Dull green stones poured out onto the carpet. "Fakes."

Kurt looked down at them, seemingly stunned, then at Red, shaking his head incredulously. "Fakes?" Kurt addressed Gator and Earl. "My old comrade just poured two million bucks worth of uncut emeralds on the floor. I'm guessing somebody tried to convince Red they were fakes. Then that somebody made the mistake of offering a paltry sum to buy them. Obviously that somebody didn't know Red like I do."

He redirected his gaze at Red. "So how'd you kill him?" He sounded as if he was having a casual conversation about the weather.

Red grew surlier. "Easy boy . . ."

Kurt ignored him. "Same way you're gonna kill these two? Same way you plan to kill me?"

"That doesn't have to happen."

"Really? Isn't that what happens to anybody stupid enough to join forces with you?"

"Hell no and you know it."

"Do I? All those years we fought side by side. Now you bring these guys here to kill me? Then what? You kill them too? Is that the new Red Alert code of honor?"

Red stuck his face close to Kurt's and yelled, "You shut the fuck up!"

Paula jumped back, an automatic reflex to Red's fury. Kurt did not flinch, stayed calm and loose. She was beginning to understand his strategy. Divide and conquer.

Gator and Earl exchanged wary glances, so maybe it was working. But what about the emeralds scattered on the carpet? What did Kurt have to do with them?

Kurt interrupted her thoughts by confronting Red again. "You got something to say, old buddy, say it."

Red struggled to regain his composure. He folded his arms over his chest just the way Kurt was doing. To Paula they looked like two big lumberjacks squaring off before a tree-climbing contest.

"Yeah, I got something to say. It's real simple, Kurt you ol' sonovabitch. Just hand over the real emeralds then all this goes away."

"Red, quit thinking with your asshole. The real emeralds are scattered around your feet. Why don't you and your flunkies just scoop 'em up and get the fuck out of here?"

Paula expected a fierce response, but Red just chuckled. "They're fake and you know they're fake. Okay, you wanna play games? We'll go about it another way."

Red strolled around like a professor giving a lecture, tapping the photos with his forefinger. "Please direct your attention to these pictures hanging everywhere. Here's how it works, ol' pard. You hand over the emeralds, the real ones, and in return, you get all these pictures. And as a bonus prize, you also get the negatives."

He removed an envelope from his inside pocket. From it he fanned out strips of negative. "Or you can choose not to hand over the emeralds . . ." He strolled over so he was facing Paula. "And these pictures go to sweet thing's hubby, her sonny-boy, her mommy-in-law, her neighbors, church, and anybody else we think might be an interested party."

Paula covered her mouth to keep from being sick.

It was just the response Red was hoping for. He grinned viciously, letting his eyes devour Paula, down, then up again, lingering over her breasts and hips. "What's the matter, sweetie? Don't want your little boy to see a picture of his mommy's pussy? Or see what a whore she is?"

That did it. Paula leaned over the sink in the bar and heaved her guts. Red, Gator, and Earl were beside themselves with laughter, enjoying the sight of a pretty woman puking.

Red clearly felt completely in control now. He turned back to Kurt. "You know, ol' buddy, the three of us studied these pictures real good. Gotta say, we admire your technique. We even wondered if maybe we might improve on it, given the opportunity. Your little whore here can decide the winner."

He turned his dead eyes on Paula. "Whadya say, honey? Or you can tell your boyfriend to just turn over the emeralds and you'll never see us again. Your choice."

68

The object of the exercise was to stay alive.

Kurt knew if he turned the emeralds over to Red, or even acknowledged that he had them, he and Paula would not stay alive very long. What these three miscreants would do to Paula first was something he couldn't allow himself to think about or he would crumble on the spot. One thing was certain, death would not come easy. These men enjoyed killing. A quick, clean kill wasn't their style. No fun in it.

Kurt had already devised then dismissed a half-dozen plans. The risk in each of them was too great for Paula. Not acceptable. She had to be saved. Not just because he loved her and needed her in his life but because she was the only person in the room worthy of being saved. The world needed a healthy population of Paulas. Civilization depended on it. As for the others in the room, the only positive contribution they could make to civilization would be to die.

Kurt had lived his life just a couple of notches above the animal level. Not far from the cave. It was women like Paula who brought men out of the cave. Taught them how to turn the sex act into making love, how to rise above being merely the most ruthless of beasts, taught them how to care and protect.

Now he had to protect Paula. Even at the cost of his life.

He would take out Earl first. He didn't need a weapon for that. In a lightning move he would break Earl's neck even before the poor slob realized he was being attacked. He had done it many times before.

Time involved: a second at most.

Then he would slam Earl's body into Gator, knocking him off balance just long enough to yank his Bowie knife from its sheath and slit his throat.

Total time to take out Earl and Gator: three seconds.

Which was more than enough time for Red to level his .357 magnum at the back of Kurt's head and blow his brains all over the hand-woven Indian carpet.

Except Red wouldn't do it that way because if Kurt was dead the emeralds might never be found. No, he would simply club Kurt over the head, tie him to a chair, and make him watch while he did unthinkable things to Paula, knowing Kurt would spill his guts to keep that from happening.

The only hope Kurt and Paula had was to convince Red he wouldn't give up the emeralds regardless of what might happen to Paula. That was going to be a hard one to pull off.

Red was visibly impatient. He started to bounce from one foot to the other the way Kurt had seen him do so many times before. "Well what's it gonna be, partner?"

Kurt frowned, showing his own impatience. He glared at Red. "Guess it all depends on the size of your balls."

Not the response Red was expecting. He was clearly jarred. "Oh great gobs of horse shit, Kurt. You know what kinda balls I got. You seen 'em in action plenty enough."

"And now you're using them for brains. Won't work. That's why you always left the thinking to me. Remember? It's the only reason you're still alive today. But now you gotta do some serious thinking for yourself, partner, even if it hurts you to do so. You too, Gator. As for you, Earl, now's your chance to show how smart you really are. Don't screw it up, pal."

Kurt did not let Paula's gape-mouthed expression distract him. He wanted Earl to question his loyalty to Red. Meanwhile, he was focused on Gator, who was clearly starting to waver.

"Whadya mean?" he said.

Kurt pressed on, his tone ominous. "To begin with, the uncut emeralds scattered around your feet are genuine. They're real."

"The hell they are," Red yelled.

"Red got bamboozled but hasn't got the balls to admit it. He knows these are the real emeralds."

"Holy shit, Kurt. If I knew these were genuine, why would I even be here? Answer me that one, oh great swami."

"Yes, why?" He turned to Gator and Earl who were beginning to look very confused. "Red's got you guys into something a whole lot bigger and deadlier than you can possibly imagine."

Red was really flummoxed now. "What the hell you talking about? Man, you're really starting to piss me off."

"Shut up, Red. It's full disclosure time."

Red slammed his fist down on the bar with such force that he cracked the bamboo top. "Full disclosure? You little shit. I don't even know what that means."

"I do," Gator said. There was a threat in his voice directed at Red, not Kurt.

Kurt stepped a little closer to Red, bearing down. “I'm betting you didn't bother to tell your buddies about Salvador Estrada, did you?”

Before Red responded, Kurt turned to Gator and Earl. “Did he?”

It was Gator who answered. “Who the fuck is Salvador Estrada and why should I care?”

Paula wondered if Kurt was pushing Red too far. She thought the big goon was literally going to explode. She’d never seen a man so full of rage. He bellowed, “This shithead's just trying to rattle you guys by throwing a lotta bullshit in your face.”

Kurt ignored him. He took a deep breath, knowing what he was about to say would change things forever between him and Paula. “Salvador Estrada hired us to steal these emeralds from the Andean Mining Federation because they tried to double-cross him in a new mining venture. Red was supposed to meet Estrada tonight in Bogotá and trade the emeralds for a certain amount of, shall we say, negotiable goods.”

To Paula, all the natural laws she had been taught since childhood were a lie. The earth was flat and the sun revolved around it. And Kurt Younger was no more than a figment of her imagination. Her head swam. She steadied herself on the bar to keep from falling over. “Kurt . . . is this true?”

The devastation in Paula’s eyes said it all. He had lost her. He was conscious of his soul departing. His only reason for existing now was to save her. “Yes.”

Red sneered at Paula. “Really had you fooled, huh? Who the fuck'd you think he was?” He laughed at her. “I know women as a rule are stupid but God almighty you take the cake.”

“Leave her alone,” Kurt barked.

“Eat my shit.”

It was Gator who broke it up. “To hell with all that. Finish the story.”

Kurt was glad to oblige. “Obviously Red blew the deal. In a couple of hours Estrada will know he's been had. He'll then take matters into his own hands. One thing you can count on, he'll come after these emeralds. And our blood. He's got a small army at his command. Thanks to Red, they'll be heading our way. It won't take long.”

Red didn’t like the way Gator and Earl were looking at him. “Okay, now that Kurt's told you boys a fancy bedtime story, it's time we get down to business.”

Kurt was about to launch a new attack. Gator saved him the trouble. He gestured to the stones on the floor and asked Red, “These the emeralds you were supposed to give to Estrada?”

“Yeah, but they're fake.”

“How do we know that?”

“Because I just told you.”

Earl jerked his head nervously from Gator to Red to Kurt then said, “But what if they're real?”

"Shut up Earl," Red screamed.

Earl reeled back as if physically struck, then to everyone's surprise adopted a defiant stance. "Sorry sir, but I gotta right to ask questions."

This made Red livid. "I tell you what rights you have, pussy face."

"Not any more," Earl said. His gun barked twice, hitting Red square between the eyes.

69

Time stopped.

Everyone was too stunned to move.

Even Kurt.

Normally he would have sprung into action before Red even hit the floor, using the distraction to take out Earl and Gator. But the unimaginable had just happened. This was Red lying on the floor.

Red.

Dead.

Impossible.

He had toppled like a Ponderosa pine. Now he was sprawled flat on his back. His eyes open, looking no different than they'd always looked. Dead. Now they really were. The two holes between his eyes resembled squashed cherries. They were no longer bleeding.

Dead.

In his state of utter disbelief, Kurt thought: that's all it took? The elaborate plan he had devised about emeralds and Estrada and a convoluted trip to Colombia wasn't necessary. All he really ever had to do was just pop Red between the eyes.

Why the hell hadn't he ever thought of that?

Kurt had to stifle an urge to laugh hysterically at the sheer stupidity of his actions. How many times did he have the chance to take Red out with one quick shot? Dozens, at least. Catch him off guard for a second. One squeeze of the trigger. Then none of the rest of this would have happened. He and Paula would be starting their new life together now, worry free.

So simple.

Why hadn't he done it?

Because it was Red. Other than himself, the most formidable fighting force he'd ever known. He had fought side by side with Red for too many blood-soaked years to doubt his cunning or his ruthlessness or his willingness to kill. Red was invincible. Indestructible. A legend among fighting men. If you were going to kill a man like Red, you'd better have a well thought out cast-iron plan. Then execute it flawlessly.

Yet Earl proved in a split-second the legend was much greater than the man. In the end, he was just a man. And two small bullets will kill a legend or a nobody with equal efficiency.

For Earl, Red was not the first man he had killed. But he was definitely the biggest score. The great Michael J. Owllart. Feared by fighting men around the world. The infamous Red Alert. Taken down by the guy everybody thought was just a lackey. A wannabe.

Wasn't that the way it always happened?

Wild Bill Hickok and Jesse James were taken down by nobodies too. Both shot in the back of the head by cowards. Earl wasn't a coward. He killed Red face to face. He looked right into the man's eyes when he pulled the trigger.

Nobody would ever think of him as a lackey again.

Gator was not good at making quick decisions. That's why he was never a member of the warrior elite. He was a good warrior, yes, a true dog of war, but not warrior elite material. To join their ranks you had to have lightning quick reflexes, be capable of making snap decisions. Kurt and Red had those qualities. Gator did not. He was aware of this particular shortcoming. Under the current situation it scared him shitless. With Red dead he was left leaderless. Not good. Not good at all. He'd always depended on a strong leader.

He never considered Earl as anything but a tag-along. A wannabe. But a second earlier he had calmly leveled his Vig M2 at Red and pulled the trigger. Two quick taps. Red came down hard, shaking the floor, rattling the glasses and bottles on the bar. Gator was left impotent.

Sure, Gator had a gun, but it was leveled at Kurt. Earl's gun was leveled at him, a move he had made even as Red was falling. Gator knew if he swung his gun toward Earl, he'd have a couple of holes between his eyes to match Red's. He remained statue still, his eyes glued on Earl, too scared to make a move, too scared to even twitch a muscle.

Because now he knew something about Earl he didn't know before.

Earl was crazy.

Huge game changer.

Paula had never seen a man murdered before. She'd seen lots of guys killed in the movies or on TV, where the body counts on one episode would rival an average American town's murder rate for an entire year. But those were actors. After the director called cut, they got up, brushed themselves off then went to their dressing rooms.

Red wouldn't be getting up.

Ever.

This was a man Paula had known for less than an hour. A man who had come out of nowhere. A man who called her a cunt then flaunted pictures of her in her most vulnerable state, threatening to destroy her life with them. Now he was splayed out on the floor. Dead.

Good.

The only thing she knew about this man called Red was that he and Kurt had evidently shared a dark, unsavory past. The only thing she knew about Kurt was that she didn't know him at all. She'd always thought of him as a rogue, an adventurer, someone who lived by his own rules. Someone who told the rest of the world to go to Hell. At least, that was the image of him she had created in her mind.

What a fool she'd been.

At the moment she only knew one thing for absolute sure. She was on her own. Once again she had given her heart to a man she trusted. Once again he ripped it apart.

Here she was on an isolated island at the tip of Florida Bay. Nobody to call for help. No police. No phone. A storm raging outside. The only means of escape was a boat locked away in a boathouse. Two men with guns stood only a few feet away. One of them had already shown he was trigger-happy. The other one looking trapped. How long before he lost control?

To make the situation even worse, she didn't know what to expect from Kurt.

She was all alone, sitting on a stack of dynamite, watching while everybody around her played with matches.

If she was going to be rescued, she'd have to do it. That meant she'd have to keep her emotions at bay. Her emotions could get her killed. She had a good brain and she was going to have to use it to survive. Her beauty wasn't going to get her out of this.

Or was it?

70

Paula coolly assessed the situation. She immediately zeroed in on the biggest, most immediate problem: Gator and Earl had weapons; she and Kurt did not.

Correction, Kurt did not.

She did.

It was a powerful weapon every beautiful woman knew she possessed starting around the age of puberty. It was potentially as deadly as a gun, knife or a grenade. Throughout history it had brought great men to their knees. It had toppled empires.

Paula had never used her feminine arsenal for any other purpose than love. But like it or not, she was fighting for her life now. She had to use the weapons available to her or very likely die. Dying was not an option.

She took a moment to gather her resolve, knowing that once she committed, she'd have to go all the way. She glanced at Kurt. He wasn't going to like what she was about to do. But that no longer mattered.

She focused on Earl. Flirt time. She tilted her head down and gazed coyly up at him. This simple gesture, she knew, made her dazzling green eyes even bigger. To complete the effect, she feigned an expression of awe then spoke with a kittenish voice. “I think that was the bravest thing I ever saw a man do.”

Kurt reacted as if he'd grabbed a live wire. “No, Paula, don't . . .”

She ignored him, noticing that Earl was responding the way she hoped he would. He was definitely standing a little taller, a little more erect. She swallowed her fear, took a step closer.

“You just proved you're the strongest, most powerful man in the room.” She smiled provocatively while fighting off the hot bile rising within her. “And strong, powerful men really get my engine going.”

Gator knew what she was doing. “You shut the fuck up, bitch.”

Paula kept her eyes locked on Earl. “I noticed how you were looking at these pictures. Like what you see, big guy?”

Earl was starting to sweat. A cocky grin transformed his face from punk loser to the playboy he'd always imagined he was. "Yes ma'am, I damn sh-sh-sure do."

Earl's eyes reflected the fantasies dancing around in his head. It made Paula cringe. Oh dear God, she thought, then mustered up the remainder of her courage and gave him a naughty smile. "Want to see the real thing?"

Kurt was about to burst. "Paula stop. You don't know . . ."

Paula cut him off but kept her eyes seductively on Earl. She continued to speak in the same breathy tone. "Kurt if you say another word, I swear to God I'll never speak to you again." She reached down, crossing her arms, grabbed the bottom of her sweater then glanced again at Kurt.

He was clearly terrified at the danger she was putting herself in. She'd never seen him so afraid, so vulnerable before.

But it was the naked, unadulterated love for her burning in his eyes that threatened to reduce her to a puddle. There was no faking that, she told herself. So what if he did some questionable things in his past? He loved her with the full force of his body and soul.

And she loved him. In flagrant defiance of caution, reason and prudent behavior, she knew she always would. She had to. That's how love worked. Kurt was her man.

Knowing that strengthened her resolve.

These thoughts occurred in less than a second. Just a slight pause as far as Earl was concerned.

In one swift movement Paula jerked her sweater over her head, tossed it aside, then stood brazenly in front of Earl, shoulders back, chest out, hands on hips.

"Holy shit," Gator said, then was pissed that he wasn't able to restrain himself.

For one of the rare times in his life, Kurt was clueless about what to do. Paula had taken any semblance of control out of his hands. Now he had no choice but to back her play.

It was a damned dangerous play.

He tried to stay poised, ready to spring into action.

The lights flickered.

Due to the tempest outside, Earl and Gator didn't seem surprised. Paula chanced a glance at Kurt. Clearly he was thinking the same thing she was. He tensed.

Lightning flooded the room followed by an explosion of thunder that shook the walls.

Earl didn't notice at all.

He couldn't take his eyes off of Paula's bulging breasts, prominently displayed in her sexiest black bra. Stuttering, he managed to ask, "How long'd it take you to grow those?"

Paula's stomach muscles tightened but she forced herself to give Earl a saucy smile. "You're joking, right? Honey, I was born a C-cup."

She stepped a little closer, lowered her voice to a husky purr. "But I've grown a lot bigger since then."

Earl's breath was quavering in anticipation.

Paula took a deep breath, which only made her breasts swell more. She wasn't trying to enflame Earl's passions further, just trying to suppress the abject fear gripping her heart that made her want to scream. She tried desperately not to let her feelings reach her eyes.

Didn't matter.

Earl wasn't looking at her eyes.

This was it.

She reached behind her back as if to unhook her bra. "Let me show you," she said, then stopped abruptly.

It was too much for Earl. "What's the matter? Come on, come on."

Paula knew what she said next would very likely get someone killed. But that was the plan. This was life or death. A quick look at Kurt. He knew it too. He was ready. She looked deep into Earl's eyes.

"I can't, sweetie." She nodded toward Gator. "Not with him watching." She pushed her breasts out, smiled invitingly. "I only want you to see."

It didn't take Gator more than a heartbeat to realize what was about to happen. He screamed, "You bitch," and swung his gun toward Earl.

But he wasn't fast enough.

Earl fired off two rounds. Unlike Red, Gator was anticipating it and swung to the side. The bullets missed him. The French doors behind him shattered. Rain blew in as if shot from a fire hose.

Gator returned fire with a short burst, missing Earl, who had dropped to his knees, but taking out a table lamp. It burst into a thousand pieces of razor sharp shrapnel. A piece of it sliced through Paula's shoulder. She winced in pain.

Kurt was already in the air, flying toward her. She grunted from the force of his tackle. It lifted her off her feet. While still in flight, Kurt twisted so that his body was under hers when they hit the floor. They skidded toward the stairs.

Gator and Earl ducked for cover, firing off random shots. Furniture cushions exploded into a snowstorm of feathers. Wall decorations danced, spun and crashed down in a cacophonous clatter. Wall planks ripped open and spewed needle-like splinters.

French doors disintegrated in a tinkling shower of glass. The storm roared in with a vengeance, despite the protection of the covered verandah. Wind plowed into the room like an air horn, howling demonically.

Kurt rolled on top of Paula, trying his best to cover every inch of her body with his own. He knew a direct hit would burrow through him into her. Hopefully he would slow it down enough so the damage to her would be minimal.

At the moment it was his only move.

Other than wait for what he knew was about to happen.

Two heartbeats later it did.

The lights went out, plunging the room into blackness.

71

The gun battle raged on. Muzzle flashes intermingled with lightning bursts brought fleeting images of the room being demolished. Stroboscopic flashes revealed Gator diving here, Earl running there, both screaming obscenities, sometimes yelling out in pain.

Kurt put his lips next to Paula's ear. “You okay?”

“I think so.”

“We gotta move before we catch a stray bullet.”

“Okay.”

“Stay low.”

Kurt pulled Paula to a crouching position. They were nearly blinded by lightning but Kurt didn't miss the black shadow on the wall behind them. He whirled to see Gator charging them, his huge Bowie knife raised to strike, screaming, “You mother fucker!” He plunged the knife down.

All the years of jungle fighting instinctively came back to Kurt. He kicked out, knocking the knife from Gator's hand. The room went black, but Kurt kicked out again at where he guessed Gator's knee was.

He hit pay dirt.

His heel tore into soft cartilage, crushing it, verified by Gator's bellowing. Kurt grabbed Paula's hand and pulled her toward the museum room. He pushed her through, slamming her back against the inside wall. Again he put his lips to her ear, although with the chaos all around, whispering was hardly necessary.

“Stay in here. Lock the door behind me. Don't open it unless you hear my voice.”

“Okay, okay, okay.”

“There's a French door in the middle of the room. Use it if you have to. Get just as far away from here as possible.”

“Oh my God, Kurt . . .”

“Don't fall apart now, baby. You're doing great.” He started to leave, then stopped. “Jesus Paula, that was the gutsiest thing I've ever seen anybody do." He started to leave again, then stopped again. Admiration radiated from his eyes. "It also scared the shit out of me."

He kissed her, lifting her off the floor. All the passionate kisses of the night before were simply a warm up to this one. She threw her arms around his neck, held him tight.

"Gotta go," he said. "Don't worry about me. Just another day at the office. Remember, lock up behind me."

Kurt felt his way to the door then rolled out. Paula was right on his heels. She quietly shut the door, located a bolt lock, and slid it home.

She stood alone in the darkness, trembling. She wished she had her sweater. Somehow having nothing on from the waist up except her barely-there bra made her feel very vulnerable. What a ridiculous thing to think about under the circumstances, she told herself, but ridiculous or not, it was how she felt.

Thank God the generator had run out of fuel. She knew immediately what was happening when the lights flickered a few minutes ago. Kurt had not topped off the propane tank on the dock. Why would he? He thought they'd be leaving in the morning and never coming back. Unwittingly, his misplaced assumptions had saved their lives.

Temporarily anyway.

Two bullets tore through the wall inches from her. Paula suppressed a scream, darted toward the interior of the room, and slammed into a display table hidden in the dark. That was it for Paula. The darkness was not only dangerous but it was too oppressive for her. She remembered seeing a hurricane lantern in here this morning. Where?

As if in response, lightning flooded the room for a split-second, rendering its bizarre contents in stark relief. It also revealed a lantern perched on the mantel. Beside it was a box of matches. Holding her hands out in front of her, Paula made her way to it, only stubbing her toe once.

Within a few seconds she had the lantern fired up and the wick trimmed to its brightest setting. A warm, soothing glow pushed away the darkness. Despite Paula's perilous situation, it brought a certain measure of relief.

On the other side of the wall she heard the unfettered fury of two great battles. One was between men, the other was between the forces of nature. Each seemed to be challenging the other for dominance. At one point a bullet ripped through the door. She jumped back, yelling, "Shit!"

Amidst the sounds of gunshots, furniture being knocked over and glass breaking, Paula heard men screaming. She heard Kurt howl a couple of times, but in anger, not pain.

"Oh God, please don't let him be hurt," she said then realized she was praying, something she hadn't done in a long time. Better late than never. "I love him, God, I love him, I love him. Please God, protect him."

Listening to the mayhem just a few feet away was maddening. Paula thought about joining in the battle, despite Kurt's warnings. It couldn't be any worse than just waiting here to see who survived.

But Kurt was right. His attention would be divided between fighting off his attackers and trying to protect her. That kind of distraction would probably get him killed.

She realized she was wringing her hands in frustration. There must be something I can do, she thought. That's when it occurred to her she was standing in the midst of hundreds of military artifacts, many of them weapons.

She tried to remember what she'd seen this morning. Definitely there were knives, swords, even spears. Any firearms? Surely there must be.

Another thud against the wall, accompanied by vicious curses, emphasized her need to hurry. She searched the room for a gun, even a sword. Something. Anything.

Lightning blasted through the French doors again. She spun around. The doors were open.

And Gator was charging through them.

72

Paula bolted away at right angles to Gator's charge, the only path open to her.

She wasn't fast enough.

His hand clamped down on her left wrist like a vise, which not only brought her flight to an abrupt halt but nearly jerked her arm out of its socket. The sharp pain made her yelp. Making matters worse, her forward momentum spun her around into Gator's waiting arms.

His hot, putrid breath in her face made Paula want to puke. She screwed her eyes shut as she always did when confronted with something truly repugnant. Because of that, she did not see Gator draw his hand back as far as it would reach.

His backhanded blow against her face was so powerful it not only made Paula see stars, it broke Gator's grip on her wrist. She hit the floor hard, rattling every bone in her body. Gator grabbed for her but she scooted under a large display table. It gave her temporary refuge from his attack.

And a second to gather her wits.

In that brief second Paula was transformed. Something hot coursed through her muscles, the way it did in the final stretch of a swim match. With it came a realization.

Her anger was greater than her fear. She was not going to lose.

On her back under the table, Gator's injured knee was clearly visible. Paula clasped both hands together until her knuckles were white, raised them as far back over her head as possible, then swung with all her might at his knee.

Gator howled. His leg caved under him and he toppled backward. Paula didn't hesitate. She rolled from under the table, raised her clasped hands over her head and smashed down on his knee again.

And again.

And again.

Gator was using invectives more colorful and inventive than Paula had ever heard, directed at women in general and her in particular.

She didn't care. Sticks and stones.

She was so intent on finishing the job Kurt had started on Gator's knee that she didn't pay attention to what he was doing with his other leg.

Big mistake.

Gator slammed his alligator cowboy boot into her stomach with the force of a piston rod on a locomotive. It drove the air from her lungs and tossed her several feet across the room. She came to a hard stop against cold metal that rumbled like the thunder outside.

She sat gasping for breath, watching Gator totter to his feet. She took satisfaction in seeing that his knee was not only a bloody pulp, but it barely supported his weight.

Unfortunately it didn't stop him from pulling his twelve-inch Bowie knife from its sheath. He brandished it before her.

Lightning flashed, temporarily blinding Paula. It was followed immediately by thunder with enough concussive force to rattle every one of the thousand or more items in the room.

When her sight returned, Gator was staggering toward her, dragging his injured leg, arms poised to attack. "So what is today, amateur hour?" he growled. "First a nobody like Earl takes out the meanest bastard who ever slung lead. Now some big-titted cunt's gonna take me out? Fuckin' ain't gonna happen, bitch." He limped another step closer, wincing when he put weight on his leg.

Paula watched him advance while concentrating on regaining her breath. Until then, no action was possible. He edged closer, savoring the moment before the kill. Rage surged back into Paula's arms and legs. Air worked its way into her lungs again, but not fast enough. Lantern light glistened on Gator's obscene knife. Paula glanced up to see she was sitting at the base of a full-sized suit of armor.

Gator reached down for the front of her bra. "I'll be havin' that boulder-holder."

Paula didn't hesitate. She rolled to her feet, darted behind the suit of armor, yelled, "Fuck you," then pushed the hundred pounds or more of metal onto him.

It avalanched down on Gator, knocking him off his feet. He pushed the heavy pieces aside while belting out a string of obscenities. His struggle made a hell of a racket, drowning out even the noise of the storm.

Paula used the diversion to scurry away. She had to find a place to observe Gator without him being able to see her. Fortunately the room, with all its exotic décor, provided several places that were suitable.

"Big fuckin' mistake. Now you've really pissed me off, you crazy bitch. Oh God I'm gonna fuck you. I'm gonna fuck you so bad." He was on his feet again, staggering around, searching for her. Lightning struck and Paula was afraid her hiding place behind a small cannon would be revealed.

"But I'm gonna tie you down first. Then I'm gonna make your pussy little boyfriend watch while I do you over and over again. Whadya think of that, Miss Big Tits?"

Paula realized she was dealing with a very diseased mind. A crazy man with a big knife. She knew her best defense was to ignore his insane rants and rely on her wits as coolly and calmly as possible. Rain lashed in through the open French doors. Paula was tempted to make a dash for it. With Gator's injury, she could easily outrun him.

But then what?

Wait for him to hunt her down? Outside amongst thick foliage, he could easily sneak up on her, then attack. One lunge with his knife was all it would take. Endgame. Gator was obviously a professional fighting man, trained to fight in a jungle environment.

She wasn't.

In the museum they were on somewhat equal footing. At least she could keep him occupied while Kurt was dealing with Earl. She heard grunts and groans from the other room, and shouts, both of pain and anger. Furniture was knocked over. Glass broken.

She heard Kurt cry out sharply, in pain this time. She listened closely; willed Kurt to say something, yell out again, anything that would let her know he was still alive.

Nothing.

Oh please God.

She glanced down at the dozen or so cannonballs stacked pyramid style just behind the cannon. Each was about six inches in diameter. Couldn't be that heavy. She lifted the one on top.

A few inches. It was unbelievably heavy.

When she realized she was going to drop it, she managed to rotate her hand under it to muffle the sound of it slamming back down on the other cannonballs.

Not a smart move.

She screamed out, "Shit," unable to restrain herself.

That did it. She heard Gator making his way toward her, erupting into a jeering, guttural laugh. "That's right, baby. Deep shit. Deep, deep shit."

Peering from behind the cannon, Paula watched him put a finger to the side of his nose and blow out a wad of snot. Her face wrinkled in disgust.

Her hand was still pinned under the cannon ball. How could something that small weigh so much? Didn't matter. She was pinned. Meanwhile, Gator was getting closer.

Step, drag. Step, drag.

Gotta do something. Fast.

She placed her other hand on the side of the ball, got into a kneeling position to leverage all her strength, and lifted.

It worked.

Gator was only a few feet away, snickering, shoving things out of his way.

Step, drag. Step, drag.

"You can either strip down yourself or I'll cut them clothes off ya. What's it gonna be?"

Paula was already on the move, attempting to circle behind him. She was taking crouching steps, having to lean back to counterbalance the weight of the ball.

Lightning flooded the room. Gator raised an arm to shade his eyes. Paula used the loud boom of thunder that followed to complete her journey behind Gator.

"I'll have the bra first. Give it up."

She took another step closer so she was directly behind Gator. Mustering strength she wasn't aware she had, Paula managed to lift the ball until she was holding it over her head. She locked her arms and legs, making it a bit easier to hold up the enormous weight.

But the effort also made her grunt.

Gator whirled around, surprised to see Paula right in front of him. His eyes went mad. "Drop it, bitch."

She did.

73

It had turned into a very frustrating day at the office for Kurt. Earl just refused to die.

When Kurt entered the room, he ran directly into Earl. That's when all hell broke loose. Kurt pinned the submachine gun against the chest of his newly emboldened adversary so the barrel pointed to the side. That didn't stop Earl from firing off a volley. All it did was further decimate the room. Muzzle flashes revealed that it was already in shambles.

As far as skill or experience was concerned, Earl was the runt of the pack. The wannabe who was little more than a lackey. Against all odds, he was still alive. Yet the man who was a living legend was now a dead legend.

Go figure.

As for Gator, he was obviously lying low. Smart move considering 'Mad Dog Earl' was on the loose. Probably hiding in the dining room or kitchen, maybe the bathroom, waiting to see who was still standing when the shooting stopped.

He might have even made a dash for it. Easy enough to do with all the sounds of the room coming apart mingled in with the caterwauling of the storm. But Kurt didn't think so. Gator wanted the emeralds.

Kurt and Earl wrestled halfway across the room like a couple of grizzlies, grunting, groaning, cursing, knocking over the few pieces of furniture still standing. Earl managed to punch the stock of his gun into Kurt's chin.

Kurt staggered back a step, losing his grip on Earl, who swung his gun around to a lethal firing position. Kurt plowed his fist into Earl's face, putting the entire weight of his body behind it.

A burst of lightning revealed Earl cartwheeling over a sofa, then the sofa toppling over onto him. Another lightning barrage picked out Red's body. Kurt dove for it, grabbed his old partner's cannon of a pistol along with all the bullets he could find.

He also helped himself to Red's shotgun and a handful of twelve gauge shells. He took the big knife too, more to keep it out of the hands of Gator and Earl than as a defensive weapon. He wasn't much of a knife fighter.

Earl opened fire again. He was running to a new position, putting down protective fire as he did so. Shrapnel from something metal sliced through Kurt's ear. He yelled out in pain then ducked down, throwing his arm over his head. In doing so, he lost his bearing on Earl's position.

Trying to get a bead on him in the darkness that now enveloped the room, or trying to hear his movements in the deafening clamor of thunder and rain, was an impossible task. He crouched behind an overturned end table, using its rim as support for the big pistol. He had no illusions the table would stop a bullet, but hopefully it would hide him from sight during the next lighting burst.

It didn't take long to find out.

The room lit up like Times Square on New Year's Eve. Kurt scanned the interior. Earl's head pop up behind the bar. Kurt promptly shot his ear off. “Damn,” he said. Earl screamed like a stuck pig. The room went black again.

Knowing his muzzle flash had given his position away, Kurt didn't hesitate to jump and roll to a new spot several feet away. Just as he anticipated, the small table he'd been hiding behind was reduced to match sticks as Earl opened up with his Vig.

The sound of the weapon was inordinately loud but was answered by an even louder bombardment of thunder. It rattled everything in the room that wasn't bolted down, which was practically everything.

Kurt was pissed at the inaccurate performance of Red's big Python .357. If the damn gun hadn't pulled to the right, Earl would be dead now. Never understood what Red liked about the weapon other than the size of hole it put in somebody.

Still there was no response from Gator. Kurt wondered if a lucky shot from Earl had taken him out. Not knowing made him uneasy. At least Paula was safe. That's all that mattered.

From a tactical standpoint, Kurt knew his best move was to take a position on the threshold of the center set of French doors. Because he believed Earl and Gator were still in the room, this was a position that would put him behind them. When the next lightning burst revealed their positions, it would be like shooting fish in a barrel.

Kurt slung the shotgun over his shoulder, kept the pistol in his hand then elbow crawled across the room. As he passed behind a sofa, his elbow clunked into something beneath it. Something metal. He eased his fingers around the object and quietly drew it out.

Gator's submachine gun.

Mystery solved. Gator wasn’t firing because he didn't have a gun. He probably lost it in a wild dive trying to avoid a fusillade of bullets from

Earl. Kurt was glad he had confiscated Red's artillery. It meant the only weapon Gator now possessed was his Bowie knife.

Good to know.

Lightning again. Kurt hugged the floor, tried to spot Earl. Couldn't. But had Earl seen him? He'd know in a second. During the following barrage of thunder, he scooted across the floor with the speed of a black mamba.

No gunfire. Earl hadn't seen him.

Just as he reached his objective, Kurt heard, despite the din of the storm, a sound that was a game changer.

Paula's scream.

Now he knew where Gator was.

Son of a bitch.

No time to contemplate what he might be doing to her. Time only to act.

Kurt jumped to his feet. He charged toward where he knew the door to the museum room was located. Any obstacles in his path would simply be knocked out of the way.

Except Earl.

He'd heard Paula's scream too and knew Kurt would run to the rescue. He moved in the darkness to intercept him with the intention of putting a bullet in his head. A lot of them.

Kurt plowed into Earl like a wrecking ball through a brick wall. The force of the unexpected impact sent his Colt Python flying. Luckily Earl lost his weapon too.

Both men crashed to the floor, fists pumping. Kurt easily deflected the roundhouse punches thrown by Earl, who fought like a drunken sailor in a barroom brawl. Kurt was more concerned about what was happening in the other room. Earl was preventing him from getting to her. That really pissed him off.

"Earl, you fucking piece of shit. I don't have time for this."

Making matters worse were the flickering blasts of lightning. They were disorienting as well as blinding. Going more by smell than sight, Kurt delivered a salvo of punishing blows to Earl's face and torso. Most men would have collapsed under such an onslaught. Not Earl. He just kept on fighting.

Who was this guy?

More sounds from the other room, this time from Gator. Kurt knew what that sound meant. He had to get to Paula and take out Gator.

Now.

To do that, he had to finish Earl off.

Lightning revealed an overturned table lamp on the floor a foot or so away. In a move that was as surprising as it was deft, Earl rolled away from Kurt, grabbed the lamp cord, wrapped it around Kurt's neck, and pulled back, putting all his weight behind it.

Which was considerable.

Kurt was flipped onto his back. He grabbed at the cord but was unable to get purchase. It was biting into his neck, cutting off his air supply.

Earl was on his feet now, dragging Kurt across the floor by the lamp cord, pulling it tighter, tighter. He was laughing, singing like a bully in a schoolyard. “I'm gonna kill you. I'm gonna kill you.”

And he was too, Kurt realized. This two-bit wannabe had already taken out Red. Now he was about to do the same to Kurt.

Earl's laughter edged into madness as he kept dragging Kurt across the room. Kurt was helpless to stop him. His brain filled with darkness from lack of oxygen.

No, it wasn't going to end like this. If it did, what would happen to Paula?

He knew what would happen to Paula.

He remembered Red's knife. It was shoved into his waistband. He pulled it free, knowing Earl couldn't see what he was doing.

He waited for the next flash of lightning.

It came a second later. He lined up his target then using all the strength he still possessed, thrust upward.

The huge blade jabbed through Earl's scrotum and continued all the way up into his intestines. Once its upward momentum stopped, Kurt gave it a half turn. Earl's scream was without doubt more horrible than any Kurt had ever heard a man make. But not as horrible as the stench that rained down over his knife hand.

None of that mattered to Kurt. Earl let go of the lamp cord. Kurt took a second to suck down several lungfulls of putrid air but his only thought was getting to Paula.

No further effort was needed on Earl. Kurt knew he had delivered a mortal blow. It would be a very painful death. He decided he would leave the knife where it was as a souvenir for Earl to cherish in Hell.

Now where was Red's gun?

A burst of lightning answered that question.

It was in Earl's hand, its barrel pointed at Kurt's face.

74

The cannonball bounced off Gator's head with a loud thunk, followed by an even louder “Fuck!” He wobbled like a sheet of tin. For a second Paula thought she'd succeeded, but somehow the bastard remained upright, even when the ball took a second bounce off his shoulder.

“Shit,” he screamed, repeating it again as the ball banged against his battered knee then crashed down on his foot. He roared, but a deafening barrage of thunder drowned him out.

Paula was surprised at how her clumsy attempt to knock him senseless had instead inflicted such grievous injury. Judging by his reaction, he was in terrific pain.

Good. But she had no time to gloat.

Despite how badly he was suffering, Gator lashed out wildly with his Bowie knife. It sliced across Paula's hip, cutting through her pedal pushers, her panties, and enough of her skin to spew a thin line of blood.

Paula was outraged. The son of a bitch had actually cut her. “You swamp rat scum-sucking low-life bastard.” It's what she'd heard her father call a pickpocket working his boat -- just before throwing him overboard. It seemed appropriate now. God how she’d like to pick Gator up and throw him overboard.

Her efforts had left him reeling, but his rage was still hitting on all eight cylinders. His knife whisked through the air again, aiming for her throat.

Paula instinctively jerked back. The blade missed her throat but its tip scratched across her chest. Not a deep cut, just enough to draw a line of blood. She screamed, put all her weight behind a savage kick to his knee, then it was his turn to scream.

His breath against her face reeked of rotting corpses. Paula jumped back, repulsed, then grabbed a cat-o-nine tails hanging nearby. She lashed Gator across the face and was shocked at how his skin split open in rivulets of blood. She hit him again but it only seemed to make him madder.

“Gimme that goddam thing.”

Paula was surprised at how easily he snatched it away from her. She knew what was coming next, turned and ran.

She only got a step before feeling the sting of the whip against her bare back. The intensity of the pain was beyond belief, as if her skin had literally been peeled off.

Paula whirled, kicking with all her might directly at his groin. "That hurt?" she asked as he screeched. "How 'bout this?" She kicked his knee again, going for maximum damage. "Yeah? Like that?"

She kicked out again and again until Gator fell screaming to the floor. Paula jumped up as high as she could then dropped down with both feet on his knee. "Drop the knife and I'll stop. Do you hear me?" She repeated the exercise, yelling, "Drop it or I swear I'll . . ."

She didn't get to finish because Gator had both his arms wrapped around her ankles and jerked up. As she fell, Paula's head collided with the corner of a mahogany display table. When she hit the floor, it spun around her, as did everything else in the room.

She was slipping into oblivion.

One part of her wanted to let it happen. Then it would all be over. The pain would go away.

Another part of her said, yeah, it'll all be over all right. And you'll be dead.

When Paula regained her senses, she was on top of Gator. His arms were locked around her, pinning her own arms to her side, making it impossible for her to fight back. Grunting like a hog in slop, Gator worked Paula up his body until they were face to face.

His was smeared with blood and spit. Thin strips of skin hung loose from it and danced in the wind blowing in through the French doors. Paula had to fight back an urge to retch.

Gator laughed contemptuously. "Yeah, you get it now, don't ya? No matter how tough you think you are, you're still just a pussy. Put on earth for just one purpose."

Paula squirmed to break loose but Gator had her in an iron grip. "For guys like me to fuck." And with that, Gator rolled the two of them over so that he was on top of her.

She felt his hardness swelling against her pelvis. He clamped his lips down on hers in an obscene kiss, pressing her skull against the floor so hard Paula was sure it would crack.

This was it.

She was trapped, unable to move. What was about to happen next was unthinkable.

Paula realized her arms from the elbows down were free. She swung them up and grabbed one of Gator's little fingers in each of her hands then jerked back hard against his wrists. She felt bones separate from their sockets.

He roared, snatching his hands away from her grasp as if from a hot skillet.

Just the reaction Paula was counting on. Free from his grip, she rolled away, jumped to her feet, and dashed to the other end of the room, putting as much distance as possible between her and Gator. It gave her a moment to consider her options.

She had to end this.

She had to kill Gator.

He was hobbling toward her with startling speed, screaming like a Zulu warrior, his knife raised overhead, ready for the killing thrust. His injuries were no longer an impediment. He was at a point beyond pain. He was charging in for the kill.

Paula noticed a stand of medieval armor nearby. She grabbed a metal shield about two feet in diameter, held it up just as Gator slashed down. His blade banged against it, skidding off.

The force of his blow knocked Paula off balance and she danced back a step. Gator slashed out again. The vibration from the impact was so severe she almost dropped the shield.

So far, so good, but Paula knew she couldn't keep fending off Gator's attack like this. She had to be able to fight back. But with what?

The solution was only a few steps away, a glistening Arabian scimitar on an ornate silver display rack. It was an especially nasty looking sword, just what she needed.

Paula fended off one more lunge, then whirled away and ran the few steps to the scimitar. She yanked it from the rack.

Gator was stunned by her move. She had a shield and a sword. He only had a knife.

No matter. She was just a woman. He laughed scornfully at her then charged.

Paula didn't hesitate. She conjured up in her mind all the swashbuckler movies she had ever seen and slashed down viciously.

Gator was surprised by her attack but responded instantly. The twelve-inch tempered steel blade of his Bowie knife proved more than adequate to fend off the scimitar's curved blade.

The ear-splitting clang of the two weapons made Paula's teeth rattle. Before she could draw back for another swing, Gator back slashed his knife. She blocked it with her shield. This left him somewhat open and Paula tried a straight in thrust with her sword, aiming for his heart.

Bad move.

Gator jumped back, at the same time slashing down, delivering a powerful blow against her sword, almost knocking it from her hand.

Now she was the one who was open and Gator was ready to exploit his advantage. To keep him from doing so, Paula slammed the shield into his face. He staggered back a step but kept his knife poised to ward off another sword thrust.

Paula spun around and hopped up onto the arm of a full size catapult. It was pulled down into the firing position and nearly parallel to the floor. She liked having the height advantage over Gator.

He simply grinned. “Ready for me to fuck you?” He snatched a double-bladed executioner's axe propped up nearby. He held it upright with one hand while his other hand brandished the Bowie knife.

The ease with which Gator climbed onto the catapult, despite his shattered knee, was unnerving. Paula had never before seen such a display of super human strength and will power.

He was relentless.

He clearly had only one purpose in life now and Paula made the decision that she’d rather die first, even if it was by her own hand. It notched up her anger several more degrees. It sparked in her eyes and said: I'll never submit.

As if the situation wasn't perilous enough, the storm let loose with a seemingly endless burst of flickering lightning that threatened to blind her.

It didn't seem to bother Gator. He advanced doggedly in surreal flashes of movement. Paula scooted back, almost lost her balance.

Gator swung the axe at her. She was able to block it with her shield, but his swing had great force behind it, knocking the shield from her hand. Now she had only one weapon while Gator had two very deadly ones.

He swung the axe again, low, trying to cut her legs from beneath her. Paula jumped high, throwing her legs out in a perfect cheerleader split. The blade sliced the air inches under them.

When she came back down, she landed badly, lost her balance and tumbled off the catapult. She fell face-first onto the floor but managed to cushion the fall with her arms. She heard Gator's boots hit the floor close by and flipped over to face him.

He stepped on her shoulder, pinning her down, then dropped the axe and leaned down with his knife. He slipped the blade under the center of her bra.

There was nothing she could do to stop him.

In a split-second, images flashed through Paula’s mind: Billy as an infant nuzzling her breast, her mother's sunny smile and the sparkle in her eye, her father's hardy laugh in the wheelhouse, Birdy singing in church -- a thousand glittering splinters of the most joyous memories of her life.

Now coming to an end.

75

Gator's head exploded, spraying blood and brains everywhere, some of it hitting Paula.

Along with little pieces of his face.

When it exploded a second time, there wasn't much left to call a head.

His legs buckled and the rest of him came down with the heft of a sailor's sea bag. Paula scooted sideways to make room for him. What remained of his face slapped down beside her like a wet rag on a drain board. It gazed at her with a stupid grin. An eyeball was hanging out.

Kurt called out, "You okay?"

He pushed his way over to her, holding Red's big gun in his hand. With his other hand he pulled Paula up. Once she was on her feet, Paula just stood there quivering like a volcano about to erupt, shaking her fists in the air; eyes screwed tight, teeth bared viciously.

"No I'm not all right!" She pounded her fists against Kurt's chest, screaming like an Amazon warrior woman.

Kurt let her get it out of her system. She collapsed against him and sobbed from the depths of her soul. As he enveloped her in his arms, she stopped him, wincing. "Don't touch my back," then continued sobbing.

When Kurt saw the welts on her back, his face flushed with anger. "Jesus," he said, then swung his gun around and shot Gator again.

Paula didn't react, but did manage to get her sobbing somewhat under control. She noticed the storm had subsided a bit, that it seemed to be moving away. She looked up at Kurt imploringly, her eyes filled with pain and anguish. "Why, Kurt? Why, why, why?"

Kurt took a deep breath. He knew she would be asking this question. He also knew if he had any chance of salvaging their relationship, he would have to answer it fully and honestly. After all she'd been through she deserved the whole truth.

When he looked deep into her eyes, he expected to see hate, loathing. He didn't. They weren't brimming over with affection, but there was a flicker of something that gave him hope.

“All I care about right now, Paula, is you're alive. If you hate me for the rest of your life, I'll understand. But even if you do, I'll love you for the rest of mine.”

She shook her head wearily. “I just want to understand.”

“I promise to tell you everything. I was going to tell you after what you had said to me in the bathtub earlier. It changed everything, made me realize what a fool I'd been. You may not believe me but it's true.”

“Why didn't you tell me?”

Kurt nodded toward Gator. “We had company.”

Paula scanned the room in all its disarray. She avoided looking at Gator. “Yes.” She buried her face in her hands as if the horror of what had happened was just too much to bear. “Oh God, Kurt . . .”

She shivered. Now that the battle was over, her body temperature was returning to normal. She crossed her arms over her chest and said, "I'm cold.”

“Yeah, lets get out of here.”

She looked at him questioningly. “Upstairs,” he said. “The bathroom. I've got first aid stuff there. We need to clean those cuts.”

“It's mostly Gator's blood.”

“An even better reason to clean it up.” He leaned over, gently touched the cut on her hip. Paula flinched. “Sorry. This one's all you. Come on.”

Kurt made a solo side trip to retrieve the lantern while Paula closed the French doors. They carefully followed a path through the rubble and out the door.

As they entered the main room it was flooded with lightning. Paula gasped -- not from the storm but the sight in front of her. If the museum was a shambles, this place looked like a bomb had gone off.

Kurt left her standing while he lit several more lanterns. The warm, friendly glow was incongruous with the naked violence of the room, not the least of which was Red's body sprawled on the floor.

“Not to worry,” Kurt said. “Maid comes on Tuesday.”

His attempt to lighten the mood didn’t work. Paula's entire body convulsed. Kurt held her, careful not to touch her back. “It's gonna be all right,” he said.

Paula looked at him wild-eyed and said, “Yeah? When?” There was an undercurrent of hysteria in her voice. “My God, Kurt . . .”

“We're alive, Paula. That's what counts. Come with me.”

They walked toward the stairs but were stopped by a loud groan from behind an overturned sofa. Kurt hurried over, gun ready. Earl was on his back in a pool of blood. He waved his gun at Kurt. “Stop.”

Kurt kicked the gun out of his hand impatiently then said to Paula, “Little bastard just won't die.”

Paula joined him. Earl was writhing, coughing, gasping, making gurgling sounds. He looked up at Paula and said in a wet, bubbling whisper, “Please . . .”

The sight of Earl with half his guts strung out around him was nauseating. She turned to Kurt. “What did he say?” He merely shrugged.

Paula leaned over Earl in an attempt to better hear. “What did you say?”

Earl spit up more blood, sucked hard for breath, then said, “Please,” again.

“Please what?”

Earl gurgled some more. “Lemme see 'em. Just once. Please.”

Paula realized what his eyes were focused on. At the angle she was leaning over, they were almost spilling out of her bra. She straightened up, crossed her arms over her chest. She looked down at Earl with utter disgust, her face ice cold, devoid of any semblance of pity.

“No.”

With that, Earl died.

76

Before heading upstairs to the bedroom, Paula and Kurt stripped off their tattered clothes, crossed the verandah, then helped each other down the steps into the cold driving rain, away from the remnants of violence and chaos and the three dead men inside the house.

The fury of the storm had moved out to the Atlantic but it still contained enough force to scour away the blood, grime, and stench of mortal combat. All that was left was fresh blood. Time to take care of that.

The bedroom was on the leeward side of the house, so even though the French doors were left open after the two had dashed out, very little rain had managed to penetrate. It was easily mopped up with a couple of towels.

With the doors closed and the room bathed in the warm, friendly glow of several hurricane lanterns, there was a sense of homeliness, a semblance of safety and security, even if it was only an illusion.

They attended to each other's wounds lovingly, tenderly, with water, alcohol and antiseptic. The cut on Paula's shoulder wasn't too deep and Kurt closed it with a large bandage. When done, both shook their heads in wonder at how much gauze and tape covered their bodies.

The knife slash on Paula's hip was too severe and would require stitches as soon as possible. Kurt first poured hydrogen peroxide on the open wound, then blew on it as she yelled, "Ow, ow, ow, ow, ow," followed by angry tears. He closed it with tightly wound bandages that at least managed to stop the bleeding.

As a precaution he gave injections of penicillin to both of them. There was morphine in his standard issue medical kit, but he knew it was important they both stayed functionally lucid, so he opted for acetaminophen tablets instead.

Medical ministrations completed, Paula pulled on a snug navy blue pullover, another pair of pedal pushers, and canvas deck shoes. The sweater Paula had worn earlier was still on the floor of the main room downstairs where she'd pulled it off. She would never touch it again; much less wear it.

Kurt handed her one of his lightweight bush jackets from the closet. Despite her statuesque physique, it swallowed her, but provided comfort along with a sense of protection. It was just what she need at the moment.

Kurt decided on full tropical combat fatigues including hat, backpack, boots and a bush jacket for himself. It wasn't much different from what most of the sportsmen in South Florida wore, whether hunters or fishermen. He loaded the outfit's numerous pockets with the survival gear he thought they might need, including a big automatic pistol clipped to his belt.

Paula watched him warily. “We going to war again?”

Kurt didn't miss Paula's deadly serious tone, devoid of even a hint of humor or sarcasm. “Not if I can help it,” he said. “I won't be caught off guard again.”

He shoved the last item in a side pocket then lit up a Camel.

Paula lit up too. “Done?”

“Except for the big stuff.”

“Good.” Paula's eyes were penetrating, unflinching. “Time you told me everything. You said you would.”

Kurt was clearly dreading this moment. He nodded. “All right.”

They sat side-by-side on the bed. The storm had diminished to little more than driving rain, gusty wind, and a distant grumble of thunder. No lightning. The alarm clock on the bedside table read 5:48.

“First off, there's something you need to understand. I've been a soldier all my life, up until about two years ago.”

“Guessed as much.”

“I'm damn proud of being a soldier. It's a job that has to be done. Always has been since one caveman decided to take something by force that belonged to another caveman.”

Conviction was in Kurt's voice and his eyes. He was opening up a part of his life to her he had never talked about before. She remained silent as he continued.

“As long as there's greed, corruption, contempt for how others think or live, or just plain old deep down evil, there's gonna be wars. And there's gonna be soldiers to fight those wars. The better the soldiers, the better the chances of victory. As long as the soldiers fight on the side of the good and righteous, they provide a valuable service to mankind.

“Think how World War Two would have turned out if our soldiers hadn't been better than the bad guys' soldiers, what kinda world we'd be living in now. I always fought on the good and righteous side, Paula. I put a lot of bad guys out of business. I have no regrets about that.”

He was quiet for a moment. It seemed to Paula that a shadow passed over his face. He took a long drag on his cigarette. "Then one day it all went bad."

"Red?"

He looked at her in surprise then nodded in the affirmative. "We went back a long way. Believe it or not, he used to be one of the good guys."

Paula had to resist a scoff as she extinguished her smoke. "I'll take your word for it."

"It's true. Real crusader for the oppressed."

"What happened?"

"I've lain awake many a night trying to figure that one out. I think his soul just shriveled up and died inside him. Can't really pinpoint what made it happen. Then one night Red did something so . . ." He waved his hands as if at a loss for words. "That was when I knew I had to get as far away from him as possible if I was going to save my own soul."

"What'd he do?"

Kurt grimaced, turned his head away.

"You promised you'd tell me everything."

He told her about the night at the campfire when the girl blew her own brains out for fear of Red. Paula sucked in her breath. She pressed her hands together in front of her mouth as if in prayer. "Oh my God, Kurt, no."

"I tried to stop it. All I managed to do was break my arm. Otherwise I would have killed Red right then and there. Paula, you've got to believe that. I'm not a monster."

She took his hand in hers. "I do believe you." She said it solemnly, without emotion, like a businessman agreeing to a deal.

Kurt told Paula how a few months ago Red had shown up out of nowhere and suckered him into a mission to rescue Sonny Stewart, one of their buddies. He explained how it had all been a plot by Red to steal two million bucks worth of emeralds and that it had turned into a bloodbath. Sonny Stewart was not a part of it. Never had been.

"But now you were."

"Up to my neck."

"Even though it wasn't your fault," Paula said.

"A fine point considering who we're dealing with."

Paula cocked her head quizzically.

"Let's just say he's a prominent citizen of Colombia who'd make Red look like a Sunday school teacher." He snuffed out his smoke." Lets also say there are no good guys in this scenario. There's no way to do the righteous thing."

Paula's mind was whirring. Pieces of the puzzle were coming together. "When did this thing that Red tricked you into happen?"

Knowing Paula, Kurt wasn't surprised by the question. "Little over two months ago."

Paula nodded in understanding. She extinguished her smoke. “That's why you didn't see me for two months.” It was a statement, not a question.

“I was busy hatching a grand scheme to get you and me safely away from here in style, while getting Red out of my hair once and forever.”

“What about your Colombian friends?”

“Fuck 'em. Like I said, there are no good guys in this. Let ‘em eat each other alive for all I care.”

“What about you? Aren't you a good guy?”

“I'm ashamed to say that for a while there I wasn't a very good guy. I’d deluded myself that I was. Turned out I was wrong.”

“How’d you find out?”

“Not how. Who.”

Paula's face flushed. She knew the answer before asking, but asked anyway. “Me?”

“You.” He stubbed his Camel out.

Paula's head was swimming. She tried to formulate a relevant question starting with “But” or “How” or “Why.” All she came up with was, “I don't understand.”

Kurt's smile was filled not only with affection, but admiration. “Paula, why did you decide to run away with me?”

“What kind of idiot question is that? I love you.” She looked somewhat miffed. “What did you think?”

“It's what you said when we were in the bathtub a little while ago.”

Paula reviewed the scene in her mind but couldn’t guess what Kurt was referring to. “Okay, what did I say?”

“You said you ran away because you were gonna spend the rest of your life doing just as you pleased.”

“Damn right I am. Glad you got the message.”

“And I was one of the things that pleased you.”

“You are. God help me ‘cause I can’t.” They both laughed at that, then she said, “All right, tell me all about this grand scheme of yours.”

“I will. But just remember it was never executed. Okay? None of this ever happened. And I had already decided it wasn't going to happen.” Noticing her skeptical look, he added. “It's all theoretical, Paula.”

“Okay.”

Kurt walked her through it, starting with setting Red up with fake jewels so Estrada would take him out. He told her who Estrada was and how he was involved. He explained the Mr. Ames subterfuge, including the little cabin cruiser hidden on the far side of the boathouse.

Paula shook her head in dismay as Kurt described rigging the *Black Jack's* hull with explosives, then told her about his plan to transfer everything, including them, to the cabin cruiser before sinking the *Black Jack* in deep water. He finished by telling her about the escape route back through the Everglades, followed by the flight out of Miami.

Paula's expression of bewilderment was about what Kurt had expected. "And you thought I would just salute obediently, say aye, aye sir, and quietly go along with this insane plan?"

Kurt took a deep breath, and said, "No, I never imagined that for a second. I knew with absolute certainty that you wouldn't."

He knew that Paula was bursting with questions, undoubtedly of the indignant kind. He held up a hand to stop her. "Let me explain." And he did. As she listened, Paula's eyes grew increasingly larger. Her mouth gaped open in utter disbelief.

"You were going to knock me out?" She waited for Kurt to respond. When he didn't she repeated it, but this time with more fury. "Kurt, you were going to drug me?"

Kurt looked sheepish, shrugged helplessly. "For your own good. I didn't like it either, but I couldn't come up with anything better."

"How about honesty? How about trusting me enough to tell me the truth?"

"I was afraid if I did that, you'd run for the hills."

"Could you blame me?"

"No."

"Because, my God, Kurt, if you'd done that to me, you would've made me your prisoner. I would've hated you for the rest of my life. What were you thinking?"

She was gazing at him with piercing intensity. Sparks danced inside her big green eyes. Not the festive kind. More like the sparks from an ignited fuse. Somehow Kurt found it even more exciting than usual.

"Ah shit, let me make it real simple." He grabbed Paula by the lapels of her bush jacket, yanked her to him then kissed her with the explosive force of a lightning bolt.

At least that's what it seemed like to Paula, but she wondered sometimes if she wasn't highly impressionable. Regardless, it left her so breathless she had to pull her face away to gasp for air. Kurt didn't relent. He grabbed her hair, jerked her back around, and captured her lips again, savoring their softness then plunged his tongue into her mouth until she completely surrendered to him.

When he pushed her away, he still held onto her lapels, keeping her close enough to look earnestly into her eyes. "Now do you understand?"

"Yes, yes, yes," she said, panting, her voice little more than a whisper. "I think."

"What do you understand?"

"That you love me. A lot."

"Only as long as I draw breath."

She smiled. Her cheeks glowed with a rosy patina. "And I love you, Mr. Younger. Can't help it. My heart belongs to you. What kind of idiot does that make me?"

Kurt took her face in his hands. "Who the fuck cares?"

They kissed very gently, lying down on the bed. Kurt gathered Paula up into his arms and she winced. “My back, my back . . .”

“Your front, your front,” Kurt replied. They both chuckled then fell fast asleep.

77

When Kurt's eyes popped open, it was dark outside. The rain had stopped, and the alarm clock read 8:05. He eased out of bed, trying not to disturb Paula, then climbed back into his clothes.

Paula shifted into a fetal position, knees pulled up, arms folded against her chest. Kurt guessed she was trying to compensate for the loss of his warmth. He pulled the covers further up over her shoulders. Keeping her eyes firmly shut, she said, "I'm still asleep." Kurt smiled, kissed her forehead, then eased out of the room.

Once downstairs he collected all the photo prints as well as the negatives in Red's pocket. Paula didn't need to see them again. He found the waterproof envelope they'd come in and slipped the pictures back inside.

The other things Paula didn't need to see were the bodies of Red, Earl and Gator. A spacious storage room was accessible from the main room. Among its varied contents were several nylon tarps. Kurt decided these would make perfect body bags.

After removing all artillery, ammo, and identification from the three corpses, he started in the museum with Gator. He scooted a number of items out of the way then spread the tarp alongside his remains. When Kurt rolled Gator onto it, what was left of his head fell off.

Kurt did not enjoy scooping up handfuls of skull and flesh and eyeballs, especially since he wasn't wearing gloves. Pieces of Gator squished between his fingers like freshly ground beef.

Kurt thoroughly washed the goo off his hands then donned rubber gloves before he working on Earl. This proved more problematic because when he tried to roll Earl onto the canvas, he came completely apart. Most disturbing was how his intestines spilled out of his body cavity.

Turned out he had a lot of intestines. They stunk like a Kansas City slaughterhouse.

Kurt fought back an urge to puke up his own guts. Instead he returned to the storage room once again, grabbed a shovel, and scraped up several loads of Earl's intestines, along with other internal organs. He dumped them on the tarp, then rolled first the legs, then the torso and head, on top of the slop.

Red's body was completely intact, just the two small holes between his eyes. Conversely, the back of his head was a gory pulp. He was the heaviest of the three corpses. To get leverage, Kurt had to kneel on the tarp beside him, grab him by shoulders and hips then give a mighty yank to roll him over.

It worked. But as Red's carcass flipped over, his arm was flung out. It came crashing down around Kurt's neck, knocking him off balance so that he fell on top of Red, ending up with his face pressed against the face of his former partner. The impact of Kurt's weight on the body pushed up air from his already putrefying innards directly into his face, like being sprayed by a polecat. Kurt gagged, almost threw up.

He didn't like the way Red was looking at him. His eyes seemed to be mocking Kurt. He tried to break loose, but the arm was wedged around his neck as if determined to hold Kurt in an obscene embrace. What was it he used to say? Partners forever.

"Fuck that," Kurt said out loud, then jerked Red's arm away and stood up. Next, he folded the tarps over each of the bodies and used Army duck tape to thoroughly seal them. When finished, all three bodies looked ready for burial at sea. Appropriate since that was exactly what was going to happen.

He pulled the bodies out onto the front verandah and fired up several hanging hurricane lanterns. They swung gently in the declining breeze, which thankfully was still strong enough to carry away the stench.

He dragged the bodies one at a time down to the dock, where he fired up more lanterns. To Kurt, the warm, festive glow washing over the three tarp-wrapped bodies was grotesquely surreal. Later he would pull the *Black Jack* alongside and heave the bodies onboard. A dance macabre indeed.

Back inside the house Kurt gathered up the fake emeralds scattered across the floor then returned them to the leather pouch Red had carried them in. He dropped the pouch on the bar and was surveying the damaged French doors when he noticed Paula descending the stairs.

She stopped halfway down, wary, as if expecting something to jump out at her. When she noticed the photos and bodies were gone, she visibly relaxed. She smiled warmly at Kurt. "Thank you."

Despite everything she'd been through, Paula looked beautiful, downright regal, in fact. Kurt noticed she was limping slightly, favoring the hip that had been knifed. It made his anger flare. The urge to unwrap Gator's corpse and unload a magazine in it was hard to subdue.

But that wouldn't help Paula. What she needed was bolstering up, so he gave her a breezy smile and said, “Fuck the whole world and the horse it rode in on.”

It broadened her smile. She cocked her fist in the air and said, “Yeah, fuck ‘em all.” She continued down the stairs. “What can I do to help?”

“You can fix us a drink. If there's a God in Heaven, a bottle of Jack survived.”

Paula crossed to the bar. Among several shattered liquor bottles was an untouched Jack Daniels Black. She brandished it saying, “I guess God loves you. Oh, and He loves me too.” She held up a bottle of Smirnoff. “Ice?”

“In the freezer below the bar. Should still have some.”

It did. Paula made drinks then handed one to Kurt. They clinked glasses. “I feel numb,” she said, followed by a big sip of vodka. “Ah, well, that helps.” She fired up a Chesterfield.

“Good. 'Cause we still got a long night ahead of us.”

“You mean cleaning up?” Paula slumped back against the bar, took another gulp. “Let's leave it for the maid on Tuesday.”

Kurt shook his head. “Cleaning up's the worst thing we can do.”

When Kurt didn't elaborate, Paula said, “Okay, why's it the worst thing we can do?”

“Look around. Obviously a battle royal took place here.”

“What's a battle royal?”

“Goes back to the Romans. It's what they called a fight to the death between three or more gladiators until only one was left standing. That's what we want them to think. Only they won't know who was left standing. That's to our advantage.”

Kurt had her complete attention now. “They?”

He took a generous pull from his whiskey then glanced at his watch. “Little over an hour ago Red was supposed to meet Estrada in Colombia and give him these.” He reached into the leather pouch, pulled out a handful of emeralds. He held them up in his palm for Paula to see.

She looked at him quizzically. “Yeah, I saw those earlier. So what?”

“Problem is, Estrada's not seeing them right now.”

“Bad, huh?”

“Very bad. He's gonna come after these emeralds. Count on it. And he's gonna come here. With a small army.”

Paula choked on her drink, then said, “You're kidding.”

“'Fraid not.”

“Well why are we standing around talking? Let's get the hell out of here.” She stubbed out her cigarette.

“Easy, easy. We've got a little time.”

“But . . .”

“Bogotá is 1500 miles away. Seven and a half hours flight time on a C-47, which is probably what they'll use.”

"Why do you say that? And what the hell is a C-47?"

"Trust me, they won't be flying Pan Am. Hard to check all that heavy artillery, inflatable assault rafts, and big outboard motors as baggage. No, they'll need an aircraft designed to carry all that gear, plus a coupla dozen troops. A C-47 is a standard military cargo plane. Twin-engine prop. A blue million of 'em were made during the war. When they were decommissioned, small military units and freight companies all over the world gobbled 'em up.

"It'll take Estrada a little while to put it all together. Four hours minimum, six at the outside. Means we've got twelve hours, maybe a little more." He clinked her glass again and winked at her. "Cheers."

Paula simply stared at him for a moment then said, "God, just when I was starting to like you again."

Kurt grabbed a handful of breast, tipped her back and said, "Like me hell, you love me." He planted a deep lingering kiss on her, then brought her back upright. Neither of them had spilled their drinks.

"Point taken," Paula said. "All right, what do we have to do?"

"Well, nothing to the house, unfortunately."

"Why not?"

"If we did any cleanup or repair, it would be a dead giveaway as to who survived the battle royal. I'd like to board up the French doors in case another storm blows in. But only the guy who owns this place would do that. Gotta keep 'em guessing."

"What a shame. Look at this beautiful rug. Ruined."

Kurt shrugged. "It's a rug." He glanced up. "At least the overhead windows aren't damaged."

Paula scanned the upper regions of the wall. "Can't say the same for poor ol' Marty the Marlin."

Kurt's prize marlin now had gaping holes punched in it from a wild burst of gunfire. "Maxine, actually. Put up one hell of a fight, she did," he said wistfully. "Took all day to reel her in."

Paula gave him a saucy look. "Nothing compared to how long it took to reel me in."

Kurt nodded, said, "True."

Paula clinked his glass. "How 'bout I freshen that up a tad." She did then nodded toward the jewels. "You want to tell me about these?"

"They're fake."

Paula twisted her mouth impatiently. "Yes, I know. So where are the real ones?"

"Safe."

"Okay, skip the lengthy explanations, just . . ."

"Paula . . ."

"What?"

"They're safe."

"Oh come on . . ."

“It's better you don't know.”

“That's what my mom said first time I asked about sex.”

“She was right. So am I.”

“Okay, let me broach a more pertinent question. Where to from here? According to you, Florida Bay'll be swarming with pirates in a few hours.”

"It will be.”

“And you've got a plan to deal with that?”

“Of course I do. The original plan.”

“Plan A?”

“The same.”

“Not plan B?”

“Never had a plan B.”

“So we're back to the one where you knock me out, throw me over your shoulder, and take me off to your cave.”

“Afraid it's not as romantic as that.”

Kurt reached inside his bush jacket, pulled out an envelope, and handed it to Paula. She opened it to find two Eastern Airlines tickets to Paris with a stopover in New York.

Paula was a little hurt. “Kurt I thought I explained to you . . .”

“We're not going there to set up house. We're just gonna hide out there till the heat dies down. Doesn't mean we can't have some fun in the meantime.” He put his arms around her. “It's a fun town. And pretty damn romantic.”

“I guess calling the cops is not an option.”

“Not a good one.”

Paula looked so vulnerable it almost broke Kurt's heart. He took her in his arms and they kissed gently, more in a show of support than affection. Kurt gazed over the room’s destruction and a sense of great loss was evident in his eyes. It confused Paula knowing he originally had planned on abandoning the house.

Then she understood. Plans had changed. This was still his home. He'd come back here, live here like before. And when the two of them were together, this is where they would live.

She put a hand to his cheek. “We can make it right again.”

He took her hand and kissed it, his swagger returning. “Damn right we can.”

Paula smiled, but looked troubled. “Something just occurred to me.”

“Yeah?”

“It's probably really stupid.”

“I promise not to laugh.”

“I was just wondering why Estrada would send a crew all the way up here from Colombia. Why not just hire some local guys?”

Kurt just stared at her for a moment. Paula thought she must have said something really dumb.

Kurt said, “Shit.”

78

“I can't believe you never thought of that,” Paula said as they were packing clothes.

“Not the way I would do it,” Kurt said. “But that may be what Estrada’s counting on. He knows I don't do hit-and-run. I do self-contained unit work. He probably will too. It's the only way to completely control the outcome of a mission.”

“What do you mean?”

“If Estrada’s not here as part of the operation, there's always the possibility the hit-and-run team will just grab the jewels and disappear into the night.”

“But?”

“Estrada knows he has the kind of reputation that would discourage anybody from double-crossing him.”

“You did.”

“Right. That's why you need to pack faster.” He spotted the porcelain egret on the dresser and picked it up. “And you don't want to forget this.”

Something clicked in Paula 's mind. She took the egret from Kurt, carefully packed it into the larger suitcase and slammed it shut. “I'm done. How much time do we have?”

“Under one scenario, hours. Under the other, none.”

“And we're assuming scenario two.”

“Got to.”

Paula took in a deep breath, blew it out. She shook her hands as if trying to get blood into them. “Okay, okay, okay.”

“I'll take the suitcases down to the dock. You hit the kitchen and pack us up some grub. There's ice chests in the storeroom.” Paula's eyes widened with panic. “We'll be outta here inside an hour. Even an experienced hit-and-run team can't get here that fast.”

“You sure?”

Kurt thought about it a second. “Pretty sure.”

"Kurt . . ."

"Move, girl. Move, move, move."

Paula said, "Yes sir," and scurried out of the room. Kurt heard her say, "Shit, shit, shit," as she took the stairs two at a time.

By a little after midnight the dock was jammed with everything they'd need for their getaway. The hurricane lanterns Kurt fired up earlier provided ample illumination. The list he'd scribbled out a little while ago was in Paula's hand. She called it out item by item.

"Food and water?"

"Check."

"Clothes?"

"Two suitcases for you, one for me."

"Booze?"

"His and hers."

"Weaponry?"

"Plenty. Plus ammo and a crate of grenades."

"Oh God, Kurt . . ."

"Come on, come on."

"First aid kit?"

"Check."

"Rigging gear?"

"Ropes, chains, clips and hooks."

"Fuel?"

"Several jerry cans.'

Flashlights?"

"Check."

"And, uh . . ."

"Three carcasses wrapped up and ready for delivery to Davy Jones' Locker."

Paula swayed, feeling ill. Kurt steadied her. She waved him off. "I'm okay, I'm okay, lets just get out of here."

Kurt grinned at her encouragingly and said, "Be right back," then scurried back up to the house. Paula was hot boxing a Chesterfield when she saw him trotting down the hill with a very big machine gun over his shoulder. Ammunition belts were slung over his other shoulder.

"Say hello to Mr. Browning," he said.

She flicked off a cigarette ash. "Boys and their toys."

Kurt laid the .30 caliber M1919 and its ammo belts down on the dock. "This toy will give anybody following us a very stern message. Stay the fuck back."

Paula surveyed all the items strung out on the dock. "We going to be able to get all this stuff on the *Black Jack*?"

"Some of it goes on the *Far Horizons*."

"The what?"

"Little cabin cruiser I told you about."

"Right, right." Her eyes got large. "Kurt, listen."

He went deathly still. His ears pricked up. He whispered, "I hear it. It's coming up the channel from the Bay. Douse these lanterns. Quick."

They did. Kurt grabbed one of the submachine guns, jammed a clip in then scooted Paula behind him. "Stay low and don't move." He cocked the gun, then silently moved to a position at the end of the dock, squatted, and waited.

The clouds had moved out. The moon was bright over the open lagoon, but because the channel cut through thick foliage, it was as black as the inside of a gun barrel.

Kurt strained to see but to no avail. But he heard the sound of something moving up the channel. It was moving fast.

Getting closer.

It came out of the mouth of the channel like a torpedo aimed directly at the dock. Kurt leveled the submachine gun at it then jerked the barrel up to keep from filling Wally full of lead.

"Wally!" The relief in Paula's laughter made Kurt and Wally laugh too. He did a back flip then stood up in the water for Paula to kiss him. "Hi, baby."

Kurt reached down, stroked him and said, "Pal you just scared the shit out of me."

Paula laughed. She leaned her forehead against Kurt's. They both laughed some more. Like children.

Kurt stood. "All right, you guys stay here. I got one last thing to do before bringing the boats around."

"Such as?"

"Hide the emeralds where Estrada's boys will be sure to find them."

"But they're fake."

"I know that. You know that. They don't know that. Not yet anyway. It'll buy us some time."

About ten minutes later, the boathouse's big doors swung open followed by the *Black Jack* easing out. It caught Wally's attention, too. He effortlessly leapt over the dock and swam over to Kurt, who responded as if he expected nothing less.

He let the *Black Jack* drift over to the far side of the boathouse where the *Far Horizons* was hidden under a cover of mangrove branches. He tossed these aside, then made fast a towline to the little cabin cruiser's bow. He closed the boathouse doors, then with Wally leading the way, cruised over to the dock.

All the items they wanted to keep were loaded into the *Far Horizons*. Everything else went into the *Black Jack*, including the three tarp-wrapped bodies. At precisely 1:00 AM they were ready to go. Kurt turned to Paula and said, "You'll have to steer the *Far Horizons* through the channel. I won't be able to tow it fast enough to keep it from swinging against the banks. When we get out to the Bay, you can transfer back to the *Black Jack*."

Paula smiled bravely and saluted.

Kurt said, "Here we go."

She kissed him. "Yes, here we go."

79

When they rounded the first bend in the channel, Paula looked back at the house and lagoon before they were eclipsed from view by the thick foliage. The enchanted island disappeared like a dream in the morning sun. Would she ever see it again?

Looking forward, she corrected her course slightly to stay in the middle of the channel. Ahead, Kurt was standing high, hands gripping the helm, feet planted about a foot apart, ready for action as always. He'd removed his bush jacket to reveal a tight-fitting black T-shirt underneath.

Wally had clearly decided that wherever Kurt and Paula were going, he was going too. He led the way most of the time, nodding back to Kurt to follow, but he would also double back to check on Paula, chattering at her. It made Paula smile. "I love you too, baby."

When they emerged into the Bay the sky was cloudless. The island was silhouetted against a bright, almost-full moon in a sky full of twinkling stars. The irony of being in such a romantic setting in the midst of the deadly scenario they were playing out was not lost on Paula.

Kurt idled the *Black Jack's* engines while Paula brought the *Far Horizons* alongside. She shut down the Evinrude then let Kurt help her onboard. She almost tripped over the bodies laid out in the stern. All thoughts of romantic settings were driven from her mind.

Kurt said, "To hell with them. They got what they had coming to them. Come up to the cockpit with me." She did and they got underway, towing the *Far Horizons* behind. Wally seemed to be glad they were both in the same boat and took a position off the port bow. Paula expected Kurt to head out to open water, but instead he steered parallel to the island.

He answered the question in her eyes. "We've gotta find the boat Red and his crew arrived in. Estrada's men aren't going to find any bodies, despite evidence of all out warfare, so they can't find a boat either. They've gotta believe all the players have fled."

Paula understood. "It also means they don't know how many people they're chasing. When they see the extent of the damage in the house, they're going to know more than two people were involved."

Kurt nodded. "The more we keep them guessing, the better for us."

Paula said, "Okay. Sorry, but I've got the heebie-jeebies. And my stomach's making sounds like an angry bear. How 'bout I fix us something to eat and a couple of drinks? I brought a nice looking ham and a there's loaf of bread. Sandwiches?"

"With lots of bite-your-ass mustard."

"Comin' up."

They found the Jon boat Red had stolen where Kurt thought it would be. It was empty except for a spare jerry can of fuel. Kurt wasn't surprised. Everything the three had brought with them would be on their persons.

It only took a few minutes to connect a tow line from the stern of the *Far Horizons*, loop it through the bow eye of the Jon boat, then run it back to the *Black Jack* where Kurt tied it off on a stern cleat. This would allow him to release the Jon boat without having to stop. During the process, Wally went from boat to boat as if inspecting to make sure the work was properly done.

"Quite a little circus train we've got going," Paula said.

"Yeah, I'm not happy about it either. Out here on open water with a big moon, I feel like one of those ducks in a shooting gallery."

Kurt eased the *Black Jack's* throttle forward and the two boats fell in line behind them. Paula noticed he had all lights turned off. She assumed under the circumstances he wanted to remain as dark as possible.

"How far?" Paula asked.

"Hours at the pace we'll be going. Gotta go round the tip of Key Largo to reach the edge of the shelf. We'll cut the Jon boat loose halfway there, close enough to wash up onshore."

They both grew quiet then, finishing their sandwiches, sipping stiff drinks, and munching potato chips that could only be described as vintage.

80

At this hour, Kurt and Paula had Florida Bay entirely to themselves.

They covered the distance from Curiosity Cove deep into Blackwater Sound without incident, but at a glacial pace because of towing two boats, one of them being the Jon boat, which was never designed for speed.

Paula was surprised that Wally was still with them. She had expected him to veer off once they cleared the island, but obviously he had other plans. At the leisurely speed they were traveling, he had no problem keeping up.

That was fine with Paula. She remembered her father saying dolphins brought good luck. Right now they needed all they could get. Her stomach was twisted in knots.

The rocky and, at this hour, shadowy coast of Key Largo loomed ahead. Kurt made a wide sweep, slinging the Jon boat toward shore then gave Paula the signal to release. She slipped the knot on the towline. Within seconds the little flat-bottomed boat was scooting toward land. Later in the morning it would make a nice prize for some old Conch. Paula pulled in the towline, coiling it as she did, always the captain's daughter.

The loss of drag allowed Kurt to pick up speed, but not as much as he would like. The *Far Horizons* was riding in the *Black Jack's* wake. Greater speed meant a more turbulent wake, which might capsize the smaller boat. Plus, the *Black Jack's* aft was weighted down with bodies and chains. Greater speed could dip it enough to take on water. A slow pace also allowed Wally to keep up. For reasons Kurt didn’t understand himself, that seemed important.

He steered north toward Jewfish Creek, which was about a mile in length. It would give them passage to Barnes Sound. From there they would take Steamboat Creek up into Card Sound, then Angelfish Creek out into the Atlantic. The continental shelf was only a few miles further. The drop off was fairly steep. It wouldn't take long before they were over deep water.

That's where he planned to drop the bodies. Once Red, Gator and Earl were taking that long dive to a place where sunlight never penetrated, Kurt intended to circle back toward the edge of the shelf until he found a spot where the water was only about a hundred feet deep.

He'd sink the *Black Jack* there so it would be easily accessible to frogmen, especially Estrada's frogmen. To complete the illusion, he'd salt the site with a sprinkling of real emeralds. Nobody would be surprised that Kurt's body wasn't found there, or the rest of the jewels. This was the legendary Florida Straits. The current was swift and deadly.

He was aware of Paula standing beside him, her fingers idly mussing his hair.

"So tell me baby, would you still have hi-tailed it outta Palm Beach if you'd known what you were getting into?"

Paula looked at him as if he had just arrived from Mars. "You're kidding, right?" She waited for a response. When she didn't get one she said, "Of course I wouldn't have."

That jarred Kurt. "You wouldn't have?"

"I don't have a death wish, Kurt. I have a life wish."

Kurt took a moment before responding. "Paula, trust me, I'm gonna fix this."

She kissed him on the cheek. "I do trust you, honey, but how are you going to fix it?"

"I think I know how to take care of Estrada."

Paula went rigid. "You mean kill him?"

"No, no. You have my word. No killing."

"What, then?"

"It's complicated but, well, I know the man. I've met him before. Several times. I know what he's made of. I know what he really wants."

"Oh Kurt, don't. He's a killer, you said so yourself."

He turned to her in his fiercest fighting stance. "This has got to be done, Paula. It's the only way we can have a life together. I'll be damned if anybody's gonna take that away from us. Anybody who tries will have me to deal with. That includes you, Miss Doherty."

This is the part where I melt like a puddle at his feet, Paula thought. She gave him her most determined smile. "All you need to know Mr. Younger, my love, my pirate, is I'd rather be running for my life with you than . . . buying eggs and milk at Wilson's."

Kurt laughed out loud. "Smart lady. I think we should drink to that."

Paula gave him a peck on the cheek. "Coming up." While she juggled booze, glasses and ice, she asked him what time it was.

Kurt checked his watch. "2:15."

Paula did the math in her head. "Thirty hours. How is that possible?"

Kurt looked at her quizzically, but all she said was, "So where will we be thirty hours from now?"

Kurt thought about it a second, then said, "On top of the Eiffel Tower sipping champagne."

Paula's eyes lit up. "The Eiffel Tower?"

"Yes ma'am."

"Tomorrow?"

"Factoring in the time change, we should have glasses in hand right about dusk, just when they're turning the lights on. All over the city."

The wonder of it danced in Paula's eyes. "The city of lights."

"It is indeed." He took a sip of his drink, then set it down. "This helps, but you know, I'm kinda hungry too."

"Okay. For what?"

"Your lips."

"You're lucky, mister. They're on special tonight."

Paula hoped hers were as tasty as his. According to the growling sounds he made, she assumed they were. "Nice and warm," he said.

"And stamped 'Property of Kurt Younger.'"

"How 'bout 'Gift of Paula Doherty?'"

She smiled, kissed him harder. "Know what I love about your lips?"

He nibbled on her bottom lip. "No, tell me."

"That they're on mine."

After that, they didn't talk for a while. Wally interrupted them with the clacking sound he made when impatient. Paula said, "Oh shut up, Wally," then looked ahead. "Entrance to Jewfish Creek coming up."

It was a familiar sight to Paula. The shadowy figure of the Overseas Highway Drawbridge marked the entrance to Jewfish Creek. It towered above them the closer they got. There was plenty of overhead clearance for both boats even though the bridge was down. Beyond it was the creek itself with walls of thick mangroves on both sides and wide enough for easy passage.

As they neared the bridge Kurt and Paula were blinded by a powerful spotlight. It was accompanied by an authoritarian voice blasting from a bullhorn. "You in the Blackjack. Heave to."

81

Kurt whipped the M1 carbine from its mount beside the helm, told Paula to get down, took aim at the light, and was about to let loose when the voice called out again with greater urgency, but decidedly less authority. “Hey, don't shoot me, I'm just the bridge tender.”

Paula was crouched down under the console with her back to the light. “Oh God, Kurt, put your gun down. That's Frankie Whipplespoon. He's been operating that bridge since George Washington was chopping down cherry trees. He knows me, dammit.”

Kurt lowered his rifle. “Is there anybody in Key Largo who doesn't?”

“Not many.”

Kurt waved at Frankie and called out, “Sorry. I guess you spooked me.”

“Spooked you?” Frankie said over the bullhorn. “Man, I'm gonna have to change my britches.”

Paula giggled. “I can't believe he said that.”

Kurt saw the silhouette of a stooped, wiry old codger with a bullhorn in one hand and a walking cane in the other. Kurt held out his hands apologetically. “Really am sorry, friend.” He wanted the tender to keep the spotlight squarely on him instead of sweeping the boat, lighting up the tarp-wrapped bundles in the back. Wouldn't take much imagination to figure out what was in the tarps. “So why did you stop me?”

“Saw you were headin' up the creek and wanted to warn you. That storm we had earlier really stirred things up. Tore up a bunch of the older mangrove trees and such. Creek's pretty littered with them. Danger of gettin' fowled. Can't guarantee passage to Barnes.”

Kurt considered his options, realized he didn't have any, and called, “Thanks for the heads-up. I'll be extra careful.”

“You do that, mister. Good luck to ya.” He turned the spotlight off then hobbled back inside his house.

Paula unfolded herself from where she was crouching and plopped down in the jump seat. “What are we going to do?”

“Gotta try to get through the creek.”

“Why don’t we turn around, head down to Tavernier, cut over to the Atlantic that way?”

“By the time we got back up to the shelf, the sun would be up. Plus, we'd be cruising up the most populated part of the island. Too much exposure. No, we gotta make it up the creek. This is already taking longer than I thought.”

Paula considered it a moment then said, “In that case, why don't I get in the bow and watch for obstructions?”

“Good idea.”

Paula made her way down from the wheelhouse, found an oar, then moved forward to the bow seat.

“What's with the oar?” Kurt asked.

“If I can push debris out of away, we're good to go. If I can't, we got a problem.”

Kurt grinned. “Beauty *and* brains.” He ignored her withering glance and throttled up, but at a slow glide, just enough to keep the *Far Horizons* from swaying behind him. Paula wedged herself into the tip of the bow seat, gripped the railing.

Kurt was more at ease on Jewfish Creek. He and Paula were hidden from view by the forest of mangroves on either side. But while that danger had temporarily passed, other dangers awaited straight ahead.

“Big one coming up,” Paula called. Kurt had seen the clump of mangrove tree branches too, dead center in the creek. He throttled back as Paula leaned over the bow with the oar and pushed against it. Luckily it gave way and she walked back on the foredeck, pushing it as far away as possible. Wally understood what she was doing and joined in, pushing the tangled remnants of the 'walking tree' toward shore.

So far, so good. Kurt looked back to make sure none of the debris worked itself back around to fowl the *Far Horizons*. Wally made sure it didn't. Satisfied, he eased the throttle open, but just enough for navigation. He knew if he had to stop suddenly, the *Far Horizons* would rear end the *Black Jack*. If so, he wanted the impact to be a bump, not a collision.

As they continued upstream they encountered several more tangled clumps of mangrove debris, old rotten stuff mostly, easily torn away by the storm. As before, Paula and Wally worked as a team to clear passage. Kurt steered around the obstacles, careful not to sling the *Far Horizons* against the opposite shore.

Paula called out, “This one's pretty big.”

Kurt throttled back as Paula jammed her oar down against the tangle of floating debris and pushed it away. But it wasn’t cooperating. Her oar was stuck and she was running out of deck space to pull it free.

Afraid she'd be pulled overboard, Paula braced her feet against the side then pushed backward with all her might. The oar broke free, but the force of her backward momentum made it swing up over her head.

Something was clearly wrong. The end of the oar was moving. Slithering. Two beady eyes and a white mouth gaping open, fangs bared. A cottonmouth, huge and clearly agitated.

Paula screamed. The viper wrapped its five-foot length around the oar in a repulsive dance of undulating muscles and slimy scales, working its way toward her. She tried to throw the oar overboard but before she could, the snake jumped onto her wrist, wrapped itself around it, then crawled up her arm.

"Kurt! Oh God!"

It coiled around her arm, its head darting up and down, its tongue flicking in and out, hissing like a vampire in a horror movie. It reached her elbow, raised its head up and stared her in the eyes. As horrific as the sight was, Paula couldn't tear her eyes away from it. "Kurt!"

"Don't move, Paula."

The calmness in his voice was almost as insane as what he was asking her to do. "What?"

The snake opened its mouth so wide that Paula was sure it would engulf her entire head. Her heart pounded. Her head was so light she knew she was about to faint.

"Kurt please . . ."

"Steady . . ."

The cottonmouth drew his head back. Paula knew it was about to strike. Instead, its head exploded, disappearing from the rest of its body. Cold blood pumped onto Paula's arm while the blast from Kurt's gun still rang in her ears.

The rest of the snake's body flopped around like an unattended garden hose. Paula threw it onto the deck then hopped up onto a bench seat to get away from it. The decapitated snake continued to slither until Kurt picked it up. He looked at it appraisingly. "Grill this baby up and we got us a real breakfast treat."

Paula leaned over the railing and threw up.

Kurt nodded, said, "Yeah, it's an acquired taste."

82

Kurt thought Paula was about to be sick again. Instead she screamed, “I hate snakes, Kurt! God almighty, I really do!”

One of Kurt's arms was outstretched holding up the snake's writhing remains while the other was wrapped around Paula's shoulders, trying to calm her. “Easy now, easy. Everything's okay.”

“Would you please just get rid of it?”

Kurt shrugged and tossed it overboard, almost hitting Wally, who gave him a puzzled look. He didn't know this game. “There, now,” he said. “All gone. Okay?”

Paula's face twisted into a grimace of revulsion, as if she'd just bitten into a lemon. She shuddered from head to toe.

Kurt realized that after everything else she'd been through earlier, the snake episode had clearly pushed her over the top. He wrapped his arms around her, hugged her, kissed her forehead. “Almost over, baby. In a little while we'll be on a big jet plane flying off to Never Land. Till then I'm not about to let anything happen to you.” He lifted her chin to make her look into his eyes. “You are my life, okay?”

Paula worked her arms free and threw them around Kurt's neck. “I'll be all right. Sorry I got all female on you. It's just I . . . I really hate snakes.”

“Okay, reading you loud and clear on that one. No snakes.”

“Thank you.” She unwrapped her arms from around his neck, swung them in circles as if doing calisthenics, and took a deep breath. “Okay, okay, I'm good. What now?”

“We're gonna swap places. You can drive this tub good as I can so you take the helm and concentrate on being the most gorgeous skipper in Florida Bay.”

As she climbed up into the cockpit, Paula marveled at how Kurt always found a way to make her feel special -- even in dire straits. She struck a pose, cocking her hip out, putting one hand on her waist, and the other behind her head. She winked at him, and said, “How’s this?”

Kurt responded with a hearty laugh that reminded Paula of her father. “You’ll do. Okay, I'll take the bow and make sure no more of those squirmy bastards get on board. If they do, I'll tie 'em up in a knot and toss 'em in the air for target practice.”

“You do that, Roy.” She glanced ahead. “But right now, you better man your oar. Debris straight ahead.”

Kurt saluted, said, “Aye, Cap'n.”

They made it out of Jewfish Creek without further mishap but there were a lot of severed mangrove branches to be pushed aside, forcing them to move at a crawl. Even though the creek was little more than a mile long, it took them a full thirty minutes to traverse it.

They now faced their longest open run, five miles across Barnes Sound to Steamboat Creek. There was scattered debris in the Sound but it was easy to scoot around, allowing them to regain their previous cruising speed.

Wally seemed to think Paula was playing chase with him. He raced through the water like a torpedo, leaping up to grab a breath, then performing an occasional barrel roll just to show off. Paula laughed at his antics, feeling better for doing so, and called to him, “Silly old dolphin.” The tension that had built up was gradually ebbing.

Kurt stepped up behind her, grabbed her pack of Chesterfields from the console, clamped one between his lips, lit it then transferred it to her lips. She took a deep, grateful drag. He shook out a Camel for himself, fired it up then gently kneaded her shoulders. “How ya doin', Cap?”

Paula groaned. “Keep that up and I'm doing just fine.” Kurt was about to swat her on the ass, but remembered the knife wound on her hip. He decided it wouldn't be such a good idea. Instead, he checked the heading. Paula was right on course.

The advantage of being in the Sound was having a flat, unobstructed field of view in all directions. Surprise attacks were not possible. The moon was bright. If company showed up, they'd see it coming from a long way off and have time to take evasive action.

Other than the purr of the engine, the splash of their wake, it was very still, very quiet. Paula looked up at the starry night with its fat moon and felt almost at peace. “Have you ever seen so many stars?”

“Every time I look into your eyes.”

Oh God, Paula thought. He knew every line in the book, along with a few that weren't. Knowing he truly meant it was what made it work. “You keep saying things like that, mister, and we're going to get along just fine.”

Fifteen minutes later they arrived at the mouth of Steamboat Creek. It was a repeat of Jewfish Creek only twice as long and half as wide. The result was that debris tended to clump together more. Paula stayed up in the cockpit, steering them through, while Kurt stood in the bow clearing passage, with Wally's help.

There were no snake attacks this time, but Kurt kept in mind that off the starboard side, Key Largo Island was rife with crocodiles. Only a mile east of their position was Crocodile Lake. If Paula didn't like snakes, he could imagine how she'd react to a croc leaping on board, a feat, unbeknownst to most, they can easily do. Kurt kept his eyes trained on anything floating in the water that wasn't a tree branch.

He hadn't traversed Steamboat Creek in quite a while. He was trying to recall any potential dangers when a red flag popped up in his mind. He turned to Paula, giving her the crossed wrists signal. She slammed on brakes and Kurt scrambled to the stern, using his oar to keep the *Far Horizons* from rear-ending them.

Paula left the engines idling then joined Kurt mid-deck. “What's up?”

“The bridge for Card Sound Road is just ahead.”

“Yeah, I know. It's low but we can make it.”

“Not what I'm concerned about. Where does Card Sound Road go from here?”

“Across the top of the island. Eventually hooks up with Highway One above town. Why?”

“Access and opportunity. The road provides access. The bridge provides the perfect opportunity for an ambush.”

Paula realized instantly that Kurt was right. She'd have never thought of it herself. Unlike Kurt, her mind wasn’t trained to think that way. “Shit.”

“Indeed.”

“Well what are we going to do? Head back down the creek? Take Barnes Sound around the end of the island?”

“Wouldn't matter if we did. Still have to cross under Card Sound Road at some point. Same situation. They can travel by truck faster than we can by boat. Plus it'd tack on two and a half, three hours of travel time while gaining us nothing.”

“Oh Kurt . . .”

“Yeah, I know. I could shoot myself for not thinking of this little squeeze play. I've been outta the game too long. I'm getting rusty.”

Paula was quiet for a moment then said, “Yeah, but on you rust looks good.” It clearly surprised Kurt. She smiled at him crookedly. “What, you think you're the only one who can do that?”

Kurt grinned too. “Lady, I think I've met my match.”

“You have. Now that we've established that, what the hell are we going to do?”

“For one thing, we've got a lotta fire power in this boat.”

“Oh great . . .”

“What we don't have is speed, which is essential, but we can fix that.”

Paula was ahead of him. “You want me to get in the *Far Horizons* and drive it so we can both go full speed.”

"It's our only chance. We'll charge the bridge, guns blazing. I'll use Big B . . ."

"What?"

"The machine gun I brought down just before we left." He lifted the M1919 up to the wheelhouse and slammed it home in the special mount near the helm. "Shoots really big bullets really fast. Settles an argument better than anything I know."

He attached an ammo belt then hopped down to the deck, grabbing Earl's submachine gun from the weapons stash. "Here, you use this." He shoved it into Paula's hands.

Paula tossed it back to him as if it was another snake. "Good grief, Kurt, I'm not going to shoot anybody."

"You're right, you won't. Doubt you'd hit anything if you tried."

"Well, thanks a lot."

"But you can damn sure make 'em duck for cover. At the speed we'll be going, that'll be good enough." He jammed a fresh magazine in, cocked it then handed it back to Paula. She reluctantly took it.

"It's ready to fire. Just point in the general direction and pull the trigger. Concentrate on spraying the bridge, not me. I'll be in front of you with the big gun makin' 'em want to kneel down and pray. Got it?"

Paula nodded. A motion in the water caught her attention. She screamed out, "Kurt! Wally!"

Kurt whipped around to see a crocodile charging Wally, who had already sensed his presence. It was clear to Kurt that Wally was going to try to take on the reptile. He snatched the gun from Paula's hands and stepped up to the railing. The croc had his mouth wide open about to lunge at Wally.

Kurt opened fire, stitching a line of holes from the creature's head to its stern. The chatter of the gun was deafening, sending a flock of sleeping egrets exploding into flight. The crock disappeared beneath the surface amidst bubbles and blood. Wally helped him along.

As the echo of the blast died away, Kurt yanked the magazine from the smoking gun, jammed in a fresh one, cocked it, and gave it back to Paula. "One thing's for damn sure. They know we're here now. Let's get moving."

83

After helping Paula onto the *Far Horizons,* Kurt slipped the knot on the towline then pulled it aboard the *Black Jack.* He nodded to Paula. "Go ahead and fire it up."

She laid the submachine gun on the front seat, moved to the stern, grabbed the pull cord on the rusty old Evinrude, and gave it a hard yank. It cranked right up. She left it idling while she made her way to the helm. When she took possession of the gun again, she noticed it had a strap. She slung it over her head so it hung at her side. Easier to handle.

She scoffed at herself. Yeah, listen to Calamity Jane here. This is nuts.

Kurt was directly across from her in the *Black Jack.* "You'll have to steer with your left hand to leave your right free to use the gun. It's gonna kick a bit, so hold . . ,"

"Don't tell me how it's going to kick, Kurt."

"It will. And if you don't keep a tight grip, it'll jump right outta your hand and shoot up the boat. Then you'll sink in crocodile infested waters."

"Okay, okay, okay."

"It's gonna be all right, Paula. This'll all be over within a minute."

"That's what old Doc Hutchinson used to say every time he gave me a shot."

"And you're still here."

Paula clearly wasn't very reassured by this. Understandable. He was having misgivings himself. She'd spent the last twenty years of her life being a housewife and mother, not a soldier. Yes, she rose magnificently to the occasion dealing with the monsters now wrapped in nylon tarps, but she didn't need to be put in that situation again. Ever.

"Look," he said. "There's another way we can do this. A better way. Turn your boat around. Get the hell out of here. Go back to your mom's place in Key Largo. Wait there till you hear from me."

"And when will that be?"

"After I get this mess cleaned up. Not long."

Paula searched deep in his eyes for any indication he wasn't telling her the truth. He didn't flinch. "That's what you want me to do?"

"It is, baby. It's the best play. Dumb of me not to think of it before."

Then she did see something, not a lie but a deep, burning love for her that was pure and true. She locked her big green eyes on him. "I'm not going anywhere, Kurt, except with you. So fire up the *Black Jack*, mister. We got a plane to catch."

Kurt and Paula's discovery of each other over the past two days was akin to the dance of the seven veils. One by one they had dropped. This was the last one. Now they stood naked before each other. Kurt said, "I promised I wouldn't let anything happen to you and I won't."

"I know you won't. I believe you."

"All right." He took a deep breath, focused on the mission. "When you see me kick it, you do the same, but stay close. No more'n ten feet back. Ride my wake."

Paula smiled encouragingly. Kurt wasn't fooled. She was scared to the core of her being.

He wasn't.

He'd faced this moment many times before. He was supremely confident that not only would he survive, he'd take out a lot of bad guys in the process.

He grasped the death grip on the M1919, double-checking that it was ready to fire. It was. The engines were still idling the way Paula had left them. All he had to do was push the throttle full forward. He did. The *Black Jack* reared up like a war horse charging into battle.

Paula's scalp tingled. This is it, she thought. She slammed the *Far Horizon's* throttle all the way open and was surprised when the little cabin cruiser almost stood up on its stern.

When the bow slammed back down it tried to find purchase in Kurt's slippery wake. It was a little tricky at first but Paula found the sweet spot and held firm.

Wally was trying to keep up with her but was gradually falling behind. He called to her, clearly wanting her to slow down. Sorry, Wally. No can do. She wished he'd turn around and beat it back home, wherever that was. She didn't want him to catch a bullet.

Then she thought with a chill: I don't want to catch one either.

Both boats were ripping through the water at maximum speed, bouncing up and down in exact rhythm. Synchronized speed boating, Paula thought. The cool breeze blowing in her face, washing it with salty spray, would have been exhilarating if she wasn't so terrified.

They rounded a bend. The bridge came into view a couple of hundred yards ahead, low, black and empty, as far as she could tell.

Paula prayed out loud, "God please don't let us get killed." Then she added, "And don't let me kill anybody."

Hundred yards.

Dead ahead.

Kurt was lined up on the center span, flying arrow-straight toward it.

Paula was lined up on Kurt.

Oh God, oh God.

Fifty yards.

She saw Kurt swivel the big machine gun into firing position, aiming it at the top of the bridge.

Paula scanned it. Nothing. Maybe it was empty. Maybe nobody was there. Oh please let it be empty.

Thirty yards.

There it was: two shadowy figures moving rapidly along the railing.

Oh shit!

Kurt opened fire. It was deafening. Paula tried to pull the trigger on her gun.

Couldn't.

The figures darted to another position. Kurt swung his gun, never taking his finger off the trigger. The figures threw out their arms, tottered for a second, then fell backwards off the bridge.

The sight of it turned Paula's spine to jelly.

They hit the water just as she passed under the bridge. Kurt was already on the other side. They floated on their backs, a surprised look in their eyes, their arms spread out.

Not their arms.

Their wings.

Paula looked down at two brown pelicans floating on their backs, torn through with big bullet holes. Their blood was staining the water red around them.

Kurt slowed to a stop and Paula pulled up beside him then throttled down. He was laughing so hard he could barely stand up. All of Paula's pent up anxiety burst loose.

"It's not funny, Kurt. You killed a couple of poor, innocent birds."

Kurt laughed even harder. "I know. It's awful."

"Oh shut up. What if they had babies?"

When he looked at her, it was obvious she was on the verge of tears. He stopped laughing. "Paula, my sweet Paula. God I love you."

Under the circumstances, she didn't quite know how to respond to that.

Wally appeared, scolding them with a cackling chatter, occasionally puffing out of his blowhole for emphasis. Kurt put his fists on his hips, exasperated at being dressed down by both of them.

"All right guys, I put a few holes in a couple of pelicans, for which I am truly, deeply sorry, but you'll notice there are no holes in you and that was the object of the exercise. Okay?"

Paula knew it wasn't Kurt; it was nerves. Hers were shot. "I want to get back in your boat now," she said. "I want you to put your arms around me and tell me everything's going to be all right."

Kurt helped her onboard and willingly complied. Paula clung to him for a long time. "We gotta go, baby."

"I know." She stepped away from him. He moved to the stern, retied the towline to the *Far Horizons,* and got under way.

84

The distance from Steamboat Creek to Little Pumpkin Creek, which was a shortcut up to Angelfish Creek, was about three miles. It meant passing through the eastern edge of Card Sound, the last large body of open water before Kurt and Paula reached the Atlantic.

Due to the adrenalin pumping events of the two previous creeks, a veil of exhaustion fell over Paula, permeating every bone in her body. She sat in the cockpit with Kurt, his right arm cradled around her while he steered with his left. Her head was tucked into the comfy spot on his upper chest just below his neck. She was dozing, purring like a cat, vaguely aware of Kurt kissing her forehead from time to time.

The part of her mind that was still awake wanted to stay just like this for the next two centuries or so, nestled in the warm strength of his body while the salty air gently caressed her face. What would be wrong with that?

She believed they were out of danger now. Perhaps they never were in danger. It was her last thought before falling into a dreamless sleep.

Kurt jarred her awake, saying, "Aw shit."

Paula's mind was muddled for a moment. Kurt was sighting through binoculars. "What's wrong?" she asked.

"Fog bank. Rolling in off the Atlantic."

He handed her the glasses. It was just shy of 5:00 AM, still very dark. Sunrise wouldn't be for another two and a half hours yet.

"I don't see any . . ." There it was. A thin, silvery line far away on the horizon. "Wonderful. How far?"

Kurt took the binoculars back, gazed through them again. "Can't tell. Hard to judge distances at sea."

Paula nodded. "So where are we now?"

He lowered the glasses, his expression saying he didn't relish having to tangle with fog. "Little Pumpkin, just below where it pours into Angelfish."

"About a mile to the Atlantic, then?" Paula asked.

"About."

A few minutes later they were cruising east on Angelfish Creek. The waterway was wide and relatively clear of debris compared to the previous two creeks.

For the first time, Paula noticed the signs of fatigue etched in Kurt's face. She kissed his cheek and said, "Want another drink?"

"Yeah. Better make it coffee."

"Ditto. Otherwise I'm going to have to hold my lids open with toothpicks." She shuffled wearily down to the deck. As she was about to enter the cabin, Kurt turned to her, saying, "Hey, just remembered, outta fresh water in the galley. You'll have to get it from one of the jugs we brought onboard."

Paula saluted. "Aye Cap'n."

Kurt turned back around just in time to see a massive tree branch jutting up from the water. "Hold on!" He swerved hard, barely missing the obstruction. Paula grabbed the cockpit ladder to keep from toppling over. They both looked aft to see if the *Far Horizons* would clear.

It didn't.

The little cabin cruiser bounced off the branch, went up on its side, and for a moment appeared poised to capsize. It plopped back down on its belly but seemed dazed. Kurt had already cut the engines on the *Black Jack*. He rushed to the stern, grabbing the oar on the way to keep the smaller boat from ramming them. He was about to tell Paula to grab the towline in order to pull the *Far Horizons* alongside, but she was already doing it.

The good news was that the little boat was still afloat. "Is it taking on water?" Paula asked,

"Doesn't appear to be." But there was a big V-shaped indent on the starboard side, luckily above the waterline. Wally examined the damage too. He shook his head in disapproval.

Kurt said, "I'm going to hop onboard and have a look below deck." He gingerly crawled over the side. Once he was stable, he held a hand out. "Flashlight." Paula passed him one. He dropped to his knees, opened the hatch, stuck his head through, and shined the flashlight's beam from bow to stern. "Amazing."

"What do you see?" She leaned forward then realized her knee was resting on one of the bodies. She hopped back, overcome with revulsion.

"No sign of damage below deck," Kurt said, his voice echoing. "Gonna give it a few minutes, watch for seepage." After the allotted time had passed, he popped his head up. "We're good." Paula sighed with relief. Kurt make his way aft on the *Far Horizons*, saying, "Okay, here's what we're gonna do."

Paula grinned. Good ol' Kurt. Always has a plan.

"I'm gonna hand you one of these spare fuel cans to put aboard the *Black Jack* 'cause it's running low. There's another spare back here, more than enough to get us where we need to go." He handed the spare over to Paula then added, "I'm gonna fire up the old Evinrude then set it at about quarter speed, enough to stabilize it in the water, but not enough to ram us."

"Good idea. Now that we're almost there, can't take any chances."

Kurt nodded in the affirmative. "Okay, take the *Black Jack's* controls. When I give you the signal, pull away. When I come up beside you, I'll hop on."

Ordinarily Paula would have thought it too risky. But considering the insane events of the past few hours, it seemed perfectly rational. Besides, if Kurt said he could jump from one moving boat to another, she didn't doubt him for a second. He could do anything. He fired up the Evinrude and waved to Paula, "Go."

Paula eased the *Black Jack* away. Kurt rushed forward to take the helm. She let him catch up with her then paced him, keeping the boats inches apart. His jump from one craft to the other was seemingly effortless. As soon as he hit the deck, Paula pushed the throttle forward until she reached a safe towing speed.

They entered into the Atlantic at 5:15. Endless water lay before them, but there was also a fog bank out there, close enough now to see without the aid of binoculars.

It only took about twenty minutes before they were over deep water. Once again Paula paced the *Far Horizons* to allow Kurt to shut down the Evinrude's throttle with the oar. Paula cut hers too.

The fog bank was now uncomfortably close, moving steadily in their direction. "Gotta hurry," Kurt said.

"What can I do?"

"See those chains over there?"

There were three coils of heavy chain about a yard away. Each had a big spring clip on the end. "Yes."

"They're too heavy for you to pick up so don't even try. Once I shift a body onto the dive platform, feed me the end of one of the chains. I'll pull it back here, wrap it around the body, then kick the bundle into the sea."

Body. Paula's face lost any semblance of color and Kurt was afraid she was about to faint. "It's almost over, baby."

"I know, I know. I'm okay." But her face remained pale. "Let's just do it."

Earl's body was on top of the corpse pile. Kurt manhandled it over the transom and onto the dive platform. Knowing how big Earl was, Paula was amazed at Kurt's strength. She fed him the end of the first chain. He pulled it over and wrapped it around Earl.

Paula made sure the chain fed smoothly, while trying not to watch what Kurt was doing. Maybe not Calamity Jane after all, she thought. The end of the chain snaked over the transom, followed by a heavy click. Kurt hopped over, joining her on deck.

"What?" Paula asked.

"The big machine goes with Earl."

"What about these other guns?"

"We'll dump 'em when we get close to the Everglades. The grass is thick and tall there." He hefted the M1919 into his arms. "But this big boy would be too easy to spot. I'll need you to hand me those ammo belts along with a few feet of rope."

"Right."

Kurt carried the machine gun out onto the dive platform then sat it down below Earl's body. He wrapped the ammo belts around Earl, tucking them securely into the chains. He tied one end of the rope around the M1919, the other end through a link in the chain. He reached under Earl, grabbed the chains for leverage then rolled him into the ocean.

A loud, heavy splash.

Goodbye Earl.

They repeated the routine with Gator, sans artillery. Another big splash.

Goodbye Gator.

Red was next. He was the biggest of the three. Kurt was clearly having trouble hoisting him up.

"I can at least get his feet," Paula said.

"No!" Kurt barked it out with such force that Paula jumped back, stunned. "I don't want you touching him."

Paula was confused and on the verge of tears. Kurt realized he had spoken too sharply and that Paula misunderstood. "I don't want you ever for the rest of your life looking at your hands knowing that at one time they touched this filthy bastard. Your hands are not to be contaminated."

It was clear to Paula that Kurt was deadly serious. She realized the anger in his voice was not directed at her but at Red and the years of savagery between them. A hot tear rolled down her cheek. She turned away so Kurt wouldn't see it.

By a super human feat of strength, fueled more by rage than muscle, Kurt wrestled the upper part of Red's body over the transom, then swung the lower part over. The stern momentarily dipped down enough to take on a little water. Paula fed him the end of the last chain. Kurt wrapped it tightly around the corpse, then clipped the ends together.

He rested on his knees a moment, hands on thighs, catching his breath. He stared intently down at Red's body. Paula wondered what was going through his mind. Nothing good, she knew. Probably a lot of regret.

Kurt stood, braced himself against the transom, then positioned his boots against Red's corpse. He said, "Burn in Hell, Red," then gave a mighty shove. There was an explosive splash. After that there was nothing but the lapping of the sea against the *Black Jack's* hull.

They were quiet for a moment, each lost in their own thoughts.
Until the first fingers of fog reached out for them.
Kurt said, “Let's get outta here.”

85

Having dumped over a half ton of chain-wrapped bodies into the bowels of the Atlantic, the *Black Jack* rode higher and noticeably smoother than before. As a result, the engines didn't labor as hard to maintain speed. Again Kurt opted to run the *Far Horizon's* engine at quarter throttle, especially since the surface had become a bit choppy.

They headed back west toward the shelf, pulling away from the grasp of the fog bank but not the sight of it. Paula hated sea fog. It was just too damn creepy.

Kurt watched the depth finder closely, then called out, "This is it." Paula was ready with the oar. She deftly closed the throttle on the old Evinrude at the same time Kurt throttled back on the *Black Jack*.

With the engines off, the silence was absolute. They rocked gently in the restless surf. It was 6:20 AM. They had cover of darkness for a little over an hour. Time to hustle.

Kurt fastened a loop of rope to the railings of both vessels enabling them to easily transfer items from one to the other. They paused for a moment, looking at each other, bonded by love, determination, and exhaustion.

Paula noticed Kurt gazing longingly at the *Black Jack*. "Do you really have to sink it?"

He gave her a grim, determined look. "Yep."

Paula nodded. It made her sad and then she thought that's dumb, it just a boat. But she knew it was more than that. It was part of Kurt, who he was. She gave up a home, twenty years of marriage, and traded it for Kurt. He was giving up his soul mate, trading it for Paula and redemption.

Kurt glanced aft then said, "We gotta step on it. Fog's crawling up our ass." Paula saw it was true. Twenty yards behind the boat, was a wall of dense grey, highlighted sporadically by silvery moonlight.

Because they'd carefully sorted the cargo between the two boats before leaving Curiosity Cove, the remaining artillery and ammo, a box of groceries, and what remained of the booze was all that had to be transferred to the *Far Horizons*. Everything else would go down with the *Black Jack*. By the time the task was finished, fog completely enveloped them, accompanied by a noticeable drop in temperature.

Visibility was zero in all directions. The fog seemed not only to suppress vision but hearing too. Because their normal voices sounded unnaturally loud, they spoke in whispers, not even aware they were doing so.

Kurt jerked his head up, fully alert, and motioned Paula to be silent. His ears pricked up, his head jerked left then right, his eyes were wary. She mouthed, "What?" He motioned her to be very still.

All she heard was the bobbing of the boats, the swirling of the fog around them, a sound she felt rather than heard.

Then she heard something else.

Voices. Men's voices.

Not casual conversation. Not friendly voices.

Threatening voices. Dangerous voices.

Speaking in Spanish.

Kurt silently untied the rope holding the two boats together and let them drift apart enough so they wouldn't knock against each other. He had held onto the submachine gun he'd given Paula earlier with the attached clip. She'd never fired it, meaning it was still ready for action.

Paula's eyes filled with the horror of what was happening. She clamped both hands over her mouth to keep from making a sound. Kurt gave her his best 'it's gonna be all right' look.

She wasn't so sure.

One of the men spoke sharply. It was little more than a husky whisper, but it spurred a heated argument among the others until the first man, obviously the leader, said, "Silencio! Silencio!" followed by complete quiet.

Kurt had been listening carefully. He held up five fingers for Paula. At first she thought he was cautioning her not to move, then realized he was saying there were five men out there somewhere.

It was that 'somewhere' that made Paula shudder. She couldn't see them. She couldn't hear them. But she could feel them. She could feel their evil. It radiated from them, penetrated the fog, and her heart. These men were cold-blooded killers; of that she was sure.

To Paula they were more terrifying than Red or Gator or Earl. Those three she could see, read their eyes, decipher their body language. It wasn't much but it was enough to enable her to fight back, to survive. These men existed in a gray void. It was like waiting for the cold finger of death. You never saw it coming.

Kurt and Paula sat motionless. She was trembling, couldn't help it. He was steely calm, coiled, ready to strike. Paula knew without doubt that of the six men circling in the fog, he was the most deadly. It was reassuring and heart chilling at the same time.

They heard impatient whispers off their port bow, close, too damn close. A moment later there were sounds of a man shifting in his seat off their starboard side. Then all was quite again. All around them, the impenetrable gray nothingness.

It was maddening.

Then it occurred to Paula: where's Wally? They hadn't seen him since the fog set in. Had it spooked him away? She didn't think so. He was out there, maybe right next to them, but he sensed danger and was taking advantage of the fog's cover. At least she hoped so.

The slapping of water against the hull would surely give their position away, she thought, then it occurred to her that the others had the same problem. The splashes against their own hull were closer and therefore louder than those coming from Kurt and Paula's boat. Small comfort.

Kurt was a statue. Only his eyes moved, scanning in all directions. Paula was sure he could remain like that for hours. Years of deadly missions taught him how. Not her, though. She was about to explode.

They heard the splashing of the surf against a hull that was not the *Black Jack's*, or the *Far Horizon's*. It was from another hull. A hull that displaced water differently, indicating a heavier, bigger craft. That they could distinguish it at all meant it was very close, no more than a few feet away.

But nothing was visible. They tried to track the sound's movement, but it was impossible to pinpoint. The fog bounced sounds around. Within the dense gloom, there was the hint of a shadow, a shape slightly darker than the fog. Just for a second. Moving parallel to Kurt and Paula maybe ten feet away. Then it was gone.

They both immediately knew what it meant.

If Kurt and Paula could see them, they could see Kurt and Paula. As if to verify this, they heard something plunk into the water nearby. Moving with the stealth of a panther, Kurt handed Paula the gun then grabbed the oar, eased it into the water, and paddled them away in a different direction.

There was another small splash.

Kurt kept paddling soundlessly. He understood what the enemy was doing. They were throwing rocks, coins; whatever was available, trying to hit the boat without giving away their own position. Clever.

The next splash was several yards off their bow. Kurt quit paddling, shipped the oar then used his hands to gently push Paula down onto the deck, placing his mouth against her ear. Even so, his whisper was barely audible. What he said froze her heart. “Do you love me?”

She placed her lips to his ear. “With all my heart and soul.”

“Do you trust me?”

“With my life.”

“Will you do what I tell you to do now?”

Paula knew where this was going. “Oh Kurt, please.”

“Will you?”

Paula swallowed the lump in her throat. She wouldn't allow herself to sob. They'd hear her sobs. But to keep from doing so almost choked her. “I don't think I can.”

“You must.”

She looked at him pleadingly, her eyes large and green and moist. Kurt kissed her cheek, her eyes, her lips, then put his own lips against her ear again and in that faint whisper said, “There's no other way.”

At that moment there was a loud swish of water followed by Wally's ear splitting chatter high above the surface. The men in the other boat shouted vile curses and opened fire. A heavy splash followed as Wally fell back into the water. The gunfire stopped, echoed through the fog, but the men still quarreled noisily among themselves, making no pretense at stealth now.

Kurt had seen their muzzle flashes. He knew they were about a dozen yards off his port bow. Their cacophony of chatter allowed Paula and Kurt to converse without putting their lips to each other's ears, which was good because Paula couldn't suppress a “Poor Wally.”

She was sad. Kurt was seething. But he had to keep it together, stay focused on the mission. “Now listen to me, baby. Sun'll be up in a few minutes. May cut through this fog, may not. Can't take a chance. We gotta get you in the other boat, now. I'll untie the towline and you paddle away from my stern as far as possible. As soon as I think you're at a safe distance, I'm gonna force their hand.”

Paula knew what that meant. “No, Kurt. There are five of them, one of you. No.”

“Now listen to me. This is how it has to be.”

Paula couldn't stop the flood of tears. “You'll be killed.”

“I won't.”

“You will, you will.”

They heard the lead man trying to get his men under control, without much success. Their position was the same as before, only maybe a yard or two further away.

Paula buried her face in Kurt's chest, pounded his shoulders with her fists. He lifted her face. The intensity in his eyes made her cringe. “I need you to be strong, Paula. That's what you can do for me right now. You've got to be strong. I know you can be. I've seen it.”

Paula tried to bring her tears under control. “I can't live without you.”

Kurt looked at her more earnestly than he'd ever done before. “Baby you know I'm not a Heaven and Hell kind of guy, but I do believe in our eternal spirits. Think how many eons it's taken for our souls to find each other. We'll never be apart again.”

The men in the other boat were settling down, obeying their leader.

Kurt grabbed her arm and lifted. “We gotta move.”

Paula wanted to protest but Kurt wouldn't let her. He was guiding her to the stern then was pulling the *Far Horizons* alongside. Before she said anything, Kurt hoisted her over the side into the other boat.

Once she was onboard he slipped the knot on the towline then put his hand behind her head and said, "No goodbyes for us."

Paula tried to appear brave but she knew it was just a facade. "No goodbyes, my love."

They kissed passionately. As they were doing so, Kurt grabbed the railing of the *Far Horizons* and gave it a mighty shove. Paula was snatched away from his embrace.

Her last image of Kurt was his deep love for her burning in his eyes.

Then he was lost to the fog.

All was eerily silent, just the never-ending dance of the surf. She found a paddle and pushed away.

A minute passed. Nothing.

Another.

Then it happened. Lights cut through the fog. Bright lights. Paula knew it was the *Black Jack's* floodlights.

The floodlights.

Kurt's shadow moved around the deck. A powerful spotlight pierced the fog. In its beam was the dark shape of another boat pulling alongside.

It was a big boat full of big men snarling, cursing and yelling. They boarded the *Black Jack* en mass.

Kurt was no longer visible.

Until he opened fire.

He was behind the spotlight, blinding them. They scurried for cover. There was none. They screamed in agony, writhed in pain, returned fire. Kurt was yelling too. The spotlight was knocked out. Kurt never stopped firing.

A bright flash.

Lightning?

No, it came from beneath the boat. A sharp crack rolled across the water, snapped in Paula's ears. She clamped her hands over her them, screwed her eyes shut.

When she opened them again, the *Black Jack* was gone. The floodlights were visible, but they were submerged now and growing dimmer as they sunk.

For a brief moment Paula was too stunned to move. Then she fired up the Evinrude. Within a few seconds she was at the sight where she'd last seen the *Black Jack*.

A few cushions were floating there, along with scraps from the hull.

The attackers' boat had taken several hits from Kurt's gun and was sinking fast.

Kurt was nowhere to be seen.

86

"Hey babe, lovely day for a dip. Care to join me?"

It was exactly what she expected him to say, arms folded over the side of the *Far Horizon*, eyes gleaming with mischief, and his usual shit-eating grin.

But it didn't happen.

Paula searched the flotsam scattered around her and called his name yet again. She was startled at how plaintive her voice sounded, like a child lost in the dark calling for her mother. "Kurt, where are you?" She clapped her hands over her ears to block out the repeats then said in a smaller voice, "I'm scared."

She couldn't stop her voice from quivering, nor stop the sobs that echoed over the water. They were thrown back at her by the fog again and again, mocking her as if there were a dozen little girls out there suffering the same fate. Cold, gray fingers of mist closed around her and seemed to tighten their grip. Paula pulled Kurt's field jacket tighter, folded her arms to keep from shivering.

"Kurt!" Again the fog taunted her. "Kurt . . . Kurt . . . Kurt . . ." Each repetition was a little quieter than the one before but the whimper of despair in her voice was just as prominent each time.

Can't be. Not possible. Kurt's invincible. He's here. Somewhere.

But there was only the formless nothingness surrounding her. Choppy surf slapped against the *Far Horizon's* hull, its hollow echo sounding as if the entire ocean was inside a giant gymnasium.

The only other sound was the breaking of her heart. It made her cry out in agony, sounding like a yelp an injured dog might make. She pounded her fists on the side of the boat in an effort to release the pain. No, she told herself. No, no, no.

She continued to putter around in what she hoped was widening circles, but with the dense fog it was nearly impossible to tell. She did her best to keep the *Black Jack's* flotsam in sight as a point of reference but that was proving increasingly difficult, and because of the swift current, not very reliable.

A chilling thought occurred to her. Maybe I'm dead and this is what death is really like, not pearly gates and a chorus of angels, but a formless, colorless mist that you swirl around in for eternity. But do the dead have to change gas cans? She had to do that a little while ago. Now she was using the spare Kurt had given her. He hadn't realized how much he'd burned by running the *Far Horizon's* motor while they were towing it.

So . . . Maybe she wasn't dead.

So . . . Maybe Kurt wasn't dead either. After all, Kurt always had a plan.

Kurt was indestructible.

The fog had a golden glow to it now, indicating the sun was up, but it did nothing to improve visibility.

He's out there, she told herself, had to be, but he'd have drifted far away by now. If Kurt was caught in the Florida Straits, he was probably well on his way to Cuba, basically a southerly direction. But which way was south? The little cabin cruiser didn't have a compass or a radio. It was a pleasure craft designed for boating and fishing close to shore, not for taking on the open seas.

Oh God Kurt, where are you?

The answer settled in her heart like a thorn.

He's gone. You know he's gone.

It hurt so damn bad she couldn't think of anything else but the pain. It was all she had now. Her head was splitting. She grabbed it with both hands and screamed, "Please God help me," but her cry echoed away into the fog.

She decided that if she didn't get out of the fog her head would explode. In desperation she opened the throttle all the way and charged ahead, even though she had no idea of where ahead was.

Kurt was gone. Wally was gone. The *Black Jack* was gone. The bad guys were gone.

Her life was gone.

She plowed through the surf, expecting any moment to crash into another boat or a bridge abutment or a rocky shoreline. She didn't care; she just had to get out of the fog. She had no idea whether she was going straight or in circles. Circles, probably. Typically that's what happened. She had no concept of time either. Hours could have passed. Days. She didn't know. Thinking rationally no longer had any relevance.

The spitting and sputtering of the rusty old Evinrude interrupted her thoughts. Then it made no sound at all. Out of fuel. No more spare cans.

She was adrift. Lost. She sat rocking in the boat, how long she didn't know. She was vaguely aware of a transformation taking place within her. She no longer felt panic.

She no longer felt much of anything, except a deep aching for Kurt.

She didn't know how long she stayed like that, didn't know when she first noticed the chugging of an approaching boat or see the spotlight beam scanning right and left through the fog until it stopped on her face.

The shadow of a boat took shape, about the same size as hers. There was somebody in the boat. Two men, maybe more. Paula was jolted back to reality. Panic lodged in her heart and turned her arms and legs to jelly. Were these more of Estrada's men? What could she do? There was a stash of guns beneath the tarp behind her, but she didn't even know how to load the damn things. This was Kurt's game, not hers.

A voice called out, "Who's there?"

She knew that voice. The boat drew nearer. Not two men. Just one very big man.

"Pappy?"

"Why, Miss Paula. My goodness, what're you doing out here? You okay?"

"Oh my God, Pappy, you don't know how glad I am to see you. I'm in so much trouble." She couldn't stop the outburst of tears.

"Hey now," Pappy was saying. "Don't you worry 'bout a thing. Pappy's here and everything's gonna be all right. Here . . ." He handed Paula his hanky. "It's clean."

She gratefully took it. "Can you tow me to my mom's place?"

"Why, of course I can. I'll just fasten a line."

"Thanks Pappy but I'm getting in your boat with you, okay?"

"Well, of course it's okay, Miss Paula. My pleasure. My pleasure indeed."

Within minutes they were under way, the *Far Horizons* tagging faithfully behind. Paula was shivering and Pappy put his massive arm around her. "Now, now, Miss Paula. Everything's all right. Pappy's got ya."

Paula was already fast asleep on his shoulder.

87

Paula studied her mother's face.

It was a sweet, tender face, always with that enigmatic Mona Lisa smile. There was a light in her eyes that even Alzheimer's couldn't diminish. It was a light that had always been there. Paula knew it came from that eternal flame of love burning in her mother's heart. A love so pure that pain, suffering or unkindness never penetrated it.

They sat on the swing in the backyard not far from the water's edge. Although her mother was unable to express it, this was clearly her favorite spot. This was where she was calmest, most at peace. She gazed out over the gentle rise and fall of the surf, not as if she was searching for anything, but rather waiting for something.

Or someone.

Paula wondered if it was her father she was waiting for, whether deep down inside the fog of her mind he still existed for her. Old Doc Hutchinson had assured Paula that wasn't the case, but when she looked into her mother's eyes, she wasn't so sure.

Maybe I'm just superimposing my thoughts onto hers, she reflected. How many days have I sat here waiting for Kurt to come galloping up on the *Black Jack*, hopping overboard into the surf where I'm waiting with outstretched arms?

Countless times, very single day.

But Kurt was gone. So was the *Black Jack*. She knew because she'd been back to the site twice now in the *Far Horizons*. It was only a matter of time before the Straits claimed it and took it God knows where. The second time she went, she borrowed a friend's scuba gear and dove down to see if the emeralds were still there.

They weren't.

Nor any sign of Kurt.

She checked daily for reports of a body found washed up anywhere in the Keys, or snagged in a fishing net. Nothing. Logic told her what had happened to Kurt and the thought of it made her shiver. But the heart has its own logic. Hers said that Kurt was still alive. If he was gone, she was sure she would know it in her heart. She would feel it. An Atlantic breeze pushed gently against them and her mother sucked it in, her chest swelling. Her eyes sparkled. She's feeling better, Paula thought. Maybe old Doc Hutchinson was wrong.

A finger of lightning danced on the horizon. A moment later thunder grumbled and rolled across the water toward them. As if on cue Birdy appeared with her mother's wheelchair, saying "'Spect we better get her inside."

As Paula pulled the wheelchair up the ramp to the back deck, heavy, fat raindrops splattered down around her, but she managed to maneuver her mother inside before the downpour started in earnest. Once Birdy got her mom settled in her usual spot, she turned to Paula, put her hands on her hips and said, "Can' decide whichah you two is more lost."

As usual Birdy hit home with such uncanny accuracy it took Paula's breath away. She burst into tears. Birdy gathered her in her arms and pressed her head into that massive, welcoming bosom of hers. She let Paula cry it out for a while then said, "C'mon honey, lets go sit out on th' porch. Time you tol' ol' Birdy all 'bout it."

It had been a week since Paula showed up at the front door that foggy Monday morning, suitcases in hand and the side of her pedal pushers black with dried blood. She had rarely seen Birdy register surprise, but this time she did, complete with wide eyes and gaping mouth. "Lawd chile, what happened?"

Paula stumbled inside and dropped her suitcases on the floor. "Nothing, Birdy. I'm just really, really tired."

Birdy wasn't buying it. "Uh-huh. Who hit you? Bill?"

"No, no, I just . . ." She staggered a couple of steps, woozy.

Birdy steadied her. "Looky here, girl, don' you faint on me. Not here. Gawd and me both could'n get you up off th' floor. C'mon over here to th' sofa."

With her last ounce of energy Paula complied, clinging to Birdy for support, mumbling, "I'm okay, I'm okay . . ."

She plopped down on the sofa then toppled right over onto her side, groaned, and was instantly sleep. Birdy removed Paula's canvas deck shoes then grabbed her ankles and swung her legs up onto the sofa. She took the cover off the back of the sofa, spread it across Paula then stuffed a throw pillow under her head. She stepped back, folded her arms over her bosom, shook her head, and said, "Lawd, Lawd, Lawd."

It was after two when Birdy nudged Paula's shoulder. "Missy. Missy, wake up. Doc's here."

Paula's eyes popped open. She sat up too quickly and the room spun. "What? Who?" Old Doc Hutchinson, stood hunched over a few steps away, his battered black medical bag in hand, his glasses perched halfway down his nose, his baggy gray pants and sea green shirt rumpled, the knot of his blood-red tie loosened, his stethoscope draped around his neck, and his bushy white hair unruly as always. He looked at Paula with kindly, tired eyes. Paula had known those eyes all her life. He was the one who brought her into the world.

Paula's injuries incurred the day before manifested themselves now in aching bones, sore muscles, and a stinging hip where she'd been cut. But she gave the doctor a bright-eyed smile. "Hi Doc, what're you doing here?"

"Don't even start," Birdy said. "I seen that nasty cut on yore hip while you wuz sleepin'. Called the Doc to come over here and stitch it up. Now lay down on yore side." Paula did and without further ado, Birdy unfastened Paula's pedal pushers and jerked them down.

"Birdy!"

"Oh hush up, chile. Doc's seen yore bare butt b'fore. He wuz the first one to paddle it."

Doc Hutchinson chuckled then carefully removed the tape and bandage Kurt had applied yesterday. "Okay," he said, scrutinizing the injury. "Birdy you'll need to get a towel or something to lay under her. There's going to be bleeding."

After injecting Paula with Lidocaine, he deftly applied sutures, his hands as steady as a twenty year old's, then cleaned the incision with an antiseptic. He was about to bandage it when Paula stopped him, saying she was going to take a much-needed shower.

"Okay," he said. "While you're doing that I'll check on your mother." He patted her on the head the way he did when she was a little girl. Paula asked, "Don't I get a lollipop?" Doc Hutchinson chuckled then followed Birdy out of the room.

Paula grabbed a suitcase and because she was so beat, used both hands to haul it upstairs to her room. She stripped down then took as hot a shower as she could stand. Although her hip was still numb from Lidocaine, she used a delicate touch when cleansing the wound. Her other cuts and bruises screamed at her in outrage. She could not hold back tears of pain. She forced herself to bear it, lathering up and rinsing off several times, then thoroughly scrubbing her hair.

When she stepped from the stall her skin glowed and was tingly. She used one towel to dry off with, another to wrap around her hair. She applied bandages to her hip, slipped on a fluffy terry cloth robe and slippers then went back downstairs.

Doc Hutchinson was standing in the foyer with his arm around Birdy's shoulder while she wept quietly. "Oh no," Paula said and ran over to them. Before she asked the question, Doc said in his gentle voice, "Your mom's still with us, Paula. But these are last days. She can go anytime." He put his other arm around Paula, gave her an encouraging hug.

That was a week ago. Now she and Birdy were on the front porch in wooden rockers fitted with all-weather cushions, gazing out at the rain.

Birdy wanted Paula to start from the time of her last visit, a little over two weeks ago. She complied, giving it to her moment-by-moment, day-by-day, leaving nothing out and being completely honest. She was surprised at how beneficial she found the exercise, organizing the events of her chaotic life during the past two weeks, putting them into some sort of logical perspective.

Birdy listened silently, never once grunting or saying, "Um-hum," the way she normally did. When Paula was finished, Birdy pulled a hanky from her bosom, wiped her eyes and blew her nose.

"I guess I screwed up pretty bad," Paula said.

Birdy patted Paula's hand. "You wuz tryin' ta find love an' happiness, Missy. That's ev'ry woman's job. Lotta women ain't strong enough or brave enough to do it. Only the special ones are. Like you."

Upon hearing that, Paula let fly with the tears. As did Birdy. They cried and hugged. The rain stopped before their tears did. Paula wiped hers away with the flaps of her shirt. Birdy used her hanky, which was now soaked.

They rocked silently for a while then Birdy said, "Pappy called an' said he has a mess a shrimp for us."

Paula nodded. "I'll go pick them up. I've got a few other things to get anyway."

She kissed Birdy then went inside, changed her shirt and did her best to repair the damage to her wrecked face. By the time she pulled Kurt's Jeep out onto the highway, the sun was out in full force.

She'd found the keys to the Jeep among the things Kurt had already loaded into the *Far Horizons* before . . . She remembered him telling her he kept the vehicle stored at Handsome Harry's Marina. Paula had grown up with Harry. After she showed him Kurt's keys, plus spent a little time reminiscing about the 'good old days', the Jeep was hers. It still carried Kurt's scent and a sense of his presence. Once she got in it, she was reluctant to get out.

When Paula stepped into Davy Jones Locker, Pappy was busy with 'Widder Jane', who was constantly berating him while he dutifully filled her order, saying, "Yessum, yessum." Widder Jane had been a widow as far back as Paula could remember. She always wore black.

While waiting, Paula browsed Pappy's eclectic selection of wares, bracing herself against a shelf or display case whenever he took a sudden turn. She noticed the porcelain egret was missing. She pointed it out to Pappy when he got free of Widder Jane.

"Oh hi, Miss Paula. Yes ma'am, I sold that to some real nice folks from up north. Fetched a pretty penny, too." He pushed his Greek sailor hat back on his head like he always did. "Wuz able to buy new tennis shoes for all my kids. One's they had wuz gettin' pretty ragged."

Paula stood on her tiptoes and kissed Pappy on the cheek. “Good for you, Pappy.”

Pappy's face flushed ruby red. After a second he said, “I got them shrimp ready for ya.”

When Paula turned into her driveway, Doc Hutchinson's station wagon was parked there. She jumped out of the Jeep and ran up the steps to the front door. Before she got there she heard Birdy wailing from inside. Doc Hutchinson pushed open the screen door for her. All he said was, “She went peacefully.”

88

The first day Birdy didn't wear black was three days after the funeral. She and Paula had lunch out back at the picnic table. Southern fried chicken. Corn on the cob. Cole slaw. Biscuits. Everything but the biscuits was left over from the funeral. As usual there was enough food to feed a brigade. Birdy drank syrupy sweet iced tea. Paula had a vodka tonic.

"Be movin' in with Lewis an' his family come Monday," Birdy said.

Paula was surprised. "But why, Birdy? This is your house much as it is mine."

"Can't stay here, Missy. Ever time I look up, I see her. Ever time I breathe in, I catch her scent. I have to let her go. Can't do that if I stay here. An' . . . I needs to be with my family. You understand." Once again tears rolled down her cheeks. She daubed at them with her napkin.

Paula put her hand on Birdy's. "Of course I do. I'm so sorry."

"Tell me, when does it quit hurtin'?"

Paula took a deep breath, fought back her own tears. "Yes, when?"

Afterwards when Paula was in the kitchen cleaning up, she saw the postman shove a letter into her box. She retrieved it and took it to the rocker on the front porch. It was from Bill.

"Dear Paula. I was so sorry to her about your mom. She was a very sweet woman. We'll all miss her. I guess Birdy's taking it pretty hard too. I was glad Billy was able to attend the funeral. He practically lives in that chick magnet you got him. I understand why you did it, but can't say I agree with your reasoning. Sorry, we can talk about that later."

No, Paula thought, we can't. But she had to admit she was mortified when Billy came roaring up to the church in his sleek red T-bird. She still bridled at calling it his T-bird. For a few brief shining moments it had been her dream car.

What really disturbed her was that Billy brought his cheerleader girlfriend with him. They stayed just long enough to wolf down some food after the service, then pecked Paula on the cheek saying they had to get back before curfew. A minute later they left with a screech of tires.

She continued reading.

“I didn't think it appropriate for me to attend considering the circumstances. I didn't want to chance upsetting anybody on a day dedicated to her memory. She was a very fine woman, Paula. Probably the finest I've ever known.”

Undoubtedly true, Paula thought.

“I want you to know I bear no animosity toward you. I understand why you did what you did. I realize I haven't been a good husband to you for a long time. Maybe I never was. You deserved better.”

Paula's mouth gaped open. My God, was it really Bill who wrote this?

“I propose we make the divorce as simple as possible. We both just want to move on with our lives. There is no rancor on my part. I hope you feel the same. For Billy's sake, I hope we can end this amicably.”

Paula let out a bark of laughter, thinking: what you really hope is I won't take you to the cleaners. Which means you still don't know anything about me.

“I realize most of the problems we had were the result of me being too focused on my business and not enough on my family. Well, I've got a second chance now with Betty. I'm determined not to make the same mistake. I've had an offer for TaylorMade Printing and I've decided to take it. Sure it'll mean we'll have to live on a tight budget, buy a smaller house in a less exclusive neighborhood, but if we're careful with our money, we'll have enough to get by on.”

Paula was hardly able to believe her eyes. She thought back to the days when TaylorMade Printing was just the two of them working out of their garage. It was Bill’s big dream. It took her a while to realize the dream didn’t include her or a family.

“It means Betty and me and the kids will have lots of time together for playing, for loving, for just being happy. I haven't told Betty yet. I'm saving it as a wedding night surprise.”

Paula doubled over in laughter. Poor, pathetic Betty. She had played out a role as old as time, plotting and planning to seduce the big boss, then grab the pot of gold at the end of the rainbow. Paula almost felt sorry for her. Almost. She continued reading.

“She really is a good kid. She takes such good care of Mama, who's living with us now in a sick room I put together for her. Betty waits on her hand and foot. By the way, Mama asks about you all the time. Can't understand why you're not here. Keeps saying you're her daughter and how she loves you.”

Of all the things Bill had written, somehow that stung Paula the most. She laid the letter down, wiped tears from the corners of her eyes. Tears for Mama Taylor? If this world gets turned anymore upside down, she thought, I know I'll just fall off. She continued to read.

"I really don't know how Betty manages it all. Besides caring for Mama and looking after the kids and making sure my meals are ready on time, she's also quite frisky in her wifely duties, if you know what I mean."

Read you loud and clear, you idiot. You had a Ferrari and traded it for an Edsel. Have a nice ride.

Bill closed the letter by saying that however she wanted to handle the divorce was fine with him, but that he hoped she understood his financial resources now were very limited.

Paula refolded the letter, then slipped it back in its envelope. She considered the fact that she was truly alone in the world now. Kurt was gone. Her mother was gone. Birdy would be gone come Monday. Her marriage of twenty years was gone. And Billy for all practical purposes was gone. Into his own head.

A chill ran over Paula, raising goose bumps. She hugged herself for warmth, even though the air around her was balmy and the sun was bright.

It did not penetrate the wretched, abject loneliness that enshrouded her.

She had run away to be a woman who did just as she pleased.

She wished she knew what that was.

89

It was Thanksgiving Day but Paula was not feeling very thankful. She wasn't feeling much of anything other than restless. And that she might explode at any moment.

She wanted Kurt. She wanted him so bad it hurt.

Yesterday had been the worst. She wandered from the living room sofa to the rocker on the front porch to the swing out back, firing up one Chesterfield after another, sucking down vodka tonics as if it were the last day before prohibition, never staying in one spot more than a few moments, then pacing, pacing like a lioness in a cage.

Billy called to say he'd be spending Thanksgiving some place up in Vermont with his girlfriend's family. He'd be sure to eat an extra slice of pumpkin pie just for her, he said. After that, they were all going snow skiing. But he wanted her to know he sure did love her and sure did miss her and sure did hope she'd have a happy Thanksgiving. Paula responded tonelessly saying, "Okay honey. Have fun. Miss you. Bye." When she hung up she felt nothing.

That bothered her.

Later in the evening, Paula stood in the dim moonlight over the place where she and Kurt made love that first night. Memories came rushing back. His lips on hers, forceful and passionate. His hands touching her, ravaging her. The feel of him inside her, hard, thrusting. She moaned. It came from a place deep and hot and wet.

God they were good together. Two bodies, two souls as one.

Paula flung her cigarette into the surf then screamed out, "Come back to me Kurt. I need you." With all her might she hurled her glass down against the rocks. But it was plastic and bounced up like a rubber ball, arced out into the Sound, and was lost. She marched around the backyard in tight circles, saying, "Why, why, why?"

She knew her emotions were getting completely out of control. To use Birdy's words, she was working herself into a tizzy. But Birdy never explained how to make a tizzy go away.

Her skin was hot to the touch and her forehead was glowing. She knew if she didn't do something quick she really was going to explode. She ran to the end of the pier, stripped down, and plunged in.

The water's chill soothed her fevered skin. She instinctively went into a racing stroke, pumping arms and legs in perfect form, trying to work the anxiety out of her muscles. She ran out of steam a quarter of a mile out in black water under a black sky. A sliver of moon was grinning at her like the Cheshire Cat.

She was pleasantly exhausted. She took a few moments to catch her breath, then got her bearings from the house lights and the ones on the pier and used a leisurely backstroke for her return.

When she got back, two men were standing at the end of the pier ogling her.

Both were fondling sweaty bottles of beer with cigarettes wedged between their fingers. Both sported shit eating grins. One was in Bermuda shorts, sandals, and a black tank top. He was leaning on the other guy. He wore denim cutoffs, sneakers, and nothing else. Bad choice, Paula thought. With that flat-chested hairless torso, you really should wear a shirt.

Tank Top spoke first. "Hey Chesty. Ain't it just the perfect night for a swim, though? Mind if we join ya?"

To their surprise, Paula showed no sign of alarm. She didn't scream or try to cover her breasts. She effortlessly treaded water, staring brazenly at them, then said, "You're trespassing on private property, boys. You need to leave."

Flat Chest clutched his heart as if Paula had mortally wounded him. "Aw come on, honey. No need to get all unfriendly like. Hell, you already naked. Why don't we get naked too and see if something good happens?"

"I'm not your honey."

Tank Top said, "Gawd what a set of tits."

"And you've seen them so it's time to leave." Even Paula was surprised at the growl in her voice.

Tank Top straightened up, hooked his thumbs in his shorts, and cocked his head belligerently. "How 'bout we don't wanna leave? Whadya gonna do about it?"

Paula's eyes were glowing green embers. She thought, if I can take on Gator, I can certainly to hell handle these redneck island boys. "What am I going to do about it?" she echoed.

Tank Top laughed sneeringly. "Yeah, whadya you gonna do about it?"

The fierceness in Paula's eyes could have melted tungsten steel from a hundred yards.

"I'm going to kick your asses."

Clearly the last thing Tank Top and Flat Chest expected the naked redhead to say. Both were momentarily speechless. Paula never wavered, never blinked, just stared them down.

Flat Chest spat and said, "Well hell, honey, no need gettin' all huffy. Just lookin' for a little fun." He motioned to Tank Top. "Hell, let's split."

Tank Top hitched up his shorts, dug a quarter out of his pocket then flipped it toward Paula. "Thanks for the show."

As they both skulked away, Tank Top took a parting shot. "You ain't the only fish in the ocean, bitch."

As the two neared the end of the pier, Paula heard Flat Chest say, "Yeah, but she's the only one that's bare ass naked and got big tits." They both laughed, then were lost to the night.

A part of Paula was disappointed. She realized she'd been spoiling for a fight.

Another part of her asked: what's come over you?

She went inside, showered, and plopped into bed, but sleep wouldn't come. She tossed fitfully. When the morning sun peaked in her window, she was still awake.

Thanksgiving day.

A little over five weeks since she'd last seen Kurt.

She spent the morning doing perfunctory housework, mainly just haunting the big, lonely house. She tried TV but it was a blur of parades and other holiday events. She picked up a magazine but put it back down after realizing she'd read the same paragraph four times.

Around noon she made herself a sandwich but only ate half of it. Not able to think of anything else to do, she just sat at the kitchen table, staring out the window.

And saw the *Far Horizons* tied up at their pier. Her pier now, bobbing lazily. As she watched, she heard Kurt whisper her name.

Or was it the wind?

She ran out onto the front porch, looked in all directions. "Kurt? Kurt where are you?" She ran over to the pier. The *Far Horizons* made a squeaky sound as it rubbed against the fenders. Paula shaded her eyes, looked to see if any boats were nearby, if Kurt was on one of them calling to her.

"Kurt?"

A runabout was trolling in the Sound. A man was standing up in it. He waved at her.

"Oh my God!" Paula bounced excitedly, waving both arms at him. "Kurt? I'm here!"

He stooped over slightly. He was reeling in a big catch, drifting a little closer to shore as he did so.

It wasn't Kurt.

It was Handsome Harry. Velma was in the boat with him. The wave Harry had given her was nothing more than being friendly. Velma waved too, calling out, "Hiya Paula. Happy Thanksgiving." True Conches, they fished virtually every day, whether it was Thanksgiving, Christmas, or Fourth of July.

Paula returned the wave halfheartedly. "Hi Velma. Hi Harry."

With his catch onboard, Harry throttled up. He and Velma were soon lost from sight.

Paula went over to the swing, plopped down, and gazed at the hypnotic sway of the Sound. Her heart hurt so bad she wondered if it truly was breaking. "Oh God help me. I can't take this. It just hurts too bad."

To make matters worse, every time she closed her eyes, there Kurt was, right in front of her, smiling at her with his roguish grin, a twinkle in his eye right where it was supposed to be.

She gazed toward the northeast, out where the shelf dropped off and beyond sight, the place where Kurt went down.

The light of realization flashed in her mind. Kurt's not there.

I know where he is.

How could I have been so stupid?

He's at Curiosity Cove.

90

Every female fiber of her body screamed it out to her. Call it intuition. Call it overwrought emotions. Paula knew it was a woman thing and her woman thing was hitting on all eight cylinders. Meaning normal logic was irrelevant. She was a woman following her most primeval instincts.

Nothing would hold her back.

She had to get to Curiosity Cove.

That's where Kurt was. She knew it.

The *Far Horizons* was waiting for her, saying come on, let's go, fill up my gas cans, load me up with water and food and emergency gear just in case, get your dad's chart that shows how to get there. And for God's sake get a compass.

Come on girl. Get moving.

It only took Paula an hour to pull together the things she needed, including fuel. She changed into shorts, a long sleeve shirt, a pair of canvas deck shoes, and wrapped a scarf around her hair. She took a seat at the rear of the little cabin cruiser then gave the chord on the ancient Evinrude a hard yank.

Nothing happened.

Paula kept jerking on the chord until she thought she'd pull her arm out of its socket. With each pull, her ire rose.

She stopped for a moment, put her fists on her hips, and yelled, "Look here boat, I'm going to Curiosity Cove whether you like it or not. If I have to yank this chord all afternoon, then by God that's what I'll do. Got it?"

For good measure she stood up and kicked the motor. She'd seen her father do that many times when something wasn't cooperating. It always seemed to work for him. Sitting back down, she yanked the chord with all her might. The Evinrude coughed twice then fired up.

"All right then," Paula said. She threw off the line, took a seat at the helm, and puttered out into Largo Sound. She cruised south toward Tavernier then west onto Tavernier Creek. It cut across the island like a big ditch, dumping her into Florida Bay. Being Thanksgiving, it was virtually clear of traffic. Paula checked her father's chart and set a heading.

The weather was brisk, the water choppy. Purple-blue thunderheads were building on the horizon. Paula didn't care. She had to get to Kurt as fast as possible. He was waiting for her; she knew it.

She opened the throttle to its maximum stop. The *Far Horizon's* bow lifted up obediently. Even though it was a shallow draft boat, Paula concentrated on the channel markers. Florida Bay was treacherous. Much of its bottom was only a few feet deep and made of hard coral. It could peel open the belly of a boat like a giant can opener.

But she was Paula Doherty, captain's daughter. She had grown up on these waters and was as comfortable in Florida Bay as Br'er Rabbit was in his briar patch.

On my way, Kurt.

The air in her face was invigorating. The *Far Horizons* bucked like a young bronco as it skimmed over the water. No matter. Paula was not about to be thrown.

She searched the horizon and there it was. A cluster of treetops was swaying in the blustery wind. The clouds overhead seemed determined to add drama to the setting. Ranging in color from deep purple to shiny silver, interspersed with shades of cobalt blue and violet, they swirled and rolled as if in a celestial wrestling match. Shafts of purest sunlight punched through them, dancing on the water's surface.

Magical, Paula thought. Anything less would be inappropriate.

She drew near to the island and pulled back on the throttle. The *Far Horizons* humbly laid down flat on its belly. Paula steered toward the channel entrance. She sucked in her breath as the tunnel closed around her.

It was relatively dark inside. And mysterious. Paula's skin tingled. Thunder rolled across the Bay, echoed through the tunnel, stirred up a cacophony of exotic bird calls.

Paula hardly heard them, so intent was she on keeping the little cabin cruiser squarely in the center of the meandering channel. Her eyes were focused straight ahead. She tried to remember whether the tunnel opened up into the lagoon around the next bend, or the bend after that, but couldn't. She felt like a child cranking a Jack-in-the-box, waiting for the clown to jump out. The anticipation was almost unbearable.

Would the house still be there? Did Estrada's men destroy it, burn it down? She said a little prayer that it would still be just as she and Kurt left it.

It had to be.

Up ahead the tunnel grew somewhat brighter, which meant the last bend was coming up. She was about to enter the lagoon. Seeing that her knuckles were white from her iron grip on the helm, she forced herself to relax.

She eased around the bend. The tunnel opened up. Just like the first time she was here, it reminded Paula of a curtain opening at the start of a play, revealing the most enchanting set she had ever seen.

The house was still there.

Intact.

It stood almost regally on the little hill of white sand above the lagoon. Paula laughed with joy. She steered the *Far Horizons* across the lagoon to the pier, shut down the motor, hopped out, and tied up. Rain began, softly at first, then great big water bombs. She was about to run up to the house when a thought stopped her.

What if somebody was there other than Kurt?

It froze Paula in her tracks. She looked closer at the house. No, it was not just as they'd left it. Repairs had been made. From her angle she saw the French doors in the main room had been replaced.

By who?

Were Estrada's men inside, watching her, waiting for her to come in so they could attack her? The horror of what Red, Gator and Earl intended to do to her -- would have done to her -- quickened her heart. A voice in her head said run, get back in the boat and get the hell out of here.

She couldn't do it.

She knew instinctively the rest of her life would be determined by what she did in the next few moments.

She walked up the hill.

Were there footprints in the sand when she first looked up at the house? The image in her mind wasn't clear enough. If there were footprints, the rain had already washed them away.

She quietly climbed the steps to the front verandah, then stopped, straining to hear. No sound or movement came from inside, but the drumming of the rain was so loud it would have obliterated anything quieter than an explosion.

Paula warily turned the doorknob. It was unlocked. She took a deep breath, pushed the door open, then jumped back, ready to run like a scalded dog at the first sign of movement.

There wasn't any.

Paula kneeled down, stuck her head through the door. She looked all around.

Nothing.

She stood up, tiptoed inside, leaving the door open in case she had to bolt. She stepped down into the main room without incident. It looked nothing like the last time she'd seen it. All the furniture except the bamboo bar had been replaced. The big beautiful rug was gone, replaced with several braided throw rugs. The bullet holes in the walls had all been repaired. The few pieces of wall décor that had been undamaged were back in place.

Paula was stunned. There was no evidence of the violence that had taken place in the room. It had been restored to its former open, comfortable, very masculine glory.

Clearly Kurt's hand was at work here because only Kurt knew what it originally looked like.

But where was he?

Convinced that the boogieman wasn't going to jump out and grab her, she called out, "Kurt?" When she didn't get an answer she called out again, "Kurt, where are you?" It was then she realized several lights were on. She heard the drone of the generator, meaning he had taken on propane.

Like a child, Paula was incapable of walking, she had to run and she ran into the kitchen. Dirty pans and dishes were stacked in the sink. She jerked open the refrigerator. It was stocked not just with beer but with fresh food. She wanted to shout hallelujah.

She ran back into the main room. Yes, a bottle of Jack Daniels Black stood proudly on the bar, about half of it gone. Had to be new; she had taken the only bottle that hadn't been smashed with them when they made their hasty departure.

Next she dashed into the museum room and it was there that she got her greatest shock.

It was empty, nothing but walls, floor and ceiling.

What did it mean?

As if in answer, the memory of that long, scary trip out to the shelf on the *Black Jack* came back to her. Kurt told her he had an idea of how to square things with Estrada so they wouldn't have to spend the rest of their lives worrying about him coming after them.

This was how he did it.

Paula told Kurt the contents of the museum room were probably worth a couple of million bucks. That's what the emeralds were supposed to be worth.

Kurt did the one thing Bill had never done during all the years they were married.

He listened to her.

Not only that, he took her at her word.

Who thought a woman's word meant anything?

Kurt did. As long as that woman was me.

She found herself laughing girlishly as she ran upstairs to the bedroom. The covers were thrown back. The mattress was lumpy, the way a man would leave a bed. She ran out onto the balcony then around back to the tub. The makeshift shelf above it was barren.

Except for a single pink frangipani in a bud vase.

Paula's hands flew to her mouth. Oh my God, he's here, he's really here.

But where?

She looked down toward the lagoon but the rain was an impenetrable wall.

"Kurt? Kurt, where are you?"

She pricked her ears, listened. A deafening timpani roll of rain blotted out all other sounds.

"Kurt? Oh please . . ."

She heard a voice, barely audible. Not Kurt's. Higher pitched. Much higher pitched. Calling to her.

Wally.

The pieces slammed together for Paula. The question of how Kurt survived without a boat. Wally. He had stayed with them the whole trip. Kurt must have clung to his good buddy Wally to reach land, not that far away.

God bless you Wally.

Paula used her long legs to take the side steps two at a time, then ran toward the lagoon. Wally kept calling to her. She laughed and cried and ran down the hill. She made out another boat tied up next to hers. Nothing like the *Black Jack* but formidable just the same.

A shadowy figure was running up the hill toward her, laughing like the buccaneer he was. She would recognize that figure from a mile away.

Kurt.

Charging like a bull.

He scooped her up effortlessly in his powerful arms, then slammed her down on the sand so hard it made her grunt, then laugh, but only for a moment because it's impossible to laugh while being bombarded with kisses. Kurt's skin was feverish, like hers. Even the cold deluge couldn't quench it.

They clung to each other and rolled over and over down the hill to the edge of the lagoon. Wally was nearby nodding his approval, slapping the water with his fins, laughing like a hyena and performing the occasional back flip.

Paula threw her head back long enough to catch her breath. "Oh my God, Kurt, why didn't you let me know you were alive?"

Kurt pulled her up to a sitting position, placed his hands on her face. Paula wrapped her legs around him so their hips were pressing together. "But you knew I was alive, didn't you?"

It took Paula by surprise. "Yes, I did."

"How did you know?"

"I could feel you in my heart."

"Damn right you could. Just like I felt you in mine. We were never apart, Paula."

"But why didn't you come for me?"

"I was waiting for you to come to me."

Paula cocked her head, clearly baffled. "What?"

"Listen to me, baby. I got us in some deep shit by assuming I had the right to make choices for you, make you live your life the way I wanted. I was wrong. You let me know I was wrong, that you were determined to make your own choices."

Paula was puzzled about where this was going. "Okay . . ."

"After everything went to hell and we almost lost our lives, I too was determined. Not to make the same mistake again. Not to come busting back into your life and tell you what our new game plan was." He took her hands gently. "Especially after I learned of your mother's death. You needed time. Space. I knew you'd figure out where I was. And you'd come when you were ready. If you still wanted me in your life. Does any of that make sense?"

Paula smiled. Her eyes sparkled green. She said, "It makes perfect Kurt sense."

Kurt laughed. More hugs, more kisses, then Paula asked, "So what about you? What have you been doing?"

"I needed time too, baby, to make things right. For us. Had to make sure you were out of danger."

"And are things right?"

"Lady, I don't think they can get any more right than this. And they're gonna stay right. My promise."

"My promise too." She sealed it with a kiss then asked, "So what's next?"

"Well, I've got these open tickets to Paris via New York City. Wanna go?"

Paula laughed. "Nothing would please me more."

"Nothing?"

They kissed, hugged, couldn't get enough of each other. Paula thought: this is the part where the rain stops and a brilliantly hued rainbow arcs over the lagoon.

It didn't happen.

In fact, it rained harder.

But it didn't matter.

ACKNOWLEDGEMENTS

Several authors who generously gave of their time and expertise as I honed this book into its final form provided invaluable assistance. That they are all women was particularly important to me since my protagonist is a spirited, independent, determined, charming, and fearless woman, which could easily describe each of them.

Marsha Roberts is my wife, a best selling author, and at least 200% woman. Her book, *Confessions of an Instinctively Mutinous Baby Boomer*, is described as an astounding work of literary genius and I have to agree. Friends who know Marsha, and who have read passages from my book while it was in the works, have said that Paula is just a 1959 version of her. Well, not exactly, but it does hit close to the mark. Did I take inspiration from her when creating Paula? You bet.

I want to thank Claude Nougat, author of the *Forever Young* series, for her objective editorial advice. She pointed out several problems in story construction, extraneous exposition, and superfluous characters. I am grateful for the time she devoted to helping me, and for her patience, friendship, and support.

Dianne Harmon, author of the best selling *Blue Coyote Motel*, combed through the manuscript with her eagle eye and caught many errors, omissions, and faulty descriptions (petal pushers instead of pedal pushers, for example). Her enthusiastic support for the book has been most welcome.

I extend my heartfelt thanks to each of these literary ladies.

ABOUT THE AUTHOR

Bob Rector has been a professional storyteller for forty years, but his background is primarily in film, video, and stage work as a writer and director.

Bob was one of the pioneers of music videos, first for *The Now Explosion* and then for *Music Connection*, which were highly popular nationally syndicated shows that preceded MTV by ten years. He created over 100 films for the top musical artists of the times.

Bob wrote and directed an outdoor-adventure feature film, *Don't Change My World*, and has won countless awards for nature and sports documentaries.

His original three-act play, *Letters From the Front,* entertained America's troops around the world for fifteen years and was the first theatrical production to be performed at the Pentagon. This beloved show, written and directed by Rector, became known as the World's Most Decorated Play.

After decades on the road (and in the air!) Bob finally settled down long enough to write his first novel, *Unthinkable Consequences.*